WORLD'S END II.

Upton Sinclair's theme is the world of the first half of the twentieth century. Readers of the other ten novels in this series will be glad to discover what has been happening to the far-flung Budd family and their friends. As with each book of this series, this one can be enjoyed for its own separate story, or as a part of the sweeping account of the era.

Each volume is published in two parts: I and II.

WORLD'S

END II.

Upton Sinclair

LCCN: 67120285

ISBN: 1-931313-13-X

Distributed by Ingram Book Com pany

Printed by Light ning Source Inc., LaVergne, TN

Pub lished by Si mon Pub li ca tions, P.O. Box 321 Safety Har bor, FL

When I say "his to rian," I have a mean ing of my own. I por tray world events in story form, because that form is the one I have been trained in. I have sup ported my self by writ ing fic tion since the age of six teen, which means for forty-nine years.

… Now I re al ize that this one was the one job for which I had been born: to put the pe riod of world wars and rev o lu tions into a great long novel. …

I cannot say when it will end, because I don't know exactly what the characters will do. They lead a semi-independent life, be ing more real to me than any of the peo ple I know, with the sin gle ex cep tion of my wife. … Some of my char ac ters are peo ple who lived, and whom I had op por tu nity to know and watch. Oth ers are imaginary—or rather, they are com plexes of many people whom I have known and watched. Lanny Budd and his mother and fa ther and their var i ous rel a tives and friends have come in the course of the past four years to be my daily and nightly com pan ions. I have come to know them so in ti mately that I need only to ask them what they would do in a given set of cir cum stances and they start to en act their roles. … I chose what seems to me the most re veal ing of them and of their world.

How long will this go on? I can not tell. It de pends in great part upon two pub lic fig ures, Hit ler and Mussolini. What are they go ing to do to man kind and what is man kind will do to them? It seems to me hardly likely that ei - ther will die a peace ful death. I am hop ing to out live them; and what ever happens Lanny Budd will be some where in the neigh bor hood, he will be "in at the death," ac cord ing to the fox-hunting phrase.

These two foxes are my quarry, and I hope to hang their brushes over my mantel.

In the course of this novel a num ber of well-known per sons make their ap - pearance, some of them living, some dead; they appear under their own names, and what is said about them is fac tu ally cor rect.

There are other char ac ters which are fic ti tious, and in these cases the au thor has gone out of his way to avoid seem ing to point at real per sons. He has given them un likely names, and hopes that no per son bear ing such names ex ist. But it is im pos si ble to make sure; there fore the writer states that, if any such coincidence occurs, it is accidental. This is not the customary "hedge clause" which the au thor of a *ro man à clef* pub lishes for le gal pro - tec tion; it means what it says and it is in tended to be so taken.

Var i ous Eu ro pean con cerns en gaged in the man u fac ture of mu ni tions have been named in the story, and what has been said about them is also ac cord - ing to the re cords. There is one Amer i can firm, and that, with all its af fairs, is imag i nary. The writer has done his best to avoid seem ing to in di cate any ac tual Amer i can firm or fam ily.

...Of course there will be slips, as I know from ex pe ri ence; but *World's End* is meant to be a his tory as well as fic tion, and I am sure there are no mis takes of im por tance. I have my own point of view, but I have tried to play fair in this book. There is a var ied cast of char ac ters and they say as they think. ...

The Peace Con fer ence of Paris [*for example*], which is the scene of the last third of *World's End*, is of course one of the great est events of all time. A friend on mine asked an au thor ity on mod ern fic tion a ques tion: "Has any - body ever used the Peace Conference in a novel?" And the reply was: "Could any body?" Well, I thought some body could, and now I think some - body has. The reader will ask, and I state ex plic itly that so far as con cerns his toric char ac ters and events my pic ture is cor rect in all de tails. This part of the manu script, 374 pages, was read and checked by eight or ten gen tle men who were on the Amer i can staff at the Con fer ence. Sev eral of these hold im por tant po si tions in the world of trou bled in ter na tional af fairs; oth ers are col lege pres i dents and pro fes sors, and I prom ised them all that their let ters will be con fi den tial. Suf fice it to say that the er rors they pointed out were cor rected, and where they dis agreed, both sides have a word in the book.

Contents:

BOOK FOUR

Land of the Pilgrims' Pride

19

Old Colonial

I

THE city of Newcastle, Connecticut, lies at the mouth of the Newcastle River, and has a comfortable harbor, not muddy except in springtime. It has a highway bridge across the harbor, and beyond it a railroad bridge, both having "draws" so that ships may go up. The Budd plant lies above the bridges, and has a railroad spur running into it. Above the plant are salt marshes, which the progenitor of the family had the forethought to buy for a few dollars an acre. Everybody called him crazy at the time, but as a result of his forethought his descendants had both land and landings, by the simple process of putting a steam dredge at work running channels into the marsh and piling earth on both sides. In the year 1917 you could not have bought an acre of this salt marsh for ten thousand dollars.

As a result, the city had only one direction in which to grow; which meant that rents were high and working-class districts crowded. The families which had owned farms in that direction had either sold them, and moved away and been forgotten, or else they had leased the land, in which case they constituted the aristocracy of Newcastle, owning stock in banks and department stores, water and gas and electric companies, street railways and telephones. As a further result, Newcastle had remained a small city, and many of the workers in Budd's lived in near-by towns and came to the plant on "trolley cars."

In fact only a small part of Budd's itself was at Newcastle. Farther up the river were dams, and here the company made cartridges and fuses. The dams had locks, and motor barges took raw materials up and brought finished products down. This enabled Lanny's grandfather to say that he disapproved of the modern tendency toward congestion in great cities. Also it enabled him to get much cheaper labor.

In the state of Ohio, once known as the "Western Reserve" and settled largely by people from Connecticut, the Budds had a powder plant. In the state of Massachusetts they had recently bought a six-story cotton mill with a dam and power plant, the concern having gone into bankruptcy because of competition in Georgia and the Carolinas; this plant was now making hand grenades. In a somewhat smaller furniture factory they were setting up a cartridge plant. In the salt marshes of Newcastle ground was being made for new structures which would enable them to double their output of machine guns. So it went; the government was advancing the money to concerns which had the skill and could turn out instruments of war quickly.

All these deals had been arranged and plans laid months in advance, and many contracts were signed before war had been declared or funds voted by Congress. By the time Lanny arrived at Newcastle, all the men of the Budd family were under heavy pressure, working day and night, and talking about nothing but the war and the contribution they were making to it. Nearly everyone in the town was in the same mental state, and this afforded an opportunity for a stranger to slip in unobserved, and have time to adjust himself to an unknown world. Nobody would bother him; indeed, unless he made a noise they would hardly know he was there.

II

Until recently Robbie and his family had occupied an old Colonial house in the residential part of Newcastle. But there was a transformation going on all over New England. Motorcars had become so dependable, and hard-surfaced roads so good, that it was getting to be the fashion to buy a farm and turn it into a country estate; your friends did the same, and collectively built a country club with a golf course, and thus had the advantages of town and country life. You got blooded rams, bulls, and boars; you produced milk and strawberries and asparagus. You were called a "gentleman farmer," and not merely had fresh air, space, and privacy, but you tried to make it pay, and if you succeeded you bragged to all your friends.

The population of such districts consisted of a "gentry," and a great number of tenants and servants, all contented and respectable, and all voting Tory, though it was called "Republican." What Lanny saw of "New" England turned out to be much like Old England. The scenery resembled that "green and pleasant land," where he had enjoyed long walks in the springtime three years ago. There were country lanes and stone walls and small streams with mill dams, and old farmhouses and churches that were shown as landmarks. To be sure, some of the trees were different, high-arching white elms and flowering dogwood soon to be in party costume; also, the dialect of the country people was different—but these were details.

The new house of the Robbie Budds stood at the head of an archway of elms more than a hundred years old. The farmhouse originally on the spot had been moved to one side and made into a garage with chauffeur's and gardener's quarters above. A new house had been built, modern inside, but keeping the "old Colonial" pattern. It had two stories and a half, and what was called a "gambrel" roof, starting at a steep pitch, and, when it got halfway up, finishing at a flatter pitch. In front of the house were big white columns which went above the second story; at one side were smaller columns over a porte-cochere.

Inside, the house was plain, everything painted white. The furniture was of a sort Lanny had never seen before; it also was "old Colonial," and he was to hear conversation about it, and learn the difference between "highboys" and "lowboys," and what a "court cupboard" was, and a "wing-chair," and a "ball and claw." Everything in the house had its proper place and to move it was bad manners. This had been explained to Lanny by his father; Esther had

strict ideas of propriety. He should not play the piano loudly, at
least not without asking if he would disturb anyone. He would
make things easier if he would go to church with the family.
Above all, he must be careful not to speak plainly about anything
having to do with the relationship of men and women; Esther tried
her best to be "modern" but she just couldn't, and it was better not
to put any strain upon her. Lanny promised.

III

He had seen pictures of her, so he knew her when he saw her
standing at the head of the stairs, with the big grandfather's clock
behind her. It was an important moment for her as well as for him,
and both of them realized it. She was becoming a stepmother, one
of the most difficult of human relationships; she was taking a
stranger into her perfectly ordered home, one from a culture foreign to hers and greatly suspected. He was young and he was weak,
yet he had a power which could not be disregarded, having entered
her husband's life ahead of her and sunk deep roots into his heart.

Esther Remson Budd was thirty-five at this time. She was a daughter of the president of the First National Bank of Newcastle, a Budd
institution. She had lived most of her life in the town, and her ideas
of Europe were derived from a summer of travel with teachers and
members of her class in a young ladies' finishing school. She was
one of the most conscientious of women, and gave earnest thought
to being just and upright. She was not cold, but made herself seem
so by subjecting to careful consideration everything she did and
said. She was charitable, and active in the affairs of the First Congregational Church, in which her father-in-law taught a men's Bible
class every Sunday morning. She guided her three children lovingly
but strictly, and did her best to use wisely the powers which wealth
and social position gave her.

To Esther at the age of twenty-one Robbie Budd had been a figure of romance. He went abroad frequently, met important people,
and came home with contracts, the report of which spread widely—

for hardly a person in that town could prosper except as Budd's prospered, and when Robbie sold automatics to Rumania, the merchants of Newcastle ordered a fresh stock of goods, and Esther's father bought her an electric coupé, a sort of showcase to drive about town in. Everybody she knew wanted her to marry Robbie; most of the girls had tried and failed, and knew there was some mystery, some story of a broken heart.

The time came when Robbie took Esther for a long drive and told her about the mysterious woman in France, the artists' model who had been painted in the nude by several men—a strange kind of promiscuity, wholly outside the possibilities of Newcastle, which in its heart was still a Puritan village. There was a child, but the woman refused to marry him and wreck his life. He had ended the unhappy affair, which was then about five years old; he had done so because he saw it preyed upon his father's mind, it could not possibly be fitted into the lessons imparted to the men's Bible class. Robbie would ask Esther to marry him, but only after she knew about this situation, and understood that he had a son and would not disown him.

The two families were working busily to make this match. Did the president of Budd's give his friend, the president of the First National Bank, some hint of the problem? Or did the latter guess what might have happened to a handsome and wealthy young businessman in Paris? Anyhow, Esther's father had a talk with her, of a sort unusual in Puritan New England. He told her the facts of life as concerning future husbands. Among the so-called "eligible" men of the town, those slightly older than herself and able to support her in the position to which she had been accustomed, she would have difficulty in finding one who had not had to do with some woman. The difference between Robbie Budd and most others was that they didn't consider it necessary to tell their future brides about the wild oats they had sown.

Esther asked for time to think all this over, and in the end she and Robbie were married. It had been thirteen years now, and they had three children, and Esther was as near to happiness as any of the "young matrons" she knew. Robbie played golf while his wife went to church, and he drank more liquor than she considered wise; but he was indifferent to the charms of the country club's seductresses, he let her have her way entirely with the children, and he gave her more money than she had use for. On the whole she could count herself a fortunate wife.

But now came this one wild oat of her husband, to be transplanted into her garden and to grow there. She was compelled to face the circumstances which had brought this about. If Lanny was going into an army, it obviously ought to be the American army; and if he came to America, and was denied his father's home, that would be a repudiation and an affront. To say that Robbie had had a previous marriage in France was one of those conventional lies that were hardly lies at all. Women would smile behind their fans, and whisper; but after all there has to be a statute of limitations on scandals.

IV

So Esther was standing at the top of the white-paneled staircase with the grandfather's clock behind her. She was tall and rather slender; she held herself erect, and was quiet and grave in manner. She had straight brown hair, drawn back from a high forehead in defiance of fashion's edicts. Her nose was a little too long and thin, but the rest of her features were regular and her smile kindly. Her brown eyes appraised Lanny, and she kissed him on the cheek. She had made up her just mind that she was going to treat him exactly like her own children, and Robbie had told Lanny that he was to call her "Mother."

She took him into her sitting room to get acquainted. He liked to talk, and was eager and friendly about it. He had been on a steamship which had been in peril of the submarines; he told how the passengers had behaved when they had struck a floating ice cake. He had been in London when it was bombed, and had a bit of shrapnel which had come through the window of a hotel room. (Of course he didn't say who had been in that room with him.) Esther, listening and watching, decided that he was intelligent, and if anything went wrong it could be explained to him. The load upon her mind grew lighter.

She took him to his room, which was in the rear. It was small, but had its own bath, and was alongside the rooms of her two boys. The walls were of pale blue, and the blankets on the single bed were the same. The rug in front of it was made by winding a long soft rope of braided rags into a spiral; his new mother explained that this was a "round-rug," and was an antique. She showed him the "highboy" in which he was to keep his shirts and such belongings. Esther knew the story of each old piece of furniture, which she had "picked up" on trips here and there in the country. Each of these adventures was important to her. As an art lover, Lanny could see that the pieces were well proportioned, and they must have been well made to be in use after a hundred years.

Outside it was warm, and the window of the room was open. There was a cherry tree close by, getting ready to bloom. A bird was singing in it with extraordinary vigor, and Lanny commented on this. Esther said it was a mocking-bird which came every season, and had arrived only a few days ago; not many of them reached New England. Lanny told about the nightingale which made its nest in the court at Bienvenu, and was treated as a member of the family. He had tried to write out all the notes it had sung, and now he would do the same for the mocking-bird. His new mother said this task would keep him busy. The mocking-bird said: "Kerchy, kerchy, kerchy, kerchy." Then it stopped and caught its breath and said: "You pay. You pay. You pay."

V

For months thereafter one of Lanny's adventures would be meeting his relatives. First came his two half-brothers, who attended a private school in town, and were taken every morning and called for in the afternoon. Robert junior was twelve, and Percy eleven; they were handsome boys, who knew how to move quietly about a well-ordered home. Of course they were curious about this new arrival from foreign parts. They took him out at once to show him their Belgian hares; also Prince, their fine German shepherd dog, which they called a "police dog," and which Lanny knew as an "Alsatian." Prince was formally introduced, and looked the new-comer over warily, smelled him thoroughly, and finally wagged his tail. That was important.

Then came Bess, who was nine; her school was near by, but she had a singing lesson that afternoon, and the chauffeur went for her after he had brought the boys. Bess was like her mother, tall for her years and slender, with the same thin nose and sober brown eyes. But she had not yet learned restraint; eagerness transformed her features. When she heard that Lanny had been where the sub-marines were she cried: "Oh, tell us about it!" She hung on every word, and Lanny found himself a young Marco Polo. "Oh, what did you do?" And: "What did you say?" And: "Weren't you dreadfully frightened?"

Lanny relived his own childhood through this half-sister. She asked him questions about his home and what he did there; about the war and the people he knew who had been in it; about the Christmas-card castle in Germany; about Greece, and the ruins, of which there were pictures in her school; about England, and the boat race, and the poor girl who hadn't had enough to eat, and the aviator who at this moment might be up in the air shooting at German planes with a machine gun—was it made by Budd's?

Not one detail escaped her; she would prove it if he left anything out the next time he told the story. And the teller became her hero, her idol; it was a case of love at first sight. He played the piano for her, he showed her how to dance "Dalcroze," and taught her the words of old songs. He made the French language come alive for her. The hour in the distant future when Bessie Budd first had to admit that this wonderful half-brother of hers was anything less than perfect would mark one of the tragedies of her stormy life.

VI

Comically different was Lanny's first meeting with his grandfather, Samuel Budd, which took place by appointment on the
second evening after his arrival. Robbie escorted him to the old
gentleman's home; impossible to subject a youth to such an ordeal
alone. On the way the father told him what to do; not to talk too
much, but to answer questions politely, and listen attentively. "It
would have been better for me if I had always followed those rules,"
he said, with a trace of bitterness.

Robbie was driving and they were alone; so he could speak
frankly, and it was time to do so. "People are what circumstances
have made them, and they don't change very much after they are
grown. Your grandfather is a stubborn person, as much so as the
bricks of which his house is built, and you might as well butt your
head against one as the other."

"I don't want to butt him," said the boy, both amused and worried. "Tell me exactly what to do."

"Well, the first thing is to get clear that you are the fruit of
sin."

From this remark Lanny realized that the quarrel which had
wrecked his mother's life and separated him from his father was still
going on, and that the wounds of it were festering in Robbie's heart.
"Surely," the youth protested, "he can't blame me for what happened then!"

"He will tell you about visiting the iniquity of the fathers upon
the children unto the third and fourth generation."

"Who says that, Robbie?"

"It's somewhere in the Old Testament."

Lanny thought and then asked: "Just what does he want me to
do?"

"He'll tell you that himself. All you have to do is to listen."

Another pause. Finally the son was moved to say: "I suppose he
didn't want me to come to Newcastle?"

"He has agreed to accept you as one of his grandsons. And I think it is important that he should be made to do it."

"Well, whatever you say. I want to please you. But if you're doing it for my sake, you don't have to."

"I'm doing it for my own," said the other, grimly.

"It's been so many years, Robbie. Doesn't that count with him at all?"

"In the sight of the Lord a thousand years are as a day."

Most of the persons Lanny had met in his young life never said anything about the Lord, except as a metaphor or an expletive. Several had said in his hearing that they didn't believe any such Being existed. But now the thought came to Lanny that his father differed from these persons. Robbie believed that the Lord existed, and he didn't like Him.

VII

The president of Budd Gunmakers Corporation had been born in a red brick mansion on the residence boulevard which skirted the edge of Newcastle. He had lived in it all his life, and meant to die in it, regardless of automobiles, country clubs, and other changes of fashion. His butler had been his father's butler, and wasn't going to be changed, even though he was becoming tottery. There were electric lights in the house, but they were hung in old chandeliers. The hand-carved French walnut bookcases were oiled and polished until they shone, and behind their glass doors Lanny caught glimpses of books which he would have liked to examine. He knew this was a very old mansion, and that political as well as business history had been made in it; but it seemed strangely ugly and depressing.

The master was in his study, the ancient butler said, and Robbie led his son at once to the room. At a desk absorbed in some papers sat a man of seventy, solidly built and heavy, as if he did not exercise; partly bald, and having a considerable tuft of whitish gray hair underneath his chin, a style which Lanny had never seen before. He wore gold spectacles, and had creases between his heavy gray eyebrows, which gave him a stern expression, cultivated perhaps for business purposes. From his desk it appeared that he had carried home with him the burden of winning a war.

"Well, young man?" he said, looking up. He did not rise, and apparently didn't plan even to shake hands.

But to Lanny it seemed that a gentleman ought to shake hands with his grandfather when he met him for the first time; so he went straight to the desk and held out his hand, forcing the other to take it. "How do you do, Grandfather?" he said; and as the answer appeared to come slowly he went on: "I have heard a great deal about you, and I'm happy to meet you at last."

"Thank you," said the old gentleman, surprised by this cordiality.

"Everybody has been most kind to me, Grandfather," continued Lanny, as if he thought his progenitor might be worrying about it.

"I am glad," said the other.

Lanny waited, and so did the old man; they gazed at each other, a sort of duel of eyes. Robbie had told him not to talk; but something came to Lanny suddenly, a sort of inspiration. This old munitions maker wasn't happy. He had to live in an ugly old house and be burdened day and night with cares. He had an enormous lot of power which other people were trying to get away from him, and that made him suspicious, it forced him to be hard. But he wasn't hard; underneath he was kind, and all you had to do was to be kind to him, and not ask anything from him.

Lanny decided to follow that hunch. "Grandfather," he announced, "I think I am going to like America very much. I liked England, and I've been surprised to find everything here so much like England."

"Indeed, young man?"

"The best part of England, I mean. I hope I shan't see anything like their terrible slums."

The elderly industrialist rose to the bait. "Our working people are getting double wages now. You will see them wearing silk socks and shirts, and buying themselves cars on the installment plan. They will soon be our masters."

"I was told the same thing in England, sir. People complain about the taxes there. The owners of the great estates say that they are going to have to break them up. Do you think that will happen in this country?"

"Apparently we plan to finance our share of the war by means of loans," replied the president of Budd's. "It is a dangerous procedure."

"M. Zaharoff talked about that. He doesn't seem to object to war loans of any size. Maybe it is because he is getting so large a share of the proceeds."

"Ahem! Yes," said the grandfather. "I am happy to say that Budd's have not conducted their affairs on the same fly-by-night basis as Zaharoff."

The art of conversation is highly esteemed in France, and Lanny had acquired it. He had heard the worldly-wise Baroness de la Tourette declare that the one certain way to interest a man was to get him to talking about his own affairs. A beginning having been made in this case, Lanny went on to remark: "I find that Budd's have a very good reputation abroad, sir."

"Humph! They want our products just now."

"Yes, sir; but I mean with persons who are disinterested."

"Who, for example?"

"Well, M. Rochambeau. He spent a good part of his life in the Swiss diplomatic service, so he's very well informed. He has been most helpful to me during the two and a half years that I haven't been seeing Robbie. Anything I didn't understand about world affairs he was always kind enough to explain to me."

"You were fortunate."

"Yes, Grandfather. Before that there was M. Priedieu, the librarian at Mrs. Chattersworth's château. He helped to form my literary taste."

"What books did he give you, may I ask?"

"Stendhal and Montaigne, Corneille and Racine, and of course Molière."

"All French writers," said the deacon of the First Congregational

Church. "May I inquire whether any of your advisers ever mentioned a book called the Bible?"

"Oh, yes, sir. M. Rochambeau told me that I should study the New Testament. I had some difficulty in finding a copy on the Riviera."

"Did you read it?"

"Every word of it, sir."

"And what did you get out of it?"

"It moved me deeply; in fact it made me cry, four different times. You know it tells the same story four times over."

"I am aware of it," said the old gentleman, dryly. "Have you read the Old Testament?"

"No, sir; that is one of the unfortunate gaps in my education. They tell me you are conducting a Bible class."

"Every Sunday morning at ten o'clock. I am dealing with the First Book of Samuel, and would be pleased to have my grandson enroll."

"Thank you. I will surely come. M. Rochambeau tells me that the best Jewish literature is found in the Old Testament."

"It is much more than Jewish literature, young man. Do not forget that it is the Word of Almighty God, your heavenly Father."

VIII

All that time Robbie Budd had been sitting in silence, occupied with keeping his emotions from showing in his face. Of course he knew that this youngster had had a lot of practice in dealing with elderly gentlemen. Colonels and generals, cabinet ministers, senators, diplomats, bankers, they had come to Bienvenu, and sometimes it had happened that a boy had to make conversation until his mother got her nose powdered; or perhaps he had taken them for a sail, or for a walk, to show them the charms of the Cap. All this experience he had now put to use, apparently with success; for here sat the leader of the men's Bible class of the First Congregational Church of Newcastle, Connecticut, who was supposed to be saving the world for democracy, and had before him a portfolio of important papers contributory to that end; but he put his heavy fist on them, and set to work to save the soul of a seventeen-year-old bastard from a semi-heathen part of the world where you had difficulty in finding a copy of the sacred Word of God.

To this almost-lost soul he explained that the Scripture was a source, not merely of church doctrine, but of church polity; and that officers of the church—including Deacon Budd—were to be thought of as exemplars of Christian doctrine, from whom others might understand the nature of Conversion and the reality of Salvation. The deacon reached into the corner of his desk and produced a small pamphlet, yellowed with age, entitled *A Brief Digest of the Boston Confession of Faith*. "This," said he, "was composed by your great-great-grandfather for popular use as a simple statement of our basic faith. In it you will find clearly set forth that central truth of our religion—that there is no Salvation save in the blood of the Cross. For that guilt incurred by Adam's sin passed on into humanity together with the colossal iniquity of the accumulated sins through the ages has made all men hopelessly evil in God's sight, and deserving His just punishment of spiritual death. Outraged by human sin, the wrath of God has only been appeased by the atoning blood shed by His Son upon the Cross, and only by faith in the blood of Christ can any man find Salvation. No righteousness of life, no good deeds or kindly words, no service of fellow-men can offer any hope of Salvation. It is belief in that redeeming blood poured out on Calvary that alone can win God's forgiveness and save us from eternal death. I recommend the pamphlet as your introduction to the study of the true Old Gospel."

"Yes, Grandfather," said Lanny. He was deeply impressed. As in the case of Kurt explaining the intricacies of German philosophy, Lanny could not be sure how many of these striking ideas had been created by his remarkable progenitors.

Having thus performed his duty as a guardian of sound doctrine, the old gentleman allowed himself to unbend. "Your father tells me that you had a pleasant voyage."

"Oh, yes," replied the youth, brightening. "It couldn't have been pleasanter—except for the collision with an iceberg. Did Robbie tell you about that?"

"He overlooked it."

"It was such a small iceberg, I suppose it would be better to speak of it as a cake of ice. But it gave us quite a bump, and the ship came to a stop. Of course everybody's mind had been on submarines from the moment we left England, so they all thought we had been torpedoed, and there was a panic among the passengers."

"Indeed?"

"The strangest thing you could imagine, sir. I never saw people behave like that before. The women became hysterical, especially those in the third class. Those that had babies grabbed them up and rushed into the first-class saloon, and they all piled their babies in the middle of the floor. No one could imagine why they did that; I asked some of them afterwards, and they said they didn't know; some woman put her baby there, and the rest of them thought that must be the place for babies, so they laid them down there, and the babies were all squalling, and the women screaming, some of them on their knees praying, and some clamoring for the officers to save them—so much noise that the officers couldn't tell them that it was all right."

"A curious experience. And now, young man, may I ask what you plan to do with yourself in this new country?"

"Surely, Grandfather. Robbie wishes me to prepare for St. Thomas's, and he's going to get me a tutor."

"Do you really intend to work?"

"I always work hard when I get down to it. I wanted to be able to read music at sight, and I have stayed at it until I can read most anything."

"These are serious times, and few of us have time for music."

"I'm going to learn whatever my tutor wishes, Grandfather."

"Very well; I'll look to hear good reports."

There was a pause. Then the old man turned to his son. "Robert," said he, "I've been looking into this vanadium contract, and it strikes me as a plain hold-up."

"No doubt," said Robbie. "But we're getting our costs plus ten percent, so we don't have to worry."

"I don't like to pass a swindle like this on to the government."

"Well, the dealers have their story. Everybody's holding up everybody all along the line."

"I think you'd better go down to New York and inquire around."

"If you say so. I have to go anyhow, on account of that new bomb-sight design."

"It seems to be standing the tests?"

They went on for quite a while, talking technical details. Lanny was used to such talk, and managed to learn something. In this case he learned that an elderly businessman who got his church doctrine and polity from eighteen hundred years ago, and his chin whiskers and chandeliers from at least a hundred years ago, would change a bomb-sight or the formula for a steel alloy the moment his research men showed him evidence of an improvement.

At last the grandfather said: "All right. I have to get back to work."

"You're carrying too much of a load, Father," ventured Robbie. "You ought to leave some of these decisions to us young fellows."

"We'll be over the peak before long. I'll hold up this vanadium deal for a day, and you run up to New York. Good-by, young man"—this to Lanny—"and see that you come to my Bible class."

"Surely, Grandfather," replied the youth. But already the elder's eyes were turning toward that pile of papers on his desk.

The other two went out and got into the car, and Robbie started to drive. Lanny waited for him to speak; then he discovered that the vibration of the seat was not from the engine, but was his father shaking with laughter.

"Did I do the right thing, Robbie?"

"Grand, kid, perfectly grand!" Robbie shook some more, and then asked: "Whatever put it into your head to talk?"

"Did I say too much?"

"It was elegant conversation—but what made you think of it?"

"Well, I'll tell you. I just decided that people aren't kind enough to each other."

The father thought that over. "Maybe it was worth trying," he admitted.

20

The Pierian Spring

I

NORMAN HENRY HARPER was the name of Lanny's tutor. He didn't in the least resemble the elegant and easygoing Mr. Elphinstone, nor yet the happy-go-lucky Jerry Pendleton. He was a professional man, and performed his duties with dignity. He prepared young men to pass examinations. He already knew about the examinations; he found out about each young man as quickly as possible, and then, presto—A plus B equals C—the young man had passed the examination. To the resolution of this formula Mr. Harper devoted his exclusive attention; his equipment and procedure were streamlined, constructed upon scientific principles, as much so as a Budd machine gun.

Nor was this comparison fantastic; on the contrary, the more you considered it, the more apposite it appeared. Experts on military science had been writing for decades about the perpetual war going on between gunmakers and armorplate makers; and in the same way there were educators, whose business it was to cram knowledge into the minds of youth, and there was youth, perversely resisting this process, seeking every device to "get by."

The educators had invented examinations, and the students were trying to circumvent them. Being provided by their parents with large sums of money, it was natural that they should use it to get expert help in this never-ceasing war. And so had developed the profession of tutoring.

This was America that Lanny had come to live in, and he wanted to know all about it. He listened to what Mr. Harper said, and afterwards put his mind on it and tried to figure out what it meant. A young man wanted to get into "prep school" as quickly as possible, in order that he might get through "prep school" as quickly as possible, in order that he might get into college as quickly as possible, in order that he might get out of college as quickly as possible. Mr. Harper didn't say any of that—for the reason that it didn't need saying. If it wasn't so, what was he here for?

Mr. Harper was about forty years of age, a brisk and business-like person who might have been one of the Budd salesmen; he was getting bald, and plastered what hairs were left very carefully over the top of his head. For about half his life he had been studying college entrance examinations. It would be an exaggeration to say that he could tell you every question which had been asked in any college of the United States during twenty years; but his knowledge approached that encyclopedic character. He knew the personalities of the different professors, and what exam questions they had used for the last few years, and so he could make a pretty good guess what questions were due for another turn. He would hold up his hand in the middle of a conversation; no, no use to know that, they never asked anything like that.

Just recently had come a revolution in Mr. Harper's profession. The educational authorities had got together and set up a body called the College Entrance Examination Board, which was going to hold uniform examinations all over the country, good for any college the student might select. There were a quarter of a million college students, and six times as many high school students, so of course they had to be handled on a mass-production basis. It was part of the process of standardizing America; everybody was eating corn flakes out of the same kind of package, and all students of the year 1917 were going to get into college because they had read Washington Irving's *Alhambra* and George Washington's Farewell Address.

Lanny Budd was, so Mr. Harper declared, the most complicated problem he had ever tackled; he became quite enthusiastic over him, like a surgeon over an abdominal tumor with fascinating complications. From the point of view of the College Entrance Examination Board, Lanny quite literally didn't know anything. One by one the youth brought his burnt offerings and his wave offerings to the educational high priest and saw them rejected. Music? No, there are no credits for music. Greek dramatists? They teach those after you get into college, if at all. The same with Stendhal and Montaigne and Corneille and so on. Molière, now, they use *Le Bourgeois Gentilhomme*—are you sure you remember the plot? Advanced French will count three units out of the fifteen you must have—but are you sure you can pass advanced French?

"Well, I've spoken French all my life," said Lanny, bewildered.

"I know; but you won't be asked to speak it, and very few of your examiners could understand you if you did. How do you say 'a tired child'?"

"*Un enfant fatigué.*"

"And how do you say 'a beautiful day'?"

"*Un beau jour.*"

"Well, now, why do you put one adjective ahead of the noun and the other after it?"

The uneducated youth looked blank. "I really don't know," said he. "I just do it."

"Exactly. But the examination paper will ask you to state the rule, or give the list of exceptions, or whatever it may be. And what will you do?"

"I guess I'll have to go back to France," said Lanny.

II

Mr. Harper decided that by heroic efforts it might be possible for this eccentric pupil to be got ready for the third year of prep school in the fall. Private academies were not so crowded as public high schools, and were better able to handle exceptional cases. But the first thing was to buckle down to plane and solid geometry, and to ancient and medieval history. Yes, said Mr. Harper, Sophocles and Euripides might help, but what really counted was facts. If a candidate were to tell a board of examiners that the Greek spirit was basically one of tragedy, how would they know whether he was spoofing them? But if he said that the naval battle of Salamis was won in the year 480 B.C. by the Athenian Themistocles, there was something that couldn't be faked.

"All right," Lanny said, "I'll go to it." That was what his father wanted, and his grandfather, and his stepmother; that was the test of character, the way to get on in America. So he put his textbooks on the little table by the open window of his room, with the door shut so that nobody would disturb him, and set to work to ram the contents of those books into his mind—names, places, and dates, and no foolish unprofitable flights of the imagination; rules, formulas, and facts, and no superfluous emotions of pity or terror.

The only company he had was the mocking-bird. This slender and delicate creature, gray with a little white, liked to sit on the topmost spray of the cherry tree and pour out its astonishing volume of song. A mystery when it slept; for no matter how late Lanny might work, it was singing in the moonlight, and if he opened his eyes at dawn, it was already under full steam. It imitated the cries of all the other birds; it said "meeauw" like the catbird, and "flicker, flicker, flicker," like the big yellow-hammer. But mostly it improvised. Of course it said no words, because it couldn't form the consonants; but as you listened you were impelled to make up words to correspond to its rhythm and melody. Sometimes they came tripping fast: "Sicady, sicady, sicady, sicady."

Then the singer would stop, and and say very deliberately: "Peanuts first. Peanuts first."

Lanny was so determined to make good that he wanted to study all the time; but Esther wouldn't have that. In the middle of the afternoon, after Mr. Harper had come and heard him recite and had laid out the next day's work—then he must quit, and go with the other young people for tennis, and for what he now learned to call a "swim" instead of a "bathe." Five days in the week he could work, mornings and evenings; and on Saturdays there would be a picnic, or a sailing party, and in the evening a dance. He had so many cousins of all degrees that he wouldn't have to go out of the family for company and diversion.

They were an astonishing lot of people, these Budds. The earlier generations had married young, and the women had accepted all the children the Lord had sent them—ten, or sometimes twenty, and then the women would die off, and the men would start again. In these modern days, of course, everything was changed; one or two children was the rule, and a woman like Esther, who had three, felt that she had gone out of her way to serve the community. But still there were a great many Budds, and others with Budd for their first or middle name. Grandfather Samuel had six daughters and four sons living; Samuel's oldest brother, a farmer, was still thriving at the age of eighty, and had had seventeen children, and most of them still alive, preaching and practicing the Word of the Lord their God, that their days might be long in the land which the Lord their God had given them.

Most of those who were not preaching the Word were employed by Budd Gunmakers Corporation in one capacity or another, and just now were working at the task of making the days of the Germans as short as possible. The Germans had their own God, who was working just as hard for his side—so Lanny read in a German magazine which the kind Mr. Robin took the trouble to send him. How these Gods adjusted matters up in their heaven was a problem which was too much for Lanny, so he put his mind on the dates of ancient Greek and Roman wars.

III

On Sunday mornings the earnest student would dress himself
in a freshly pressed palm beach suit and panama hat, and at five
minutes before ten o'clock would be among those who thronged
into the First Congregational Church. This building occupied a
prominent position on the central "square" of Newcastle; a large,
two-story structure, built of wood and painted white, with a high-
pitched roof and rows of second-story windows resembling those
of a private residence. What told you it was a church was the
steeple which rose from the front center; a square tower, with a
round cylinder on top of that, then a smaller cube and then a very
sharp and tall pyramid on that. Topping all was a lightning rod;
but no cross—that would have meant idolatry, the "Whore of
Babylon"—in short, a Catholic church. There were stairs inside the
steeple, and windows so that you could look out as you climbed.
Robbie said the original purpose was so that the townsmen could
keep watch against the Pequot Indians; but there was a twinkle in
his eye, so Lanny wasn't sure.

The men's Bible class was one of the features of Newcastle life.
It is not in every town that you can meet the leading captain of
industry face to face once a week, and have a chance to ask him a
question. So many took advantage of this opportunity that the
class was held in the main body of the church. Many of the leading
businessmen attended, most of the Budd executives old and young,
and everyone who hoped ever to be an executive. It was a business
as well as a cultural event.

Did the teacher of this remarkable class have any cynical ideas
as to what caused so many hard-working citizens of his town to
give up their golf and tennis and listen to the expounding of ancient
Jewish morality and Swiss and Scottish theology? Doubtless he did,
for his faith in his Lord and Master did not extend to the too many
children of this Almighty One. It was enough for Samuel Budd
that they came; having them at his mercy for one hour, he pounded
the sacred message into them. If they did not take their chance,

it was because the Lord had predestined them to everlasting damnation, for reasons which were satisfactory to Him and into which no mortal had any business trying to pry. If they chose to sit with blank faces and occupy their minds with how to get a raise in salary, or how to get their wives invited to the Budd homes, or what make of new car they were going to purchase—that also had been arranged by an inscrutable Divine Providence, and all that a deacon of the stern old faith could do was to quote the texts which the Lord had provided, together with such interpretations as the Holy Spirit saw fit to reveal to him at ten o'clock on Sunday morning.

IV

The regular service followed the men's Bible class; which meant that the ladies had an extra hour in which to curl their hair and set on top of it their delicate confections of straw and artificial flowers. The war hadn't changed the fashions, nor the fact that there were fashions; all that elegance which had fled from Paris and London was now in Newcastle. The chauffeurs drove back to the homes for the ladies, and they entered with primness and piety, but now and then a sidelong glance to be sure that gentlemen standing in the sunshine on the steps were properly attentive.

That little heathen, Lanny Budd, had never attended a church service before, except for a wedding or a funeral; but he did not reveal that fact. The rule was the same as for a dinner party: watch your hostess and do what she does. He stood up and sang a hymn, from a book which Esther put into his hand, the number of the hymn having been announced twice by the minister. Then he bowed his head and closed his eyes while the Reverend Mr. Saddleback prayed. "Thou knowest, O Lord," was his opening formula; after which he proceeded to tell the Lord many things which the Lord knew, but which the congregation presumably didn't. Also he asked the Lord to do many things for the congregation, and it seemed to Lanny that the Lord must know about these already.

A well-trained choir sang a florid and elaborate anthem, this being Newcastle's substitute for grand opera. A collection was taken up, and Grandfather Budd passed the plate among the richest pew holders up front, and kept an eagle eye upon the bills which they dropped in. Finally Mr. Saddleback preached a sermon. Lanny had hoped that he would explain some of the difficult points of Fundamentalist doctrine, but instead he explained the will of the Lord with regard to Kaiser Wilhelm and his *Kultur.* "And surely your blood of your lives will I require; at the hand of every beast will I require it, and at the hand of man; at the hand of every man's brother will I require the life of man. Whoso sheddeth man's blood, by man shall his blood be shed. And I, behold, I establish my covenant with you, and with your seed after you." The Reverend Mr. Saddleback turned his pulpit into a Sinai, and thundered such awful words, and they seemed a direct message to Budd Gunmakers Corporation, which in the spring of that year 1917 had enlisted all its lathes and grinding machines, its jigs and dies and other tools, in the allied services of the United States government and the Lord God Almighty.

V

Lanny took time off to write letters home and tell his mother and Marcel how things were going with him. To cheer them up he went into detail about the martial fervors which surrounded him. Beauty sent him affectionate replies, and told him that Marcel was painting a portrait of Emily Chattersworth, and wouldn't let her pay him for it; it was his thanks for what she was doing for the poilus. Marcel was in a state of increasing suspense and dread, because of the failure of the French offensive in Champagne, in which his old regiment had been nearly wiped out. Beauty couldn't say much about it, but doubtless Robbie would have inside news; and he did.

Also Lanny wrote to Rick and to his wife. From the former he had a cheerful post card, beginning "Old Top," as usual. From

Nina he learned that Rick had made a dangerous forced landing, but fortunately behind the English lines; he was a highly skilled flier now, what they called an "ace." Also Nina said that the baby was real and was making itself known. She told him about her examinations, and he told about those for which he was being prepared. In his letters he permitted himself to have a little fun with them.

He wrote the Robin boys in the same strain, and they told him about their school work, which for some strange reason they loved. He wondered if it was a characteristic of the Jews that they enjoyed hard labor; if so, it gave them an unfair advantage over other races. Lanny found that they bore that reputation in Newcastle; they had little stores in the working-class districts of the town, and kept them open until late hours, and now and then were fined for selling things on the Sabbath—the Puritan Sabbath, that is. They sent their children to the schools, where they persisted in winning prizes; there were so many of them crowding into Harvard that they had been put on an unadmitted quota. Members of the New England aristocracy would say to their complacent sons: "If you don't buck up and work, I'll send you to Harvard to compete with the Jews." Lanny wrote that to the Robins, knowing that it would make them chirp.

The salesman of electrical apparatus in Rotterdam forwarded another of Lanny's letters to Kurt; a very careful one, in which Lanny told all about his studies, but didn't mention the U.S.A. He just said: "I have gone to visit my father's home. Write me there." Kurt knew about Newcastle; and in due course a letter came, by way of Switzerland, as usual. Kurt said that he was well, and had gone back to his duties, and was glad to hear that his friend was keeping his mind on matters of permanent interest and benefit. That was all; but Lanny could read between those lines, and understand that even though Kurt was now fighting America, he didn't want Lanny to be fighting Germany!

Midsummer; and Nina wrote again. Rick had had a week's leave, and had come home; she had been to The Reaches with him—and, oh, so happy they had been! So happy they might be all their lives, if only this cruel slaughter would end! The baronet and his wife had been kind to her, and Rick was a darling—they had boated and bathed and played croquet. And the heavenly nights, with music on the river, and starlight trembling on the water, and love in their hearts! It all came over Lanny in a wave of melancholy longing; he too had had love in his heart, and had it still—but the granddaughter of Lord Dewthorpe was the poorest of correspondents, and her letters were skimpy, matter of fact, and wholly lacking in charm. Taking care of wounded men all day left one tired and unromantic, it appeared. Old England had had too much of war, and now it was New England's turn.

VI

Perhaps the letter from Nina, and Lanny's continual thinking about it, may have had something to do with the strange experience which befell him a few nights later. When Lanny went to bed he was tired in both mind and body, and usually fell asleep at once, and rarely wakened until the maid tapped on his door. But now something roused him; at least, he insisted that he was awake, fully awake, and no amount of questioning by others could shake his certainty. He lay there, and it seemed that the first faint gray of dawn was stealing into the room—just enough light so that you could know it was a room, and that there were objects in it. The mocking-bird hadn't noticed the light, and the crickets had gone to sleep, and the stillness caught Lanny's attention; it seemed abnormal.

Then a weird feeling began to steal over him. Something was happening, he didn't know what it was, but fear of it began to stir in his soul, and his skin began to creep and draw tight, so it seemed. Lanny stared into the darkness, and it appeared to be taking form, and he began to wonder whether the light was daylight or something else; it seemed to be shaping itself into a mass at the foot of his bed, and the mass began to move, and suddenly Lanny realized it was Rick. A pale gray figure, just luminous enough so that it could be clearly seen; Rick in his flier's uniform, all stained with mud. On his face was a grave, rather mournful expression, and across his forehead a large red gash.

It came to Lanny in a sort of inner flash: Rick is dead! He raised his head a little and stared at the figure, and a cold chill went over him, and his teeth began to chatter, and his eyes popped wide, trying to see better. "Rick!" he whispered, half under his breath; but maybe that was a mistake, for right away the figure began to fade. Lanny cried again, half in fright and half in longing: "Rick! Speak to me!"

But the pale form faded away—or rather it seemed to spread itself over the room, and when it did, Lanny could see that it was the beginning of dawn and that objects were slowly looming in the room. All at once the mocking-bird tuned up and the other little birds outside began to say: "Cheep, cheep," and "Twitter, twitter." Lanny lay sick with horror, saying to himself soundlessly: "Rick is dead! Rick is dead!"

He did not go to sleep again. He lay till the sun was nearly up, and then put on his clothes and went into the garden and walked up and down, trying to get himself together before he had to meet the rest of the family. He tried to argue with himself; but there was no making headway against that inner voice. It was the first great loss of his life. He had to wrestle it out with himself—and he knew that he hated this war, and all wars, now and forever; just as Beauty had done in the beginning, and as Robbie still did in the depths of his heart, though he had stopped saying it.

VII

Impossible that Robbie and Esther should not notice his distraught condition. He said that he had slept badly—he didn't want to discuss the matter before the children. But after they had gone to their play he told his father and stepmother. As he had expected, Esther hated the idea. Hers was a practical mind and her beliefs in supernormal phenomena were limited to those which had been ratified and approved by biblical exegesis. The visit of Emmaus was all right, because it was in the Bible; but for there to be an apparition in the year 1917—and in her home!—that could be nothing but superstition. Only Negroes, and maybe Catholics, let themselves be troubled by such notions. "You just had a dream, Lanny!" insisted his father's wife.

"I was exactly as wide awake as I am right now," he answered. "I feel sure something dreadful has happened to Rick."

He wanted to cable Nina; and Robbie said he would send it—his name being known would speed matters with the censors. He promised to attend to it the moment he reached the office, and to prepay a reply, because Nina didn't have much money. "What news about Rick?" he sent; and in course of the afternoon his secretary called the house and read Lanny the reply: "Rick reported well last week's letter."

Of course, Lanny said, that didn't tell him anything. He insisted upon a second message being sent, with reply prepaid: "Advise immediately if trouble." For two days Lanny waited, doing his utmost to keep his mind upon his studies, so as not to forfeit the respect of his stepmother and her friends. Then came another cablegram from Nina: "Rick badly hurt great pain may not live prayers."

Somehow it was that last word which broke Lanny down and made him cry like a baby. He was quite sure that Nina was not a religious person; she was looking forward to being a scientist—but now the same thing had happened to her that had happened to Beauty in those dreadful hours when Marcel's life hung upon a thread. She was praying; she was even moved to cable for Lanny's help!

Could Lanny pray? He wasn't sure. He had listened to the Reverend Mr. Saddleback praying and had been inclined to take the procedure with a trace of humor. But now he would be glad to have anybody's help to keep Rick alive.

Esther, of course, was much affected by what had happened; in this crisis their two so different natures came to a temporary understanding. Her pride was humbled, and she had to admit that there were more things in heaven and earth than were dreamt of in her philosophy. If something in Rick's soul had been able to travel from France to Connecticut, why might not something from Lanny's go back to France? As it happened, prayers for the sick and afflicted were in accord with the doctrines of Esther's church; so why should not the congregation be requested to pray for a wounded English officer—especially since their own boys were not yet being killed?

"Spare no expense in helping Rick," cabled the practical Robbie. "Keep me advised by wire." He arranged for Nina to have unlimited credit for cabling—you can do that kind of thing when you are one of the princes of industry. Nina replied that her husband was in a base hospital abroad, and she could not get to him; they just had to wait—and pray.

It was some time before she herself knew the story and could write it to Lanny. The English troops had been making an attack, and Rick had been assigned to the defense of another plane which was doing "contact flying"—that is, observing the advance of the troops, and sending information by wireless so that the artillery barrage could keep just in front of them. Rick had been attacked by three German planes and had been shot through the knee; he was forced to make a landing behind the enemy's lines, and his plane overturned—that was when he had got the gashed forehead. The attack being under way, the Germans had not found him; he had dragged himself into a shell hole and hidden, and for two days and nights had lain, conscious only part of the time, hoping that the British might advance and find him. This had happened—but meantime his wound had become infected, and he was suffering dreadfully; it was a question whether his leg could be saved, or whether he could survive having it amputated.

VIII

Men were being killed by thousands every day; but still the work of the world had to go on. Lanny had to wipe the tears from his eyes, shut from his mind the thought of his friend's suffering, and acquire information about the conquests of King Alexander the Great. Hosts of men had been mutilated in those wars; not with machine-gun bullets, but with arrows and spears, just as painful, and as liable to cause infection. All history was one river of blood—and who could live if he spent his time weeping upon its banks?

Lanny had managed to become interested in his job. He was young, and nothing could be entirely a bore. Mr. Harper came every day and heard him recite, and was pleased with his progress, and told Esther, so the youth enjoyed a glow of satisfaction. He was making good; he was taking the curse off himself—and he was getting an education. "Drink deep," a poet had sung of the Pierian spring. Here in America it had been dammed and piped, and the water was metered and duly paid for at a fixed price; you turned a spigot, and drew so many quarts at a time, and when you had drunk it five days a week for ten weeks, that was called a "unit." Ancient history, one unit; medieval history, one unit; algebra one, geometry one; elementary French two, advanced French three, and so on.

Lanny read the announcement, made by the Yale authorities, that the university would now require military training. The slogan "For God, for Country, and for Yale" would become "Yale for God and Country." But Robbie said not to worry, this war wasn't going to last forever, and after Yale had won it, everything could go on as before. Mr. Harper insisted that a unit would always be a unit; it was the indestructible particle of the educational world. So Lanny memorized the dates of Charles Martel the Hammer, and of Charlemagne and the Holy Roman Empire.

No more apparitions came to him. He learned by the more expensive medium of the cable that Rick was still alive; then that he had been brought to England; then that he was having an opera-

tion, and then a second—he was going to be one of those cases which
constitute a sort of endowment for surgeons and hospitals. Lanny,
of course, had written Nina all about his vision; Rick admitted that
when he had crashed he had thought about Lanny—because Lanny
was so afraid of crashes, and had told him about Marcel's.

Later on Nina wrote that Rick was back at his father's home,
and she was helping to take care of him. "Write him affectionate
things and cheer him up," she said. The knee is a difficult place to
heal, and if Rick was ever to walk again, it would be with a steel
brace on his leg. Poor, proud, defiant, impatient aesthete, he was
going to be a pitiful, nerve-shaken cripple; his wife would be one of
those devoted souls—millions of them all over Europe—who were
glad to get even part of a husband back again, and have that much
safe from the slaughterman's ax.

IX

Every time Lanny went swimming or boating, he saw great towering iron chimneys, pouring out billowing clouds of smoke. At
night, if he sat on the front porch, he saw down the vista of the
elm trees a dull red glare in the sky. That was Budd's; that was
the plant, the source of all Lanny's good things, and one of the
places where the war was being won. From earliest childhood he
had listened to discourses about its functions and ownership—those
precious pieces of paper called stock certificates, which guaranteed
safety and comfort to whoever held them, and to his children and
his children's children. Robbie, man of business and of money, had
been wont to preach little sermons, playful yet serious; he would
see a ragged old beggar slouching along in rain or snow, and would
say: "There, but for the plant, go you!"

Of course Lanny wanted to see it, and Robbie promised to arrange it. As soon as they heard the proposal, Junior and Percy put
in their clamors; they had seen it before, but no one could see it
enough. And then Bess, loudest of all—why did she have to be left
out of everything? Bess had heard about votes for women, and de-

clared that she believed in them from now on. Hadn't she just had
her tenth birthday party, and got better marks than either of her
brothers in school? The father said, all right, he would have one
of his secretaries take Saturday morning off and escort the four of
them.

They drove through the great steel gates of the plant, guarded
now by armed men, for there had been explosions in American munitions plants, and German agents were known to be active. They
were led from one huge building to another, and saw white-hot
steel being poured from giant ladles amid blinding showers of
sparks; they saw golden ingots being rolled into sheets, or cut by
screaming saws, or pounded and squeezed in huge presses. The clat-
ter and clamor was deafening to a stranger. Their escort said that
munitions were noisy at two periods of their career, the beginning
and the end; he said that men got used to both, sooner or later. The
foreman on the floor could tell in a moment if anything went
wrong, because one of the familiar sounds was missing or out of
tune.

They were taken through rooms as big as railroad sheds, in which
traveling cranes overhead brought heavy parts, and electric motor
trucks brought other parts, and men working in long lines assembled heavy machine guns, which were on wheels. A gallery ran
about the rooms, from which you could look down upon the
crowded floor, and it seemed a place of hopeless confusion; but the
secretary assured them that every motion made by one of those human ants had been studied for weeks in a laboratory, and that the
movements of each piece of machinery were timed to the second.

They walked through long rooms like corridors, in which such
things as time fuses for anti-aircraft shells were made. Women and
girls sat at a table which the children thought must surely be the
longest in the world; on top of it was an endless belt, gliding silently.
The object being manufactured started from nothing, and each
worker added a bit, or maybe just turned a screw, until, at the far
end, the completed products were slid onto trays, and taken by
truck to a part of the plant where shrapnel shells were loaded. That

place was remote, and visitors were not permitted there—not even members of the family.

Lanny was interested in time fuses, but still more interested in women and girls. He saw that they all wore uniforms, and that the motions of their hands were swift and unvarying; most of them never took their eyes from the job, and if they did, it was only for the fraction of a second—even when there was a good-looking young man in the line of vision. They were riveted to this task for seven hours and forty minutes every day, with twenty minutes for lunch, and Lanny wondered what it did to their minds and bodies. The secretary assured him that all this had been studied by experts, and the speed of the belt precisely adjusted so that no one would become weary. It was a pleasant thing to hear, but Lanny would have been interested to ask the girls.

Of course he might have gone out at night, in the parts of the town where the picture theaters and the bright lights were, and it would have been easy to "pick up" one of them and get her to talking. But Lanny wasn't roaming the streets at night; he was studying and earning credits with his family, as well as with St. Thomas's prep school. All he would know about the Budd plant was what a friendly but discreet young secretary saw fit to tell him. This was wartime, and every department was working in three eight-hour shifts. Those who couldn't stand the pace went elsewhere.

X

Lanny took his ideas and impressions home and thought them over in his leisure hours. He was proud of that large institution which his forefathers had built; he understood Robbie's dream, that some day his oldest son might become the master of it. Lanny put the question to himself: "Do I want to do that?" The time to decide was now; for what was the sense of shutting himself up in a room and learning the dates of old wars if his business was going to be with new ones?

It seemed to him that, if he meant to become a maker of muni-

tions, he ought to go into the plant and begin learning from his
father and his overburdened grandfather all about steel and alu-
minum and the new alloys which were being created in the labora-
tories; about slow-burning and quick-burning powders, and the
ways of grinding which made the subtle differences; the various
raw materials, their prices and sources of supply; money, and how
it was handled and kept; and, above all, men, how to judge them,
how to get out of them the best work they were capable of performing. This was the education which a captain of industry had to
acquire. It was grim, tough work, and it did something to those
who undertook it.

First of all Lanny ought to make up his mind on the subject of
war. Did he agree with his father that men would go on fighting
forever and ever, because that was their nature and nothing could
change it? Did he agree with his grandfather that God had ordained
every war, and that what happened on this earth was of little importance compared with eternity? Was he going to adopt either of
those beliefs—or just drift along, believing one thing when his
father talked to him, and another when he saw Rick's image at the
foot of the bed?

One thing seemed plain: if you were going to be happy in any
job, you had to believe in that job. Robbie said it was enough to
know that the money was coming in; but Lanny was watching his
father more closely, and becoming sure that he was far from happy.
Robbie was by nature sociable, and liked to say what he thought;
but now he kept silence. His heart was unwarmed by all this blaze
of patriotic excitement which possessed the country, the newspapers
full of propaganda, the streets blaring music and the oratory of
"four-minute men" and salesmen of "liberty bonds." The airplanes
were going to be driven by "liberty motors," and you ate "liberty
steak" and "liberty cabbage" instead of hamburgers and sauerkraut.
Robbie hated such nonsense; he hated still more to see the country
and its resources being used for what he said were the purposes of
British imperialism.

This attitude didn't make for contentment either in his work or in his home. As it happened, Robbie's wife was growing more martial-minded every day; she was believing the atrocity stories, putting her money into liberty bonds, helping to organize the women of Newcastle for community singing, for rolling bandages, nursing, whatever doings were called for by patriotic societies and government officials. It happened that President Wilson was the son of a Presbyterian minister, and that Esther's mother was the daughter of one. Esther read the President's golden words and believed every one of them; when Robbie would remark that the British ruling classes were the shrewdest propagandists in the world, a sudden chill would fall at the breakfast table.

21

The Thoughts of Youth

I

LANNY didn't meet his grandfather again for quite a while. He saw him in church, but made no attempt to catch his eye; just dropped his dollar bill into the plate and knew that his good deed had been credited for that day. The old gentleman was absorbed in the task which the Lord had assigned him, and he stayed in his big mansion, with an old-maid niece to run it, and rarely went anywhere except to his office. But he managed to keep track of the members of his big family, and if they were doing anything of which he disapproved, he let them know it. "Silence means consent," remarked Robbie, with a smile.

He added: "I showed him Mr. Harper's report on your progress."

"What did he say?"

"He grunted and said you were a clever lad, but a chatterbox. Of course that's not to be taken too seriously. It's not according to his nature to give praise."

Lanny met others of his uncles and aunts; sometimes in church, sometimes when they came to the house and stayed to meals. Robbie would tell him about these people—always when the two were alone, because Robbie's view of his relatives was often touched with mischief. They were a cranky lot; an old family which had had money for generations and could indulge their whims however extravagant. Some were satisfied to stay in harness, and make more money, even though they had no need of it; but others took up special duties, such as endowing missionaries and having the Bible translated into Torgut or Bashkir or some other unlikely language; or exploring the river Orinoco and bringing home black orchids; or traveling to Southern Arabia and making friends with a sheik, and purchasing blooded horses to drive about town and to breed from.

Great-Uncle Theophrastus Budd came calling on his way home from a convention of reformers. He was the eldest of the brothers of Grandfather Budd, and was known as a philanthropist; his cause was euthanasia, which meant the painless ending of the lives of the aged. He was getting pretty aged himself, and Robbie said that his heirs were waiting for him to practice what he preached. Great-Aunt Sophronia, an old maid, lived in an ancient house with many cats, and when Lanny went to call at her request, he found her in the attic with a dustcloth over her hair, sorting out family treasures in an old trunk. She had found moths in it, and was hunting them with a fly-spat, and invited Lanny to help her, which he did, and found it a pleasant diversion. This old lady had a sense of humor, and told her new grandnephew that some years ago she had lost interest in life, and had found to her surprise that this had made her quite happy.

These odd people had a way of quarreling bitterly and never making up. Uncle Andrew Budd and his wife had lived in the same house for thirty years and never spoken. Cousin Timothy and Cousin Rufus couldn't agree upon the division of their family farm, so they had cut it in halves and lived as neighbors, but did not visit. Aunt Agatha, Robbie's eldest sister, went off and took up residence in a hotel, and forbade the clerk at the desk ever to announce any person by the name of Budd. That was New England, Robbie said; a sort of ingrown place, self-centered, opinionated, proud.

II

One whom Lanny met only in the most formal manner was his Uncle Lawford. The meeting took place in church, where members of the family would exchange greetings in the aisles, or as they walked to their cars. When an occasion arose, Esther said: "Lawford, this is Lanning, Robbie's son." And Uncle Lawford shook hands and inquired: "How do you do?"—politely, as became two children of the Lord meeting in His holy place. That was all.

He was a peculiar-looking man, heavily built, with broad square shoulders and rather short bandy legs. He was close to fifty, and his gray hair was thin on top; he had a square bulging forehead, and on his face a look that Robbie said was "sour," but to Lanny it seemed as if someone had just said something to hurt Uncle Lawford's feelings. Robbie said that was perhaps the case; Lawford couldn't stand the least opposition in anything, and Robbie's way of making jokes annoyed him beyond endurance.

These two might have let each other alone, but business affairs wouldn't permit that. Every policy that Robbie advocated was opposed by the older brother. The father had the final say, and if he came to Robbie's view, Lawford would withdraw into himself. He was "vice-president in charge of production," and was vigilant and competent, but he took the job as a dog does a bone—going off into a corner by himself, and growling at any other dog that comes near.

Lanny said: "If I had anything to do with Budd's, I'd be bound to run into him, wouldn't I?"

"I'm afraid so; but I'd back you, and I think we'd win."

"Suppose Grandfather Budd should die—how would that work out?"

"It'll be up to the stockholders; there'll be a hunt for proxies."

"Do members of the family own most of the stock?"

"Not outright, the plant's grown too big. But we have enough to keep control, especially with our friends in the town."

Lanny went off and thought about all that. To follow his father's occupation would mean to take up these ancient grudges and make himself the object of these festering hates. Did he want to do it? Or did he want to hurt his father by refusing to do it?

III

Important to the youth was his meeting with his Great-Great-Uncle Eli Budd, youngest and only surviving uncle of Grandfather Samuel. He lived in a town of the interior called Norton, and was eighty-three, and still hale. He sent word that he wanted to meet his new kinsman, and since he was the head of the family, his wish was a command. Lanny was to motor there on Saturday morning, and come back on Sunday evening; and Esther told him not merely how to behave, but where on the trip he would see a famous old "overhang" house, and an old mill which Esther's grandfather had built, and a churchyard with the headstone of the progenitor of all the Budds. "The churchyards are among the most interesting places in New England," said Lanny's stepmother.

The main street of the village of Norton was broad, and deeply shaded with great elms; its residences were white, and none had fences or hedges, but stood in a continuous well-kept lawn, with elms and oaks and maples averting the summer's glare. They were dignified old houses with well-proportioned Colonial doorways, and no unseemly noises ever disturbed their peace inside or out. In one of them the old gentleman lived with his second wife, some thirty years younger than himself, and one unmarried daughter—there were many such in New England, because so many of the young men went away. The family lived frugally, upon a small income, because this retired preacher valued independence more than anything else in the world. "The Budds will all tell you how to live if you will let them," he said to Lanny, with a dry smile.

He was a man of more than six feet, his frame slender and unbowed. His hair was snow-white and long, his face smooth-shaven, with a large Roman nose and deeply graven lines about the mouth. His neck was long and the cords stood out on it, and the skin was like withered brown parchment. But his eyes were still keen, and his step though slow was steady. He had learned how to live, and to limit his desires and keep his spirit serene.

Lanny felt as soon as he entered the house that here was a place ruled by love. Great-Great-Aunt Bethesda was a Quaker, gentle, quiet, like a little gray dove. She said: "Has thee had a pleasant trip?"—and this was something new to Lanny, and awakened his curiosity. He knew that the old gentleman was a Unitarian, and that this had been a scandal in its time, and still was to Grandfather Samuel, and perhaps to Stepmother Esther. One glance about was enough to tell him that Eli was a scholar, for the walls were lined with books that had been read and lived with.

Sitting in this patriarch's study, Lanny was invited to talk about himself, and didn't mind doing it. He was able to guess what would interest his relatives: the natural beauty of the place where he had lived, and the cultivated persons he had met, especially the old ones, such as M. Anatole France, and M. Priedieu, and M. Rochambeau. Eli Budd questioned him about his reading; and when Lanny named names, he didn't say: "All French writers." He had read them himself, and made comments on them, and was able to discover from Lanny's remarks that he had understood what was in them.

Between these two there took place that chemical process of the soul whereby two become one, not gradually, but all at once. They had lived three thousand miles apart, yet they had developed this affinity. The seventeen-year-old one told his difficulties and his problems, and the eighty-three-year-old one renewed his youth, and spoke words which seemed a sort of divination. Said he:

"Do not let other people invade your personality. Remember that every human being is a unique phenomenon, and worth developing. You will meet many who have no resources of their own, and who will try to fasten themselves upon you. You will find others eager to tell you what to do and think and be. But it is better to go apart and learn to be yourself."

Great-Great-Uncle Eli was a "transcendentalist," having known many of the old New England group. There is something in us all, he said, that is greater than ourselves, that works through us and can be used in the making of character. The central core of life is personality. To respect the personality of others is the beginning of virtue, and to enforce respect for it is the first duty of the individual toward all forms of government, all organizations and systems which men contrive to enslave and limit their fellows.

I V

Youth and age went out and strolled in the calm of twilight, and again in the freshness of the morning. They sat and ate the frugal meals which two gentle ladies prepared for them. But most of the time they just wanted to sit in the book-walled study and talk. Lanny had never heard anyone whose conversation satisfied him so completely, and old Eli saw his spirit reborn in this new Budd from across the sea.

Lanny told about his mother, and about Marcel; about Rick and his family, and about Kurt; he even told about Rosemary, and the old clergyman was not shocked; he said that customs in sexual matters varied in different parts of the world, and what suited some did not suit others. "The blood of youth is hot," he said, "and impatience sets traps for us, and prepares regrets that sometimes last all our lives. The important thing is not to wrong any woman—and that is no easy matter, for women are great demanders, and do not scruple to invade the personality." Great-Great-Uncle Eli smiled, but Lanny knew he was serious.

Free-thinker that this old man was, he was nevertheless a product of the Puritan conscience, and wanted men and women to become

pure in heart. As Lanny listened, he began to recall a certain afternoon upon the heights by the church of Notre-Dame-de-Bon-Port.
His friend Kurt Meissner had not merely voiced the same ethical
ideas, but had justified them by the same metaphysical concepts.
Lanny mentioned that to the ex-clergyman, who said there was
nothing strange about it, because New England transcendentalism
had stemmed directly from German philosophical idealism. Interesting to see a son of New England bringing home another load of it,
a century later!

Eli bade Lanny have the courage of his vision. Without it men
would be dull clods, and life would become blind greed and empty
pleasure-seeking. "God save the Budds if they were never anything
but munitions makers and salesmen!" exclaimed Eli; and these words
pierced to the center of Lanny's being. When the time came for
him to depart, this gentle yet hardy old man gave him a volume
of Emerson's essays inscribed by that great teacher's fine and sensitive hand. Emerson had been merely a name to Lanny; but he
promised to read the book, and did so.

V

Lanny drove up to Sand Hill, where St. Thomas's Academy is
situated, and took his examinations with success. The fact that the
name of Budd was signed to all his papers was not supposed to have
anything to do with his passing; nor the fact that one of the school's
largest brownstone buildings had been paid for out of the profits
which Budd Gunmakers had derived from the American Civil War,
and another from the profits of the Spanish-American War. St.
Thomas's was a part of the Budd tradition, and the family's right to
send its sons there was hereditary. Lanny asked his father about the
matter of his not being quite properly a Budd, and Robbie said he
had entered him as his son, and that was that; it wasn't the custom
to send over to France for marriage certificates.

The beautiful old buildings stood in a park having lawns and shade
trees like an English estate. They were of dull old red brick with

Boston ivy on the walls, making a safe home for millions of spiders and bugs. In one of the dormitories Lanny shared a comfortable room and bath with a cousin whom he had met on the tennis courts, but with whom he had little else in common.

Lanny had played with boys, but always a few at a time; he had never before been part of a horde. He discovered that a horde is something different, a being with a personality of its own. Being young and eager, he was curious about it, and every hour was a fresh adventure. He awoke to the ringing of an electric bell, went to breakfast to another ringing, and thereafter moved through the day as an electrically controlled robot. He acquired knowledge in weighed and measured portions; memorized facts and recited them, forgot many of them until the end of the month, relearned them for a "test," forgot them again until the end of a term, relearned them once more for "exam"—and then forgot them forever and ever, amen.

In addition to this part of his life, scheduled and ordained by the school authorities, the horde had its own life which it lived during off hours. This life centered upon three things: athletic prowess, class politics, and sex. If you could run, jump, or play football or baseball, your success was probable; if you could talk realistically about girls, that would help; if your family was notably rich and famous, and if you had Anglo-Saxon features, good clothes, and easy manners, all problems were solved. Entering the third year, Lanny was jumping into the midst of school politics, and had to be looked over and judged quickly. His cousin, belonging to a fashionable set, was ready to initiate him, and would be provoked if Lanny didn't display proper respect for the fine points upon which his friends based their judgments. "Be careful, or they'll set you down for a 'queerie,'" said this mentor.

VI

Robbie had asked Lanny not to play football, saying that he was too lightly built for this rough game. It was another of those cases in which the father expected him to be wiser than himself. Robbie didn't want Lanny to smoke or drink. He was willing for him to have a girl now and then, but wanted him to be "choosy" about it. He had wished Lanny to attend his grandfather's Bible class and his stepmother's church—even though Robbie himself wouldn't do it, and paid a price for refusing. All this was hard to fathom.

As it happened, Lanny could run, and liked to, and he was a good tennis player, so he would never be entirely a "queerie." But he had many handicaps to success at St. Thomas's. He had just come from abroad, and that made him an object of curiosity. He pronounced French correctly, which could only be taken as an affectation. He had read a great many books, and his masters discovered this fact and brought it out in class, hoping to waken a desire for culture in these "young barbarians all at play." That was hard on Lanny.

His first disillusionment came with the discovery that class sessions at St. Thomas's were rather dull. They consisted mainly of the recitation of lessons studied the night before, and if you had studied well, you were bored listening to other fellows who had studied badly, and you were only mildly entertained by their efforts to "get by" with a wisecrack. Rarely was there any intelligent discussion in class; rarely anything taught about which either masters or pupils were deeply concerned. They were preparing for college, and all instruction was aimed like a gun at a target; they learned names, dates, theorems, verb forms, rules, and exceptions—everything definite and specific, that could be measured and counted.

Lanny found that he was expected to assemble now and then with his cousin's "set." These were called "bull sessions," and there would be some talk about the prospects of beating Groton or St. Paul's at football, and some about the wire-pulling of a rival set; but sooner or later the talk would turn to sex. Lanny was no Puritan—on the contrary, he was here to study the Puritans; and what troubled him was that the element of mutuality or idealism appeared to be lacking in their relations with girls. Shrewd and observant young men of the world, they knew how to deal with "gold diggers," "salamanders," and other deadly females of the species. Both boys and girls appeared to regard the love market as they would later in life the stock market—a place where you got something for nothing.

One of the characteristics of the horde is that it does not allow you to be different; it persecutes those who do not conform to its ideas and obey its taboos. There was a sensitive younger lad named Benny Cartright, whose father was a well-known portrait painter; he found out that Lanny was interested in this subject, and would cling to him and ask yearning questions about the art world abroad. There was a son of Mrs. Bascome, well-known suffrage lecturer; this youth wore horn-rimmed spectacles and was opposed to war on principle. More than a year ago Robbie had told his son about the secret treaties of the Allies, in which they had distributed the spoils of war among themselves; now these treaties were published in the New York *Evening Post*, and this chap Bascome brought them to Lanny in the form of a pamphlet.

So, despite his cousin's warnings, Lanny became more queer, and this was in due course reported back to the family. The grown-ups also were a horde, and watched the young and spied upon them— just as the masters in this school were expected to do. St. Thomas's had a "rule book," and your attention would be called to section nine, paragraph six; if you disregarded the warning, attention would be called more sternly, and if a third warning had no effect, you might be "sequestered."

Among the masters at St. Thomas's was one who taught English, a slender and ascetic young man who was trying to write poetry in his off hours. By accident he discovered that Lanny had not merely read the Greek dramatists but had visited that country. They talked about it after class, and from this developed a liking, and Lanny was invited to the master's room on several occasions. This was a form of queerness with which the horde had never before had to deal, and they didn't know quite what to make of it. They applied to it a rather awful term out of their varied assortment of slang; they said that Budd was "sucking up to" the somewhat pathetic Mr. Algernon Baldwin—who got only eight hundred dollars a year for his earnest labors in this school, and had an invalid mother to take care of.

VII

There came a cablegram from Juan, making a happy little jingle, though this was probably not intentional: "Girl both well Marcel." Later came a letter—since one could not count upon the cable these days. Beauty had a lovely little baby girl, and had named her Marceline. The painter was exceedingly proud of himself, after the fashion of fathers. He had persuaded Beauty to the unprecedented course of nursing the baby herself; a matter of hygiene and morality upon which he laid much stress. He had got the idea out of Rousseau.

Then came a letter from Mrs. Eric Vivian Pomeroy-Nielson, announcing that she was the mother of a baby boy. Said Nina: "I won't say much about him, because everything about new babies has been said a million times already. I send a picture." So Lanny had a pair to set up on his bureau; he wrote to each of the mothers about the other, suggesting that they get in touch and start making a match.

Nina revealed that poor Rick had had another operation, his third; still hoping to get rid of pain in what was left of his knee. They were living at The Reaches. Sir Alfred was helping with war work, and riding around to places most of the time. They were saving food, because the submarine blockade was pinching England badly.

Lanny went home for Thanksgiving and read this letter to his father, who said that the submarines were being countered by the system of convoying ships. The U-boats didn't dare show themselves in the neighborhood of destroyers, because of the effectiveness of depth bombs. So with the help of the combined navies great fleets of vessels were crossing the Atlantic in safety. The top men at Budd's knew all about it, having to adjust their system of loading to the sailing dates of convoys.

Father and son talked also about the second Russian revolution, which had just occurred. The government of Kerensky, trying to go on with the war, had been overthrown by a group called Bolsheviks—a Russian word which nobody had ever heard before. These were out-and-out revolutionists, confiscating all property and socializing industry. Robbie said this overturn was the most terrible blow the Allies had yet received; it meant that Germany had won half the war, and the job of the United States had been doubled. "It may mean even more than that," he added. "Those forces of hatred and destruction exist everywhere, and they're bound to try the same thing in other countries."

"Do you suppose there are Bolsheviks in this country, Robbie?"

"Thousands of them; they're not all Russians, either. Your Uncle Jesse Blackless is some such crackpot. That's why I was determined he shouldn't get hold of you."

"You mean he's an active Red?"

"He used to be, and this may stir him up again. He may be behind these mutinies which have been happening in the French army."

"But that's crazy, Robbie. Don't they know the Germans would march straight in and take the country?"

"I suppose they figure that the same sort of agitation is going on among the German troops. If that fire once got to blazing, it might spread everywhere."

"Gosh! Do you suppose we have such people in Budd's?"

"If there are, they keep pretty quiet. Father and Lawford have ways to keep track of agitators."

"You mean we have spies?"

"Nobody can expect to run an industry unless he knows what's going on in it. This thing in Russia has set all the agitators crazy." Robbie thought for a moment, then added: "Those secret treaties of the Allies have put a powerful weapon into their hands. They say to the workers: 'Look what you're fighting for! Look what's being done to you!' "

"But you said that too, Robbie!"

"I know; but it's one thing for you and me to know such facts,

and another for them to be in the hands of revolutionists and criminals."

"There's a chap in school who has a copy of those treaties and
talks about them a lot. He says everything that you do."

"Watch out for him," replied the father—his sense of humor
failing him for once. "Some older and shrewder persons may be
using him. These are dangerous times, and you have to watch your
step."

VIII

Lanny went back to school, and it wasn't long before he walked
into the very trap against which his father had warned him. There
was a Mrs. Riccardi, a well-to-do society lady of the town of Sand
Hill who sometimes gave musicales in her home. She found out that
Lanny had studied "Dalcroze," and begged him to come and tell
her friends about it. Lanny brought Jack Bascome and Benny Cartright to this affair, and it wasn't long before Bascome was talking
against the war to Mrs. Riccardi. He told her about the secret treaties, and gave her the pamphlet, and she passed it on to others. Of
course rumors of this were bound to spread. The country was at
war, and people who found fault with France and England were
lending aid and comfort to the enemy, whether they realized it or
not.

On a Sunday evening Lanny and his two "queeries," Benny and
Jack, went by invitation to the home of this wealthy lady, and there
was Mr. Baldwin, and another schoolmaster of aesthetic tastes, and
several other persons, including a young Methodist preacher with
the unfashionable name of Smathers. Lanny had never heard of
him, but learned that he had been pastor of a church in Newcastle—
in the working-class part of the city, known as "beyond the tracks."
He was a gentle, mild-voiced person, and in the course of the evening Lanny learned that he had got into the newspapers when there
had been a strike of the workers in the Budd plants, and he had
helped to organize a relief kitchen for the wives and children, and

had made speeches and been chased down an alley and clubbed by mounted police.

Of course Lanny ought to have known better than to ask questions of such a man. The man tried to avoid answering them, saying that he didn't wish to give offense to a member of the Budd family; but that was a challenge to Lanny's integrity; he had to declare that he couldn't possibly be offended by the truth. So Mr. Smathers said, all right, if he asked for it he could have it. The other members of the company gathered round to hear what this "radical" young minister might have to say to a son and heir of Budd Gunmakers.

What Mr. Smathers said was that Budd's didn't allow their workers to organize. They had refused to let the strikers speak on the streets and had suppressed their papers; they had had the town council pass a law forbidding the distribution of handbills. Later on they had shut down the strike headquarters and had the leaders arrested on various charges. They had brought in an army of guards, whom they had made into "deputy sheriffs," and provided with arms and ammunition—made by the Budd workers for their own undoing. So the strike had been broken, and now no one could talk union in any Budd plant; workers who breathed a word of it were instantly fired.

Could all that be true? asked Lanny; and the Reverend Mr. Smathers replied that everybody in Newcastle knew that it was true. The businessmen justified it by saying that it was necessary to keep the workers from being led into violence. "What that means," said the minister, "is that large-scale private industry will destroy what we in America call political democracy, and our liberties are doomed. It seems to me that is something about which American citizens ought to be making up their minds."

Lanny could only thank Mr. Smathers for speaking frankly, and say that he had lived abroad, and hadn't even heard about the strike, which had taken place in the summer of 1913, while he was at Hellerau. Strange to think of such things going on at the very time that he was learning to enact the role of one of Gluck's furies! Such a graceful and charming fury he had been—and taking it for granted that tragic and cruel things happened only in operas and dramas, and that you were doing your duty to mankind when you learned to enact them beautifully!

Lanny didn't tell Mr. Smathers how his father had admitted to him that Budd's maintained a spy system. Nor did he say what he knew about his Uncle Lawford, who had had the handling of that strike. A somber person was this "vice-president in charge of production"; both he and the president of the company would know that whatever they did to protect Budd's and its profits was the will of the Almighty, and that whoever opposed them was an agent of Satan—or perhaps of Lenin and Trotsky, two personal devils who had suddenly leaped onto the front pages of American newspapers.

IX

Of course those who had been present that evening went out and talked about it. From the point of view of a hostess it had been a great success; people would be eager to come to a home where such dramatic incidents took place. The reports spread in ever-widening circles, and did not follow the laws which govern sound and water waves, but grew louder and bigger as they traveled. So came a new experience for the new pupil of St. Thomas's Academy.

One morning he was called from class to the office of the headmaster, Mr. Scott. This gentleman was tall and gray-haired, firm but kind in manner. With him were two severe-looking gentlemen whose clothes made them known as persons of importance. One was large and heavy, with scanty hair, and was introduced as Mr. Tarbell; Lanny learned afterwards that he was an important banker from the state capital, chairman of the board of trustees of the school. The other was a young businessman of the keen, go-getter type, an official in one of the big insurance companies. Mr. Pettyman was his name, and he also was a trustee.

Lanny was quickly made aware that this was a grave occasion. They had come, said the headmaster, to make inquiries about Mr. Baldwin, concerning whom certain reports were being circulated:

they wished Lanny to tell them all he knew about this master.

The request brought the blood to Lanny's cheeks. "Mr. Baldwin is a gentleman of the very highest type," he said, quickly. "He has been most kind to me, and has given me a great deal of help."

"I am pleased to hear you say that," replied the headmaster. "Is there anything you could report that would do him harm?"

"I'm quite sure there is not, sir."

"Then I know you will be glad to answer any questions these gentlemen may ask you."

Lanny wasn't exactly glad, but he realized at once that if he hesitated, or seemed to be lacking in frankness, it would be taken as counting against his friend.

Mr. Tarbell, the banker, spoke in a slow and heavy voice. "It is being reported that Mr. Baldwin has talked in a way to indicate that he is out of sympathy with the war. Has he said anything of the sort to you?"

"Do you mean privately, or in class?"

"I mean either."

"In class I have never heard him mention the war. Privately he has sometimes agreed with things I have said to him."

"What have you said to him?"

"I have said it's a war for profits, and that for this reason I find it hard to give it any support."

"What reason can you have for saying that it's a war for profits?"

"I have seen the evidence, sir."

"Indeed! Who has shown it to you?"

"My father, for one."

The banker from Hartford appeared taken aback. "Your father has said that in so many words?"

"He has said it a hundred times. He wrote it to me continually while I was living in France. He warned me on no account to let myself forget that it's a war to protect big French and British interests, and that many of them are trading with the enemy, and protecting their own properties to the injury of their country."

"Ahem!" said Mr. Tarbell. Words seemed to have failed him.

"And what is more," persisted Lanny, "Zaharoff admitted as much in my presence."

"Who is Zaharoff?"

It was Lanny's turn to be surprised. "Zaharoff is the richest man in the world, sir."

"Indeed! Is he richer than Rockefeller?"

"He controls most of the armament plants of Europe, and my father says this war has made him the richest man in the world. Now he is keen for the war to continue—'*jusqu'au bout*,' he said. My father had a letter from Lord Riddell the other day, saying that was Zaharoff's phrase."

"And this man admits that his motive is profits?"

"Not in those words, sir, but it was the clear sense of many things he said."

"You know him personally, you mean?"

"I was in his home in Paris last March, with my father, and they talked about the war a great deal, as businessmen and makers of munitions."

X

The banker dropped the embarrassing subject of a war for profits. He said it had been reported that Mr. Baldwin had attended a social gathering in Sand Hill, at which there had been a great deal of Bolshevik talk by a notorious preacher named Smathers. Had Lanny been there? Lanny said he had been at Mrs. Riccardi's, if that was the place that was meant. He had heard no such talk; he had come away thinking that the Reverend Mr. Smathers was a saint, which was something different from a Bolshevik, as he understood it.

"But didn't he criticize Budd Gunmakers Corporation and its conduct of the strike?"

"He told what had happened—but only after I had asked him to."

"Do you accept what he told you?"

"I have in mind to ask my father about it, but I haven't seen him since that time."

"Did Mr. Baldwin take any part in that conversation?"

"I don't recall that he did. I think he listened, like most of the others."

"And did he say anything to you about it afterwards?"

"No, sir. He was probably afraid of embarrassing me."

"Did he know that Mr. Smathers was to be there?"

"I have no idea about that, sir. I was invited by Mrs. Riccardi, and I didn't know who else was coming."

"There were other pupils of St. Thomas's present?"

"Yes, sir."

"Who were they?"

Lanny hesitated. "I would rather not say anything about my fellow-pupils, sir. I have said that I would tell you about Mr. Baldwin."

The young go-getter, Mr. Pettyman, took up the questioning. He wanted to know about the master's ideas, and what was the basis of Lanny's intimacy with him. Lanny replied that Mr. Baldwin was a lover of poetry, and had written some fine verses, and had given them to Lanny to read. He had lent him books. What books? Lanny named a volume of Santayana. It was a foreign-sounding name, and evidently Mr. Pettyman hadn't heard of it, so Lanny mentioned that the writer had been a professor of philosophy at Harvard.

In a kind and fatherly way the banker reminded the impetuous lad that the nation was at war. "Our boys are going overseas to die in a cause which may not be perfect—but how often do you meet absolute perfection in this world? There has never been a war in which some persons didn't profiteer at the expense of the government. The same thing happened in the Civil War, but that didn't keep it from being a war to preserve the Union."

"I know," said Lanny. "My father has told me about that also. He says that was how J. P. Morgan made the start of his fortune—by selling condemned rifles to the Union government."

So ended the questioning of Lanny Budd. He didn't realize what an awful thing he had said until later, when he told his father about it, and Robbie manifested surprise mixed with amusement. Mr. Tarbell's great bank was known as a "Morgan bank," and the House of Morgan was just then the apex of dignity and power in the financial world—it was handling the purchases of the Allied governments, expending about three thousand million dollars of their money in the United States!

22

Above the Battle

I

LANNY came home for Christmas. The war was not allowed to interfere with this festival; a big tree was set up in the home, and elaborate decorations were hung. Everybody spent a lot of time thinking what presents to give to relatives who obviously didn't need anything. Lanny, a stranger, sought the advice of his stepmother, and they went to the town's largest bookstore and tried to guess what sort of book each person might care for. By this method the well-to-do got reading matter enough to occupy their time for the rest of the year.

Lanny remembered his Christmas at Schloss Stubendorf, where people ate enormously, but were frugal in other spending. Here in New England it was the other way around—it wasn't quite good form to stuff your stomach, but Yankee ingenuity had been expended in devising toys to please the children of the rich, and adults were swamped under a flood of goods incredibly perfect in workmanship. On Christmas morning the base of the tree was piled with packages wrapped in multicolored paper and tied with ribbons. Pipes and cigars, bedroom slippers, silk dressing gowns, neck-

ties—these were standard for the men—while ladies received jewels,
wristwatches, silk stockings, veils and scarves, handbags and vanity
cases, elaborately decorated boxes of chocolates and candied fruits
—everyone had such quantities of these things that it was rather a
bore opening parcels, and you could read in their faces the thought:
"What on earth am I going to do with all this?"

Robert junior and Percy were two friendly and quite normal
boys, living rather repressed lives at home. Esther considered all
forms of extravagance as bad taste, and tried to teach this to her
children; but she was fighting the current of her time, in which
everything grew more elaborate and expensive, and a vast propaganda for spending was maintained by thousands of interested
agencies. Here came this flood of goods, bearing the cards of uncles
and aunts and cousins and school friends and even employees; the
boys became surfeited, and couldn't really appreciate anything.

Lanny had his share of goods and of bewilderment. Good heav-
ens, three sweaters—when already he had several hanging in his
clothes closet! More neckties, more handkerchiefs, more hair
brushes; an alligator-skin belt that was too heavy for comfort; newly
published books that some clerk in a store had said would appeal to
a youth. And in the midst of all that superfluity, a gift from Great-
Great-Uncle Eli—a much worn copy of Thoreau's *Walden,* appearing as misplaced as its author would have been in this fashionable
company. Henry David Thoreau, telling you how to live in a hut
on a diet of cornmeal mush and beans, in order to have your spirit
free and your time not in pawn to commercialism! Old New
England and new New England met in the Budd family drawing
room, and neither was much interested in the other.

II

Lanny had sent his great-great-uncle the handsomest book he
could find in the local store, a "de luxe" copy of *Don Quixote* with
the Doré illustrations. There came now an invitation to spend a
week-end with the old gentleman, and to bring Bess along. Esther

wasn't entirely pleased by the intimacy between her daughter and her stepson, but Lanny promised to drive very, very carefully on the snow-covered roads, and Bess was so thrilled and Robbie so pleased that the mother couldn't forbid the visit.

Between Lanny and his stepmother lay a temperamental gulf that nothing could ever bridge. Lanny was guided by his love of beauty, whereas Esther had to think carefully about everything she felt or did, and bring it into conformity with rigid standards. A few times in the afternoon she had come in to find her stepson playing the piano in a loud and extravagant manner, completely absorbed in it; Esther had stood and listened, uneasy in her mind. She had never heard such music, at least not in a drawing room, and to her it was disorderly and unwholesome. Impossible to believe that anyone could let himself go like that and not sooner or later misbehave in other ways.

Bess with her excitability had been something of a "problem child" to her mother; and now came this youth from abroad to stimulate that tendency. Bess would listen to his playing with a rapt expression, as if transported to some strange land where her mother had never been. Bess wanted to play like Lanny, she wanted to dance like him—and wear a one-piece bathing suit in a drawing room while doing it! She chattered about the places her romantic half-brother had visited, the people he had met, the sights he had seen, the stories he told her. Books on child training which Esther conscientiously read all agreed that you shouldn't be saying "Don't! Don't"—and so Esther didn't. But uneasiness troubled her heart.

On that lovely winter ride, snugly wrapped in fur robes, Lanny told the child about the wonderful old gentleman she was going to meet. Great-Great-Uncle Eli had once helped slaves to escape; his friend Thoreau had gone to jail for refusing to pay taxes to a slave-catching government, and when the poet Emerson had come and asked: "Henry, what are you doing here?" Henry had answered: "Waldo, what are you doing out of here?" Some of them had gone to live in a colony called Brook Farm, in order to be independent and have more wholesome lives. "What is a colony?" demanded

Bess; and then: "Oh, what fun! Are there any colonies now? Could we go and live in one, do you suppose?"

These two reincarnations of New England idealism arrived in the village of Norton in the proper mood to appreciate their venerable relative. The sweet little Quaker wife and the spinster daughter made them at home, and Bess sat for hours at the old man's feet. She couldn't understand all his long words, but she knew that what he said was good. When the two young people drove home again they had this new bond between them, as if some ancient prophet had anointed them with holy oil.

III

The last winter of the war was the darkest and most dreadful. For three years and a half all the ingenuities of man and the resources of science had been devoted to the ends of destruction. Both sides now had many kinds of poison gases: some which penetrated the clothing and tormented the skin, some which destroyed the lungs, some which blinded men, or made them vomit unceasingly. These gases were put into shells, and whole battlefronts were drenched with them. The Germans had flame throwers, which killed the man who used them as well as those in front. The British and French had tanks, "big Willies" and "little Willies," which advanced in front of the troops, spitting fire and death.

The poet's vision had come to reality, and there rained a ghastly dew from the nations' airy navies grappling in the central blue. Squadrons of swift fighting craft darted here and there; they swooped from the clouds and machine-gunned the marching troops; they raided behind the lines and dropped bombs upon railroads and ammunition dumps. The Zepps were fought with explosive bullets, and so great was the peril that the crews of two vessels destroyed them at home in order to avoid going out in them.

Everything had become bigger and more deadly than ever before. The Germans constructed enormous siege guns, known as "Big Berthas," and set them up in a forest behind Laon, and were firing shells into Paris from a distance of seventy-five miles. At first people had refused to believe such a thing possible; but now they were being fired every twenty minutes, and on Good Friday one of their shells struck a church and killed and wounded nearly two hundred persons, many of them women and children.

For the U-boats there were depth bombs, and nets across all the principal harbors and channels. The Americans were furnishing seventy thousand mines, which were being laid in a chain across the northern entrance to the North Sea, from the Orkney Islands to the coast of Norway, a distance of nearly three hundred miles. That made one for every twenty feet. Also the British had devised the "Q-boats"—old tramp steamers with concealed armor sent out to wander in the danger zones. A submarine would rise and open fire with shells—for they tried to save their torpedoes for bigger craft. Some of the men of the "Q-boat," the "panic-crew," would take to the boats; the "sub" would come closer to complete her job—and suddenly portions of the steamer sides would drop down, disclosing six-inch guns which would open deadly fire.

America was getting ready, upon a scale and with a speed never before known in history. You could feel the spirit of the country hardening in the face of world-wide danger. People talked about the war to the exclusion of everything else; even at St. Thomas's, even at the "bull sessions," the fellows discussed what was going on, and what part they hoped to have in it. The draft age was twenty-one, but you could volunteer younger, and now and then some upper classman would pack up his belongings and move to an officers' training camp.

Lanny was now eighteen, and his father worried over the possibility that his emotional temperament might take fire. Whenever the youth came home over Sunday, Robbie would sound him out to see if the bacteria of propaganda had found lodgment in his mind; if so, he would be subjected to a swift prophylaxis. "Did you ever hear of Lord Palmerston?" the father would inquire. "He was Prime Minister of England during our Civil War, and he said: 'England has no enduring friendships. She only has enduring interests.'"

Robbie and Esther didn't agree about England, or about America either, and Robbie's rule was to let her say anything she pleased, uncontradicted. He did the same thing with his friends; of course they all knew that he had special opportunities to get information, and their curiosity was aroused, but all he would say was that he made weapons for those who wanted to fight and had the cash. Now and then old Samuel would caution his son: "Tend to business and let fools shoot off their mouths." No one ever found out what the president of Budd Gunmakers thought about this war; all they knew was that he made munitions twenty-four hours every day, including the Lord's.

As a result of all this Lanny wasn't entirely happy through the war period. People weren't satisfied to let you think your own thoughts; they considered it their duty to probe you, to cross-examine you, and if you were wrong to try to set you right. At school the fellows decided that Lanny was lacking in appreciation of the land where his fathers died; his fashionable cousin told him so, and they agreed to have different roommates the following year. At the same time Lanny was deprived of the companionship of Mr. Baldwin, for the young master had been advised to confine his teaching to the subject of literature, and to avoid contacts with his pupils outside the classroom.

I V

There came a letter which gave Lanny an extraordinary thrill. The envelope was addressed by typewriter, with no sender's name, but with a United States stamp and a New York postmark; inside was a long missive from Kurt Meissner! At first Lanny wondered, had Kurt come to New York; but then he realized that his friend must have known somebody in a neutral country who was coming.

Anyhow, here was a real letter, the first Lanny had had from Germany since the outbreak of the war. Kurt gave the news about himself and his family. He was a captain of artillery, and had been twice wounded, once with a bullet through the thigh, and the second time having pieces of ribs torn out by a shell fragment. He was not at liberty to give the name of his unit or where it was stationed; only that he was writing from a billet in a town behind the front, while having a few days' recuperation. All three of his brothers had been in the war; one had been killed during the early invasion of East Prussia, and another was now at home recovering from a wound. Kurt's father had an important government post. His sister had married an officer, and was a widow with two babies.

Kurt told about the state of his soul, which was uncomplicated, and oddly like that of Marcel and of Rick. The country was at war, and it was necessary for a man to put aside everything else, and to help to overcome an arrogant and treacherous foe. Kurt said he was as much interested in music and philosophy as ever, but his duties as an artillery officer left him little time to think about these subjects. After the Fatherland had emerged victorious, as surely it must and would, he would hope to hear that his American friend had been able to go on with his studies.

This led to the main purpose of the letter, which was to plead with Lanny to resist the subtle wiles of the British propaganda machine. Kurt wasn't afraid that his friend might get physically hurt, for it was obvious that the British would be driven into the sea and the French would lose Paris long before the Americans could take any effective part in this war. But Kurt didn't want his friend's mind distorted and warped by the agents of British imperialism. These people, who had grabbed most of the desirable parts of the earth, now thought they had a chance to destroy the German fleet, build their Cape-to-Cairo railroad, keep the Germans from building the Berlin-to-Bagdad railroad, and in every way thwart the efforts of a vigorous and capable race to find their place in the sun.

It was to be expected that France would hate Germany and make war upon her, because the French were a jealous people, and thought of Germans as their hereditary enemies; they were pursuing their futile dream of getting Alsace-Lorraine with its treasures of coal and iron. But Englishmen were blood kinsmen to the Germans, and their war upon Germany was fratricide; the crime of using black and brown and yellow troops to destroy the highest culture in Europe would outlaw its perpetrators forever. Now the desperate British militarists were spending their wealth circulating a mass of lies about Germany's war methods and war aims; what a tragedy that Americans, a free people, with three thousand miles of ocean between them and Europe's quarrels, had swallowed all this propaganda, and were wasting their money and their labor helping Britain to grab more territory and harness more peoples to her imperial chariot!

Lanny took that letter to his father, and they read it together, and Robbie pointed out how its arguments resembled those which you could read every day in the Newcastle *Daily Courier*—but with everything turned around! Each saw his own side, and was blind to the other fellow's. "You write Kurt and tell him that you are going on with your studies," said the father; and added: "Phrase it carefully, because you can't tell who may read a letter nowadays."

V

Now and then Lanny would write to his mother, reciting his adventures in the land of the pilgrims' pride: all the strange kinds of people he was meeting, and how different it was from Provence. Knowing how Beauty was interested in human beings, he went into detail about his stepmother: a good woman, but so inhibited—a word Lanny had learned from the conversation of Sophie, Baroness de la Tourette, who was very different from Esther Remson Budd, and would have been a scandal if she had ever come to Newcastle. Lanny left no doubt that he preferred Juan as a home, but he was doing his job here as his father wished.

Beauty wrote once or twice a month, nice gossipy letters. Baby Marceline was thriving upon her natural diet, and Beauty herself was well, and as happy as one could expect to be in these sad days. More and more widows on the streets, more and more *mutilés* for Emily Chattersworth to crowd into her place. Prices were rising, and fear was universal—Beauty said she couldn't write all the alarming things that were reported. Everywhere an American went he heard one question: "When are your soldiers coming?" The Germans were preparing an enormous offensive by which they hoped to end the war; and poor France had scraped the bottom of the national pot for man power. There just weren't any more young men, hardly any middle-aged ones; you didn't see them on the streets, you didn't see them in the fields. "Oh, Lanny, I am praying to God it may be over before you grow up!"

Marcel would send a message, or scribble a line or two on the bottom of the page. Marcel didn't discuss the war, or his own problems; he would say something about the state of Lanny's soul: "Remember you are an artist, and don't let the Puritans frighten you." He would say: "I am painting a *chasseur* parting from his mother; it looks like this"—and he would give a little pencil sketch. He would say: "*Seine Majestät* is worried," and make a comic drawing of the figure most hated in France. Lanny treasured these sketches, and showed them to his father, but not to anyone else. His stepmother would of course disapprove of his having a stepfather; if Lanny's mother had been a woman with a sense of propriety she would have expiated her sin by living a celibate life.

But Beauty had been born without that sense. Beauty had a husband of a sort, and was making the most of him. She talked about his work upon every occasion, fought for it, and intrigued to get it shown and recognized—a custom in France, and possibly not unknown in other lands. When some critic called Marcel Detaze a painter with a future, Beauty purchased all the copies of that paper she could find, and cut out the article and sent it to her friends. Marcel still didn't care for being "promoted," but his wife had won the right to do what she could.

Her main struggle was to keep him from going back into the army. She would say, over and over: "The Americans are coming, Marcel! They are making a real army! They mean to finish it!" She would find things in the British and American papers and magazines and bring them to him. She wrote to Robbie, asking him to tell her what was going on, in such a way that Marcel would be convinced, and so be willing to stay at home and leave the saving of France to men who didn't happen to be geniuses.

VI

The new masters of Russia, the Bolsheviks, made peace with the Germans at Brest-Litovsk, an action regarded as treason by almost everybody in the Allied lands. It set the Germans free in the east, and enabled them for the first time to have an actual superiority of numbers on the western front. Their long-prepared offensive was launched in the middle of March; first against the British on the Somme, a front of nearly fifty miles. They brought up masses of artillery, and mountains of smoke shells and gas shells; they overwhelmed the British and drove them back with a loss of some three hundred thousand men. They attacked again farther north, and pushed the weakened British lines almost to the sea. Then they fell upon the French, and drove them again to the river Marne, close to Paris, as in the early days of the war.

This desperate fighting lasted for about three months, and all that while the French people lived in an agony of suspense, waiting hour by hour for news of the collapse which seemed inevitable. Frenchmen and Britons were dying by hundreds every hour, sometimes by thousands; and hopes were dying even faster—among them those of poor, tormented Beauty.

The first news came to Lanny by mail; no use to cable, since there was nothing to be done. "Marcel has gone," wrote the mother. "He stole away at night, leaving a letter on my pillow. I made it too hard for him, I suppose; he couldn't face any more scenes. Do not worry about me, I have got myself together. I've been living this over and over for the past two years, and never really believed I could escape it. Now I don't torment myself with hope; now I know I shall never see him again. They will take him into the army, and he will die fighting. I have to reconcile myself to the fact that one cannot have happiness in these times.

"Of course I have little Marceline," the letter went on. "That is why she was brought into the world, because in my secret heart I knew what was coming. I am still nursing her, but I have been going over to Sept Chênes every afternoon. There are such pitiful cases. I don't know what to think about the war, or what to expect. It seems impossible that the Germans can ever be driven out of France. Shall I have to watch the spectacle of American boys coming over and being sacrificed for nothing? Have I got to live to see my only son drawn into it? Am I going to hear the same phrases from you that I listened to from Marcel's lips?"

While Lanny was reading that letter, he knew that Marcel must be in the thick of the fighting. He was a trained man, and the fact that part of his face was gone wouldn't count in a time like this. They would give him a uniform and a gun, assign him to a regiment, and put him into one of the *camions* that were being rushed to the front.

And so it turned out. Marcel wrote letters to his wife, full of quiet certainty and peace; he was doing the thing that he had to do, that he was made to do. He wrote about the sights he had seen in Paris; about the men in his outfit, some too old and some too young, some veterans just out of hospital. He wasn't allowed to tell where he was going, but presently he was there, and the boche was in front of him, and still advancing, and had to be stopped.

And that was the end. There came no more letters. The enemy advanced, and was not stopped—at least not yet. Of course there remained the possibility that Marcel might have been taken prisoner; his friends had to wait until the war was over, and then wait some more; but they never heard from him. Later on Lanny made inquiries, and learned that Marcel's company had been defending one of those trenches which had been turned into shell holes; presumably he had stayed there, firing his rifle as long as he could hold it and see the enemy. He had been buried in an unmarked grave, along with many of his comrades; his dust would enrich the soil of *la patrie*, and his soul would inspire new generations of Frenchmen with a love of beauty, and with pity for the blunders and sorrows of mankind.

VII

Lanny came home for a week-end, and found a surprise letter. He had failed to let Jerry Pendleton know he was in the United States, so the letter had crossed the ocean and come back. His old tutor had been picked in one of the early drafts and trained in Camp Funston. Now he was a sergeant, a machine-gun expert giving special training to a group in Camp Devens and expecting soon to move on, to a destination not supposed to be mentioned in soldiers' letters. But Jerry said: "I'm going to see Cerise if I have to bust a gut"—which wasn't exactly keeping military secrets!

Lanny was greatly excited, for he had heard a lot about Camp Devens; it was where some of his classmates had gone, and others were planning to go at the end of the term. It was in Massachusetts, some three hours' drive from Newcastle. "Oh, Robbie, can't I go and see him? Right away, before he sails!"

"Send a wire and find out if he's still there," said the father. Lanny did so, and the reply came in a jiffy: "Delighted advise coming quickly visitors one to five any day." Jerry, economical fellow, had got in his exact ten words.

Lanny was all in a fuss. He must go the next day, which was Sunday. Wouldn't Robbie go with him? Jerry Pendleton was a grand chap, and perhaps was using the Budd gun, and might be able to tell Robbie things. The father said, all right, they'd make an excursion of it. Esther said to take the boys. Of course Bess started her clamor, and Robbie said: "Send Jerry a telegram to prepare tea for five!"

New England was beautiful at that time of year; the spring flowers up in the woods, and the trees a shimmering pale green. The rivers ran brown with floods from the distant hills, but the bridges were strong, and most of the roads were paved. The young people chattered with excitement, having heard a lot about this marvelous "cantonment," as it was officially called. There were sixteen of them scattered over the United States, and they had grown like the beanstalk in the fairy tale—last June there had been nothing, and two months later there had been accommodations, complete with all modern improvements, for six or seven hundred thousand men.

They arrived at the gates of the new city at one, and found their host waiting for them. The army was proud of its great feat, and visitors were made welcome. Jerry was bronzed by the sun and seemed taller, certainly he was broader, and a fine advertisement for military training; handsome in his khaki uniform with leggings and his service hat with a flat brim and strap. He was serious, and proud of the place, showing it off as if he owned it. It was a regular city, with avenues named A, B, C, and cross streets 1, 2, 3. Its buildings were mostly one-story, all alike, of unpainted pine siding; there were fourteen hundred buildings in Camp Devens, and the stuff had all been cut to a pattern. Jerry said that when the carpenters got going they aimed to make a record of one building every hour, and boasted of a world's record when they averaged one every fifteen minutes.

Now forty thousand doughboys swarmed all over the place: keen, clean-cut fellows, all smooth-shaven—and all having had chicken and mashed potatoes for their Sunday dinner. Another world's record was being made, an army without liquor; since it had put in the plumbing before anything else, there wasn't any disease and wasn't going to be. All this the machine-gun expert told them while standing on the running board of the car, guiding Robbie through the traffic of trucks, motorcycles, and mule wagons which were like old prairie schooners with khaki tops.

Jerry took them to his own building, which he said he had in strict privacy with some thirty other men. The long room had a low ceiling, and a pleasant smell of fresh pinewood. Everything was as clean as in a hospital; the cots were of black steel and the floors were swept and scrubbed daily. Jerry showed them the messroom, where they had better food than most of the men had ever seen in their lives. He took them to the drill grounds, where you could watch thousands of men exercising—"and believe me, we get plenty of it," said the red-headed sergeant.

"Yes," he added, "the machine guns are Budd's." He took them to the place where he gave instruction with real trenches, and rocks and trees and brush for cover. Jerry showed some of the drill, and sang a doughboy song: "Keep your head down, Fritzie boy!"

He and Robbie had technical details to talk about, while the young people stood and listened in awe. Yes, it was a grand gun; Jerry doubted if anybody in Europe had one as good. "I've studied some of them," he explained. "I have to teach something about them, because a soldier never knows what he may run into on the battle-field."

This man's army was learning fast, and it was going to do the job. Its training was all for attack, the sergeant affirmed. "We aren't going over there to sit in trenches. We teach the men how to capture positions, and to go on from there to the next one."

"The Germans have pretty good machine guns," cautioned Robbie.

"We expect to flatten them out with artillery, and then get them with hand grenades. There's one thing they lack, and that's a life-time's practice at throwing a baseball. Most of our fellows can land a grenade onto a target the first throw. Every time you hit the nigger you get a good seegar!" Jerry grinned, and added: "I don't know if you ever went to a county fair in Kansas."

VIII

All the time Lanny kept thinking: "Marcel ought to be here and see this!"—a thought which had a tendency to diminish the pleasure of his visit. It was gratifying to meet an old friend, and find him bronzed and handsome, astonishingly matured and full of vigor; but when you thought how he might be three months from now—like Marcel, or Rick, or Lanny's gigolo—the crowded cantonment took on a different aspect. They watched those proud, upstanding fellows marching on the drill ground, and Lanny saw a troubled look on his half-sister's face, and guessed that she was thinking the same thoughts. She was only ten years old, but children always know when there is dissension in a home, and Bess understood how her father felt about this war, and how Lanny felt.

On their way home the two boys prattled gaily about the wonders they had seen. They were Budds, and made machine guns, and in their fancy used them freely. They had learned to make sounds in imitation of the weapon's chatter, and as the car rolled along they discovered solid ranks of Germans charging out of some farmer's woodlot, and mowed them down without the slightest qualm. They wanted to know all about the men they had seen being entrained from the cantonment; what embarkation camp they were taken to, and what kind of transports they boarded, the time it took to get to France, the chances of a submarine sinking them.

Their father didn't worry about them, because they were too young to get into this mess. But he wanted to be sure that Lanny hadn't been seduced by all the glamour. Making war is an ancient practice of mankind, and it is always impressive to see a job done with vigor and speed. So Robbie waited for something to come out of his eldest's thoughtful mood; and when it did, he got a pleasant surprise.

Said Lanny: "Do you suppose that when school's over you could find me some job in the plant for the summer?"

"What sort of a job, son?"

"Anything where I could be useful, and learn something about the business."

"You really think that would interest you?"

"Well, everybody's doing something, and a fellow doesn't feel comfortable just to be playing round."

"If you make a good record at school, Lanny, nobody's going to question your right to a summer vacation."

"If they knew how little real work I have to do, they might. And if you're going to tell a draft board that I'm needed to make munitions, hadn't I better know something about it?"

"It'll be two years and a half before you have to consider that problem."

"I read that they're thinking of lowering the draft age. So if you don't want me in, you'd better get busy and fix up an alibi."

"We'll think about it," replied the father; and added, with a smile: "It would make something of a hit with the president of Budd's!"

23

Midsummer-Night's Dream

I

EXAMINATIONS came at St. Thomas's, and Lanny passed with good grades, and checked off his list several subjects about which he would never have to think again.

He had now spent fourteen months in Connecticut; and during that period more than a million Americans had been ferried across to France. Jerry Pendleton and fifty thousand other sergeants were ready to try out the idea that German machine-gun nests could be wiped out by baseball players throwing Budd hand grenades. During the fourteen months' period the plants had been working day and night without let-up. Smoke billowed from their chimneys, the workers toiled like swarms of ants, and the products were piled by the million in warehouses in France and behind the fighting front. The doughboys had had a sort of tryout at the battle of Cantigny, and now were being moved into position to stop the German advance on Paris.

Such was the news in the papers when Lanny sat down to discuss with his father the problem of how to spend the summer. He still wanted to go into the plant; and when Robbie asked his ideas, he said: "Why shouldn't I take a job like anybody else, and see how it feels to put in an eight-hour day?"

"Beginning at the bottom of the ladder?" smiled the father.

"Isn't that the accepted way?"

"Accepted by the fiction editors. You'd be set down in one corner of one room, and learn six motions of your hands, and do them say eight hundred times a day for three months. You would learn that it is very fatiguing."

"I thought I might learn something about the people I was working with."

"You'd learn that nine out of ten of them don't know anything but their six motions, and don't care about those. You'd learn that they are making a lot of money, and don't know what to do with it except to buy fancy shirts and socks and a second-hand car. You can learn all that by going down on Center Street any evening."

This was discouraging. "I didn't like to suggest going into the office, Robbie, because I don't know anything, and I saw that everybody was so busy."

"Both those things are true. But, first, tell me what's in your mind. Do you want to become a Budd executive, and live out by the country club? Or would you rather learn my business in Europe? In other words, do you want to make munitions or sell them?"

"I thought I ought to know both jobs, Robbie."

"You have to know something about both if you're going to know either; but they are highly specialized, and you have to concentrate. It's like choosing your major and minor subjects when you go to college."

"Well, you're asking if I want to be with you, or with Uncle Lawford. You know what I'll say to that."

"Then why not start in my office, and see everything in the plant from there, as I do?"

"Can you make sure I won't get in the way?"

"I'll make mighty darn sure of it," said the father. "If you get in my way, I'll tell you, and if you get in other people's way, they'll tell you."

"That's fair enough."

"All right then; here's my idea for the summer: have a desk in my room, and sit there and study munitions instead of sines and cosines or the names of English kings. When I interview callers you listen, and when I dictate letters, you get the correspondence and follow it back until you understand the deal. Study contracts and specifications, prices and discounts; get the blueprints, and what you don't understand ask me about. Learn the formulas for steel, and when you know enough to understand what you're seeing, go down to the shop and watch the process. When you know the parts of a gun, take it apart and see if you can put it together again. Go to the testing grounds and watch it work—all sorts of things like that."

Lanny listened in a glow. "Gee, Robbie, that's too much!"

"How far you get will depend on you. This much ought to be certain—in three months you'll know whether you're really interested and want to go on. Is that a deal?"

"You bet it is!"

"I'll tell my secretaries to give you whatever papers you ask for, and you'll make it your business to turn them back to the person you got them from. You mustn't touch the files yourself, because there can't be any blundering in them. If there's anything else you want, ask me, because everybody in the place is working under heavy pressure, and they wouldn't like you if you tripped them up. One thing you know already—you won't ever breathe a word to anybody about what you learn on this job."

II

For a while Lanny was like a sailorman who has dug up an old chest full of Spanish doubloons and jewels; he couldn't get enough of looking at them and running them through his hands. All those mysterious things that he had heard his father discussing with army

officers and ministers of war were now unveiled to him. One of the
first that came along was a lot of reports from the firms abroad
that had leased Budd patents for the duration of the war; also the
secret reports that Bub Smith was sending on the same subject. It
was like being turned loose amid the private papers of Sherlock
Holmes! Lanny dreamed of the day when he might be able to call
Robbie's attention to some discrepancy in the reports of Zaharoff's
companies, something that Robbie himself had overlooked in the
rush of affairs. But he never had that luck.

His new job brought him the honor of an invitation to dine at
his grandfather's. He and Robbie went together, and the old gentleman said: "Well, young man, I hear you have kept your promise."
Just that, and no more.

They talked about the war developments, and ate a New England
boiled dinner served by an old-maid servant under the direction of
an old-maid relative. Later in the evening the grandfather said:
"Well, young man, you have attended my Bible class. Have you
learned anything?" Lanny said that he had; and at once the other
launched on a discourse having to do with the one certainty of
Salvation through Faith. He talked for five minutes or more; and
then he turned to Robbie and remarked: "Well, number 17-B gun
seems to be holding up pretty well in France."

Lanny was so absorbed in his new researches that he wanted to
get to the office early, and wanted to stay at night when something
kept his father. But Esther intervened again, and Robbie agreed—a
growing youth ought not to work more than an eight-hour day,
and Lanny ought to get some tennis and a swim in the pool at the
country club before dinner. So it was ordered; and so the way was
prepared for another stage in a young man's expanding career.

The Newcastle Country Club had purchased two large farms and
built a one-story red brick clubhouse, close enough to town so that
businessmen could motor out now and then for a round of golf before dinner on summer evenings. Besides the Budd people, there
were officials of other manufacturing concerns, of utilities and
banks and the bigger stores; several doctors and lawyers, the local

newspaper publisher, and a few gentlemen of no special calling. The ladies came in the afternoon to play bridge, and in the evenings there were dances, and now and then some entertainment to relieve the boredom of people who knew one another too well. When you have lived all your life in a town, it may seem dull and commonplace; but when you are young, and a stranger, the commonest varieties of gossip take on the aspect of lessons in human nature.

There were several "sets" in this club: groups of persons who considered themselves superior to others, whether because they were richer, or because their families were older, or because they drank less, or because they drank more. There were a few who regarded themselves as clever; they were younger, and had the ideas called "modern." Since the western part of Connecticut is a suburb of New York, there were "smart" people, who did what they pleased and made cynical remarks about the "mores" of their grandfathers. You couldn't very well keep them out of a club, because some of them belonged to the "best" families.

Of course such a group would be interested in a handsome youth who had lived abroad, and spoke French fluently, and could talk about Cannes and Paris and London, Henley and Ascot and Longchamps. He played the piano, he danced well, and if he did not smoke or drink, that made him all the more an object of curiosity; the bored ladies imagined that he must be virginal, and they made themselves agreeable, and worried because he insisted upon staying in a dull office and couldn't be lured away for a *tête-à-tête*.

It was the practice of the club to give dramatic performances during the summer, in an open-air theater built in a woodland glade. There was a "dramatics committee," and hot arguments as to what sort of plays should be given. The smart crowd wanted modern things, full of talk about sex; the conservatives demanded and got something sentimental and sweet, suitable for the young people. In view of the conditions prevailing, they had given a war play called *Lilac Time*, which had been the success of the previous season in New York.

This summer everybody was supposed to be absorbed in war work. The businessmen went to their offices early and stayed late. The women spent their spare time rolling bandages, knitting socks and sweaters, or attending committee meetings where such activities were planned. But there were a few whom these efforts did not satisfy; perhaps their hearts were not in the killing of their fellow human beings, or in arousing the killing impulse in others. One could not say this, in the midst of all the patriotic fervors; what one said was that the cultural life of the community must not be allowed to lapse altogether, and that overworked executives who were forgoing their customary month of vacation ought to have some gracious form of entertainment.

So it was that the dramatics committee had summoned its courage and undertaken a production of *A Midsummer-Night's Dream*, which provides a variety of outdoor diversions and has charming music. The committee cast about for players suited to the various roles, and invited Lanny to become one of two lovelorn gentlemen who wander through a forest in the neighborhood of Athens. No one on the committee knew that Lanny himself had been a lovelorn gentleman for a couple of years. He still was—for only a few days ago he had received a letter from his erstwhile sweetheart, mentioning casually in the course of other news that she was about to be married to the grandson of the Earl of Sandhaven, who had been recalled from the "Mespot" front and was now attached to the War Office in London.

Lanny said he didn't think he'd have time to rehearse a play; but the committee assured him that the work would be done in the evening—of necessity, since the part of the Duke of Athens was to be played by a stately vice-president of the First National Bank, and the part of Bottom was entrusted to a member of the town's busiest law firm. Lanny's family gave their approval, and thereafter he dined at the club with other members of the cast, and on the stage of the open-air theater he alternately pursued and repulsed a beautiful damsel whose father managed the waterworks of the city of Newcastle. To his rival for her favor he recited:

"Lysander, keep thy Hermia; I will none:
If e'er I loved her, all that love is gone."

Lanny could say this well, because he had only to imagine that Lysander was the heir to an English earldom, and that Hermia's last
name was Codwilliger, pronounced Culliver.

III

America is the land of mass production and standardization;
whatever it is that you want done, you will find somebody ready
to do it according to the latest improved methods—if you have the
price. If you want to raise funds for charity by means of amateur
theatricals, you will discover that there are firms which specialize
in showing you exactly how to do it. They will send you a director
to take charge; they will rent you scenery and costumes, or provide
experts to make them; they will advise you what play to give, and
if you choose a modern one they will arrange about the copy-
right; they will have tickets and programs printed—in short they
will do everything to smooth the development of whatever his-
trionic talent may be latent in Osawatomie, Kansas, or Deadwood
Gulch, South Dakota.

The director of the Newcastle Country Club production of *A
Midsummer-Night's Dream* came from New York; a tall young
man of aesthetic appearance, wearing spectacles, and hair a bit
longer than was usual in the town. He had an absentminded manner and a habit of making oddly humorous remarks. He took a
liking to Lanny, and told him about a part of New York called
Greenwich Village, where young people interested in the arts for-
gathered, writing plays on a little oatmeal and producing them on a
shoestring. Walter Hayden was a discreet person, who valued his
job, and never exercised his sense of humor upon anything in Newcastle; but he made general remarks to Lanny about the odd position of a stage director whose actors were all rich people accustomed to doing what they pleased, so that only by the exercise of

patience and tact could things be got a little less than terrible.

After the first 'two or three rehearsals, there began to spread in the polite assemblage an uneasy sense that something was lacking in the Newcastle Country Club version of *A Midsummer-Night's Dream*. One of the "swank" young matrons found an opportunity to draw Lanny aside and ask whether he did not think it barely possible that Adelaide Hitchcock was less than completely adapted to the role of Puck? Adelaide was a lovely young girl with a wealth of wavy brown hair and large soulful brown eyes which turned quite often in the direction of Lanny Budd. She had a shapely figure, and everything that was needed to make a fairy, so long as she stood silent and motionless; but when she spoke her lines there was no life in them, and when she came onto the stage it was as a young lady entering a drawing room, and not in the least as a dancing sprite, the incarnation of mischief.

Now if Lanny had been more at home in Connecticut, he would have stopped to reflect that the Hitchcock family was prominent in his father's city, and that Adelaide's mother was first cousin to Lanny's stepmother. But he was thinking about art, and he said that in his opinion Adelaide with wings on her shoulders would make a great addition to the train of Queen Titania; but for the part of Puck they needed a boy or girl who could act; and if it was a girl, it ought to be one with a boyish figure, without hips.

They talked about various members of the younger set and couldn't think of anybody. Lanny asked if there wasn't some teacher of dancing in the town who could make a suggestion; then suddenly Mrs. Jessup recalled that she had seen a play given by the students at the high school, and in it was a girl who had "stolen the show" by the extraordinary verve of her acting. Lanny said: "Why don't you bring her here and let the members meet her?" Again he showed that he was not at home in Connecticut; for in this old-fashioned city the daughters of the aristocracy did not attend the free high schools, and girls who attended these schools were rarely invited to country clubs.

Mrs. Jessup went off to find this girl, whose name was Gracyn

Phillipson and whose mother was an interior decorator, having a little shop and her living rooms above it. Before Mrs. Jessup went, she told her friends that Lanny had made the suggestion, thus giving him full credit for what happened. Later on it would be said that she was an "intriguer," and had manipulated matters to this end; but how could Lanny know about that?

IV

Gracyn Phillipson came to the club late the next afternoon, and Lanny was there as he had promised. One glance, and you could see that she was made for the role of Puck; a tiny, slender figure, with no hips that you would notice; a quick, eager manner, a voice full of laughter, and feet that danced of themselves. To be sure she was a brunette, and Lanny had somehow thought of fairies as blond; but when you came to consult the authorities, you couldn't find anything definite on the point.

Several of Mrs. Jessup's smart friends, having been told that Lanny Budd was interested in this young lady, had assembled to meet her. As the quickest way to bring out her "points," someone asked her to dance. A record was put on the phonograph, and of course it was up to a gallant youth to escort her onto the floor. If he had been discreet, he would have found some other partner for her and would have sat and studied her with a cold professional eye. But Lanny had a weakness for dancing, and it may be that the intriguers were taking advantage of that.

Anyhow, there were the two young persons on the floor, and an extraordinary thing happened. Lanny hadn't had a real dance since coming to the land of the pilgrims' pride, and he had missed it. The dancing that was done at the club was so subdued that it amounted to little more than taking a lady in your arms and walking about the room with her, backing her for a while and then reversing and letting her back you. People did this to the pounding of ragtime music which exercised a hypnotic effect, so that you might have been watching a roomful of automatons, electrically controlled so that they didn't bump into one another as they wove here and there.

But if you are young and full of fire you can dance fast and freely to any music. You can take three steps while others are taking one; you can bend and turn and leap—in short you can express the joy that is in you. And if you have in front of you a girl who is the very soul of motion, who watches you with excitement in her eyes, and reads in your face what you are going to do— that is something to wake you up and get you going. A few tentative steps, a few quick words, and the two bodies were swaying together, they were bringing grace and charm into being—they were creating a dance.

The watching ladies of course had seen dancing on the stage; there was a thing known as "society dancing," all the rage just then. But that dancing was carefully rehearsed; whereas these two young creatures had never seen each other before, and you could see that they were inventing something to express their pleasure in the meeting. It was stimulating, indeed it was almost improper—and that is what it became when the story started on its thousand-legged way through the city of Newcastle.

Was Gracyn Phillipson really what she seemed to Lanny that afternoon? Did joy really bubble up in her like water in a mountain spring? Lanny gave no thought to the question, and would have had no means of getting the answer. If Gracyn was acting—well, it meant that she was an actress. And surely nobody was expecting her to write *A Midsummer-Night's Dream.*

After the dancing there was tea, and this alert young creature revealed that it was the hope of her life to get on the stage. Mrs. Jessup had told her about the play that the club was producing, and she said that she would be tremendously honored by a chance to appear in it. Yes, she knew a little about the part of Puck; she had loved Shakespeare since childhood. Miss Phillipson didn't exactly say that she carried an assortment of Shakespearean roles about in her head; and of course there was the possibility that she had sat up most of the night learning Puck.

Anyhow, when Mrs. Jessup said: "Could you give us an idea of how you would do it?" the answer came promptly: "I'd be glad to, if it wouldn't bore you." No shyness, no inhibition; she was an actress. Right there in the main room of the clubhouse, with other ladies sipping tea or playing bridge, and gentlemen passing through with their golf bags, Gracyn Phillipson enacted the scene in which Puck replies to the orders of King Oberon to torment the lovers: "My fairy lord, this must be done with haste."

Presently came the place where Demetrius enters, wandering in the forest. Lanny being Demetrius, Gracyn gave him a sign, and he recited his challenge to his rival. Puck answered in the rival's voice, taunting him:

> "Thou coward, art thou bragging to the stars,
> Telling the bushes that thou look'st for wars,
> And wilt not come?"

Gracyn managed to produce the voice of an angry man from somewhere in her throat. She put such energy and conviction into the playful scene that ladies at the tables put down their tea cups or cards, and gentlemen rested their golf bags against the wall and stood and listened. Everybody could see at once that this was an actress; but why on earth was she exhibiting herself at the Newcastle Country Club?

V

Rumor with its thousand tongues took up the tidings that Robbie Budd's son had interested himself in a high-school girl, and was trying to oust Adelaide Hitchcock from the role of Puck and to put his *protégée* in her place. He had had this *protégée* at the club and had danced with her and played a scene with her, and now the dramatics committee was requested to give her a chance to show what she could do. Lanny was calling it a matter of "art"; the thousand tongues each said that word with a different accent, indicative of subtle shadings of incredulity and amusement. "Art, indeed! Art, no less! Art, if you please! Art, art—to be sure, oh, yes, naturally, I don't think!"

The rumor came to Adelaide Hitchcock in the first half-hour. She rushed to her mother in tears. Oh, the insult, the humiliation—making her ridiculous before the whole town, ruining her for life! "I told them I was no actress; but they said I could do it, they made me go and learn all those silly verses and take all that trouble getting fitted with a dress!"

Of course the mother hastened to the telephone and called her cousin. "What on earth is this, Esther? Has your stepson gone out of his mind? What a scandal—bringing this creature to the club and making a spectacle of himself before the world?"

Esther had made a strict resolve that if ever there was anything serious to be said to Lanny, it would be said by his father; so now she told Robbie what she had heard. She took the precaution of adding: "Better not mention me. Just say that you've heard it."

Robbie led his son to his study after dinner and said: "What's rhis about you and an actress, kid?"

Lanny was astonished by the speed with which rumor could operate, with the help of a universal telephone system. "Gosh!" said he. "I never met the girl till this afternoon, and I never heard of her till yesterday."

"Who told you about her?"

"Mrs. Chris Jessup."

"Oh, I see!" said the father. "Tell me what happened."

Lanny told, and it was interesting to compare notes and discover how a tale could grow in two or three hours. Robbie couldn't keep from laughing; then he said: "It would be better if you didn't have anything to do with this fight. You see, Molly Jessup and Esther have been in each other's hair of late; it had to do with the chairmanship of some committee or other."

"Oh, I'm sorry, Robbie! I had no idea of that."

"It's the kind of thing you get in for the moment you have anything to do with women's affairs. Just sort of lay off this Miss Pillwiggle, or whatever her name is, and let the women fight it out."

"It'll be rather awkward," said the young man. "I've expressed the opinion that she can act; and now people will be asking me about it, and what shall I say?"

"Well, of course, I wouldn't want you to violate your artistic conscience," replied the father, gravely. "But it seems to me that when you find you've spilled some fat into a hot fire, you're justified in stepping back a bit."

It was Lanny's turn to laugh. Then he said: "Strictly between you and me, Robbie, Adelaide is a stick."

"Yes, son; but there are many kinds of sticks, and she's an important one."

"A gold stick?"

"More than that—a mace of office, or perhaps a totem."

VI

The dramatics committee assembled, and Miss Gracyn Phillipson, alias Pillwiggle, showed how she would propose to enact the role of Puck, alias Robin Goodfellow. After the demonstration had been completed, the committee asked the advice of Mr. Walter Hayden, and this experienced director of the rich replied that it was his practice to leave such decisions to the members; he would give his professional opinion only upon formal request. This having been solemnly voted, Mr. Hayden said that Miss Adelaide Hitchcock was endowed with gifts to make a very lovely fairy with wings on her shoulders; whereas Miss Phillipson was an actress and something of a find, who might some day reflect credit upon her native city.

Adelaide declined to put wings on her shoulders, and went away in a huff, declaring that she would never darken the doors of the country club again. The rehearsals went forward, and every evening for the next ten Lanny watched Gracyn Phillipson manifest enraptured gaiety upon the dimly lighted stage of a woodland theater. Every evening he staggered about in mock confusion, seeking to capture her, and crying:

"Nay, then, thou mock'st me. Thou shalt buy this dear,
 If ever I thy face by daylight see."

He hardly knew her as a human being; he was under the spell of
the play, a victim of enchantment, and she the fairy creature who
poured into his eyes the magic juice which transformed the world.
"But, my good lord, I wot not by what power!—"

The long-awaited evening came, and Gracyn was trembling so
that she was pitiful. But the moment she danced onto the stage
something took hold of her—"I am that merry wanderer of the
night!" She swept through the part in triumph, and lifted an
amateur performance into something unique. The audience gave
her a polite ovation.

Then next day—and the spell was broken. Lanny was an appren-
tice salesman of armaments, and Gracyn was a poor girl whose
mother kept a shop and lived over it. The members of the club
had had an evening's diversion, the Red Cross had got a thousand
dollars, Lanny had made some enemies and Gracyn some friends;
at least so she thought, but she waited in vain for another invitation
to the club, and the painful realization dawned upon her that it took
more than talent to crash those golden gates.

It was too bad that Lanny had to justify the gossips. Now that
it was no longer a question of "art," he had no excuse for seeing
this young female. But he was interested enough to come and take
her driving in his car, and investigate her as a human being. He
discovered a quivering creature devoured by ambition, a prey alternately to hopes and fears. She wanted to get on the stage; how
was it to be done? Go to New York, of course. Mr. Hayden had
promised her introductions; but wasn't that just politeness? Didn't
he do that to young actresses in every town he visited? Already he
was on another job—and doubtless telling a stage-struck amateur
that she had talent.

So far in Newcastle Lanny had lived a restricted life and hadn't
met a single person outside his own class. But the impulse to get
interested in strangers was still alive in him; and now he met

Gracyn's friends, a group of young people with feeble and pathetic yearnings for beauty, and having no idea where to find it. Several were working in factories during the summer months, earning money to go to college; others had taken commercial courses in school, and now were taking jobs in offices, knowing themselves doomed to the dull round of business life. Most of them had never seen a great painting, or a "show" except vaudeville and cheap "road shows," or heard music except jazz dances and the bellowing of a movie theater organ.

And now came Lanny Budd, an Oberon, master of magic. Lanny could sit at the little upright piano in the Phillipson home and, without stopping to think for a moment, could cause ecstasy to flow out of the astonished instrument; could weave patterns of beauty, build towering structures of gorgeous sound. He would play snatches of Chabrier's *España*—and Gracyn, who knew nothing about Spanish dancing except for pictures of girls with tambourines, would listen and catch the mood. She would say: "Play it again"; the young people would pull the chairs out of the way and she would make up dance steps while he watched her over his shoulder. Among the country-club crowd everybody had so much and was bored with everything; whereas here they had so little and were so pathetically grateful for a crumb of culture and beauty.

VII

Lanny took to being out frequently in the evening; and of course the watchful Esther did not fail to make note of it. Once more, she would say nothing to her stepson but only to his father. Robbie didn't feel the same way about a young man enjoying his evenings, provided he had done his job during the day; but Robbie understood his wife and tried to please her, and said he would speak to the boy.

What he said was: "I hope you're not getting in too deep with that girl, Lanny."

"Oh, it's quite innocent, I assure you, Robbie. Her mother sits in one room and paints watercolor designs for house decorations; I play the piano and Gracyn dances and her young friends watch. Then we make cheese sandwiches, and twice we've had beer, and felt bohemian, really devilish."

"Couldn't you do that with some of our own crowd?"

"It just happens that I haven't met any of them who take my music or dancing seriously."

"They are a rather frozen-up lot, I suppose."

"The trouble with most of them is they have no conversation."

Robbie repressed a smile, and asked: "Aren't you ever alone with the girl?"

"I've taken her driving two or three times; that's the only way she'd ever see the country. But we talk about the theater; I've told her books to study, and she has done it. Her whole heart is set on being an actress."

"It's a dog's life for a woman, son."

"I suppose so; but if you're really in love with art, you don't mind hard work."

"What usually happens is that a woman thinks she's in love with art, but really it's with a man. You mustn't get her into trouble."

"Oh, no, Robbie; it won't be anything like that, I assure you. I've made up my mind that I'm through with love until I've got my education, and know what I want to be and do. I had some talk with Mr. Baldwin, my master at St. Thomas's, and he convinced me that that's the wisest way to live."

"Maybe so," said the cautious father; "but sometimes the women won't let you, and it's hard to say no. You find you've got your foot in a trap before you realize it."

So Lanny had to go off and consider in his mind: was he the least bit in love with Gracyn Phillipson, or she with him? He was sure that if he had been thinking of falling in love, he'd have chosen some girl like Adelaide, who was soft and warm, and obviously made to melt in your arms. It would have been a wiser choice, because his parents would have been pleased, and her parents, and they would have a lovely church wedding with brides-

maids and orange blossoms and yards and yards of white veils
spread all around her like a pedestal. But he hadn't been thinking
about love, he had been interested in acting, and in music and
dancing and poetry and the other arts that Shakespeare had woven
into an immortal fairy tale. Gracyn was boylike and frank and
interested in the same things, and they had made a pleasant friendship on that basis.

If she'd been thinking about anything else, she'd have let him
know it. Or would she? She was an actress; and might it be that
she was acting the part of boylike frankness? Acting is a tricky
business, and a woman might fool herself as well as others. Gracyn
wanted a start in life, and could surely not be unaware of the fact
that Lanny might give it to her. His father could get her a start if
he chose to take the trouble. Gracyn must have thought of this;
and would she think that Lanny was careless and indifferent to her
needs? Would she be too proud to hint at it, or take advantage of
their friendship? If so, she must be a fine person, and Lanny was
putting her to a severe test.

VIII

He took her driving the next evening, that being the only way
she could ever see the country. They followed the river drive, and
a full moon was strewing its showers of light over the water;
fireflies were flickering, and the world was lovely, as well as
mysterious. Over in France the doughboys had begun their long-
expected drive, and the newspapers were full of their exploits;
which lent a strange quality to any happiness you felt—as if it were
something you had no right to, and that might disappear while
you held it in your hands.

"Gracyn," said Lanny, "I've been thinking that if you're going
to get a job this season, you ought to be in New York now. while
the managers are getting their fall productions ready."

"I know, Lanny; but I can't!"

"What I thought was, I'd ask my father to back you to the

extent of a trip there. He saw your performance and liked it a lot."

"Oh, Lanny!" The girl caught her breath. "Oh, I couldn't let you do that!"

"It wouldn't break him."

"I know—but I haven't the right——"

"You can call it a loan. Anybody starting in business borrows money and pays it back out of his earnings. You surely won't fail to earn something; and it would make me happy if I could help you."

"Oh, Lanny, what a darling you are!"

"You'll do it, then?"

"How could I say no?"

"I haven't asked him, you understand; but he's never refused to do anything within reason."

"Lanny, I'll work so hard—I'll have one reason more for making good!"

"I know you'll work; the chances are you'll work too hard and do yourself up."

The road passed a wooded point, and came to an open spot with a tiny bay. "Oh, Lanny, how lovely!" whispered the girl. "Stop for a bit."

They drew up by the roadside, as young couples were doing along ten thousand rivers and streams of America. They sat looking over the water, strewn with shimmering bright jewels; and Gracyn put her hand on Lanny's and murmured: "Lanny, you are the kindest, sweetest man I've ever known."

"It's easy for me to be generous with money I don't have to earn," said he.

She answered: "I don't mean only that. I mean a lot, lot more than that."

He felt her hand trembling, and a strange feeling which he had learned to know began to steal over him. When she leaned toward him he put his arm about her. They sat so for quite a while; until at last the girl whispered: "Lanny, let me tell you how I feel."

She waited, as if it were a question; he answered: "Yes, dear, of course."

"I think you are the best person I've ever known, and I'll do anything I can to make you happy—anything in this world. You have my promise that I'll never ask anything of you, never make any claim upon you—never, never!"

So there was Lanny mixed up with the sex problem again. His father had said: "It's hard to say no." Lanny found that it was impossible.

24

The World Well Lost

I

THERE had come a post card from Sergeant Jerry Pendleton in France. "We are ready. Everything fine. Watch our smoke!" And right after that the big news began to come in. The Americans hit the spearhead of the German advance on Paris, at a little village called Château-Thierry, difficult for doughboys to pronounce. The Americans furnished two divisions for the great attack at Soissons, which caught the Germans on the flank, and cut the supply lines of their advancing armies. The same fellows that Lanny had met and talked with; they had been training for a new kind of fighting, to attack and keep on attacking, and take machine-gun nests in spite of losses—and now they were doing it! In the few days of that battle the Germans sent in seven divisions to stop the First Division of the Americans, and when they failed, their leaders knew that the tide of the war had turned.

From that time on there was one battle that went on day and night for three months. The fifty thousand sergeants led their million and a quarter men, and the machine guns mowed some of them down and left them crumpled and writhing on the ground—but others got close, and threw their hand grenades and silenced the guns. After three days of such attacks, one of the battalions from Camp Devens, a thousand strong, came out with two hundred men unwounded. But they had taken the positions.

People read about these exploits with pride and exultation, or with shuddering and grief, according to their temperaments. Lanny, who knew more about war than anybody else he met, was of two moods in as many minutes. A poet had expressed his state of mind in alternating verses:

I sing the song of the great clean guns that belch forth death at will.
Ah, but the wailing mothers, the lifeless forms and still!

At the country club Lanny had met officers who were now in France, directing this all-summer and autumn battle, and he was proud of these stern, capable men and the job they were doing. As the poet had said:

I sing the acclaimèd generals that bring the victory home.
Ah, but the broken bodies that drip like honey-comb!

A letter from Nina: "It is so dreadful, the way poor Rick has to suffer. I do not know how he can stand it. They are going to have to take out another piece of bone. Perhaps they ought to take the whole leg, but the doctors are not able to agree about it." And then one from Beauty, with words of apology for the tear stains which marred it. These were the days when she was waiting in vain for some message from Marcel; she had to pass a still longer period, clinging to the hope that he might have been captured, and that she would get word through the organization in Switzerland which exchanged lists of prisoners.

One day there came in Lanny's mail a carefully wrapped package from France, and when he opened it, there was a charming little figure of a dancing man carved in wood. M. Pinjon, the gigolo, was back in his native village and wished to greet and thank his old friend. He didn't suggest that Lanny might interest some rich Americans in giving little dancing men as Christmas gifts; but of course Lanny knew how happy the poor cripple would be if this were done. Kind-hearted persons would take duties like this upon themselves—even while they knew how pathetically futile it was.

II

Gracyn Phillipson didn't take the trip to New York; at least not right away. The morning after her understanding with Lanny she received a letter from Walter Hayden. He had meant his praise, it appeared. He was at the town of Holborn, thirty or forty miles away, about to direct a show for the Red Cross ladies there. It was a war play, and had a "fat" part for a leading lady; the committee were dubious about their local talent, and Hayden had told them about his "find" in Newcastle. They couldn't pay any salary, but would guarantee her fifty dollars' expenses for two weeks if she cared to come. It would be a chance for her to have Hayden's direction in a straight dramatic role, and the experience might be very helpful to her. The girl was wild with delight, and phoned Lanny that she was leaving by the first train.

So now the youth had another art project to be absorbed in. When he finished his study of contracts and specifications for Budd fuses furnished to the United States navy, he did not go to the country club to play tennis, but motored to Holborn and took Gracyn Phillipson to dinner—an inexpensive procedure, since she was too excited to eat. Then he drove her to the hot little "opera house" where the rehearsals were held, and watched the work, and criticized and made suggestions, and drove home late at night. On Saturday afternoon he went and stayed overnight and on Sunday took her to the beach.

This again was supposed to be "art"; and again the gossips wouldn't believe it. It was too bad that there had to be truth in their worst suspicions. There are persons who believe in the ascetic life, and when their stories of renunciation are told, as in Browning's *Ring and the Book,* they make noble and inspiring literature. But Lanny Budd had been brought up under a different code, and his leading lady also had ideas of her own. On the stage she was acting a part of conventional "virtue," and pouring intense feeling into it; but when she and Lanny were alone, she embraced him with ardor, and did not trouble to fit these two codes to each other.

Lanny felt free and happy, so long as he was in Holborn; but when he started on the long drive back to the home of Esther Remson Budd, a chill would settle over his spirit, and when he put his car in the garage and stole softly up to his room, he felt like a burglar. His stepmother didn't wait up for him, but she knew the worst—and, alas, the worst was true. She never said a word to him about it, but as the days passed, their relationship grew more and more formal. Esther saw herself justified in everything she had feared when she had let this bad woman's son into her home; he had that woman's blood and would follow her ways; he belonged in France, not in New England—at any rate not in her home, making it a target for the arrows of scandal. From that time on Esther would count the days to the latter part of September, when Lanny would be going back to school.

The thing made for unhappiness between her and her husband also. Robbie didn't feel as she did; Robbie had met the girl, and thought she was the right sort for Lanny to have at this stage of his life. He couldn't say that to Esther, of course; he had to pretend that he didn't know what was going on—at the same time knowing that Esther didn't believe him.

III

This interlude with Gracyn was a strange experience for Lanny. She was a "daughter of the people," and his acquaintance with these had been limited to servants and his childhood playmates in France. She had hardly any tradition of culture; her mother had been a clerk who had married her employer late in his life and inherited his small business. Gracyn had gone through school as Lanny was doing, bored with most subjects and forgetting them overnight. She had lived through four years of world war and it had become known to her that America was helping England and France to fight Germany; but she hadn't got quite clear about Britain and England, she didn't know which side Austria was on, and if you had mentioned Bulgaria and Bougainvillaea, she couldn't have told which was which. She was all the time pulling "boners" like that, and never minded if you laughed. "Don't expect me to know about anything but acting," she would say.

When she was a child in school she had posed in some tableaux, representing "Columbia," and "Innocence," and so on, and it had set her imagination on fire; she had discovered a way of escape from the harassments of daily life, with a mother always in debt and very rarely a good substantial meal on the table. She found that she could lose herself in a world of imagination, full of beautiful, rich, and delightful people—"like you, Lanny," she said. She had driven her childhood friends to act in stories which she made up and in which she played the princess, the endangered and adored one. She haunted the local "opera house," to which traveling companies now and then came; she learned that sometimes they would use a child to walk across the stage in a crowd scene, or to be dressed up and petted by some actress playing the mother. Thus she had watched plays from the wings, absorbed in the story, and, no matter how humble her part, she had lived it.

She was passionate and intense in whatever she did; making love to her was like holding a live bird in your hand and feeling the throbbing of its heart. Her emotions came like waves rolling on the ocean, sweeping a boat along; but they passed quickly and were succeeded by another kind of waves. Lanny would become aware that she was no longer loving him, but was thinking about love to be enacted on the stage. It would be one of the principal things she had to do, of course; and while she did it she would start to talk about it from the technical point of view. She had studied the fine points of the actresses she had been able to see; also the favorites of the motion picture screen, and Lanny found it startling in the midst of a *tête-à-tête* to be told that Gloria Swanson heaved her bosom thus and so when she was manifesting passion, and the audiences seemed to like it, but Gracyn thought it was rather overdone, and what did Lanny think?

It was unfortunate that two great crises had come piling into the life of this highstrung creature at the same time: the arrival of her Prince Charming, and the dawning of her stage career. It made too much excitement to be packed into one small female frame, and she seemed likely to burst with it. As it happened, the career part had a time-schedule that could not be altered; she had to be on hand for rehearsals, and she had to know her lines and every detail of her "business" as the exacting Mr. Hayden ordered it. So love-making had to be put off to odd moments, and food and sleep were neglected almost entirely.

Lanny had to put up with many things which his fastidious friends would have found "vulgar." He had to keep reminding himself all the time that Gracyn was poor; that she had had no "advantages"; that things which he took for granted were entirely new and strange to her. It was desire for independence which made her want to eat in cheap "joints," and to stay in a lodging-house room which not merely had no conveniences, but was dingy, even dirty. If she talked a great deal about money, that, too, was part of her fate, for money governed her chance to act, to travel, to know the world and be received by it. If she seemed ravenous for success, lacking in poise and dignity—well, as Lanny drove back to his luxurious home, he would reflect that the founder of Budd's must have had some lust for success, some intensity of concentration upon getting his patents, raising his working capital, driving his labor, finding his customers, getting his contracts signed. Because Lanny's progenitor had fought like this, Lanny himself could be gracious and serene, and look upon the still-struggling ones with astonishment mildly tinged with displeasure.

Lanny came to realize that he was not merely a lover and a

possible backer; he was a model, a specimen of the genus "gentle-man" in the technical sense of the word. He was the first that Gracyn had had a chance to know and she was making full use of her opportunity. She watched how he ate, how he dressed, how he pronounced words; she put him through interrogatories about various matters that came up. What was "Ascot"? Where was "the Riviera"? She had heard of Monte Carlo, because there was a song about a man who broke the bank there. She knew that the fashions came from "gay Paree," but she didn't know why it was called that, and was surprised to be told that the French pronounced the name of their capital city differently from Americans. Indeed, this seemed so unlikely that she wondered if Lanny wasn't making fun of her!

IV

The role which had been put before this stage-struck girl was one for which her Prince Charming was oddly equipped to give help. It was an English play, the leading lady being a war nurse in a base hospital in France. She was a mysterious person, and the interest of the play depended upon the gradual disclosure that she was a lady of high station. She became the object of adoration of a young wounded officer whom she nursed back to recovery; but she did not yield to his love, and the audience was kept in suspense as to the reason until the last act, when an officer who turned up at the hospital was recognized as the husband who had deserted her several years back. Of course her sense of duty prevailed— otherwise the play would not have been chosen by a group of society ladies of this highly moral town of Holborn. The handsome young adorer went back to the trenches in sorrow, and one learned from the play that war affords many opportunities to exhibit self-renunciation.

"Are there really women who would behave like that?" Gracyn wanted to know. Lanny said, yes, he was quite sure of it; nine-tenths of the ladies who saw the play would at least think that it was their duty to behave like that and would shed genuine tears of sympathy. He said that his stepmother would be one of them; and right away Gracyn wanted to know all about Esther Remson Budd.

Still more important, she had to have information about the manners of an English lady, a being entirely remote from her experience. Lanny was moved to tell her that he had known an English war nurse whose grandfather was an earl, and who was soon to marry the grandson of another. Straightway Rosemary began to be merged with Esther in the dramatic role—a very odd combination. Gracyn, of course, had a nose for romance, and after she had asked a score of questions about Rosemary—where Lanny had met her, and how, and what he had said and what she had said—she asked him pointblank if he and the girl hadn't been lovers, and Lanny didn't think it worth while to deny this. The revelation increased his authority and prestige.

He wouldn't let Gracyn tell Walter Hayden about this aspect of the matter. But the director knew that Lanny had lived abroad and possessed a treasure of knowledge about fashionable life. Together they pumped him and built the production on his advice—costumes, scenery, business, dialect, everything. The young society man of Holborn who took the part of the "juvenile"—that is, the wounded officer who fell in love—became Rick with his wounded leg, plus a few touches of Lanny himself. The French officer who lay in the next bed took on the mannerisms of Marcel Detaze. The comic hospital servant acquired a Provençal accent like Leese, the family cook at Bienvenu. Gracyn Phillipson received the "juvenile's" lovemaking with all the ardor of Rosemary Codwilliger, pronounced Culliver; but instead of being a "free woman" she became the Stern Daughter of the Voice of God of Wordsworth's "Ode to Duty." That part of her was Esther Remson Budd; and she was so sorrowful, so highminded, so eloquent, that some of the ladies of the college town of Holborn had tears in their eyes even at rehearsals.

So Lanny became a sort of assistant director, and gave an education as well as receiving one. He lived a double life, one lobe of his brain full of stage business, and the other full of munitions contracts and correspondence. He left the office at five, and was in Holborn by six, had supper with Gracyn and sometimes with Hayden, attended the rehearsal, and was back in bed by midnight. He saw the play growing under his hands and it was a fascinating experience, enabling him to understand the girl's hunger for a stage career. He told his father about it, and Robbie was sympathetic and kept his uneasiness to himself. He surely didn't want his son drawn into that disorderly and hysterical kind of life; but he told himself that every youngster has to have his fling and it would be poor tactics trying to force him.

V

The great day in the evening drew near. The frightened amateur players had rehearsed a good part of the previous night; but Lanny hadn't been able to stay for that, he had to leave them to their fate. He invited several of his friends to the show; Robbie promised to bring others, but Esther politely alleged a previous engagement. Rumors had spread concerning the dramatic "find," and the wealth and fashion of one Connecticut valley was on hand; the Red Cross would have another thousand dollars with which to buy bandages and medicines.

Lanny had thought he knew Gracyn Phillipson by now, but he was astonished by what she did that evening. Every trace of fright and uncertainty was left in the wings like a discarded garment; she came upon the stage a war nurse, exhausted with her labors and aching with pity, yet dignified and conscious of her social position. All the incongruous elements had been assembled into a character— it might not have satisfied an English lady of society, but it met New England ladies' ideas of such a person. They believed in her noble love for the young officer, and when she made her sorrowful renunciation their hearts were wrung.

The actress had shifted her names around, and appeared on the playbill as "Phyllis Gracyn." The director considered that better suited for the electric signs on Broadway, for which he now felt sure that it was destined. Lanny listened to the excited questions of people about him: "Who is she? Where does she come from? How did they find her?" When the show was over, they crowded behind the scenes to meet and congratulate her. Lanny didn't try to join them; she had told him to go home—all she wanted was to crawl into bed in her lodging-house room and sleep a full twenty-four hours.

When he heard from her again she was in New York. Walter Hayden had advised her to come without delay. She wouldn't have to bother Lanny for money, because she had saved the greater part of her fifty dollars. She would write him as soon as she had something to tell. As he knew, she wasn't much at letter-writing; she was always running into words that she wasn't sure about.

Lanny returned to the armaments business and found it now lacking in glamour. He had satisfied the first rush of curiosity, and had discovered that contracts are complicated and that when you have read too many they become a blur in your mind; at least that was the case with him, though apparently not with his father. Lanny kept thinking about speeches in the play, and the way Gracyn had said them. They had got all mixed up in his mind with Rosemary, Rick, and Marcel; and it made him sad.

He went back to tennis and swimming at the country club. He had become a figure of romance in the eyes of the debutantes and the smart young matrons; he had had an affair with a brilliant young actress and might still be having it. More than one of them gave signs of being willing to "cut her out," but Lanny was absent-minded. It was August, and the papers reported a heat wave in New York; how was that frail little creature standing it? She was meeting this manager and that, she wrote; hopes were being held out to her; she would have good news soon. But not a word about love! Did she think that the Stern Daughter of the Voice of God might be opening Lanny's mail?

The war kept haunting him. Every time he went home he looked for a cablegram about Marcel, but nothing came. He thought about

the monstrous battle line, stretched like a serpent across northeastern France; the mass deeds of heroism, the mass agony and
death. The newspapers fed it to you, twice every day; you break-
fasted on glory and supped on grief——

I sing the song of the billowing flags, the bugles that cry before.
Ah, but the skeletons flapping rags, the lips that speak no more!

VI

September, and there came an ecstatic letter from Gracyn. She
had a part; a grand part; something tremendous; her future was
assured. Unfortunately, she couldn't tell about it; she was pledged
to keep it a strict secret. "Oh, Lanny, I am so happy! And so grateful to you. I'd never have made the grade if it hadn't been for you.
Forgive me if I don't write more. I have a part to learn. I am going
to be a success and you'll be proud of me."

So that was that; very mysterious, and a trifle disconcerting to a
young man in love. A week passed, ten days, it was almost time
to go back to school. Lanny found that he was glad, for it wasn't
comfortable living in Esther's home when he knew that she didn't
want him and was watching him all the time, anxious when he made
the children happy, when he had too much influence over them.
He knew that he had ruined himself with his stepmother and that
nothing he could do would ever restore him to her favor.

All right; he might as well be hanged for a sheep as for a lamb;
he decided suddenly that he wanted to see the great city of New
York. He had had only a few hours there on his arrival, and only
one trip with his father the previous summer. He hadn't seen the
great bridges, the art galleries, the museums—to say nothing of the
theatrical district, where many new plays were being got ready.
He mentioned it to his father, who said all right. He sent his trunk
to the school by express and packed a suitcase and took a morning
train to the metropolis.

He had the bright idea that he would surprise Gracyn; so he

took a taxi to the address to which he had been writing. He found it was a poor lodging house—and that she had moved from there a month ago, leaving no address. Her mail was being forwarded by the post office; but at the post office they wouldn't give the address—he would have to write her a letter and wait for a reply. After thinking it over he decided to call Walter Hayden's office. The director was away on an assignment, but his secretary said, yes, she knew about Phyllis Gracyn, she was rehearsing at the Metropole Theater—she had the leading part in *The Colonel's Lady*, a new play by somebody who was apparently somebody, although Lanny had never heard the name.

He drove to the theater. You don't have to send in your card during rehearsals; one of the front doors is apt to be unlocked, and you can walk in and look around. Lanny did so. Since the auditorium was dark no one paid any attention to him; he took a seat in back and watched.

Gracyn was on the bare stage with perhaps a dozen other persons, mostly men: a director, a couple of assistants, a property boy, and so on—Lanny was familiar with the procedure by now. The place was hot, and all the men were in their shirtsleeves and mopped their foreheads frequently. Gracyn was sitting in a chair watching the work; when her cue came she would get up and go through a scene.

Another war play; the men sat at small tables and it became apparent that they were supposed to be doughboys in a wine shop somewhere behind the lines. Gracyn was a French girl, daughter of the proprietor—her father scolded her for being too free with the soldiers. When he went off she teased them and some of her lines were a trifle crude—evidently it was a "realistic" play. The doughboys sang songs, one of them "Madelon," in translation. "She laughs—it is the only harm she knows."

Gracyn was doing it with great spirit. Oh, yes, she could act! Lanny had never seen the American boys in France, but he recalled the scene with the French soldiers when he and his mother motored to see Marcel. He thought: "I could have given the director a lot of help." But they wouldn't let Gracyn tell what she was doing. And yet the secretary at Hayden's place had known about it and had told it freely. Very strange!

VII

Lanny didn't want to disturb her. He waited until the rehearsal was over and she was about to leave. Then he came down the aisle, saying: "Hello, Gracyn."

She was startled. "Lanny! Of all people! Where on earth did you come from?"

"Out of a taxi," he said.

"How did you find me?"

"Your secret appears to have leaked."

She came into the auditorium to join him. She led him back, away from the others, and sat down. "Darling," she said, swiftly, "I have something that's dreadfully hard to tell you. I couldn't put it on paper. But you have to know right away." She caught her breath and said: "I have a lover."

"A *what?*" he exclaimed. When he took in the meaning of her words, he said: "Oh, my God!"

"I know you'll think it's horrid, but don't be too mean to me. I couldn't help it. It's the man who's putting up the money for the show and giving me this part."

The youth had never been so stunned in all his life. He was speechless; and the girl rushed on:

"I had a chance, Lanny; I might never have had another. He's a big coffee merchant, who happened to see my performance in Holborn. He lives in New York and he invited me to come. He offered to take me to a good manager and find me a part—right away, without any waste of time. What could I say, Lanny?"

The youth remembered his mother's phrase. "You paid the price?"

"Don't be horrid to me, Lanny. Don't let's spoil our friendship. Try to see my side. You know I'm an actress. I told you I didn't know anything else, I didn't care about anything else—I wanted to get on the stage, and I'm doing it."

"There isn't any honest way?"

"Please, darling—use your common sense. This is New York. What chance does a girl stand? I'd have tramped the heels off my shoes going to managers' offices, and they wouldn't even have seen me. I'd have called myself lucky to get a part with three lines—and I'd have spent a month or two rehearsing, going into debt for my board while I did it. The play might have failed the first week, and I'd have twenty dollars, maybe thirty, to pay my debts with. Believe me, I've talked to show girls these few weeks, and I know what the game is."

"Well, it's all right," he said. "I wish you success, and the highest salary on Broadway."

"Don't sneer at me, Lanny. Life has been easy for you. You were born with a gold spoon in your mouth, and you've no right to scorn a poor girl."

"I'll do my best to remember it. Thanks for telling me the truth."

"I'd have told you before, Lanny; but it was so hard. I hate to lose you for a friend."

"I'm afraid you have done so," he said, coldly. "Your angel might be jealous."

"I know it's a shock, darling. But you know so little about the stage world. Somebody had to give me a start. You couldn't have done it—you surely know that."

Said he: "It may interest you to hear that I was thinking of asking you to marry me."

Did this startle her? If so, she was a good actress. "I haven't failed to consider that. But you have to go to school, and then to college—that's five years, and in that time I'd be an old woman."

"My father would have helped me to marry, if I'd asked him."

"I know, dear, but can't you understand? I don't want to be a wife, I want to be an actress! I couldn't think of settling down and having babies, and being a society lady—not in Newcastle, not even in France. I want to have a career—and what sort of a life would it be for you, tagging along behind a stage celebrity? Would you enjoy being called Mister Phyllis Gracyn?"

He saw that she had thought it all out; and, anyhow, it was too late. No good saying any unkind words. "All right, darling," he said—it was the stage name. "I'll be a good sport, and wish you all the luck there is. I'm only sorry I couldn't give you what you needed."

"No, Lanny dear," she said. "It's thirty thousand dollars!" And there wasn't any acting in what she put into those words!

VIII

The sun was going down as Lanny climbed onto the top of one of the big Fifth Avenue busses, which for a dime took you uptown, and across to Riverside Drive, and up to where the nation had built a great granite tomb for General Grant, in the shape of a soap box with a cheese box on top. Part of the time Lanny looked at the crowds on the avenue, and at sailboats and steamers on the river; the rest of the time he thought about the strange adventure into which he had blundered. He decided that he wasn't proud of it, and wouldn't tell anybody, excepting of course Robbie, and perhaps Rick or Kurt if he ever saw them again.

He told himself that he had made himself cheap. That little tart—well, no, he mustn't call her names—she had her side, she had her job to do and might do it well. But he mustn't let himself blunder like that again; he must know more about a woman before he threw himself into her arms. A man had to have standards; he must learn to say no. Lanny thought about the number of times he had said yes to Gracyn Phillipson, and in such extravagant language. He writhed with humiliation.

He didn't want to go home in that mood, and he didn't want to go to school ahead of time, so he put up at a hotel, and spent his time in the museums and art galleries. He looked at hundreds of paintings—and all the nudes were Gracyn, except those that were

Rosemary. He told himself with bitterness that they were all for sale, whether for thirty-thousand-dollar shows on Broadway, or for three dollars, the price of the pitiful painted ones who hunted on that Great White Way in the late hours of the evening. Rosemary's price would be a title and a country estate, but she was being sold just the same; it didn't matter that the bargain would be solemnized by a bishop in fancy costume, and proclaimed by pealing chimes in St. Margaret's. Would he ever meet one that didn't have her price? And how would he know her—since they were all so hellishly clever at fooling you?

There was another hot spell in New York, and he looked at the crowds of steaming people. The women wore light and airy garments and the young ones tripped gaily; but all the men who wanted to be thought respectable had to wear hot coats, and Lanny pitied them and himself. It was the time of year when "everybody" was supposed to be out of town; but there was an enormous number of "nobodies," and Lanny marveled how nature had managed it so that they all wanted to live. There were more Jews than anywhere else in the world and he might have satisfied his curiosity about that race if he had had time. There were great numbers of soldiers, and foreigners of every sort, so New York didn't seem very different from Paris. He found a French restaurant and had his dinners there and felt at home; he wished his mother were with him—what a comfort to tell her about Gracyn and hear her wise comments!

IX

The young man went back to St. Thomas's, and forgot his troubles in the pleasure of meeting his schoolfellows and hearing stories of where they had been and what they had done. He had a firm resolve to buckle down and make a record that would please his father and grandfather, and perhaps even his stepmother. It was pleasant to have your work cut up into daily chunks, duly weighed and measured, so that you knew exactly what you had to do and were spared all uncertainties and moral struggles.

The Americans had begun their attack in the Argonne, a forest full of rock-strewn hills and deep ravines thick with brush, one of the most heavily fortified districts in the war zone, and considered by the Germans to be impregnable. The doughboys were hammering there, and fifty thousand of them would be killed or wounded in three weeks. It was the greatest battle in American history, and it was a part of Lanny's life; his friends were in it, and his heart. There came now and then a post card from Jerry Pendleton—that fellow had been fighting every day and almost every night for a month and hadn't been touched. Now he was back in a rest camp, enjoying the peace his valor won. Somehow Lanny couldn't think of wounds and death in connection with Jerry; he was the wearer of some sort of Tarnhelm and would come out safe and whole to tell Lanny about it.

Also a letter from Nina. She had a brother who had been in the fighting south of the Somme and had got what the British called a "blighty" wound, one that brought him home and kept him out of danger for a while. Rick had had his operation, and this time they really hoped for better results. There were even a few lines from Rick to prove it; nothing about wounds, of course, you'd never know if Rick was suffering. "Well, old top, it looks like Fritz is really in trouble. Moving out and no time to pack his boxes. Cheerio!"

Beauty was always a dependable correspondent, and managed to smile through her tears. No word from Marcel yet. M. Rochambeau had written to friends in Switzerland, asking for information. M. Rochambeau said that Germany was cracking; discontent was breaking out everywhere inside the country. President Wilson's propaganda was having a tremendous effect; his "Fourteen Points" left the German people no reason for fighting. Baby Marceline was thriving, and all the world agreed that she was the most beautiful baby in the Midi.

Lanny knew, of course, that all this was an effort on his mother's part to hide her grieving for Marcel. What was she going to do when the war was over? He had made up his mind that his stepfather was dead; and Beauty was not a person who could live alone. Sometimes he wondered, had he made a mistake in bringing about that marriage? What would he have done if he had known that Marcel was going to be a *mutilé* inside of one year and a corpse in less than four? Maybe she should have taken the plate-glass man after all!

X

The Allied armies continued their grinding advance. The Hindenburg line was cracked and the Germans forced to retreat. First Bulgaria collapsed, then Turkey, then Austria; there came a revolution in Germany and the Kaiser fled to Holland—all that series of dramatic events, culminating in the day when everybody rushed into the streets of American cities and towns, shouting and singing and dancing, blowing horns and beating tin pans, making every sort of racket they could think of. The war was over! There wasn't going to be any more killing! No more bombs, shells, bullets, poison gas, torpedoes! The boys who were still alive could stay alive! The war to end war had been won and the world was safe for democracy! People thought all these things, one after another, and with each thought they shouted and sang and danced some more.

Even at St. Thomas's Academy, the place of good manners, there was a celebration. Lanny got his father on the telephone; they laughed together, and Lanny cried a little. He sent a cablegram to his mother and one to Rick. People were behaving the same way in France, of course. Even those cold and aloof beings, the gentlemen of England, were rushing out into the streets embracing strangers. It had been a tough grind for the people of that small island; they hadn't been in such danger since the days of the Spanish Armada.

A couple of weeks later came Thanksgiving Day and Lanny went home. One of the first things his father said was: "Well, kid, I guess I'm going to have to go back to Europe pretty soon. There'll be a lot of matters to be cleared up."

Lanny's first thought was: You can cross the ocean and enjoy it! You can walk on deck and look for whales instead of submarines!

One needed time for that to sink in. Then he said: "Listen, Robbie—don't be surprised. I want you to take me with you."

"You mean—to stay?"

"I've thought it all over. I'll be a lot happier in France. I can get much more of what I want there."

"Aren't you happy here?"

"Everybody's been kind to me, and I'm glad I came. I had to know your people, and I wouldn't have missed the experience. But I have to see my mother, too. And she needs me right now. I don't think she's ever going to see Marcel again."

"You could visit her, you know."

"Of course; but I have to think of one place as home, and that's Juan."

"What about the business?"

"If I'm going to help you, it'll be over there. You'll be going back and forth, and I'll see as much of you one way as the other."

"You don't care about going to college?"

"I don't think so, Robbie. I've asked people about it and it isn't what I need. I was going through with it on account of the war, and to please you."

"Just what is it you want—if you know?"

"It isn't easy to put into words. More than anything else I want art. I've lived here a year and a half and I've heard almost no music. I haven't seen any good plays—of course I might see them in New York, but I haven't any friends there, all my best friends are in England and France."

"You'll be a foreigner, Lanny."

"I'll be a citizen of several countries. The world will need some like that."

"Just what exactly do you plan to do?"

"I want to feel my way. The first thing is to stop doing all the things that I don't want to do. I'm in a sort of education treadmill. I make myself like it, but all the time I know that I don't; and if I dropped it and went on board a ship with you I'd feel like a bird getting out of a cage. Don't misunderstand me, I don't want to loaf;

but I'm nineteen, and I believe I can direct my own education. I want to have time to read the books I'm interested in. I want to meet cultured people, and know what's going on in the arts—music, drama, painting, everything. Paris is going to be interesting right now, with the peace conference. Do you suppose you can manage to get me a passport? I understand they let hardly anybody go."

"I can fix that up all right, if you're sure it's what you want."

"I want to know what you're doing, and I want to help you—I'll be your secretary, run your errands, anything. To be with you and meet the people you meet—don't you see how much more that's worth to me than being stuck in a classroom at St. Thomas's, hearing lectures on modern European history by some master who's a child in comparison with you? Everything they have is out of books, and I can get the same books and read them in a tenth of the time. I'll wager you that on the steamer going across I can learn more modern European history than I'd get in a whole term in school."

"All right," said the father. "I guess it's no use trying to fit you into anybody else's boots."

XI

Lanny motored up to the school to pack his belongings, and say good-by to his masters and his fellow-pupils, who thought he was the luckiest youth in the state. Then he came home and started saying farewell to people at the country club and to the many members of the family. Most of all he wanted to see the Reverend Eli Budd; but fate had other plans about that. There came a telegram saying that the patriarch had passed away peacefully in his sleep, and that the funeral would be held two days later.

Lanny motored up to Norton with Robbie and his wife and an elderly widowed cousin who was visiting them. The Budd tribe had assembled from all over New England—there must have been two hundred of them in the little Unitarian church, where the deceased had been the minister for fifty years of his life. The Budd men were all grave and solid-looking, all dressed pretty much alike, whether they were munitions magnates or farmers, bankers or clergymen. They listened in silence while the present minister extolled the virtues of the departed, and when they came outside, where the first snowflakes of the year were falling, the older ones agreed that the Budd line was producing no more great men. When the will was opened, everyone was puzzled because the old man had left his library to his great-grandnephew, Lanning Prescott Budd. Some of them didn't know who that was, till the whisper went round that it was Robert Budd's bastard, who was now going back to France and would probably take the books with him.

Robbie had got the passports, and the steamer sailed two days later. The son went over to the office and said good-by to all the executives and secretaries who had been kind to him. He had had to see a good deal of his Uncle Lawford in the office, and he now went in and shook hands with that morose and silent man, who unbent sufficiently to say that he wished him well. Lanny called on his grandfather at his home, and the old gentleman, who had aged a lot under the strain of the war, didn't make any attempt to seem cheerful. He said he didn't know how Robbie could be expecting to drum up any more business in Europe now; they had munitions enough on hand to blow up the whole continent, and he wasn't sure but what they might just as well do so.

"There's going to be hell to pay at home," he warned. "All our workingmen have got too big for their breeches, and we've got to turn a lot of them off when we finish these government contracts. They've been watching that lunatic asylum in Russia, and they'll be ready to try it here when they find we've nothing more to give them. Better take my advice and learn something about business, so you can take care of yourself in a dangerous time."

"I'm planning to stick close to my father, sir, and learn all that he'll teach me."

"Well, if you listen to me you'll forget all this nonsense about music and stage plays. There are temptations enough in a young man's life without going out to hunt for them."

"Yes, Grandfather," said the youth, humbly. This was a rebuke, and he had earned it. "I don't think there'll be much pleasure-seeking in France for quite a while. They are a nation of widows and cripples, and most of the people I know are working hard trying to help them."

"Humph!" said Grandfather Samuel, who wasn't going to believe anything good about France if he could help it. He went on to talk about the world situation, which was costing him a lot of sleep. Forces apparently beyond control had drawn America into the European mess, and it wasn't going to be easy getting her out again. American businessmen would be compelled to sell more and more to foreigners. "We Budds have always been plain country people," declared the grandfather. "Not many of us know any foreign languages, and we distrust their manners and their morals. We can use someone who knows them, and can advise us—that is, if it's possible for anybody to live among them and not become as corrupt as they are."

"I'll bear your advice in mind, sir," replied the youth. "I have learned a great deal from my visit here, and I mean to profit by it."

That was all, but it was enough, according to the old gentleman's code. He wouldn't try to pin anyone down. Lanny had been to Bible class, and had had his chance at Salvation; whether he took it or not was up to him, and whatever he did would be what the Lord had predestined him to do. The Lord would be watching him and judging him—and so would the Lord's deputy, the president of Budd Gunmakers.

XII

There remained the partings from Robbie's own family. The two boys were sorry indeed to see him go, for he had been a splash of bright color in their precisely ordered lives. He found time for a heart-to-heart talk with Bess, the only person in Connecticut who shed tears over him. She pledged herself to write to him, and he promised to send her pictures of places in Europe where he went and of people he met. "Some day you'll come over there," he said;

and she answered that Robbie would have to bring her, or she would come as a stowaway.

As for Esther, she kissed him, and perhaps was really sorry. He thanked her with genuine affection; he felt that he had done wrong and was to blame for the coldness which had grown between them. He would always admire her and understand her; she would always be afraid of him.

Father and son went to New York by a morning train. Robbie had business in the afternoon, and in the evening Lanny had another good-by to say. Through the newspapers he had been following the fortunes of a dramatic production called *The Colonel's Lady*, which had opened in Atlantic City the beginning of October and had scored a hit; it had run there for two weeks, and had then had a successful opening at the Metropole Theater. Lanny wanted to see it, and Robbie said, sure, they'd both go. Their steamer had one of those midnight sailings which allow the pleasure-loving ones a last fling on the Great White Way.

Lanny didn't want to meet "Phyllis Gracyn"; he just wanted to see her act. He got seats for the show, for which one had to pay a premium. They were well down in front, but Gracyn probably didn't see the visitors. They followed the fortunes of a French innkeeper's daughter who was fascinated by the brilliance of an American "shavetail," but wasn't able to resist the lure of a French colonel, whose jealous wife involved him with a German spy in order to punish him. Out of this came an exciting melodrama, which was going to hold audiences in spite of peace negotiations.

Lanny was interested in two things: first, the performance of Gracyn, which wasn't finished by any means, but was full of energy and "pep"; and, second, the personality of the young American officer. Evidently the play was one of those which had been written at rehearsals, and Gracyn had had a part in it. Lanny had taught her, and she had taught the author and the young actor; so there were many touches in which Lanny recognized himself—mannerisms, phrases, opinions about the war, items about the French, their attitude to the doughboys and the doughboys' to them. There were even a few third-hand touches of Sergeant Jerry Pendleton in this Broadway hit!

"Well, you did a good job," said Robbie. "Charge it up to education and don't fall in love with any more stage ladies."

"I've made a note of it," said the dutiful son.

"Or else—note this: that if you'd had thirty thousand dollars, you might have licked the coffee merchant!"

They were in the taxi on the way to the steamer; and Lanny grinned. "There's an English poem supposed to be sung by the devil, and the chorus runs: 'How pleasant it is to have money, heigh-ho, how pleasant it is to have money!' "

"All right," replied the father. "But you can bet that poet had money, or he wouldn't have been sitting around making up verses."

On board the steamer; and one more farewell to say. Standing on the deck, watching the lights of the metropolis recede, Robbie pointed to an especially bright light across the bay and said: "The Statue of Liberty."

She had come from France, and Lanny was going home. She waved her torch to him, as a sign that she understood how he felt.

BOOK FIVE

They Have Sown the Wind

25

The Battle Flags Are Furled

I

THERE was only one steamer a week to France at this time, and those who traveled on it were carefully selected persons, able to show that they had important business, of a kind the authorities approved. In theory, the world was still at war, and it was not in tended that Americans should use the peace conference as a propa ganda platform, or for sightseeing tours. But Robert P. Budd knew the people at the War and State Departments; they talked to him confidentially, and when he asked for passports they arranged it at once.

The first thing Robbie did on a steamer was to study the passenger list. He was an extrovert; he liked to talk with people, all sorts, and especially those who were familiar with his hunting ground. There was no printed list in wartime, but he borrowed the purser's list, and went over it with Lanny, and told him that this man was "in steel," that one "in copper," and a third represented a Wall Street banking group. Near the top he read: "Alston, Charles T.," and remarked: "That must be old Charlie Alston, who was in my class at Yale. He's a professor now, and has published a couple of books on the geography of Europe."

"He'll have to begin all over again," ventured Lanny.

"He was a 'barb,' and I didn't know him well," added the father. "I remember him as a rather frail chap with big spectacles. He was an awful grind, and most of us considered it unfair competition. However, he's made good, I suppose."

December is apt to be a rude month on the Atlantic, and there

479

were vacant seats in the dining saloon, and one or two at the captain's table. Robbie glanced at the place card alongside him, and read "Professor Alston." He asked the captain, and learned that his former classmate was an adviser to the peace delegation, but had been unable to sail with the presidential staff because of an attack of influenza.

The third day out, the sea was quieter, and the professor appeared on deck; the same frail little man, wearing his large spectacles. The only thing Robbie didn't recall was that his complexion was yellow with a slight tinge of green; perhaps that would change when he was able to keep food on his stomach. The professor was glad to see his classmate; it appeared that when you had known somebody in college, you felt a peculiar sentimental bond. Alston had looked up to the handsome, rich, and popular Budd as to a shining light on a mountain top; so now to have him sitting in a deckchair asking questions about the coming peace conference and listening with deference to his replies—that was a sort of promotion.

Also the professor was interested in a fresh incarnation of the handsome, rich, and popular Budd; a youth of nineteen, resembling in many ways the one whom Alston remembered. Lanny was lighter in build and faster in mind, more accessible than his father and more eager to learn. The fact that Charles T. Alston had never "made" a fraternity in college and had earned a scant living by waiting on table in a students' boarding house—that didn't mean anything to Lanny. But that he was a storehouse of vital facts, and had been chosen to help the American peace commissioners in their efforts to make Europe a saner place to live in—that made him a great personage in Lanny's eyes. He listened to the conversations between the two elders, and at other times, when Robbie was exchanging shop talk with the "big men" of steel and copper and banking, Lanny would be strolling the deck with the specialist in geography, keeping one hand under his arm to steady him when the ship gave a lurch.

II

It wasn't long before the professor entrusted the youth with his confidence; he was troubled by doubts whether his linguistic equipment—so he called it—was adequate to the task he had before him. "My knowledge of French is that of a student," he explained. "I have read it a great deal, but, as you know, it is a different language to listen to."

Lanny perceived what the shy little man wanted, and presently made the suggestion that they carry on their conversations in French. After that Lanny could have all the professor's time and all his stock of information. Once more he had found something that was better than going to college.

Professor Alston found that he could understand nearly everything that Lanny said; but would it be as easy to understand a Frenchman? Lanny knew that it was a common experience of his American friends to be able to understand American French but not French French. So he undertook to talk like a Frenchman—a matter of running his words together, taking many syllables for granted. The professor braced himself for the shock, and every now and then would ask him to stop and say it over again.

Toward this suddenly developing intimacy the older Budd felt something less than enthusiasm, and Lanny was interested to probe into his attitude. What was wrong with Professor Alston? Well, for one thing, he was a Democrat with a capital D, and his success was political. Alston was one of the crowd whom Woodrow Wilson had brought in, as part of his program to make over the world. Before the war had come along to divert his mind, the Presbyterian President had put forward a program of national reform which, if you would believe Robbie Budd, amounted to taking control of business out of the hands of businessmen and turning it over to politicians. And of course the least hint of this caused sparks to dance before Robbie's eyes.

Now the President was carrying his attitude into international affairs; he was going to settle Europe's problems for it, and to that end had picked out a bunch of theorists like himself, men whose knowledge of the world had been derived from books. The diplomats, the statesmen, the businessmen of Europe were going to be preached at and lectured and put in their places. In America this had been called "the New Freedom," and in Europe it was "the Fourteen Points," but by any other name it smelled as sour to the salesman of Budd Gunmakers.

"But, Robbie," argued his son, "a lot of the Fourteen Points are what you yourself say ought to be done."

"Yes, but Europe isn't going to do them, and it's not our business to make them."

"But what harm can it do to give them advice? Professor Alston says"—and Lanny would repeat some of his new friend's statistics regarding the economic unity of Europe, which was being crippled in so many ways by its political subdivisions. Robbie didn't deny the facts, but he didn't want to take them from a "scholar in politics." The scholar's place was the classroom, or his own cloistered study, where he would be free to write books—which Robbie wouldn't read!

III

However, the scholar was in politics—and no way to get him out until the next election. The former president of Princeton University had got the whole civilized world for his classroom, with hundreds of reporters eagerly collecting every word that he might speak, and paying fortunes to cable it to China and Peru. He had caused to be assembled a troop of his kind, a sort of general staff of peace, which, under the name of "The Inquiry," had been working more than a year to prepare for the time when the war drums throbbed no longer and the battle flags were furled.

The task of organizing this "Inquiry" had been passed on by the President to his Texas friend, Colonel House, who in turn had put the president of another college in charge. Some two hundred scholars had been selected and set to work accumulating a huge mass of data. Elaborate detail maps had been prepared, covering every square mile of Europe; statistics had been dug up, both in libraries and in the "field," as to populations, languages, industries, resources —every question which might arise during the making over of the world. Several carloads of material had been boxed and loaded onto the transport *George Washington*, together with many of the learned persons who had helped to prepare it, and all had been conveyed to the harbor of Brest under the escort of a battleship and half a dozen destroyers.

Professor Alston had been left behind, laid up with the dreadful "flu" which had come in the wake of war; a mysterious scourge which science was powerless to explain, and which many looked upon as a judgment of Providence upon the disorderly nations. The frail professor was hardly well enough to travel, but was worrying himself because of what might appear a shirking of all-important duties. Robbie Budd consoled him by saying: "You won't find all the problems settled when you get to Paris. You may not find them settled when you leave. Your learning may be saved for the next conference."

The professor didn't have his feelings hurt. "Yes, Budd," he answered, patiently. "That's what makes our task so hard—the dreadful weight of skepticism which rests upon so many minds."

IV

The curtain was about to rise upon the last act of the great world melodrama which Lanny Budd had been watching through four and a half impressionable years. During the eight days of the steamer voyage his new friend helped him to peep through the curtain and see the leading characters taking their positions. This melodrama differed from others in that it was not written, it was to be played impromptu, and only once; after that it would be precedent, and would determine the destinies of mankind perhaps for centuries. Each of the actors hoped to write it his way, and no living man could say what the *dénouement* would be.

Professor Alston talked about history, geography, and those racial and language differences which made such a complex. As a scientist, he was dedicated to the truth; he said that he had but one thought, to understand men and nations, and help to bring about a peace that could endure because it was just and sound.

That was the way Lanny wanted things to be; that was his dream, to find some method which would bring his friend Rick and his friend Kurt together, now that the war was over. For hours on end, helping the professor to practice his French, the youth asked questions, and showed himself so eager and understanding that on the last day of the voyage, when the steamer was in sight of the lighthouse of Pointe de St.-Mathieu, the frail scholar was moved to inquire: "Lanny, how would you like to have a job?"

"What sort of job?" asked the other, surprised.

"The State Department, which is my employer, has not seen fit to allow me the services of a secretary; but the nearer I get to France, the more I realize how I shall need one. It's going to be some time before I recover my full strength, and the duties before me are certain to be heavy."

"But a secretary has to know shorthand and typing, doesn't he?"

"Your knowledge of languages and of European ways would count far more with me."

"Don't you think I'm rather young for such a task?"

"You are older than you look. The main thing is that I can trust you. I couldn't pay you what you would consider an adequate salary——"

"Oh, I wouldn't let you pay me, Professor Alston!"

"I'll try to get the department to foot the bill. But in any case I would insist upon your being paid. It'll be one of those all day and most of the night jobs that one does because they're urgent, and because they're interesting. You'd meet a lot of important people, and you'd be on the inside of affairs. I should think it ought to be worth a year in college."

"It sort of takes my breath away," said Lanny. "It would be the first time I ever earned anything."

"What do you suppose your father would say?"

"He wants me to meet people; but he's all the time hoping I'll begin to take hold of the munitions business."

"Well, there's a competition between your father's business and mine right now." The professor was smiling.

"My father won't fight you," replied Lanny, seriously; "but he'll wait, feeling sure that the forces on his side will lick you."

"Perhaps I'd better be the one to put the proposal to him," said the professor. "I don't want him to think I'm trying to steal his son."

Robbie was broader-minded about it than they had foreseen. He saw the advantages which such an opening would give to Lanny. That was the way young Englishmen began their careers in politics and diplomacy; and Robbie wasn't afraid of his son's being led astray by the peace-makers. He said that the same men who made the peace would be making the next war, and Lanny would have a chance to meet and know them. "I'm going to be all over Europe during the next couple of months," added the wise father. "I'll tell you things and you can tell me things."

Lanny thought about that. "Listen, Robbie. If I'm going to be on the payroll of the government, I'll have to work for it, and there may be things I can't tell."

The other was amused. "That's O.K. by me," he said, in the slang of the day. "But this job won't last forever, and when it's done, we'll join forces again."

V

Lanny took the job. Because he liked his new boss, he became not merely secretary, but male nurse, valet, and handyman; he helped the professor to get his things packed, and to get on board the boat train, and to get to his hotel. Oddly enough, the one which Robbie had always patronized, the Crillon, had been taken by the United States government for the use of the Peace Commission and its advisers. Lanny and his professor could have rooms there, but Robbie couldn't—not for love or money. A symbol of the new order of things, under which businessmen were being ousted from the seats of authority and replaced by scholars in politics!

Lanny found himself, with hardly any warning, thrust into the midst of a beehive, or antheap, or whatever simile best indicates a great number of creatures in a state of violent activity. It has always been the practice of scholars and specialists to meet in congresses and conventions, and they always feel that what they are doing is of vital importance; but it may be doubted if any group of such persons had ever before had such good reason to hold this conviction. Some fifty American scholars, plus librarians and custodians of documents and typists and other assistants, several hundred persons in all, had been appointed to remedy the evils of Europe, Asia, Africa, and Australasia, which had been accumulating for no one could say how many hundreds of years. All the world had been told that the evils were to be remedied, and all but a few skeptical ones believed it, and waited in suspense for the promises to be kept. The fate of hundreds of millions of persons for an indefinite future might depend upon the advice which these scholars would give; so the learned ones carried in their souls a colossal burden of responsibility, and never in the history of mankind had so much conscientiousness been crowded into one structure as was to be found at the junction of the Rue Royale and the Place de la Concorde at Christmas time of the year 1918.

The first few hours for Lanny Budd were a blur of faces, names, and handshakes. He met so many persons that he gave up trying to keep them in mind. But quickly they began to sort themselves out. Professor Alston's immediate associates were eager to tell him all that had happened during the two or three weeks he had lost. Alston informed them that Lanny was to be his confidant, and so he had a front seat at the rising of the curtain upon the fateful last act of the great world melodrama.

The art work of the ages to which this production most nearly approached was the story of Daniel in the lions' den. The title role was taken by the scholar from Princeton, and the scholars from

Yale, Harvard, Columbia, and other institutions were gathered in his train, striding with bold miens but quaking hearts into an arena filled with British lions, and with tigers, hyenas, jackals, crocodiles, and other creatures whose national affiliations had better not be specified. Each of these creatures had jaws dripping with blood, and under its claws lay other creatures, equally fierce, but now torn, bleeding, and near to death.

Such was the aspect of the world at the conclusion of the greatest of recorded wars, and the task of Daniel and his associates and advisers was to persuade the victorious ones to abandon at least a part of the prey they had seized, and permit it to be hospitalized and have its wounds attended and be set upon its feet again, under solemn pledges to abandon its predatory ways and live thereafter in a millennial state of brotherhood and legality. If into this description there creeps a trace of mockery, it is due to the fact that Robbie Budd was sojourning at the Hotel Vendôme not far away, meeting his son at intervals, and hearing his description of the academic gentlemen and their activities. If it had been an assemblage of steel, oil, and munitions manufacturers meeting to apportion the trade of the world, Robbie would have taken its decisions with seriousness; but to his mind there was something inherently comical about any large group of college professors. The kindest comparison he could make was to the behavior and conversation of a flock of elderly hens in a chickenhouse when the fox comes sneaking round at night.

VI

When Lanny got to know the members of the American staff, he found that some were according to his father's imagining, but the little group of Alston's intimates had a point of view which included Robbie's far more than Robbie's included theirs. They were informed concerning munitions manufacturers and salesmen, and the part which these played in the beginning and continuing of wars. They knew it so well that they were a bit uneasy at the idea of having their intimate conversations listened to by a son of Budd's. They had to sound him out and watch his reactions for a while before they would completely trust him.

Besides academic persons the staff included a number of young men of independent means who were playing at politics and diplomacy in what they were pleased to consider the "people's cause." Lanny discovered that these fellows knew about Zaharoff, and the de Wendels, and the Briey Basin, which had come out of the war without any serious bombing. They knew about the politicians and propagandists both official and unofficial who now surrounded them. Their conversation was full of jokes about being flimflammed and bamboozled and hoodwinked, short-changed or sold a gold brick or a gross of green spectacles. They watched suspiciously every person who approached them, and received a compliment as if it might be a loaded hand grenade. Many had their wives with them, and these helped to mount guard.

The concern of many had been aroused at the outset by the fact that there was no peace conference under way, and no sign of getting ready for one. The French government had requested that President Wilson should arrive by the fourteenth of December and the President had done so. They had given him a grand reception— the people of Paris turning out and making it the most tumultuous in history. But nothing had been said about a conference; the French hadn't even named their delegates.

The more suspicious of the staff put their heads together. What did it mean? Doubtless they had wanted to get the President over here so that they could wine him and dine him and tell him that he was the greatest man in the world. They would study him, discover his weak points, and see what they could do with him. They offered to take him to inspect the war zones, and the meaning of that was obvious; they would stir up his emotions, fill him with the same hatred of the Germans which they themselves felt. Meanwhile the military men would go on weakening Germany, taking out of the country all those things which the armistice had required—five thousand locomotives, as many trucks, and a hundred and fifty thousand freight cars. Germany would be blockaded, and its remaining stocks of food exhausted—in short, those who wanted a Carthaginian peace would be getting it.

Within the Allied lines there was a struggle getting under way between those who wanted to make peace and those who wanted to wage the next war. In general the French were on one side and the Americans on the other, with the British wavering between the two. Lloyd George, who had become Prime Minister during the war, had only a faction behind him, and had seen the opportunity to cement his power by throwing the country into a general election—the "khaki election," it was called, because of the spirit in which it was carried on. Lloyd George had promised that the Kaiser should be tried, and at the hustings the cry had arisen for him to be hanged. The German people must somehow be made to suffer, as the British and French and Belgians had done. But there was a liberal element among the British representatives in Paris, especially the younger ones, who were sympathetic to the American program of peace with reconciliation. These, of course, wished to meet and know the Americans. Was it proper for the Americans to meet them? Or would that, too, be "propaganda"?

VII

Lanny had sent his mother a telegram upon his arrival in Brest, mentioning the exciting tidings that he had got a job. It meant that he could not come to Juan—at least, not until he had finished solving the problems of Europe. He wrote, suggesting that she should come to Paris.

Of course Beauty had to see her boy; and Robbie thought it would be a good thing if she left home for a while. He didn't take much stock in her efforts at rehabilitating broken Frenchmen; that was all right for women of a certain type, but not for Beauty, who was made for pleasure. Writing to Lanny, she protested that everything in Paris would be so dreadfully expensive; and Robbie answered in his usual way, by giving their son an extra check to send her. It was one of his ways of educating Lanny, helping him to realize how pleasant it was to have money, heigh-ho!

The mother was still clinging to the hope that she might hear some word about Marcel. She told herself that she could carry on her search better from Paris; if it brought no results, she could help to promote interest in his paintings, a labor of piety which intrigued her mind. Lanny could assist her, now that he was meeting so many important and influential persons. In short, life once more began to stir in the bosom of Mabel Blackless, once Beauty Budd, and now Madame Detaze, *veuve*.

She ordered her trunks packed, and oversaw the job, exclaiming over the dowdiness of everything she owned; she hadn't bought a thing for years, and would simply *have* to do some shopping in Paris! Should she give up hope and put on black for Marcel, and how would she look? Leese and Rosine of course had views which they expressed freely. Beauty would repeat her injunctions for the care of Baby Marceline, now a little more than a year old and safely weaned; the two servants would renew their pledges, and Beauty would by turns be grieved at leaving her new baby and excited at the prospect of meeting her old one.

Lanny was at the Gare de Lyon, and they rushed together; then they held each other apart, to see what twenty months had done. "Oh, Lanny, you're grand! What a great tall thing you've grown!" And: "Oh, Beauty, you've been breaking the rules! There are ten pounds more of you!"

She blushed as she admitted her sins. "But I'll soon lose it here in Paris, with the prices I'm told they're charging." They had lunch together at the hotel, and Beauty inspected the *addition*, which included fifty francs for a chicken. She exclaimed in horror, and said she would live on pear and endive salad from now on. One felt guilty to eat anything at all, with so many people starving all over Europe.

Such a myriad of things they had to talk about! Lanny had to tell about Esther and her family, and the rest of the Budd tribe, a hundred details that he had been too busy to write. He had to tell about Gracyn, that horrid creature, so Beauty adjudged her; there were women like that, and they filled a mother's heart with distress. Beauty inspected him anxiously for any signs that his life had been ruined; but he assured her that he was all right, he had learned a lot, he was wiser as well as sadder, and meant to live a strict ascetic life from now on, devoting himself to bringing peace to Europe. Beauty listened gravely; she had heard other men make such resolutions, but had rarely seen them kept.

She told him about the baby, how she looked and what she ate and the delightful sounds she made. She told him about the wounded men she had been visiting at Sept Chênes. "I don't know what I'm going to do with them, Lanny, now that the war is over—it's just like having a lot of relatives." She told about Emily Chattersworth, whose château was still given up to *mutilés*. "She's living in town now, and you must go and see her—she can be so helpful to you and your professors—she knows everybody and likes to bring people together—that's really her forte, you know."

"Don't bother," smiled the youth. "My professors are meeting several times as many people as they want to."

"Oh, but I mean the right ones, Lanny. That's the way to get things done here in France. Emily will arrange to take your Professor Alston direct to Clemenceau himself, and he can explain just how he thinks the peace ought to be settled." It was going to be as simple as that!

VIII

President Wilson and his wife went shopping in Paris. She was a buxom lady who was devoted to him and took the best possible care of him, and wore in his honor a gorgeous purple gown and a hat with purple plumes. Everywhere they appeared there were ovations; the people of Europe rushed to manifest their faith in him, their hope, their adoration. It was something entirely spontaneous, unforeseen by the politicians and not a little disturbing to them. For this man talked about Democracy, and not merely before elections;

he spoke as if he really believed in it—and these were dangerous times, when words were liable to explode, like the shells which were buried in the fields of France and went off in the faces of the peasants who tried to plow. This man talked about freedom of the seas which Britannia boasted of ruling; he talked about self-determination for those small peoples whom the statesmen of Europe were bent upon ruling.

President Wilson and his wife went to London, arriving on the day after Christmas, which the British call "Boxing Day." Enormous throngs welcomed them, and the government provided a royal banquet at Buckingham Palace, making it the most gorgeous spectacle ever seen in that land of pageantry. Britain was the only country left in Europe that could put on such a show. The empire of the Tsar was now a land of starving proletarians, and the realm of the Kaiser was ruled by a saddlemaker; but Britannia still had the money, and her field marshals and generals and admirals and lord mayors still had the costumes. Before this shining assemblage the lean Presbyterian professor stood in his plain black clothes, and talked about the rights of the people; also, he failed to tell the lords and masters of the realm that they had won the war, an offense which they wouldn't forget.

President Wilson and his wife returned to Paris, and he made a speech before the Chamber of Deputies, and failed to praise the heroism which France had displayed. It was hard for his hearers to understand that this was a peace man, who had been forced into war with bitter reluctance, and now had but one thought in his mind, to make such a calamity impossible for the future. He went to Italy, and the hungry and tormented people turned out in a demonstration which frightened the ruling classes. Everywhere it was the same throughout Europe, in defeated lands as well as in victorious ones; the peasants cut out newspaper pictures of this new redeemer and pinned them onto the walls of their huts and burned candles before them. In Vienna the children who were dying wholesale of the diseases of malnutrition smiled happily and said: "It will soon be all right; President Wilson is coming." Never had a living man held so much power in his two hands; never did a living man have so many prayers said for him and to him.

Many among the staff of advisers had considered that it was a mistake for the President of the United States to come to Europe at this time. Professor Alston was among these; he didn't say much about it, wishing to be tactful, but Lanny knew what he thought, and why. If the President had remained in Washington, and had the proposals of the peace delegates submitted to him, his decisions would have come as from Mount Sinai; but when he descended into the arena, he would be just one more contestant, and would sacrifice his prestige and authority. He who had had no training in diplomacy would be pitted against men who had had little else since childhood. They knew a thousand arts of which he was ignorant; they would find out his weak points, they would brow-beat him and weary him and trap him into unwise concessions.

Reading now about the President's triumphal tour, Lanny wondered if this would alter his chief's opinion. But Alston said it was a tragic fact that these millions of people were confused in their minds and easily swayed. They wanted peace, but also they wanted national gains at the expense of others, and they could be whipped up to excitement by a venal press, and by politicians who secretly served financial interests of a selfish kind. What the outcome of these struggles would be, no man alive could foretell; but it was going to be a grim fight, and all of them would have to stand together and back their great leader to the best of their abilities. So thought and whispered the technical advisers of the American Commission to Negotiate Peace.

26

The Parliament of Man

I

THERE was not much holiday spirit in Paris that Christmas. Half the women were in mourning, and the other half doing the work of their men, who were still under arms, many of them in Germany, guarding the bridgeheads of the Rhine. The season was inclement, with cold and rain; food and fuel were scarce and disorganization general. The very rich were richer, but everybody else was poor, and anxiously peering through a curtain of fog to discern what new calamities lay ahead.

The little staff of official Americans were of course well looked after; not merely sheltered and warmed and fed, but provided with every sort of technical assistance: an elaborate courier service, a post office, a telephone and telegraph service of their own, a printing plant, a wireless station which could send a message all the way around the world in the seventh part of a second. Something like a million and a half dollars had been expended to guarantee their security and efficiency. While the President was away on his tours, the experts busied themselves preparing what was known as the "Black Book," an outline of the territorial settlements which the Americans would recommend to the President. It was highly confidential, and many persons wanted very much to know what was in it.

This had the effect of intensifying the siege being laid to the Hotel Crillon. Not a physical siege, of course, for the place was well guarded, and you couldn't get in without a pass; but a diplomatic siege, a social siege, waged with the ancient weapons of

494

elegance and prestige, of courtesy and tact for which Paris was famed. Did anybody know a member of the American staff? And would it be possible to give the said member a dinner party, or invite him to tea, or to a salon, or to hear some music, or to see some pictures? The American professors had a hard time making excuses to all the people who wanted to tell their national troubles. The professors were disposed to be reserved, especially at the outset; bearing in mind that they were not negotiators, but advisers to negotiators.

Lanny Budd was only a semi-official person; and, besides, he had connections in Paris of a sort which few others enjoyed. Professor Alston couldn't very well expect him not to meet his own mother and father, or the friends whom he had known since childhood. And of course the effect was to constitute him a "pipeline" into the Crillon. A great many persons found out that Madame Detaze, widow of a French painter, had a son who was a translator or something to the American staff; so at once Madame Detaze became a popular hostess. "Oh, Madame, I have heard so much about that charming son of yours! So brilliant, so wise beyond his years! I'd love to meet him—couldn't you arrange it? Oh, right away, within the next few days!"

Nothing of that surprised the mother; she had always known that her son was all that! So Lanny would be asked to meet dreamers and propagandists, fortune hunters and impoverished aristocrats from places whose names he had to look up in the atlas—Kurdistan and Croatia, Iraq and Mingrelia, Cilicia which must not be confused with Silesia or Galicia, and Slovenia which must be distinguished from Slovakia. Earnest strangers would appeal in the name of President Wilson's doctrine of "self-determination of all peoples"; and Lanny would take their stories to the experts at the Crillon—and like as not would learn that these same people were busily engaged in oppressing some other people, even perhaps killing them wholesale!

II

Beauty called the hotel, saying: "Lanny, I've just met the most delightful young English officer—he's been in Arabia for years, even before the war, and tells such interesting stories about it. You know, they wear robes, and gallop across the desert on beautiful horses, and take long journeys on camels. They say he has an Arabian sheik or something with him, and he's going to bring him to Emily's for tea. Couldn't you run over?"

So Lanny, who for the last six hours had been working without a break at making abstracts of several French reports on conditions in the Ukraine, said yes, and in the drawing room of Mrs. Chattersworth's town house he met a figure out of the *Arabian Nights:* a man of thirty or so, with a mild face, long and thin, such as painters have imagined for Jesus Christ. He had a black beard and mustache and very beautiful dark eyes, and wore a robe of soft gray silk edged with scarlet, and a four-cornered turban with a hood having a flowered pattern. His father was Sherif of Mecca and King of the Hejaz—at least he said the British called his father "king," but it was silly, for the father traced his ancestry back to the Prophet, more than twelve hundred years ago, and what was any "king" in the world compared to that?

The Emir Feisal, as this young man was called, spoke no English; what he said was translated by the officer who was his companion and friend. The latter's name was Lawrence, and the two of them had been fighting the Turks and Germans all over the sun-scorched deserts of Arabia, and in the end had swept them out of the country. Colonel Lawrence was about thirty-one and seemed even younger, having the manner of a gay schoolboy. He was stocky, with sandy complexion much burned, and very bright blue eyes. He and his friend had a keen sense of humor and exchanged many jokes during the translating.

But they had a serious purpose, having come to Paris to tell the story of the heroic fight which their people had waged for freedom, and to present to President Wilson the claims they held under the terms of his Fourteen Points—Number 12, to be precise, which specified that "the Turkish portions of the present Ottoman Empire should be assured a secure sovereignty, but the other nationalities which are now under Turkish rule should be assured an undoubted security of life and an absolutely unmolested opportunity of autonomous development."

It seemed impossible to misunderstand that. The Emir put it up to Lanny Budd, having been told that he was a compatriot of the great Democrat and a member of the Crillon staff. He begged to be told what Lanny thought about the prospects, and the secretary-translator, speaking unofficially, of course, replied that he had no doubt whatever that President Wilson meant to stand by his promises. It was hard to see how any question could be raised, because the Fourteen Points, with only two reservations, had been expressly accepted by the Allies as the basis of the armistice with Germany. Having given this assurance, Lanny shook hands with the gay young warriors from the sun-scorched lands and they parted the best of friends; the youth went back to his inaccessible hotel and told his chief about it—which of course was what Feisal and his companion assumed that he would do.

Alston smiled a rather wry smile and said that this question of the Hejaz was one of the battles which had to be fought out in the Peace Conference. Lawrence had promised, and the British government had ratified the promise, that the Arabian peoples would have their independence as the price of their support against Turkey and Germany; but unfortunately there was a great deal of oil in Mesopotamia, and a pipeline was proposed to run through Syria; also the British government had promised a lot of Arab territory to the French—it was one of those "secret treaties." The French were now in possession of the land and it wasn't by any means sure that they could be got out without another war. Moreover, there was another Arab chieftain, Ibn Saud, who had driven the Turks out of eastern Arabia—and what about his claims?

All of which went to show how very inadvisable it was for a youthful translator of the American Commission to meet figures

out of the *Arabian Nights* and cause them to believe that they had
assurances of things which they might or might not be going to get!

III

Life does strange things to human beings. Charles T. Alston had
been raised in a small farming community of Indiana, and here he
was, a specialist in geography, ethnography, and allied branches of
learning, helping to decide the destinies of men in lands whose very
names were unknown to the people of the Hoosier state. In his
village as a boy he had attended a tiny Congregational church,
which could not afford a regular pastor but had the services of
students from a near-by church school. One of these students had
eaten fried chicken and cornmeal mush in little Charlie Alston's
home, and had helped to awaken in him a longing for knowledge.
Thirty-five years had passed, during which Alston had never seen
him; but here he came strolling into the Hotel Crillon—having been
in the interim a doctor of divinity, a professor of "Applied
Christianity," a Socialist agitator, and finally one of the trusted
agents and advisers of President Wilson in Europe.

Lanny watched him while he talked to his old friend, and thought
he was one of the strangest-looking men he had ever known. His
unusually sweet and kindly features had not merely the pallor of
marble, but seemed to have its texture. His hair, mustache, and
beard were jet-black. He was obviously not in good health, and
his whole aspect was pain-driven, haunted not merely by his own
griefs but by those of mankind; his manner was quiet, his voice
low, and his language apocalyptic. He rarely smiled, and when he
did so, it seemed to be reluctantly, as a concession to other people's
ways. A sense of impending doom rested upon his spirit, as if he
saw more of the future of Europe than any of the persons he met.

George D. Herron was his name; and later on Alston told Lanny
about the tragedy which had broken his health and happiness. He
had been one of the leaders of a movement called "Christian
Socialist," seeking to bring justice and brotherhood in the name of

the proletarian carpenter. A clergyman and professor in a small college of Iowa, Herron had been unhappily married, and had fallen in love with the dean of women of his college. He had left his wife—something not in accord with the ethics prevailing in the "corn and hog belt." The enemies of his dangerous ideas had taken this opportunity to ruin him, and he had been expelled from his job in the college, and had gone abroad with his new wife to live.

That had been a long while ago, and the unhappy professor and his great sin had been pretty well forgotten. In Europe he had come to know working-class leaders, pacifists, humanitarians— those whose spirits could not rest while their fellow-men were being butchered, mutilated, starved, frozen, drowned in mud, and fed upon hate and falsehood. Living in Geneva, he had been accessible to both sides in the war, and friends and strangers had come to him from Austria and Germany, to sound him out and use him as a means of communicating with the Allied lands. First he had reported to the American embassy in Switzerland, and later to the President direct. He had had something to do with the shaping of the Fourteen Points and had outlined a plan for the forming of a League of Nations. This Socialist agitator who had been driven from his own country in disgrace now possessed the freedom of the Crillon, and could have audiences with the President at a time when the latter was so overburdened that not even the members of his own Peace Commission could see him.

The second time that Lanny met Herron he was walking on the street toward the hotel. He walked slowly, because he suffered from arthritis. Lanny joined him, and he started talking about some of the developments of the day. When they reached the hotel, Lanny waited politely for the elder to go through the revolving doors. He had entered the moving space, when a large military man, coming the other way in haste, pushed the doors violently, and a carved wooden cane which Herron was carrying got caught in the doors and cracked in two. When Lanny came through, his friend was standing with the pieces in his hand, gazing at them and exclaiming: "My Jerusalem cane!"

"Is it valuable?" asked the youth.

"Not to anyone but me. I bought it when I was young and visited the Holy Land. It has been precious to me as a souvenir of deeply felt experiences."

"Oh, I'm sorry," said Lanny, sympathetically.

The other still held the broken pieces. "I am not superstitious," he continued; "but I will tell you a curious incident. When I was leaving home, my sixteen-year-old son asked me why I was carrying that cane, and I said, half playfully: 'I am going to Paris to set up the kingdom of heaven, and this staff from the country of Jesus is a symbol of my purpose.' 'See that they don't break it, Father!' said my son."

The professor looked at the pieces a moment or two longer and then called a bellboy and gave them to him to dispose of. "*Absit omen!*" he remarked to Lanny.

I V

It was the twelfth of January before the "Supreme Council" held its first session, in the hall of the dingy old Foreign Office on the Quai d'Orsay, just across the Seine from the Crillon. The gray stone structure kept some of the most vital secrets of France, and had high iron railings and heavy gates. Only important personages were admitted to the opening ceremony, but Lanny and his chief were among them, because some of the American delegates might need information about geography. Lanny's duty was the carrying of two heavy portfolios of maps and other data; he would take them with him to many important gatherings, but rarely would open them—instead, he would keep his ears open, and stay close behind his chief; now and then the latter would touch his knee, and Lanny would lean over and whisper what some excited Frenchman was saying. This kind of assistance was not uncommon among the American officials; neither President Wilson nor his closest associate, Colonel House, knew French, and there always had to be whisperers behind their chairs.

The council hall was splendid and impressive, having on the floor a heavy Aubusson carpet, pearl-gray with large red roses; red damask curtains at the windows, superb Gobelin tapestries on the walls. The ceilings were high, and the lights were set in enormous chandeliers. A great many tables were laid end to end in the shape of a square U, covered with green baize, and pink silk blotters which were changed every day. The chairs were gilded, with silk upholstery, and all this splendor was guarded by *huissiers* wearing silver chains.

At the bottom of the square U sat Georges Clemenceau, Premier of France, a squat little figure with a strange head, bald and flat on top. He had broad humped shoulders, a short neck, sallow complexion, white walrus mustaches, thick, shaggy eyebrows, and a long, square-tailed black coat. At his back was a fireplace with a crackling fire—you would always find that wherever he sat, for he was seventy-eight, and diabetic, and his blood was growing chilly. Over the fireplace was a figure of Peace holding up a torch—perhaps to warm his soul, which may also have grown chilly. Always he wore gray silk gloves on his hands, because he suffered from eczema.

Near him sat President Wilson, stiff and erect, with lean ascetic face and shining glasses. Beyond him was the Prime Minister of Britain with pink cherubic features and a little white mustache. Next to him was Balfour with his air of aristocratic boredom, cultivated not for this occasion but for life. The other personages tapered off down the line. In the background were generals wearing uniforms and medals, and potentates in the varicolored robes of the East. Marshal Foch was there, and General Pershing, and other military men, because the first matter in hand was the renewal of the armistice, which was for a month at a time, and each time the Marshal had thought of some new ways to tighten the screws upon the hated foe.

After that they took up the question of representation at the conference, and the future methods of procedure. It was supposed to be a deliberative assembly, but after a few sessions it became apparent that everything had been fixed in advance. Someone would make a proposal, and while he was speaking Clemenceau would sit with hands folded and eyes closed, and no one would know whether he was asleep or not. But the moment the speaker finished, the chairman would raise his heavy eyelids and say: "Any discussion?" —and then, before anybody could get his wits together to answer, he would bring down his gavel and snap out: "*Adopté!*" Said Professor Alston to Lanny: "He's fighting the next war."

V

At the head of President Wilson's Fourteen Points stood the phrase: "Open covenants of peace openly arrived at." Taking this statement at its face value, American press associations, newspapers, and magazines had sent their correspondents to Paris, and there were now a hundred and fifty of them in a ravenous condition, having waited a whole month for something to happen. The rest of the world had contributed twice as many; and now they were informed that no press representatives would be admitted to sessions of the conference, but that they would get "handouts" from a press bureau. When they got their first one they found that it contained exactly forty-eight words.

A howl went up that was heard, quite literally, all the way around the world. The hundred and fifty Americans appointed a committee and stormed the American press bureau; a war began that did not end with the Peace Conference, but was continued into the history books. Men took one side or the other—and from that choice you could know what part they were going to play, not merely in this particular melodrama, but in all the others which were to follow upon its heels.

France had been at war for four bloody years, had suffered grievous wounds, and now stood with one foot upon her deadly foe. During these four years the people of France had been under a complete censorship; officials and military men between them had decided not merely what should be done but what should be said and thought. Now suddenly it was proposed to lift this censorship and turn people loose to reveal secrets and criticize policies—in short, to say what they pleased, or what the enemy might hire them to say. "What?" cried the shell-shocked officials. "Open the sessions of the conference, and let newspaper men hear the wrangles of the diplomats, and tell the whole world about national ambitions and demands? If you do that, you will have a series of new wars on your hands—the Allies will be fighting among themselves!"

To this the believers in open covenants openly arrived at replied that the affairs to be settled by the conference were the affairs of the people, and the people had a right to know what was being planned and done. Democracy could not function unless it had information. The only way of lasting peace was to turn the conference into a means of education, an open forum where problems were threshed out in the sight and hearing of all.

So the debate raged; and like everything else with which the assemblage dealt it was settled by compromise and evasion. It was agreed that the press should be admitted to the "plenary sessions"; whereupon these were turned into formal affairs to ratify decisions already worked out by the so-called "Council of Ten." When the press took to clamoring against the secrecy of the "Council of Ten," the real work was transferred to a secret "Council of Four." Presently this became a "Council of Three," and this holy trinity not only told no pressmen what it was doing, but to make sure that they couldn't find out, it employed but one secretary and kept but one record.

VI

Of course only a small portion of the people of Paris were occupied with the Peace Conference. The common people, mostly women and elderly men, worked at their daily tasks, and gave their thoughts to getting food with prices steadily rising. The well-to-do had their cares also, for it was a violent world, exposed to sudden unforeseeable changes. Only speculators throve; and whenever

Robbie met his son he had stories to tell about what these were doing.

The munitions industry was shot to pieces, reported the salesman. Budd's had been forced to close down; all that magnificent plant which had been like a beehive—its chimneys were empty and its gates were locked. "But I thought we still had contracts with the government!" exclaimed the youth. The father answered that it didn't pay to run big plants for a few orders, and they had canceled the contracts on the basis of part payments.

"But what will all those working people do, Robbie?"

"I hope they saved their money. For us the war ended too soon. Nobody could foresee that Germany was going to collapse like that."

"We still have those fine new plants, haven't we?"

"What are plants if you can't run them? They're just a drain; upkeep, insurance, and taxes—the government soaks you as hard whether you're making anything or not."

"I never thought of that," confessed Lanny.

"Your grandfather isn't thinking about anything else very much."

Robbie was sending home long reports, mostly without a gleam of hope. There were plenty of people who wanted to go on fighting, but where were they to get the money? Who would want to finance new wars? And, anyhow, the fighting would be done with munitions already manufactured. There were mountains of it piled up all over France, and on the Italian front, and the Balkan front, and the Palestine front—everywhere you looked on the map. It could be bought for almost anything you wanted to offer.

"I've been trying to interest Father in buying some as a speculation," added Robbie. "But he says we're not going into the junk business. I can't very well do it myself while I'm the European sales agent of our firm."

In Lanny's mind was a vision of that depressing old Colonial house in Newcastle, with a worried and overworked businessman sitting at a desk piled high with papers—and having in one drawer a bundle of pamphlets setting forth the Confession of Faith of his grand-father. "What does he expect to do, Robbie?"

"We've got to figure out ways to turn some of the plants to peacetime uses. And that's going to cost a lot of money."

"Well, we made it, didn't we?"

"Most of it was distributed as dividends, and people aren't going to put it back in unless we can show them new ways of making profits."

"Surely, Robbie, there's going to be a demand for every sort of goods! People are clamoring for them all over."

"It doesn't matter how much they clamor, unless they've got money. The ones that have money daren't risk it when there's so much uncertainty—and when those in authority can't make up their minds about anything. We've got a President who spent his time studying Latin and Greek and theology when he ought to have been learning the elements of finance and credit."

Robbie said that Clemenceau and Lloyd George were every bit as ignorant about economic questions; he wanted businessmen and financiers called in to advise. With one-third of Europe in revolution, and another third hanging on the brink; with tens of millions of people not knowing where to get their next day's bread; with trade disorganized, railways broken down, river transport sunk, harbors blockaded, and millions of men still kept out of production, liable to revolt and go home, or to start shooting one another—the man to whom they all looked for guidance had brought a shipload of specialists in geography and history and international law, and only a handful who knew finance, production, or trade.

VII

The telephone rang in Lanny's room, and he heard a voice, speaking English with a decided foreign accent: "Can you guess?" Someone in a playful mood; he kept on talking, and Lanny, who had heard so many kinds of accents in his young life, tried his best to think, but nothing stirred in his memory. "Five years ago," said the stranger. "On a railroad train." Lanny groped in his mind. "I got on at Genoa," said the voice; and suddenly a light dawned, and the youth cried: "Mr. Robin!"

"Johannes Robin, Maatschappij voor Electrische Specialiteiten, Rotterdam—at your service!" chuckled the voice.

"Well, well!" said Lanny. "What are you doing here?"

"A little business, which will be a secret until I see you."

"And how are the boys?"

"Fine, Lanny, fine—do I call you Lanny, even though you are grown up to a young gentleman?"

"You bet you do, Mr. Robin. I'll never forget the favors you have done me." In the course of the last four years Mr. Robin had mailed six or eight letters to Kurt in Germany, one of them only a week or two previously. That was how the trader knew that Lanny was in Paris, and his address.

Of course Lanny wanted to see that friend, even busy as he was with all the affairs of Europe. "I'm going to have lunch with my father," he said. "Wouldn't you like to join us?"

"Sure, I like to meet your father," said the dealer in electrical gadgets. Lanny told him where to come.

Johannes Robin was somewhat stouter than Lanny remembered him; he had spent money on his clothes and looked the picture of prosperity. He was the same exuberant fellow, who liked to talk about himself; but Lanny, more observant now, got the feeling that he was not entirely at ease. He wanted very much to please these two rich Americans, and was never quite sure whether he was doing it. His handsome dark eyes moved from Lanny's face to Robbie's and back again, and his smile was deprecating and hesitant, as if to say: "I hope you don't mind if I am so proud to know you."

He was genuinely glad to see the youth and exclaimed over how big he had got. Of course he wanted to tell about those two boys at home, and he had some more snapshots of his family group, which he presented apologetically—they wouldn't take up much room. They talked about Kurt Meissner; Lanny had had no answer to his last letter, and was worried about it. A captain of artillery could have been killed during the last days of the war just as well as at any other time. Robbie said that the Americans had been attacking just as hard between seven in the morning when the armistice was signed and eleven when it went into effect.

With Lanny's father Mr. Robin became the businessman, who had traveled over Europe and knew its affairs, and could tell interesting stories about money-making in wartime. From his safe retreat in the Low Countries he had made quite a lot, in spite of the British blockade; nothing to compare with Mr. Budd's affairs, he said modestly, but enough to constitute success for one who had been born in a ghetto hut with a mud floor. Robbie liked that attitude—he liked people to be what they were and not pretend to be something else; so he and the Jewish importer got along pleasantly. They agreed that business would pick up again, if only the diplomats would quit their stalling; they agreed on many things that ought to be done—and Lanny listened, picking up bits of information which he could take back to his chief, to atone for taking a couple of hours off in the middle of a busy day.

VIII

Before those two had finished their bottle of wine they knew each other well enough for Jascha Rabinowich, alias Robin, to make a confession. "Mr. Budd, I have some ideas in my head that just don't let me rest. You know the feeling perhaps: there is money to be made, so much money, and I see how it can be done at once, but later on it will be too late."

Yes, Robbie knew the feeling, and gave permission for his new acquaintance to tell him what he had in mind. It turned out to be the same thing that had been interfering with Robbie's sleep: all that mass of munitions and other supplies which had been manufactured at enormous cost, and which were now lying about—"Have you seen them, Mr. Budd?"

Robbie smiled. "My son sees them on the Place in front of his hotel." It was packed with rows of cannon of every type, howitzers, mortars, field-guns—captured German pieces with the marks of war on them, and now rusting in the rain.

"It is terrible, Mr. Budd, all those goods which cannot even be covered up: shells that they were ready to fire, boots they were going to wear. Now they do not know what to do with it all. To take things back to England—that is possible; but all the way to America—will it pay the cost of crating and shipping?"

"We have been figuring on it, and it won't," said Robbie Budd. "The army has a commission here, trying to dispose of the stuff."

"Well, Mr. Budd, I am a man who knows how to sell things. I know dealers all over Europe. And I have ideas. I wake up in the middle of the night, because one has stung me, like it might be—what is it?—*abeille*——"

"A bee," said Lanny.

"For example?" said Robbie.

"Well, hand grenades; there are millions of them——"

"We made a quarter of a million for our army."

"And now they are somewhere out in the mud of Lorraine. You know what they look like; I don't need to describe them."

"What would you do with them?"

"First I unload them. I have a mass of black powder, which I put up in bags. I know a man who supplies mining companies in Chile, Peru, all those countries. Then I cut off the handles; tomorrow I will find something to do with them. Then I have a little round metal box; it has a pretty shape, it sits up on end; I cut a slot in the top, and there you are."

"What is it?"

"It is a children's bank, where they drop their pennies, their *pfennigs*, their *sous*, their *soldi*—in every country they have little coins for the poor."

Robbie and his son couldn't keep from laughing. Such an odd idea: a hand grenade, the quintessence of destructiveness, made into a children's bank, the symbol of thrift. Swords into plowshares and spears into pruning hooks!

Mr. Robin laughed too, but only for a moment. "You don't know what a market it is, Mr. Budd. You don't know the homes of the poor, as I do."

"But they have no money now."

"They will get these small coins; and they will starve themselves and save—maybe to pay off a mortgage, maybe to buy a cow, or for a girl's dowry—such things as the peasants hope for. A bank is something sacred, it comes next to the crucifix; it teaches virtue, it is a witness and a reminder; the family that has it has something to live for. If there is peace, on next Christmas Day a million peasant women will give such banks to their children."

"Christmas is a long way off, Mr. Robin."

"You would not say that if you knew the novelty trade. Next summer we start to travel for our Christmas trade; and meantime I am finding the agents, I am sending them the samples and the circulars and the contracts; and all that I have to get ready. If I have a couple of hundred thousand banks that have cost me only a few cents each, I know I can sell them, and just where and how. And that is only one small deal, Mr. Budd. I will find a hundred bargains, and a use for each."

"Have you thought about storage costs?"

"In the old city where I live are hundreds of warehouses, and no longer will they be full of goods when ships can go directly into Germany. They are on the canals, and goods come by the rivers or the sea—there is cheap transport to every part of the world. All that is needed is cash to buy—and to do it quickly, before someone else snaps up the bargain. I am so certain of the profits that I am offering to go fifty-fifty with you; I will give all my time and experience, I will do the work, and pay you half the profits. We will form a company, and your name will be kept out of it—I know that you do not want your name in small business like this. It will be a quick thing—in a year it will be over, and I would not dare to tell you how many hundred percent we will clear, because then you would be sure that I must be a swindler."

IX

Lanny watched these two traders, smoking their cigars and knocking the ashes into the dregs of their coffee cups; he amused himself trying to guess what was going on in their minds. He himself kept silent, knowing that this wasn't his job. He personally would have been willing to trust the Jewish dealer, because he liked him. But Robbie didn't like Jews; his view was that of society people who don't want them in their fraternities or clubs. Robbie would sometimes make playful remarks based upon the assumption that Jews went into bankruptcy freely, and set fire to their warehouses and stores when the season became slack. "Fur stores burn in February" —all that sort of thing.

Would Mr. Robin be aware of that attitude? Lanny guessed that this shrewd fellow knew everything that concerned himself and his affairs; he would anticipate the attitude of fashionable gentiles listening to his business "spiel" and watching the play of his hands and shoulders.

"Look, Mr. Budd," said the dealer in gadgets. "I come to you a stranger, and perhaps I have nerve to talk money to you. But I have business connections, I have a reputation in my home city; my creditors and bankers will tell you. But more important yet is that you should know me as a man. If I may speak to you frankly, and from my heart, and not feel that I am boring you . . . ?"

"I have been interested in you ever since Lanny told me about you, Mr. Robin."

"Perhaps he told you that I come from a Polish ghetto, and that I have suffered poverty and worked bitterly hard, and paid for everything that I have gained. Now I have had some success, and if I am cautious I and my loved ones do not have to worry the rest of our lives. But I have brains and I like to use them. It is a game that we play, you and me, all of us; you know what I mean?"

"I know."

"It is a pleasure to rise in the world, to meet new people, educated people, those that have power. I know that I will always be a Jew, and carry the marks of the ghetto; I know that my accent is not right in any language, that I talk with my hands, and that I say things that are not in good taste, so I do not expect ever to shine in drawing rooms. But I expect that businessmen will recognize me, and that I will be able to do things that are worth while. And now through a chance I have met a big businessman——"

Robbie raised his hand. "Not so big, Mr. Robin!"

"I am telling you how it seems to me. You live in a world far above mine. Maybe you are not really better than me, but the world thinks you are, and I, with my ghetto memories, look up to you. I look at your son and I think: 'I would like my boys should be like him.' And if I persuade you to go into a deal with me, I have a chance to make good in a new way. If I cheat you, I will get some money quick, but then no more. You will say: 'The little kike!'— and that is the end. But if I make good, then I have your respect. You tell your friends: 'I don't care what you say about the Jews, I know one that's straight, I would trust him with the crown jewels' —or whatever it is that you value in America, the Statue of Liberty, shall we say?"

"I am touched by your confidence, Mr. Robin," smiled the American. "I will try to be worthy of your ideal."

"I will tell you something more, Mr. Budd—if I am not boring you?"

"Not at all."

"You have seen the little pictures of my two boys. How I love those boys is something I cannot tell any man. I would give my life if it would spare them unhappiness. Those boys were not born in a ghetto, and its marks are not on them. For them I imagine the finest things in the world. The little one, Freddi, is a quiet lad, and studious; he will be a professor, perhaps. But the other, Hansi, his choice is made; he lives for the violin. He will not be some obscure fellow in an orchestra; he has fire, he has temperament, and he works so hard, I know that he will be a virtuoso, a concert performer. You think, perhaps, it is a fond father's dream; and maybe so, but to me it is real."

"I understand," said Robbie, who also had a dream.

"Then one day I meet on the train a little American gentleman, and I talk with him. He is going to visit in a German castle; he has good manners, and what is more, he is kind; he plays the piano, he reads, he has traveled and met famous people, his talk is far beyond his years; it comes to me as incredible that a boy should know so much, and talk so like a man of the world. I go home and tell my boys about him, and how they wish they had been on that train and met that Lanny Budd! Then a year or two passes, and one day I get a letter, with a picture of himself and his mother in front of their home; my boys they pin it up on the wall, and all the time they are talking about that wonderful Lanny Budd. They write him little notes, and he answers, and they are saying: 'Some day we shall meet him!' They are saying: 'Do you think that he would like us, Papa? Do you think he would mind that we are Jews?' Perhaps you have never thought about how it is to be a Jew, Mr. Budd?"

"I am interested to understand," said Robbie, politely.

"If you are an orthodox Jew, you have your faith, your ancient laws and customs, and that is enough; you are not interested in any-one but Jews, because you know that the rest is accursed. But if it happens that you learn modern ideas, and decide that the Sabbath is a day like any other day, and that ham will not hurt you if it is well cooked, and that it is all rubbish that you should not eat meat and butter from the same dish—then you are done with the old religion and you are looking for something else to take its place. You wish to live in the world like other people; to be a man among men. If somebody says: 'I do not want you in my home because you are ignorant, and stupid, and you bore me'—that is all right, that may be true, and you cannot complain. But if someone says: 'I do not want you in my home because you are a Jew'—that is not fair, and that hurts. But of course every Jew hears it, and a Polish Jew most of all, because that is supposed to be a very low kind. Every Jew wishes to meet gentiles, and to live among gentiles, but no Jew is ever quite happy, or quite sure; every Jew is thinking: 'Is there something wrong here?' or perhaps: 'Have I done something

I shouldn't?' But he cannot ask, because that is not done; and when I say this to you, I have to think if it will displease you."

"Not at all," said Robbie. It was a concession on his part.

"So little Hansi is thinking: 'I will play the violin better and better, and then some day, when I meet the wonderful Lanny Budd, he will wish to play duets with me. He will really judge my music, and not as the rich boys do at school, my Jewishness.' That is what my Hansi has said to me; and now, should I smash his dream that the wonderful Lanny Budd might wish to play music with him? Shall I have to hear him say: 'No, Papa, I cannot have Lanny Budd for a friend, because his father says that you are not honest in business, that you took advantage of him when he trusted you'? So you see, Mr. Budd, I should have to go straight, even if it was against my nature."

"A new kind of business credentials, Mr. Robin!" said the other, smiling. "How much money would you say you could use to advantage in this business?"

"It is hard to know in advance. You understand that the buying will always be a spot-cash proposition. I would say a hundred thousand dollars should be in the bank. I would report to you what I am doing, and if I saw a use for further sums, you could judge each proposition on its merits."

Robbie had never told his son just how much money he had made in the last few years; so Lanny was startled when his father said: "I guess I could find a hundred thousand without too much trouble. You give me the references you speak of, Mr. Robin, and I'll look into them, and if they are what you tell me, I'll take a flier with you."

Lanny was pleased, but he didn't say so until they had dropped the dealer at his hotel. Then he chuckled and said: "You're in the junk business, Robbie!"

27

The Federation of the World

I

THE Peace Conference had begun its sessions. They had long debates as to whether they should debate in the English language or the French, and finally decided that they would use both, and have everything translated back and forth. They had a bitter controversy over the question whether they were going to try the Kaiser for his crimes; they had solemnly announced that they would do so, but the Kaiser was in Holland, which wouldn't give him up, and gradually the debate petered out—there were so many more urgent problems. Their armies were costing several million dollars a day, and so many women wanted their men back home!

President Wilson had set it as the first item on his program to establish a League of Nations and get it going. Everything else depended upon that, for without it you couldn't be sure that any arrangements you made would last a year. Premier Clemenceau had publicly sneered at the idea; what he believed in was the "balance of power"—which meant a group of nations strong enough to lick Germany. He and the President were now meeting daily, testing out each other's sparring power; meanwhile the American professors had to live upon scraps of gossip. Was it the Premier or the President who had been frowning when they emerged from the conference room that day?

The guessing grew hot when the problem of a League of Nations was assigned to a commission. That, obviously, represented Clemenceau's effort to shelve and forget it. But Wilson countered by appointing himself as one of the American members of the League of Nations Commission. Naturally he became chairman of it, since it was his idea and his hobby; when he began attending its daily sessions, he hadn't time to attend any other sessions, and so Clemenceau was left to fume and fret. The Americans rubbed their hands with delight. The Big Chief was really going to fight!

Everybody in the American staff began talking League. Even those who were supposed to be busy on other assignments couldn't keep their fingers out of the pie. Such a colossal enterprise, the most momentous in history! The poet Tennyson had sung about "the Parliament of Man, the Federation of the World," and all these professors had learned the verses in school. How much of sovereignty was each nation to part with? What representation was each to have? Should the little ones have equal power with the big ones? And what about the colonial peoples? What about the national minorities?

President Wilson had a draft of the League somewhere among his baggage. Several members of "The Inquiry" had their drafts. The British, having an "Inquiry" of their own, had prepared a layout, of which a prominent feature was that each of the British dominions should count as a separate nation and have its own delegates. The French had a plan, of which the most important feature was an international army, to make sure that Germany could never again invade France. All these plans had to be put together, in spite of their being incompatible.

II

Lanny Budd had been assigned to a room on the top floor of the Crillon, on the courtyard, along with two other secretaries. But after a couple of weeks the three were moved out to a near-by hotel, to make room for more important persons who kept arriving from America. However, Lanny still had his meals in the hotel dining room, because Professor Alston wanted him. Under the regulations he was allowed to have one guest each day. He would invite his father to meet the staff and convince himself that they were not so tender-minded as they had been imagined. He would give his mother a chance to exercise her charms upon a susceptible group of gentlemen a long way from home and not having much opportunity to enjoy feminine society.

It had been only a little more than six months since Marcel had disappeared into the furnace of war; but Beauty's grief was less, because, as she explained to Lanny, she had suffered so much of it in anticipation. This suffering had given her dignity, without depriving her of those weapons of earlier days. She was still on the good side of forty, and deducted a couple of years more in her thoughts about herself. She couldn't very well deduct more, with a son seated at her side, several inches taller than herself!

Beauty was far too much a woman of the world to pretend to knowledge before these professors; she chose the line of calling herself an ignoramus and deploring her wasted youth. "Oh, Professor Alston," she would exclaim, "do make these wonderful ideas of yours work, so that we women in Europe won't have a nightmare pouncing down on us every generation!" It was an old practice of hers, in dealing with the male sex, to ask each about his own work, listen attentively, and express admiration. This proved as effective with scholars as with those of higher station, and Beauty might have eaten all her meals at the expense of the United States government if she had cared to accept the invitations showered upon her.

She told these learned ones about her friend Emily Chattersworth, and many of them knew the name; the older ones remembered the banking scandal, back in the bad old days when pirates had sailed the high financial seas. Mrs. Emily had rented a town house, and had teas every Thursday, and a salon on a modest scale on Sunday evenings; with her permission, Beauty invited Lanny's chief, and he went, and met important people: a member of the French cabinet, or a general just returned from service in Salonika; an English statesman who had flown from London that afternoon, or a Russian grand duke who had escaped from the Bolsheviki by way of Siberia

and Manchuria. A youth who had access to social opportunities such
as these was considered an unusually good secretary.

III

One of the persons whom Lanny saw most frequently was George
D. Herron. This prophet of the new day came to see Alston, and
they talked, and Lanny listened. Herron seemed to take a fancy tɔ
the youth, perhaps thinking of him as a possible convert. They sat
on a bench by the embankment of the Seine, and the older man in-
terpreted the events of the time in accordance with his peculiar
ideas.

The only Socialist Lanny had met so far was that editor who had
taken such unfair advantage of a boy's indiscretion. It appeared that
Herron had called himself a Social-Democrat a couple of decades
ago, and had helped to found the Socialist party in the United
States; but the war had brought a violent reaction, and Social-
Democracy was now in his mind a part of "Germanism," the arch-
enemy of the soul of man. It based itself upon materialism, denying
freedom and respect for the personality. Herron's vision was of a
society transformed by brotherhood and love; he found those quali-
ties embodied in Jesus, and that was why he called himself a Christian Socialist, even while rejecting the dogmas of the churches.

On this subject he talked with the fervor of the prophets of old.
For him all thinking led to the basic question whether mankind
could be saved from sliding into an abyss of barbarism, a new Dark
Age of materialism and hate. The late war had brought us close to
the edge, and new wars now on the horizon might carry us over.
He pointed to the fall of empires throughout history; what was
there to save us from a similar fate? Only a vision of spiritual things
which a few great souls had caught, and for the sake of which they
had martyred themselves and must continue to do so.

To this tormented soul the League of Nations represented the one
hope of preserving justice and peace in the world, so that the higher

faculties of man might survive and be propagated. In the spring of the previous year he had written President Wilson an urgent letter on behalf of the project, and a considerable correspondence had resulted. In Paris, Wilson showed him his draft of the League, and asked his suggestions. This was known to the advisory staff, who looked upon this strange interloper with a mingling of curiosity and alarm. Perhaps he wasn't a scandalous person, but all America believed him to be that—and what would America say as to the sort of company its college professors were keeping in Paris?

It happened that Robbie Budd came to lunch and sat at table with Herron, Alston, and Lanny. The black-bearded prophet was in his most apocalyptic mood. Said he: "The salvation of the world from Germanism depends upon the salvation of Germany from her ancient barbarian self. The final value of our military success, the proof that we are worthy of it, must lie in its redemptive power. We have won a victory over the German people and we have now to win the German people to that victory. What we do must be infused by such spiritual purpose as will enable the German people to see the divine reason for it, and to enter co-operatively into the judgments and workings of that reason."

When Lanny had been alone with his new acquaintance, listening to such words, he had been much impressed; but now he heard them through the ears of his skeptical father and they made him wriggle uncomfortably. Robbie was a self-contained man, and knew how to keep quiet when he wanted to; but when he was alone with his son, he exclaimed: "My God, who is that nut?" When Lanny told him that the fervid orator was one of President Wilson's trusted advisers, Robbie was ready to go home and tell America that it was being governed from a lunatic asylum. The United States Senate—now safely under control of the Republican party—ought to send a committee to Europe to take charge of the peace-making!

Of course Robbie couldn't expect to keep his son in cotton wool. Lanny was in the world now and had to meet crackpots and fanatics along with sane businessmen. But at least he was going to have his father's advice. In detail, and with as much conscientiousness as any

Christian Socialist, Robbie explained that the ruling class of Germany had tried to grab the trade privileges of the British Empire, and had failed. They would try again whenever they got the chance; it was life or death for one group or the other, and would continue to be that so long as men used steel in making engines, and coal and oil—not hot air—to run them with. Lanny listened, and decided that his father was right, as always.

IV

It was a time of strain and anguish, and really it wasn't easy to know what to think or do. Lanny had shared in his own soul the griefs of the people of France and could understand their dread of a wicked government which had inflicted them. For Lanny the soul of France was embodied in the memories of his stepfather; and always he tried to imagine, what would Marcel have felt about the peace-making and the various problems which kept arising in connection with it?

One thing seemed certain: Marcel would not have approved the deliberate starving of women and children. The Germans had assumed that the blockade would be lifted when they signed the armistice; but the French had no such thought. Nothing was to go into Germany until she had accepted and signed the peace terms which France meant to lay down. But the treaty wasn't ready yet, and meanwhile children were crying with hunger.

To the members of the American delegation this seemed an atrocious thing. They protested to the President, and he in turn to Clemenceau—but in vain. Herbert Hoover, who had been feeding the Belgians, wanted also to feed the defeated peoples; he did finally, as a great concession, get the right to send a relief mission to Austria —but nothing to Germany. Marshal Foch stood like a block of concrete in the pathway. Lanny saw him coming out from the conference room where this issue was fought over; a stocky little man with a gray mustache, voluble, talking with excited gestures, demanding his pound of flesh. He was commander-in-chief of the

Allied armies and he gave the orders. A singular thing—he was a devout Catholic, went every morning to mass, and kneeled to a merciful redeemer who had said: "Suffer the little children to come unto me, and forbid them not." Little French children, of course; no little German children!

This was one of the things which tormented Herron. He talked incessantly about a "Carthaginian peace," such as the Romans had imposed when they razed a great city to the ground and drove its population into exile. If France imposed a peace of vengeance upon Germany, it would mean that "Germanism" had won the war; it would mean that France had adopted Germany's false religion, and that the old France of the Revolution, the France of "liberty, equality, fraternity," was no more. The black-bearded prophet suffered so over the hunger of the blockaded peoples that he couldn't eat his own food.

He would come to the Crillon to consult with Alston, whom he trusted because he had known him as a lad. A sense of agonized impotence possessed him; to see the world drifting to shipwreck, and know what ought to be done, but be helpless to get it done; to give advice and have it accepted—but not acted upon. To see intrigue, personal jealousy, factional strife, blocking the hopes of mankind. There was all that sort of thing at the Crillon, of course; there were those who had the President's ear, and others who sought to get it, and pulled wires and flattered and fawned. There were some who were not above repeating scandals and raking up old tragedies. "Of course I'm a marked man," said Herron. "I cannot be recognized publicly; but that doesn't change the fact that I know Europe better than any of those whom the President is meeting."

V

Many times in these days Lanny had occasion to recall the words which the Graf Stubendorf had spoken, concerning "the dark cloud of barbarism in the eastern sky." In five years that cloud had spread until it threatened to cover the firmament; it was of the hue of

Stygian midnight, and its rim was red and dripping a bloody rain. No longer the Russian Tsar with his Cossacks and their whips, no longer Pan-Slavism with its marching hosts, but the dread Bolshevism, which not only formed armies, but employed a new and secret poison which penetrated the armies of its enemies, working like a strong acid, disintegrating what it touched. A good part of the secret conferences going on in Paris had to do with this peril and how to meet it. There were some who thought it made no difference what decisions the Peace Conference took, because it was all going to be swept away in a Red upheaval throughout Central Europe.

As the friends of Lanny Budd portrayed it to him, two evil creatures had been spewed up from the Russian cesspool, and had managed to seize power. They were still holding on to it—in spite of the fact that the newspapers reported Lenin as shooting Trotsky and Trotsky as poisoning Lenin about once a week. They had led the workers and peasants in a campaign of massacre, and the nobility and land owners of the Tsar's realm had fled, counting themselves lucky if they had a few jewels sewed up in the lining of their coats. Paris was full of these refugees, with pitiful and ghastly tales to tell; Lanny heard some of them, and his mother, in her incompetent way, made efforts to help the victims. It seemed to her sympathetic soul unbearable that people who had never had to work and so didn't know how to work should suddenly find themselves without money to pay for their meals. Robbie had to tell her more than once that his fortune was not equal to supporting the Russian aristocracy in the state to which it had been accustomed.

Of course Europe had to protect itself against this Red menace, said Lanny's friends; and so the Allied armies had established what they called a *cordon sanitaire* around the vast former empire of the Tsar. The Japanese and the Americans had seized Vladivostok and the eastern half of the Trans-Siberian railway. The British and Americans had occupied Archangel and Murmansk in the far North, blocking all commerce by that route. Along the European land front the Allied troops stood on guard, and French and British officers were busy organizing anti-Bolshevik Russians, and providing them with arms and money and sending them into the Ukraine, Russian Poland, and the Baltic provinces. This fighting had been going on for a year now, and each day Lanny read in the papers of "White" victories and was assured that soon the dreadful menace would be at an end.

But it was like a forest fire, whose sparks flew through the air; or perhaps a plague, whose carriers burrow underground and come up through rat-holes. The emissaries of the Bolsheviks would sneak through the sanitary cordon, and creep into the slums of some city of Central Europe, telling the hungry workers how the Russians had made a revolution, and offering to help do the same. The armies would catch many of them and shoot them; but there were always more. Even before the armistice, a Jewish "Red" by the name of Eisner had seized the government of Bavaria; in Berlin two others named Liebknecht and Luxemburg—the latter a woman, known as "Red Rosa"—were carrying on a war in the streets, seeking to take power from the Socialist government which had arisen in Germany after the overthrow of the Kaiser. In Hungary it was the same; a member of the nobility who called himself a Socialist, Count Karolyi, had given his estates in an effort to help the poor of that starving land, but now a Bolshevik Jew was leading a movement to unseat him and set up soviets on the Russian pattern.

Always it was a Jew, people pointed out to Lanny; and this kindled to flame the anti-Semitic feeling always latent among the fashionable classes of Europe. "What did we tell you?" they would say. "The Jews have no country; they are seeking to undermine and destroy Christian society. It is a worldwide conspiracy of this arrogant people." Robbie said something along this line; and Lanny grinned and replied: "Be careful, you've got a Jewish partner now!"

Robbie made a wry face. His Anglo-Saxon conscience troubled him, and his aristocratic feelings resented the odor of the junk business. But Johannes Robin had bought a couple of hundred thousand hand grenades, and had already sold the powder before he had got it extracted. The prospects looked excellent; and Robbie Budd just couldn't bear to sit on a big pile of money and not make use of it—the use, of course, being to make more money.

V I

One day when Lanny went to lunch he found at his table a young army officer, introduced as Captain Stratton; handsome, well set up, as they all were, full of smartness and efficiency. Military uniforms were plentiful in the Crillon dining room, as all over Paris; someone had counted up the soldiers of twenty-six different nations to be found in the capital at that time. Captain Stratton was connected with the Intelligence Service of the army, and it was his special task to watch out for any efforts of the Bolsheviks among the dough-boys. It was a confidential subject, but the officer was in the midst of persons who had a right to know what was going on.

He talked interestingly about his work. He said that the slum denizens were in a state close to madness, with hunger, the fever of war, and the vision of sudden power. It couldn't be said that they were without training for power, for they had a sort of discipline of their own; in fact, they had a whole culture, which they called "proletarian," and which was to replace our present culture, called "bourgeois." A truly frightening thing, said the officer, who before the war had been a rising young architect in Chicago. "I was never afraid of the Huns," he declared, "but I admit that I'm afraid of these Reds."

Just recently, he went on to tell, he had come upon evidence of the activities of a press on which had been printed leaflets addressed to the denizens of the Paris slums, calling upon them to rise against the profiteers and seize the food which was in the depots, and which the bureaucrats were refusing to release. The captain had one of these leaflets with him; it ended with a string of slogans followed by exclamation points, and was signed by the *Conseils des Ouvriers de St.-Denis.* "They don't say Soviets," remarked the officer. "But that's what the word means."

Then even more startling news: he expected to have proof that these agitators were preparing an appeal to the American troops to break ranks and go home. These troops had enlisted to oust the Kaiser, and why should they stay to hold the workers of Europe in slavery to landlords and money barons? It was a plausible argument.

"Surely you're going to stop that!" exclaimed one of the professors.

"We'll have to," replied the officer. "But it's a bit awkward, because the fellow who is most active in the matter happens to be an American."

"What difference does that make?"

"Well, my God, if you arrest an American Red in Paris, you can't keep it away from the newspapers; then all the agitators at home will be swarming like hornets."

Professor Davisson, who specialized in the Balkan languages, and had just come back from a mission to the Bulgarian front, expressed the opinion that the unprintable scoundrel ought to be dealt with by military law at once. To this Alston interposed a question: "What's the use of having licked the Germans if you have to sacrifice American free speech in the process?"

"Do you think that free speech means the right to overthrow the government which protects your free speech?" demanded Davisson.

"Free speech doesn't overthrow governments," answered the other. "It's the lack of free speech."

"You mean you'd let Bolsheviks incite our troops to mutiny?"

"They wouldn't get anywhere, Davisson—not unless there was something wrong with what the army was doing."

So they argued, and got rather hot about it, as men were apt to do these days; until one of them, wishing to dissipate the storm clouds, asked of Captain Stratton: "What sort of fellow is it that's printing the leaflets?"

"He calls himself a painter, but I don't know if he works at it. He's lived most of his life over here, and I guess he's absorbed what the Reds call their 'ideology.'"

"Budd knows a lot of painters here," said Lanny's employer. "What's the man's name?"

"I don't think I'm at liberty to tell that," replied the captain. "Perhaps I shouldn't have said as much as I have."

"It'll all be confidential," said Professor Davisson, and the others nodded their confirmation. As for Lanny, he kept up a pretense of interest in his food, and prayed that nobody would notice the blood that had been stealing into his cheeks and throat, and even, so he felt, to the roots of his hair.

VII

When the party broke up, Lanny said to his chief: "I wish you'd take me upstairs to your room for a minute. There's something important I want to tell you." When they were alone, he explained: "I can't be sure, but I think the man Captain Stratton was talking about is my uncle, Jesse Blackless."

"The heck you say!" exclaimed the startled professor.

"I thought you ought to know right away, because it might prove embarrassing if it comes out."

Lanny told briefly about this "red sheep" of his mother's family. "There aren't apt to be two American painters who are such active Reds. I know he's in Paris now, because he came to see my mother, to advise her about the best way to arrange for an exhibition of my stepfather's paintings."

"Well, well!" said the professor. "A trifle awkward, I must admit."

"It could be terribly so. I'm afraid there's nothing for me but to quit before the story breaks."

The older man smiled. "No, you don't get off so easily! I assure you, I need you too badly. We'll work out some other solution."

"But what can it be?"

"Let me think. Do you suppose you could get hold of this uncle of yours?"

"I suppose he'll have left his address with my mother."

"Well, we'll have to be quick, before the army people grab him."

"What do you want to do with him?"

"First, we'll have a talk with him and see what his ideas are, and how much he knows. Then I thought it might be well to take him to Colonel House, and possibly to the President."

Lanny could only stare, wondering if he had heard aright.

"You see," explained his chief, noting his expression, "there are two ways to deal with social discontent—one is to throw it into jail and the other is to try to understand it. The President has had to do some of the former under the stress of war, but I'm sure that in his heart he much prefers understanding. Right now, I happen to know that he's deadlocked with the French over the question of what's to be done about Russia. Can you keep a really important secret?"

"I've been keeping a lot of them, Professor."

"I had a tip this morning which I believe to be straight—that the President is thinking of moving for a conference with the Bolsheviks at some neutral place. So you see, it might be in order for Colonel House or someone who represents him to get in touch with these people, to find out what their attitude would be. Do you suppose you could find your uncle today?"

"First I'd have to get my father's consent," replied the youth. "I gave him my word that I'd not have anything to do with my uncle. That was five or six years ago, and he mayn't feel the same now."

"Tell him it's an order from the boss," smiled Alston.

VIII

Needless to say, Robbie Budd didn't like it a bit when his son brought him that proposition. Lanny couldn't tell the whole story, being under orders regarding the "Intelligence" aspect of it; he could only say that the peace experts wanted to talk with some Bolsheviks, to know what concessions they were willing to make. To the salesman of armaments it seemed an outrage that any government should be willing to do anything with such scoundrels but shoot them; however, Lanny pointed out that the Allied troops.

were clamoring to go home, and statesmanship required that some compromise should be worked out. So quickly was a youth of nineteen catching the official tone!

Robbie didn't smile, for he wished his son to take his duties seriously. "All right," said he. "But I want you to know, I'll be damned unhappy if I see you getting mixed up with that blatherskite Jesse."

"Don't worry," answered Lanny. "This is a job, and I want to do it as capably as I can, and maybe it'll take me to the President."

Beauty gave her brother's address, up on the Butte Montmartre, where painters and other irregular people lived. Beauty scented a mystery in her son's inquiry and it was cruel to have to put her off; but Lanny just said that one of the professors was interested in painting and might buy something. No use trusting any secrets to Madame Detaze, *veuve!*

Taking the address to his chief, Lanny said: "I've been thinking this matter over and it occurs to me that it may be awkward if I don't tell my uncle about the army people. If later they should jump on him—he'd be sure to think I'd been helping to trap him or something."

"I've thought of that also," replied the other. "I'm going with you to see him, and then I'll have a frank talk with Captain Stratton. If the Crillon is interested in the man, Intelligence will lay off, of course."

The taxis were back from the war and were being driven about the streets of Paris by homicidal maniacs. Lanny and his chief were whirled down the Rue Montmartre, and Lanny pointed out the window of the restaurant through which Jaurès had been shot. Alston said that the French authorities might have been glad to have the help of that great orator now, while their workers were seething with discontent. The cab whirled round a corner and down a crooked street—another "cabbage patch," with crowded old buildings. It was one of the rare days when the sun shone in January, and slatternly women were leaning out of windows, and swarms of children playing all but under the wheels of the taxi.

Lanny explained to his chief that Uncle Jesse didn't have to live in
such a place, for he enjoyed a modest income from an inheritance.
Apparently he wanted to be close to the people. Alston said there
were men like that; sometimes they were saints, and sometimes a
bit crazy, and sometimes both.

IX

"Entrez," called Jesse Blackless, at their knock. He was sitting
in an old dressing gown by the open window, working on a manuscript. Beside him was a table, looking like the one which Lanny
remembered in the cabin on the Riviera; the remains of a meal, a
tobacco pouch and a bad-smelling pipe, a great quantity of books
and papers which apparently were never moved or dusted. The
canvas cot which served as a bed was unmade, and there was an
open book on the floor beside it, as if it had been laid there when
the reader was ready to go to sleep. An overcoat thrown over a
chair, an umbrella on it—in short, general disorder and the absence
of the feminine touch. There were unframed paintings on the walls,
but no easel and no smell of paint. Apparently Uncle Jesse had
given up art for politics.

He looked startled when his nephew came in, followed by a
strange gentleman. He put his manuscript away in a hurried manner and his eyes moved to the door, as if he expected a couple of
gendarmes might follow.

"Hello, Uncle Jesse," said the youth.

"Hello," returned the other, not rising.

"Uncle Jesse, this is Professor Alston, my chief at the Crillon."

"How do you do?" said the painter; but he didn't offer to shake
hands, and he didn't say: "Have a seat"—which, indeed, would have
been difficult, since the only extra chair was piled with papers. His
manner said: "What's this?"

"Uncle Jesse," explained Lanny, "Professor Alston asked me to
bring him to you because he has an important proposition to put
and he hopes you'll be kind enough to hear it."

The painter, of course, knew that his nephew had been avoiding him for years and that this had been at Robbie's orders. He knew also that the youth had taken a job with the peace-makers. He looked over the mild and bespectacled professor, whose physical vigor hadn't improved much under the strain of hard work in damp and chilly Paris. There was no abatement of the uncle's hostile manner as he said: "All right. What is it?"

Frankly, but at the same time tactfully, the scholar explained the efforts of the American commission to bring at least a partially sane peace out of an insane war. President Wilson was being opposed, not merely by all the jealousies and greeds and fears of Europe, but by the reactionary elements at home, the big-money interests and our newly awakened militarism. Just now there was a crisis over the subject of Russia and a decision might be taken at any hour. The President wanted to get the warring factions together in a council hall; while the French and British military men wanted invasions on a big scale.

"I don't know whether you have heard it or not," said Alston, "but Winston Churchill is in Paris now, for the purpose of urging a real war to put down Bolshevism. Foch has been demanding it from the day of the armistice, and the whole French General Staff is with him. Clemenceau is beginning to waver—and of course Lloyd George wavers all the time."

"What's the use of telling all this to me?" questioned Uncle Jesse.

The professor looked about him uneasily, and asked: "May I sit down? I have not been well."

The painter knew that he hadn't been a gentleman, and he stood up. "Have my chair," he said.

"This is all right," replied the other, and sat on the edge of the cot. Lanny pushed some books aside and rested on a corner of the table.

"Mr. Blackless, nobody in our staff at the Crillon wants any more war; and there's a group of us who are convinced that concessions have to be made and an armistice **brought** about in Russia before there can be any real peace. That doesn't mean that we are sympathetic to Bolshevism, but it does mean that we have studied the forces which brought on the revolution, and we don't consider it possible to set back the clock of history. My own position is entirely that of a scientist——"

"What sort of a scientist?"

"I am a geographer and ethnologist, but just now I have been set the task of finding out what some of the peoples of Europe want."

"You have your hands full, Professor."

"No doubt of that; and I have the right to ask for the help of every well-meaning man."

"What leads you to think that I am well-meaning?"

"I think it of every man, Mr. Blackless, until he shows me otherwise. I assume that you don't want to see any more war in Europe."

"You assume incorrectly, Professor."

"You *do* want war?"

"I tell the workers to fight for their rights, and I hope they will do so until they have overthrown the capitalist system."

"But surely you can't think that the Russians can defeat the Allied armies, if they decide seriously to fight!"

"My answer is that if the Allied armies believed they could defeat the Russians, they'd be fighting right now. I take your visit as a sign that the Allied leaders are beginning to find out what the rank and file of their troops are thinking and saying. Lloyd George and Clemenceau will have to face it, and even Foch and the lineal descendant of the Duke of Marlborough."

So Lanny and his employer knew that they had found a real Bolshevik; one who could tell President Wilson exactly what was in the hearts of men and women who were risking their lives trying to make revolutions throughout Europe!

X

Jesse Blackless appeared to be showing the effects of mental strain. The lines around his eyes were more plentiful and those at the sides of his mouth more deeply graven. He was balder than ever, but the bare scalp wasn't so bronzed—he had, presumably, been living in cities and wearing a hat. He was even more gaunt and his voice seemed hoarse, as if he had been talking a lot. Doubtless he had much to say to proletarians, as he called them; but with bourgeois persons like Lanny and his chief he didn't care to be bothered—or so his manner seemed to say. He didn't argue, he told you, and there came that disagreeable twist of the mouth. Lanny had always disliked this strange man, and did now; but he had to admit that he had convictions and stood by them.

Just now the painter was convinced that the Bolsheviks had Central Europe in their grasp. He announced it defiantly; but Alston, who had inside knowledge, stopped him with the remark: "That is all right for a stump speech or a manifesto; but are you sure it's the attitude of Lenin? Mightn't it be that he'd like a little time to collect his forces?"

The painter eyed his visitor sharply, and decided to take a different tone. "Just what is it you propose, Professor?"

"First, that you should understand me. I know you are suspicious, and doubtless you have reason in many cases. But you waste time if you suspect me. I am a scholar who doesn't like bloodshed and has come over here to help make peace. In this visit to you I have no authority from anybody. I came on my own impulse, when Lanny told me about his uncle. Knowing the situation at the Crillon, I thought some of my superiors might like to confer with you."

"A fine time I'd have explaining to my friends if I took up with the Crillon!"

"Don't your friends trust you, Mr. Blackless?"

"A certain distance; but not that far!"

"There's no reason why you shouldn't tell them in advance that you are going, and why. There is nothing secret about my visit. You will see that I ask you no questions—who your associates are, or anything of that sort. I take it for granted that you may know where to find some persons who are in touch with the Bolsheviks and could discuss with us the basis for a conference."

"Suppose I should go to the Crillon and not come out again?"

The professor smiled. "Be reasonable, Mr. Blackless. Undoubtedly the French military authorities know your address, and can come here just as well as I can. That goes for the Americans also. I can't give you any guarantees—except that anything that happens to you won't be of my doing. On the other hand, if the Crillon should invite you to come and talk to them, it would certainly be a bonafide invitation to a conference and would confer immunity upon you for the time being."

Said Jesse Blackless: "I think the man you need to talk with is Sazonov." This was the former Foreign Minister of the Tsar, now in Paris, and the remark was, of course, a sneer.

"We don't have to go to any of the Whites," replied Alston, patiently. "They come to us in droves. They tell us they will have nothing to do with assassins and bloody-handed murderers, and so on. They demand that we give them unlimited arms and money so that they can crush the Reds. That happens to be the idea of the military men, including some of the Americans, I am sorry to say. But fortunately it is the civil authorities who have the decision. Trust me, Mr. Blackless, and help me to get your point of view before the Council of Ten, right now while the subject is up for settlement."

"You mean, it's your idea that the Bolsheviks shall come to Paris and sit down with the Whites?"

"Not in Paris—Clemenceau would never allow that. It would be somewhere close to Russia, and far from here."

"You think the Whites would come?"

"I'll put it crudely, Mr. Blackless, as you seem to prefer. The Allies are the paymasters."

Uncle Jesse smiled one of his crooked smiles. "And you imagine that we would give up to the Whites—is that it?"

"At a conference, Mr. Blackless, both sides have to give up something, unless the conference is to fail. But first there has to be a conference—that is the most difficult point."

The painter considered for a while longer. Finally he said: "All right, Professor. I'll talk to some other persons, and let you hear from me in a few hours."

28

The Red Peril

I

THERE were five members of the American Commission to Negotiate Peace. President Wilson was of course its head, and the French government had lent him a palace to stay in, the home of the Princess Murat. The second member was Mr. Lansing, Secretary of State, who did not agree with his chief about the League or anything else very much; he was a lawyer, and thought that things ought to be done according to juridical formulas which he had learned. He spent his time recording his objections in a diary; also making comical little sketches of the other diplomats. To him and his fellow members had been assigned apartments on the second floor of the Crillon, looking out on the Place and having the highest ceilings, the biggest chandeliers, and the most gilt and pink upholstery.

One of these others was General Bliss, a bluff and kindly old soldier who gave good practical advice when asked. Another was a veteran diplomat, Mr. Henry White, who owed his appointment to the fact that etiquette required that the Republican party should have representation on the Peace Commission. Mr. White was so old that the Republicans had forgotten him, but he was in the history books and nobody could question his credentials. He had been in Paris at the time of the Franco-Prussian War and the Commune, nearly fifty years back, and he liked to drive people around and show them the places and tell what he had seen; but he wasn't seeing very much now.

The fifth member was of a retiring nature, but that didn't prevent his suite from becoming the most frequented of all. Two naval yeomen in uniforms and white caps stood guard at the door, and in the anterooms you would see the great ones of the earth coming and going at all hours, and many cooling their heels, waiting in hope of an interview. The name of this commissioner was Colonel House. He was not a military man, but the kind known as a "Kentucky colonel"—although he came from Texas. He was a frail little gentleman of sixty or so, and had never enjoyed health enough to be a warrior, or even to engage in the turmoil of politics; he didn't like crowds and shrank from publicity as a mole from sunlight. What he liked to do was to consult and advise and persuade; he liked to sit behind the scenes and pull wires and manipulate the actors. Being wealthy, he could indulge in this hobby; he had made several governors of his home state, and then had picked out the head of a college as a likely "prexy" for the forty-eight states. He had promoted him and "put him over," and was now his friend and authorized agent in most of the peace negotiations.

He had come to Europe before the outbreak of the war. He had come more than once during the conflict, trying to work out ways to end it. He was gentle and unassuming, and never sought anything for himself; people compared him to a little white mouse—and right now the words of this mouse were backed by most of the money and most of the food in the world. America had financed the last year and a half of the war, and America must finance whatever peace there was to be. What did America want? What would America accept? The answer was: "See Colonel House."

So it came about that through the doors where stood the naval yeomen, polite yet impressive with their side-arms, came diplomats and politicians and journalists from pretty nearly every nation of the earth. In those anterooms you saw uniforms worthy of the most expensive grand opera production: gold and cream and scarlet, rose-pink, sky-blue. You saw civilian costumes out of the gorgeous East, Near and Far: burnooses, mantles, and togas, turbans, fezzes, and sugarloaf hats. You saw Koreans and Malayans, Kabardians and Lezghians, Buriats and Kirghiz, Kurds, Persians, Georgians, Azerbaijan Moslems, Assyrian Christians, and all the varieties of Syrians —Moslem, Druse, and Greek Orthodox. Had ever in the history of Texas a stranger fate befallen one of its sons than to be receiving this stream of day and night callers, and to know that his smile was a matter of life and death to their peoples?

II

To this Mecca of peace-seekers now came Professor Alston, bringing the tidings that he had established contact with certain of the extremely elusive Bolshevik agents in Paris. Might it be that this would offer to President Wilson and his staff an opportunity of sounding out the revolutionaries and judging the probabilities of success for any conference?

The little white mouse found that interesting. It was the sort of thing he liked to do. He pinned his faith upon quiet talks and under-standings among key people. That was the way the Democratic party was run in Texas; that was the way a college president had been nominated for President of the United States; that was the way peace was now to be brought to Europe. When the details had been agreed upon, the results would be proclaimed, and that would be "open covenants openly arrived at."

Of course these revolutionaries couldn't come to the Crillon. Where had Alston met this painter? The professor described the room, and the Texas colonel smiled and asked if it would be possible to get some extra chairs into it. He said they would go that very evening, as soon as he could get away from a reception he had promised to attend. He told the professor where and when to call for him. They would say nothing to anybody about it; they would take along Alston's translator, who already knew about it. The colonel didn't speak French, unfortunately, and it might be that the Bolsheviks wouldn't know English.

A first-class thrill for a youth just embarked upon a diplomatic career. He was going to the top right at one bound! He was going to help with the most exciting problem of the conference; to have a hand in settling the destinies of a hundred and forty million people—and incidentally to shake the gory paws of those murderers, assassins, fiends in human form, creatures whom the resources of the English language were inadequate to describe. So Lanny had been hearing, and he pictured them as pirates with bushy black whiskers, and pistols and daggers in their belts. He hurried off to tell his uncle of the appointment and make sure the little white mouse wouldn't have to sit on the cot!

Uncle Jesse said he could borrow chairs from neighbors in the tenement. "We poor help each other out," he explained, with one of his wry smiles. He added: "Keep your eyes open, Lanny, and see if you can't learn something."

"Thank you, Uncle Jesse," replied the youth. "I'm learning a lot, really."

"It won't please your father," continued the other. "I've known him since before you were born, and I've never known him to learn anything. He's going to be an unhappy man, with the world changing as it is."

Lanny wouldn't discuss his father with this uncle whom he didn't like. But he went off thinking hard, and wondering: Was Robbie really narrow-minded and set in his opinions? Or was this Bolshevik propaganda?

III

That evening Alston and his secretary strolled to the Hotel Majestic, residence of the British delegation, where a grand reception was being held. Promptly at eleven the colonel emerged, and a sturdily built man in civilian clothes fell in behind him and accompanied him to his car, and, after the others had got in, took his seat alongside the chauffeur. So far as Lanny knew, this man never spoke once, but he watched, and no doubt had a gun handy.

Huddled into one corner of the car, Lanny listened to the conversation of one of the most powerful men in the world. The youth was intensely curious about this soft-voiced and kind-faced little person. What was it that had lifted him from obscurity in a region of vast lonely plains inhabited by long-horned cattle which one saw in the movies? Lanny gathered that the Texas colonel's leading characteristic was a desire for information; he went right to work to pump Alston's mind, asking him about all the problems on which he had been specializing. Sooner or later the little white mouse might have to settle them. He had a way of shutting his eyes for a few moments when he wanted to impress something upon his memory. Presently he was asking questions about Georgia—not the state in America, whose problems had been settled long ago, but the portion of Russia in the Caucasus mountains, famed for its lovely women.

"Those people have one great misfortune, Colonel House," remarked the professor. "They are sitting on one of the world's great oil deposits."

"I know," said the other. "It may explode and blow us all to kingdom come." He asked many more questions, and then said: "Do you suppose it would be possible for you to look into this matter and let me have a report?"

"Why, I suppose so," said the professor, both surprised and pleased. "They've got me loaded up with work already, though."

"I know; but we all have to do more and more. This Georgian business complicates the Russian problem, and we'll have to find a way to settle it. What do you say?"

"I am honored, of course."

"Perhaps we'll have a committee and put you on it. I'll have to put it up to the President."

So fate gave another turn to Lanny Budd's destiny. He was going to meet the mountaineers of the Caucasus and learn about their manners and customs—but not their lovely women, alas, for they hadn't brought any of these to Paris.

I V

There were three Russians in the tenement room when the Americans entered; at least Lanny supposed they were Russians, but he discovered that one was a Frenchman and another a Lett. He had been sure they would be big, bewhiskered, and fierce; but he found that only the Frenchman had hair on his face, the black beard trimmed to a point of which you could see thousands on this Butte Montmartre; he wore glasses on a black cord and his face was abnormally pale—he was a journalist who had served a term in prison for opposition to the war. The Lett appeared to be some sort of workingman, and was smooth-shaven, blond, and quiet. The Russian was a scientist, not much bigger than the colonel from Texas; he had spent several years in Siberia and his fingers trembled as he lighted the cigarettes which he smoked with great rapidity.

Only the Frenchman knew English, so the conversation was carried on largely by him. The Russian knew French, and the Lett knew Russian; there was a good deal of whispering back and forth, and when the conversation in English was going on, the other two Bolsheviks listened with a strained expression, as if they could understand by trying harder. They were obviously anxious. They, too, knew that they were in the presence of one of the most powerful men in the world.

Lanny helped the Frenchman with a word now and then, and sometimes asked him in French just what he was trying to say. The Russian, who was apparently their "big man," became impatient at the English conversation, and moved his chair behind Jesse Blackless and whispered for him to repeat in French what was being said. So Lanny, who sat next to his uncle, would hear English with one ear and French with the other, which kept his mind on the jump. However, he got his impressions, and the first was that these seemed like decent fellows in serious trouble; it was hard for him to believe that they had been committing the crimes that his mother's fashionable friends had told about. Afterwards, when he talked over his impressions with his chief, the idea was suggested to him that in civil wars it is often the most earnest and conscientious persons who do the killing.

One thing was certain: the Bolsheviks weren't going to make any of what Professor Alston called "stump speeches." Presumably they had talked it over in advance and decided to lay their cards on the table. They had no authority to speak for their government, and no way to communicate with it quickly; but they were certain that it wanted peace, and would be willing to pay any price short of giving up their "workers' state." Just as they had gone to Brest-Litovsk nearly a year ago and given in to the power of the German armies, so now they would do so for the Allies. The Whites might keep what they held; there was land enough in the interior of Russia, and the workers would build their state and show the world what they could do; only they must have freedom to trade with the outside, so that they could get goods and repair their shattered industry.

They spoke without emotion of the sufferings of the Russian peasants and workers under the lash of the Tsar, and in the civil war now raging. They reported that Petrograd was starving; a hundred thousand persons had died in the past month, and not a baby under two was left alive. The Soviets wanted peace; they would meet the Whites anywhere, and accept any reasonable terms. They had again and again declared their willingness to pay off their debts to the capitalist nations, including the monstrous debt which the Tsar had incurred to arm their country in the interest of French militarists and munitions makers. Poor as they were now, they would pay the interest in raw materials. Lanny was surprised by this, for the French newspapers were incessantly repeating that the debt had been repudiated; this was the reason for the French clamor for the overthrow of the Soviets. "You know what our newspapers are," said the Frenchman, shrugging his shoulders; "our reptile press —I worked for it until my soul was poisoned."

V

"Well, Alston, what do you think?" asked the colonel, when they were in their car again.

"If you want my opinion," said the professor, "I think the civil war should be stopped at any cost."

"Even if it means letting these people have a chance to establish their regime?"

"If their ideas are not sound, they will fail in the end."

"Perhaps. But won't that mean another war?"

"That's a long way in the future, Colonel."

The other turned to the young translator, whose eager competence he had observed. "What do you think, Budd?"

This gave Lanny a start, and he flushed. He had sense enough to know that the great man was being kind and that it would be the part of wisdom for a youth to be brief. "What struck me was that those fellows have all suffered a lot."

"No doubt about that," replied the gentleman from Texas. "We who live under an orderly democratic government find it hard to realize what men endured under the Tsar."

Colonel House didn't tell them what he himself thought. They learned the reason later on—that he disapproved of the proposed conference and didn't think it could succeed. But the President wanted it, and he was the boss; Colonel House never gave his opinion unless and until it was asked for. He said now that he would report what the Bolsheviks had said, and they would await the decision.

What happened was soon known to all the world. The President of the United States sat down before his well-worn typewriter— it being one of his peculiarities that when he had something important in his mind he liked to type it with his own fingers. He wrote as follows:

"The associated powers are now engaged in the solemn and responsible work of establishing the peace of Europe and of the world, and they are keenly alive to the fact that Europe and the

world cannot be at peace if Russia is not. They recognize and accept it as their duty, therefore, to serve Russia in this great matter
as generously, as unselfishly, as thoughtfully, as ungrudgingly as
they would serve every other friend and ally. And they are ready
to render this service in the way that is most acceptable to the
Russian people."

The document went on to summon all groups having power in
Russia or Siberia to send representatives to a conference. President
Wilson took it to the Council of Ten next afternoon, where it became the subject of much debate. Some still demanded that an army
be sent into Russia to overthrow the Bolsheviks; but when it came
to a showdown, they wanted the soldiers of some other nation to
go. Lloyd George asked the question all around: "Would your
troops go? Would yours?" Not one statesman dared say yes, and
so in the end the program offered by Wilson was adopted unanimously.

Where should the proposed conference be held? Various suggestions were made, one being the island of Prinkipo, in the sea of
Marmora, near Constantinople. This afforded the overworked delegates a few moments of relaxation. Some refused to believe that a
place with such a musical-comedy name could actually exist; but it
was shown as a tiny dot on a map. When the council voted for it, the
august Arthur Balfour, philosopher and scholar as well as statesman,
was moved to a musical-comedy effusion:

> Oh, let us go
> To Prinkipo,
> Though why or where we do not know!

VI

This vote of the Supreme Council was one of the factors which
decided Robbie Budd to go back to Connecticut; for the proposed
war on Russia had offered about the last chance remaining for a
salesman of munitions. Robbie had his sources of information, and
had tapped them all and made certain that any money which

America might lend to the smaller nations would be hedged about with restrictions, that it was not to be spent for arms. If England and France wanted any fighting done, it would obviously be with the stocks they already had on hand. In short, the cards were stacked against Budd's, and Robbie might as well go home with the bad news.

They would have to convert the plants to the uses of peace; but what uses? Every field was already crowded; if you decided to make automobile parts or sewing machines, you entered into competition with concerns which had been making these things for some time, and knew a thousand tricks that you had to learn. Everybody agreed that Europe would constitute an unlimited market, as soon as peace was declared; but the trouble was, Europe had so many factories of its own, and they would all be seeking the same markets. It was reported that the peace treaty was going to require the demilitarization of the German arms plants; which would mean that Krupp's also would be making automobile parts and sewing machines!

In short, the manufacture of munitions was a precarious business. When danger came, public officials rushed to you for help, and expected you to exhaust yourself working in their service; but the moment the danger was over they were done with you. You heard nothing but the clamor of demagogues that you had made too much money—when the fact was that you stood to lose everything by the sudden collapse of your business. Robbie said this with bitterness, and his son, who was now meeting other men and hearing other points of view, realized more clearly the curious antinomy in his father's mental make-up. Robbie hated war, and called the people fools for being drawn into it; yet when they stopped fighting, he was without occupation, and wandered about like a boy with whom other boys wouldn't play!

It wasn't his fault, of course; he hadn't chosen to be born a Budd. Said his son: "Why can't we convert our plants for good and all, and make things that would have a steady market and not go *kaput* all of a sudden?"

What was needed was new inventions, creating new demands. Some lay in the future, but they hadn't yet come over the horizon— and meanwhile there was only the junk business. Oddly enough, the most promising deal that Robbie had been able to make since the armistice was the one with Johannes Robin, who was setting out to prove himself a first-class businessman. What he was doing and planning was going to bring in a large sum; but because it consisted of a number of small items, Robbie would never be proud of it, and to the end it would remain in his mind the sort of business for a Jew.

VII

Just before sailing, Robbie called up his son and inquired: "Would you like to meet Zaharoff again? I've an appointment with him, and he always asks about you."

The old gray wolf was still on his way up in the world. Last year he had been made a Grand Officer of the Legion of Honor, and he was soon to receive the Grand Cross, usually reserved for kings. He had invited Robbie to call, and father and son drove to the palace on the Avenue Hoche, close to where President Wilson was being housed. The duquesa served tea again; only this time, since Lanny was a grown young gentleman and budding diplomat, she did not take him out into the garden but left him to attend the business conference.

Robbie had guessed that the Greek ex-fireman was still haunted by his dream of monopolizing the armaments industry of the world; and it turned out that this guess was correct. He said that now had come the time of the seven lean years, and those whose barns were small would be well advised to make friends with those whose barns were capacious. Zaharoff had taken the trouble to accumulate a lot of information about Budd's; he knew what dividends they had paid and what reserves they had kept; he seemed to know about the different plans which the president of the concern had been con · sidering for the conversion of the plants, and the approximate cost of such procedure. Old Samuel Budd never came to Europe, either for business or pleasure, but Zaharoff had seen a picture of him; he even knew about the men's Bible class, and spoke of it with urbanity as an original and charming hobby.

The aging Greek with the velvet-soft voice explained that Budd's was in munitions alone, whereas the several hundred Vickers companies were in everything basic in modern industry: iron and steel, copper, nickel, and all the non-ferrous metals, coal and oil and electric power, shipping and finance. "When you have such an organization, Mr. Budd, you can turn quickly from war to peace, and back again at will; you have the money, the connections, the techniques. Whereas a small concern like Budd's, off in a corner by itself, is at the mercy of the financiers, who don't do anything for love."

"I know," said Robbie; and didn't ask whether Zaharoff was going to do it for love.

The American was more cautious than he had been five years ago. He knew that his people were in a dangerous position, and he knew that Zaharoff knew it. He listened while the old man with the white imperial suavely explained that such things as family and national pride were out of date nowadays; what counted was money. The really big kind was international, and was without prejudice; it did, not what it chose, but what it had to do. In times of stress, such as lay ahead of them, little business was swept into the discard and factories went on the bargain-counter like—"Well, like field-guns right now," said Zaharoff.

The munitions king seemed actually on the way to realizing his life's dream. Vickers now completely controlled Schneider-Creusot in France, Skoda in Bohemia, and the Austrian, the Turkish, the Italian plants. Its biggest rival, Krupp, was to be put out of the trade entirely. If Lanny had ever been uncertain as to why Zaharoff was standing so valiantly by the demand for war to a finish, he had the answer now.

"How unwise for you, Mr. Budd, with your isolated small business, to stand outside the great world movement! You might come in on terms that would be both honorable and profitable"—the speaker showed his delicacy of feeling by the order in which he placed these two words. "You have done us an important service in the war, and this is a way we can show our gratitude. It had better be done at once, before the stresses of business competition begin to weaken the ties of friendship. You will understand what I mean, I am sure."

"Yes," said Robbie, "I understand." And he did. He promised to go back and put the proposition before his father and brothers. "I'd rather not attempt to guess what their reaction will be," he added.

So the tactful Grand Officer of the Legion of Honor began to talk about the Peace Conference and what it was doing. He said that President Wilson was perhaps a great statesman and certainly a high-minded gentleman, but that some of his projects were hardly in accord with the interests of either Robert Budd or Basil Zaharoff. He turned to the boy who had now grown into a statesman, and asked how he was enjoying his excursion into diplomatic affairs. When Lanny revealed that his chief was a geographer, and was engaged in preparing a confidential report on Georgian affairs, the munitions king couldn't conceal his interest. Georgia was Batum, and Batum was oil; and already Zaharoff was on the scene, and fully intending to stay!

He began telling Lanny things, hoping that Lanny would be led to tell more important things without knowing that he was doing so. When they were ready to leave, the old man insisted upon summoning his duquesa to bid them farewell, and he said in her presence that Lanny must not let the work of peace-making deprive him entirely of social life; he should come and see them some time, and meet Zaharoff's two very lovely nieces. There must have been some secret signal which Zaharoff gave the lady, for she instantly joined in and pressed the invitation. Neither of them mentioned that the two young ladies were expected to share the fortune of the richest man in the world; but Lanny knew that it was so, and knew that all the world speculated as to whether Zaharoff himself had children by a secret marriage in that past which he did so carefully. It was rumored that he had a son in Russia and that this young man had come to England to seek recognition, but in vain.

When the two Americans were alone in the taxi, the father chuckled, and said: "Look out for yourself, kid!"

"That really was a bid, wasn't it?" inquired the youth.

"A royal command," declared the other. "You can make a bigger deal than I can. All you have to do is arrange for a regiment or two of doughboys to help the British protect Batum from the Bolsheviks!"

VIII

Lanny settled down to his new work, which was studying the manners and customs of the Georgians. They had several delegations in Paris, and word spread, quite literally with the speed of lightning, that Professor Alston at the Crillon had been charged with deciding their fate. They all came at once—even though many of them were not on speaking terms with one another. They were large, tall men with wide mustaches, and for the most part wore their national costumes—some because they had no others, and some because they had learned that it was good propaganda. The costumes included long coats of hairy goatskin, high soft boots, and large bonnets of astrakhan. Their French and English were rudimentary, and those who spoke the difficult native tongue would become so excited that they forgot to stop and give their translators a chance. Their idea of persuading you was by a kind of baptismal rite; they would put their faces close to yours and talk with such vehemence that they enveloped you in a fine salivary spray, which went into your eyes and which good manners forbade you to wipe away.

When they couldn't get hold of the professor, his secretary would do, so Lanny submitted to this rite for hours at a time. He had to meet various groups and individuals and sort them out, and try to discover what it was which caused them to sit glowering at one another. They all hated and dreaded the Bolsheviks, but differed as to the way to resist them and who was to rule after the victory had been won. There were aristocrats and democrats, land owners and peasants, clericals and Socialist intellectuals, all the warring groups, as in French politics. All were acutely aware of the treasure which lay beneath the surface of their country, and some were thinking what a noble civilization could be built with its help. But unfortunately these were idealists who lacked experience in oil production; on the other hand, those who had the experience were in the pay of some foreign interest seeking concessions. All these lied shamelessly, and Lanny, who hadn't had much experience with liars, had to work hard for every fact he reported to his chief.

The plight of the little country was precarious. Toward the end of the war the Germans had seized it, along with the Ukraine; the armistice had forced them to vacate, and the French had sent a small army into the Ukraine, while the British had taken Batum on the Black Sea and Baku on the Caspian, and were policing the railroad and the pipelines by which the oil was brought out. But meanwhile the Bolsheviks were swarming like bees all about them, using their dreadful new weapon of class incitement, arousing peasants and workers against the invasion of "foreign capitalism." They were now driving the French out of Kiev, and literally rotting their armies with propaganda. How long would the British armies stand the strain? Men who had set out cheerfully to unhorse the hated Kaiser considered that they had done their job and wanted to go home; what business had their rulers keeping them in the Caucasus to protect oil wells for Zaharoff the Greek and Deterding the Dutchman?

It was that way all over Eastern and Central Europe. The soldiers and sailors of Russia had overthrown their Tsar, the soldiers and sailors of Germany had driven their Kaiser into exile, and now the soldiers and sailors of the Allies were demanding: "What is all this about? Why are we shooting these peasants?" In Siberia the American troops were meeting the Reds and feeling sorry for them, exactly as Lanny had felt for those he had met in his uncle's tenement room. The armies were disintegrating, discipline was relaxing, and officers were alarmed as they never had been by the German invasion.

So, of course, the elder statesmen in Paris were having an unhappy time; their generals in the field were pulling them one way and the great industrialists and financiers at home were pulling them the other. Coal and oil, iron and copper—were they going to let the Reds take these treasures and use them to prove that workers could run industry for themselves? There was a clamor for war in all the big-business press, and in the parliaments, and it turned the Peace Conference into a hell of intrigue and treachery. To be there was like walking on the floor of a volcano, and wherever you thrust your staff into the ground, it began to quake, and fumes shot out and boiling lava oozed up.

IX

The Georgian question, with which Lanny was occupied, was one of the hottest spots. Since the province had been a part of the old empire of the Tsar, the Georgians had been invited to send delegates to Prinkipo. President Wilson had proposed this conference, and the Council of Ten had unanimously voted it—and that had included the French. But now, what was this that the excited Georgians were stammering into the face of the shrinking Lanny Budd? They were trying to find out from him if there was going to be any Prinkipo, if the Americans really wanted it, if it was safe for the Georgians to attend. When the youth questioned them he learned that Pichon, the French Foreign Minister, had been telling them that it was all a mistake, there wasn't going to be any conference, the Bolsheviks wouldn't come and couldn't be trusted if they did.

Lanny reported this to his chief, and both of them tried to find out more. It appeared that the French were advising all the Russian Whites in Paris to oppose the proposal and refuse to attend; they were saying that the Reds had fooled Wilson into believing in their good faith; but France was not to be fooled, and would continue to support the Whites with arms and money, and if they held on they would have their estates and fortunes returned to them. More than once French agents went so far as to threaten the Georgians that, if they supported Prinkipo, they would themselves be regarded as Bolsheviks and expelled from France. So these strangers in a strange land didn't dare whisper the truth to an American until he had pledged his word not to name the source of his information. "What shall we do, Mr. Budd? Will President Wilson protect us?"

And here was Winston Churchill, powerful war minister, scholar, and orator, appearing before the Supreme Council to denounce the Bolsheviks and demand war upon them in the name of humanity, Christianity, and his ancestor, the fighting Duke of Marlborough. Here was Lord Curzon, whom his associates described as "a very superior purzon," making his appeal especially for Georgia—his lordship had visited that mountainous land in his youth, and had romantic memories of it, and didn't want these memories disturbed by dialectical materialism.

And Zaharoff! He appeared before no councils, for he was neither scholar nor orator, and had no ancestors to boast of; but he had powerful voices to speak for him. If you could believe Robbie Budd, one of these voices was that of the squat little Frenchman with the white walrus mustaches and black skull-cap who sat at the head of the conference table and choked off debate with his "*Adopté!*" Robbie said that "the Tiger" had been Zaharoff's friend for years, and both his brother and his son were directors in Zaharoff's companies. If you wanted to understand a politician you mustn't pay too much attention to his speeches, but find out who were his paymasters. A politician couldn't rise in public life, in France any more than in America, unless he had the backing of big money, and it was in times of crisis like this that he paid his debts.

X

A day or two after Robbie sailed for home, Lanny received a confirmation of his "royal command"; a little note from María del Pilar Antonia Angela Patrocino Simón de Muguiro y Berute, Duquesa de Marqueni y Villafranca de los Caballeros. She didn't sign all that, of course. She requested the pleasure of his company at tea the following afternoon; and Lanny showed the note to Alston, who said: "Go by all means and see what it's about." So, looking his best in formal afternoon attire, the youth alighted from a taxicab in front of 53, Avenue Hoche, and presented his hat and stick to the black-clad butler, and was escorted upstairs to the drawing room with the Spanish masters on the walls and the elaborate tea service on an inlaid Louis Quinze table.

Zaharoff's two nieces were as shy and as strictly brought up as Lanny had imagined them; they had large dark eyes and long lashes which they lowered like curtains when a handsome young American gazed too directly. They were clad alike in blue chiffon tea gowns, and blushes came and went in all four of their cheeks. It was evident that they found their visitor interesting; he had come recently from a far-off land which they saw enlarged and glorified on the motion-picture screen. It really seemed as if Lanny was considered what the French call a *parti*, an eligible person. He was expected to display his charms, and gladly did so.

He entertained three fashionable ladies with stories of the leading personalities of the greatest show on earth. More than once it had happened that he had been waiting in anterooms when the great ones had come forth chatting, and he had heard what they said; also he knew the anecdotes which were going the rounds. Thus, Arthur Balfour and Clemenceau had appeared at some function, the former with his "topper" and all the trimmings, the latter in a bowler hat. His lordship in a spirit of *noblesse oblige* had remarked: "I was told to wear formal dress"; to which "the Tiger," with his mischievous twinkle, replied: "So was I."

Also the story of Premier Hughes of Australia, a labor leader who had fought his way up in a rough world; a violent little man who had become deaf, and carried with him a hearing machine which he set up on the table. He defied President Wilson, declaring that what his country had got it meant to keep. This delighted Clemenceau, for if Australia kept what she had got, it would mean that France might keep hers. So when they were arranging for another session, Clemenceau remarked to Lloyd George: "Come—and bring your savages with you!"

XI

Presently the master of the house came in, and tea was served; he too was interested in the stories, and it was like a family party. Until finally the ladies arose and excused themselves, and Lanny was alone with the old gray wolf.

It was really a fascinating thing to watch; most educational for a young man with a possible future in the diplomatic world. The perfection of a Grand Officer's technique: the velvety softness of manner, the kindness, the cordiality, even affection; the gentle, insinuating voice; the subtle flattery of an old man asking advice from a young one; the fatherly attitude, the strong offering security to the weak. Won't you walk into my parlor? It is warm, and the cushions are soft, and there is no sweeter honey provided for any fly.

What the munitions king wanted, of course, was for Lanny to become his spy in the Crillon; to circulate among the staff, ask questions, pick up valuable items, and bring them quickly to his employer—or should we say his friend, his backer, perhaps his father-in-law? Nothing was said about this directly; it is only in old fairy stories that the king says: "Go out and slay the seven-headed dragon, and I will give you my daughter's hand." In the modern world men have learned to convey their meaning with a glance or a smile.

Lanny had read of the Temptation on the Mount in two synoptic narratives. In that ancient trial Satan had shown all the kingdoms of

the earth, but had overlooked the greatest treasure of all. Perhaps
the high mountain had been a bad choice and it would have been
wiser to invite his victim to the home of one of the rich and mighty
of the kingdom, and let him see dark eyes peering seductively from
behind the curtains of a seraglio.

Lanny had inspected what Zaharoff had to offer and he knew that
it was good. These young women had been brought up in a con-
vent and were unspoiled by the world; their hearts were in a susceptible state, and Lanny could have made himself agreeable and
stood a chance at either. He had only to bring his daily meed of
news and the way would have been made smooth for him; he would
have been left alone with the one of his choice and they would have
looked at engravings together, played music, strolled in the garden,
and whispered the secrets of eager young hearts.

Of course Zaharoff may not have meant it seriously; but why
not? He might have done worse. A youth who was pleasing and
intelligent, who had got himself a start in the great world, and with
a fortune behind him, could have gone to the top in diplomacy,
politics, finance. And what more could the youth have asked? Either
one of the young women would have made him a good wife. He
was uncertain as to their parentage, but it seemed reasonably certain
that they were normal and sound. He had seen that the old man was
fond of them, and would make a helpful father-in-law; it wouldn't
be long before Lanny would be in control of the greatest fortune
in the world.

All he had to do was to be as tactful as the munitions king himself. He didn't need to say: "I accept your offer and will betray my
trust." No, no; his speech would have been: "I appreciate your position, and how greatly you are inconvenienced by the blundering of
the diplomats. If at any time I have information that will be of use
to you, I'll be most happy to bring it—of course purely as an act of
friendship, and without any thought of reward." That was the way
Robbie hired his agents—those of the high class, who got the biggest
pay.

XII

Such things were being done all the time in the great world; and why didn't Lanny accept? Was it because he knew how his father despised Zaharoff? Not entirely; for Lanny's father despised President Wilson, yet Lanny had come to think that President Wilson was in many ways a great man; not equal to his present tasks, perhaps, but far better than the politicians with whom he was dealing. Lanny was coming to think highly of many of the Crillon staff; he had even permitted himself to have good thoughts about the Bolsheviks he had met, although his father couldn't find words enough to denounce them.

Was it because he wasn't impressed by the young ladies? He couldn't say that, because he hadn't seen enough of them; and young ladies are always interesting to investigate, at the least. You met them everywhere you turned here in Paris, where so many of the young men were in the ground with white crosses over them, or else living in barracks along the German frontier, or in Salonika and Odessa and Syria and Algiers—so many places you couldn't keep track of them.

Was it perhaps because Lanny had in his heart an image of an English girl with broad brow and smooth, straw-colored hair and a gentle manner reminding him of his mother? That girl was married now to the young nobleman in the British War Office. Did she love her husband? Was she going to be a true and faithful wife? Or would she continue getting her ideas from "free women"? Lanny knew that the women had at last got the ballot in Britain, so Rosemary wouldn't have to carry any more hatchets into the National Gallery. When she wrote, it was one of her brief, uncommunicative letters; he would have to go and see her, before he would know how to think about her in the future.

Nobody could have been more polite than Lanny to his elderly host. He said that nobody really knew whether there was going to be any Prinkipo conference; the French were working against it—

Lanny smiled inwardly, well knowing that Zaharoff was one of the hardest of the workers.

"There's no doubt," the youth added, "that President Wilson means what he says, the American troops are going to find a way to withdraw from the fighting." And when Zaharoff brought up another subject, he replied: "I really don't know what's going to happen at Batum. The British can't seem to make up their minds. Have you heard the bad news as to the troubles of the French in the Ukraine?"

All that was sparring, of course; and Zaharoff knew it. He knew what it meant when Lanny explained that, unfortunately, on the few occasions when he did get advance news of the Crillon's intentions, it was always confidential, and so his lips were sealed. The munitions king realized that he had wasted his afternoon. He didn't show any signs of irritation, but brought the interview politely to a close and parted from the youth on terms which would make it possible for the duquesa to invite him again.

But she didn't; and Lanny didn't see those shy and well-bred young ladies for quite a while—until he met one of them as the wife of a Belgian lawyer who was said to be in Zaharoff's confidential service. He learned that the other one had married a nobleman and gone to live in Constantinople, where she had become celebrated for the protection she offered to the pariah dogs of that city. The wheel of fate had made a circle, and a portion of Zaharoff's fortune had returned to the place from which it had made its not so creditable start!

29

A Friend in Need

I

THE Supreme Council was now going ahead under full steam. They were hearing the claims of the small nationalities, and it was proving a tedious process. As the Americans reported it, Dmowski, presenting the case of Poland, began with the fourteenth century at eleven o'clock in the morning, and reached 1919 at four in the afternoon. Next day came Beneš to present the claims of the Czechs, and he began a century earlier and finished an hour later.

Professor Alston had to be there, for no one could say at what moment an American commissioner might beckon to him and ask some question; Lanny had to be there, because of the heavy portfolios, and also because the professor's French couldn't cope with the outbursts of Clemenceau, who used not merely the slang of the boulevards, but that of the underworld—many of his ejaculations being so obscene that Lanny was embarrassed to translate them and the recorders of the proceedings had to be told to expurgate them.

A weary, weary ordeal! You couldn't lounge or tilt back in a frail gilded chair a couple of hundred years old; you had to sit stiff and motionless and tell yourself it was a history lesson. But did you want to know all that history? Lanny would close his eyes and remember the beach at Juan, the blue water sparkling in the sunshine, and the little white sailboats all over the Golfe. He would summon up the garden with the masses of bougainvillaea in bloom; he would remember the piano, and yearn over those boxes of books which he had had shipped from the home of Great-Great-Uncle Eli and which some day he was going to have the delight of unpacking. Did he really want to be a person of distinction, live in the *grand monde*, and submit to endless, unremitting boredom?

He would open his eyes and watch the faces of the old men who were here deciding the destinies of the nations. Clemenceau sat shrunken into a little knot, the hands with the gray gloves folded over his stomach, the heavy lids covering his weary brown eyes. Was he asleep? Maybe so, but he had an inner alarm clock, for the moment anyone said anything against the interests of his beloved *patrie* he was all alert, bristling like the tiger he was named for. The pink, cherubic Lloyd George quite frankly dozed; he told one of the Americans that two things had kept him alive through the ordeal of the war—naps were one and the other was singing Welsh hymns.

Woodrow Wilson was unsparing of himself, and as the weeks passed his health caused worry to his associates. He was attending these Council sessions all day, and in the evenings the sessions of the League of Nations Commission. He was driving himself, because he had to sail on the fourteenth of February to attend the closing sessions of the Congress, and he was determined to take with him the completed draft of the Covenant of the League. A thousand cares and problems beset him and he was getting no sleep; he became haggard and there began a nervous twitching of the left side of his face. Lanny, watching him, decided never to aspire to fame.

The oratory became intolerable, so the Council picked out the talkers, and appointed them on what was called the "Clarification Commission," where they could talk to one another. Altogether there were appointed fifty-eight commissions to deal with the multiplicity of problems, and these commissions held a total of 1646 sessions. But that didn't remedy the trouble, because all the commissions had to report—and to whom? Where was the human brain that could absorb so many details? Hundreds of technical advisers assembling masses of information and shaping important conclusions —and then unable to find a way to make their work count!

All the problems of the world had been dumped onto the shoulders of a few elderly men; and the world had to crumble to pieces while one after another of these men broke down under the strain. There was that terrible influenza loose in Paris, striking blindly, like another war. It was the middle of winter, and winds came storming across the North Sea, tempered somewhat by the time they got to Paris, but laden with sleet and snow. It would cover the mansard roofs and pile up on the chimney pots; it didn't last many hours, and then the streets would be carpeted with slush, and the miasma that rose from it bore germs which had been accumulating through a thousand years of human squalor.

II

Early in February the Bolshevik government announced its willingness to send delegates to the Prinkipo conference. That put it up to President Wilson to act, if he was going to stand by his project. A few days later Alston told his secretary an exciting piece of news: the President had decided to name two delegates, one an American journalist, William Allen White, and the other Alston's old-time mentor, George D. Herron!

The official announcement was made a day or two later and raised a storm of protest from the "best" people back home. The New York *Times* led off with an editorial blast exposing the Socialist ex-clergyman's black record; the Episcopal bishop of New York followed suit, and the church people and the women's clubs rushed to the defense of the American home. It was bad enough to propose sitting at a council table with bloody-handed thugs and nationalizers of women; but to send to them a man who shared their moral depravity was to degrade the fair name of Columbia the Gem of the Ocean. All this was duly cabled and printed in Paris, and reinforced the efforts of the Quai d'Orsay to torpedo the Prinkipo proposal.

Herron, who had gone back to his home in Geneva, now returned to Paris, deeply stirred by the opportunity which had come to him. No longer would he have to sit helpless and watch the world crumble. He saw himself arbitrating this ferocious class war which had spread over one-sixth of the globe and was threatening to wreck another huge section of Europe. He was busy day and night with conferences; the newspaper men swarmed about him, asking questions, not merely about Russia and the Reds, but about free love in relation to the Christian religion, and whatever else might make hot news for the folks at home.

The Socialist prophet was all ready to go to work. But how was he to do it? He had never held an official position, and came to Alston for advice. How did one set about working for a government? Where did one go? If he was to set out for Prinkipo, presumably he would have a staff, and an escort, and some funds. Where would he get them?

Alston advised him to see Mr. Lansing. That was easy, because the Secretary of State didn't have much to do in Paris. Formal and stiff, his feelings had been mortally wounded because so few persons paid attention to him. But he didn't want the attention of Socialist prophets; he looked on Herron as on some strange bird. He was as cold as the snowy night outside, as remote as the ceiling of his palatial reception room with the plaster cupids dancing on it. He had received no instructions about the conference, didn't approve of it, and was sure it would prove futile.

President Wilson was driven day and night trying to get ready for his departure, and Herron could find nobody who knew or cared about the musical-comedy place called Prinkipo. The Supreme Council had passed a resolution, but unless there was someone to fight for it and keep on fighting, it would be nothing but so many words. Alston explained the intrigues of the French as he knew them. Herron, a simple man to whose nature deception was foreign, was helpless against such forces. People fought shy of him, perhaps because of the scandal freshly raked up, but mainly because he was believed to sympathize with the Reds. In a matter like that it was safer to lie low—and let Marshal Foch and Winston Churchill have their way.

III

Over at the Hotel Majestic was the British staff, almost as large as the American; and from the outset they had been coming over to make friends. The Americans did their best to keep on their guard, but it was difficult when they found how well informed and apparently sincere the Englishmen were. They had such excellent manners and soft agreeable voices—and, furthermore, you could understand what they said! A Frenchman, or a European speaking French, talked very rápidly, and was apt to become excited and wave his hands in front of you; but the well-chosen words of a cultivated Oxford graduate slid painlessly into your mind and you found yourself realizing how it had come about that they were the managers of so large a portion of the earth. If a territory was placed in the hands of such men, it stood a chance to be well governed; but what would happen if the Italians got it—to say nothing of the Germans or the Bolsheviks!

The British members of commissions of course had young secretaries and translators carrying heavy portfolios, and Lanny met them. They reminded him of Rick and those jolly English lads with whom he had punted on the Thames. One of them invited him to lunch at their hotel, an ornate structure which seemed to be built entirely of onyx; the dining room was twice as big as the Crillon's, and in it you saw the costumes of every corner of the empire on which the sun never set. The English youth, whose name was Fessenden, had been born in Gibraltar, and was here because of his fluent Spanish and French. He was gay, and had the usual bright pink cheeks, and Lanny exchanged eager confidences with him; each was "pumping" the other, of course, but that was fair exchange and no robbery.

What was this business about Prinkipo? Lanny told how anxiously Dr. Herron was trying to find out. The English youth said his government hadn't appointed any delegates, so presumably they thought it was going to fizzle. One more of those "trial balloons." Fessenden's chief had said that the only way it might be made to work would be for President Wilson to drop everything else and go there and put it through. But of course he couldn't do that. "Don't you think perhaps he's a bit too afraid of delegating authority? One man just can't make so many decisions by himself."

That was the talk all over Paris; three of the peace commissioners were figureheads, and Colonel House had been weakened by an attack of flu. That was no secret, and Lanny admitted it.

"All of us," said the Englishman, "at least all the younger crowd, were hoping Wilson could put it over. Now we're a bit sick about it."

Lanny answered cautiously. "One hears so many things, one doesn't know what to believe."

"But there are definite things that you can be sure of. It seems as if your President just doesn't know enough about Europe; he does things without realizing what they mean. At the outset he agreed to let the Italians have the Brenner! Shouldn't he have asked somebody about that before he spoke? Of course it's important for the defense of Italy; but if you're going to distribute the world on the basis of strategic needs, where will you stop?"

"I don't know much about the Brenner," admitted Lanny.

"It's a pass inhabited almost entirely by German people; and what is going to happen to them when the Italians take them over? Will they be compelled to send their children to Italian schools, and all that sort of rot?"

Lanny smiled, and said: "Well, you know it wasn't we who signed that treaty with the Italians."

"True enough," admitted Fessenden. "But then it wasn't we who brought up those Fourteen Points!"

That was why it was a pleasure to meet the English; you could speak frankly, and they didn't flare up and deliver orations. It was true they wanted the Americans to pull some chestnuts out of the fire for them, but it was also true that they would meet you halfway in an effort to be decent. The best of them had really hoped that the American President was going to bring in a new order and were saddened now as they discovered how ill equipped he was for the tremendous task.

Lanny didn't tell his English friend an appalling story which Alston's associates were whispering. The Supreme Council was planning to recognize a new state in Central Europe called Czecho-slovakia, to consist principally of territories taken from Germany and Austria. The Czechs, previously known as Bohemians, had a patriotic leader named Masaryk, who had been a professor at the University of Chicago and a personal friend of Wilson. An American journalist talking with Wilson had said: "But, Mr. President, what are you going to do about the Germans in this new country?"

"Are there Germans in Czechoslovakia?" asked Wilson, in surprise.

The answer was: "There are three million of them."

"How strange!" exclaimed the President. "Masaryk never told me that!"

IV

Lanny was worried because he hadn't had any letter from Kurt. After he had been in Paris a month, he wrote again, this time to Herr Meissner, asking that he would kindly drop a line to say how Kurt was. Lanny assumed that whoever the mysterious person in Switzerland might be who had been remailing Kurt's letters to Lanny, Kurt's father would be able to make use of him. Lanny followed his usual practice of not giving his own address, for fear the letter might come into the wrong hands; he just said that he was to be addressed at his mother's home.

Lanny sent his letter in care of Johannes Robin, in Rotterdam, and there came in reply one from Hansi Robin, saying that his father had forwarded the letter as usual. Hansi was now fourteen, and his English was letter-perfect, although somewhat stilted. He told Lanny how his work at the conservatory was progressing, and expressed the hope that Lanny's career in diplomacy was not going to cause him to give up his music entirely. He said how happy he was that his father had become a business associate of Lanny's father and that they all hoped the adventure was going to prove satisfactory. Hansi said that his brother joined in expressing their high regard and sincere good wishes. Freddi, two years younger, added his childish signature to certify that it was true.

Lanny put that letter into his pocket, intending to forward it to his father the next time he wrote; and maybe that was the reason why for the next two or three days his thoughts were so frequently on Kurt Meissner. Lanny was sure that he would get a reply, for the comptroller-general was a business-like person, and it would be no trouble for him to dictate to his secretary a note, saying: "My son is well, but away from home," or: "My son is ill," or whatever it might be. Every time Lanny called for his mail he looked for a letter with a Swiss stamp.

And of course he thought about Schloss Stubendorf, and Kurt's family, and Kurt himself, and wondered what four and a half years of war had done to him. What would he be doing now, or planning? Would he be able to go back to music after battle and wounds, and the wrecking of all his hopes? Around him Lanny saw men who had become adjusted to war and couldn't get readjusted. Some were drinking, or trying to make up for lost time by sleeping with any woman they could pick up on the streets—and the streets were full of them. Would Kurt be like that? Or was Kurt dead, or mutilated as Marcel had been? What other reason could there be for his failure to communicate with the friend to whom he had pledged such devotion? Could it be that he now hated all Americans, because they had torn Germany's prey from out of her jaws?

Such were Lanny's thoughts while taking a walk. Such were his thoughts while he sat in the stuffy, overheated rooms at the Quai d'Orsay, attending exhausting sessions whenever a geographer was likely to be needed. While furious and tiresome quarrels were going on over the ownership of a hundred square miles of rocks or desert, he would turn his thoughts to the days when he and Kurt were diving and swimming off the Cap d'Antibes; or the holiday at the Christmas-card castle, which he saw always as he had seen it the first morning, with freshly fallen snow on its turrets shining in the newly risen sun. There were so many beautiful things in the world—oh, God, why did men have to make it so ugly? Why did they have to rage and scream and bluster, and tell lies so transparent that a geographer and even a secretary were made sick to listen.

Kurt was only a year older than Lanny, but he had seemed much more; he was so grave, so precise in his thinking, so decided in his purposes, that Lanny had honored him as a teacher. For nearly six years the American had kept that attitude; and now, when Kurt didn't write to him, he was worried, puzzled, hurt. But he kept telling himself that he had no right to be. There was bound to be some reason, to be explained in good time.

V

The streets of Paris were full of picturesque and diverting sights: dapper young officers in Turkey-red pants, looking as if they had just stepped out of bandboxes; poilus trudging home from the front, unshaven, mudstained, bent with weariness; elegant ladies of fashion tripping from their limousines into jewelers' and coiffeurs'; pathetic, consumptive-looking grisettes with blackened eyebrows and scarlet lips. The glory of La Ville Lumière was sadly dimmed, but there had to be ways for the foreigners to enjoy themselves. There were always crowds of them in the fashionable restaurants, no matter how often the prices were raised; always lines of people trying to get into every place of entertainment. So many had made money out of the war—and they had to have pleasure, even though their world might be coming to an end.

The strolling youth would note these things for a while, and then again be lost in thoughts about the problems of the peace. What was the conference going to do with Upper Silesia? That territory was full of coal mines and many sorts of factories; the French wanted to take it from Germany and give it to Poland— so that in the next war its coal would serve the purposes of France, and not of her hereditary and implacable foe. There was a commission to decide all that, and Professor Alston had been asked to attend it; when Lanny finished his walk he would hear arguments concerning the destiny of the Meissner family! A translator, of course, could take no open part, but he might be able to influence his chief by a whispered word, and his chief might influence the higher-ups in the same way.

So thinking, Lanny strolled on—into what was to prove the strangest adventure of his life up to that time. He had come to a street intersection and stood to let the traffic by. There came a taxi, close to the curb, and as it passed it was forced to slow up by another vehicle ahead. In the taxi sat a single passenger, a man, and at that moment he leaned forward, as if to speak to the driver. His profile came into clear view; and Lanny stared dumfounded. It was Kurt Meissner!

Of course it was absolutely impossible. Kurt, an artillery captain of the Germany army, riding in a Paris taxicab while the two countries were still formally at war! It must be somebody else; and yet from the first moment Lanny knew it wasn't. It hadn't been merely a physical recognition, it was some kind of psychic thing; he knew that it was Kurt as well as he knew that he himself was Lanny Budd. Could this be another apparition, like the one he had seen of Rick? Did it mean that Kurt was dead, or near to death, as Rick had been?

The cab was moving on, and Lanny came out of his daze. His friend was in Paris, and he must get hold of him! He wanted to shout: "Kurt! Kurt!"—but the traffic was noisy, and Lanny's training kept him from making a public disturbance. He began to run, as fast as he could, dodging the pedestrians, and trying to keep his eye on that cab. Perhaps he could catch it at the next crossing; but, no, it was going on faster. Lanny was despairing, when he saw a vacant cab by the curb. He sprang in and cried: "Follow that cab! Quick!"

Taxi drivers have such experiences now and then. It means a pretty girl, or perhaps a fashionable married lady—anyhow, some sort of adventure. The driver leaped into action, and presently

they were weaving their way through the traffic, Lanny peering
ahead, to pick out one cab from all the others. He made sure he
had it, because he could see through the rear window the passenger's gray fedora, which had been a part of the image stamped
upon his mind in one quick flash.

VI

They had turned onto the Boulevard Haussmann, with much fast
traffic, so there was nothing to do but follow; meanwhile Lanny
had a chance to think, and get the aspects of this problem sorted
out in his mind. Kurt in Paris, wearing civilian clothes! He couldn't
be on any official mission, for there were no enemy missions in
France; there had been a lot of talk about having the Central
Powers represented at the Peace Conference, but the talk had died
down. Nor could Kurt be here on private business, for no enemy
aliens were being given passports into France. No, his presence
could mean only that he was here on some secret errand, with a
false passport. If he were detected, they would try him before a
military court and stand him against a wall and shoot him.

Lanny's next thought was that he, a member of the Crillon staff,
had no business getting mixed up in such a matter. He ought to tell
his taxi driver that it was a mistake, and to turn back. But Lanny
hadn't learned to think of himself as an official person, and the idea
that he couldn't speak to Kurt just didn't make sense. Whatever
his friend might be doing, he was a man of honor and wouldn't do
anything to get Lanny into trouble.

Kurt's cab turned off the boulevard, into the Neuilly district.
"I can drive up alongside him now," said Lanny's driver; but
Lanny said: "No, just follow him." He would wait until Kurt got
out, so that they could meet without witnesses.

Watching ahead, Lanny saw the passenger turn round; evidently
he discovered that he was being followed, for his cab began turning corners rapidly, as no sane taxicab would have done. Lanny
could imagine Kurt saying: "Ten francs extra if you shake off that

fellow behind us." Lanny said; "Ten francs extra if you don't let that fellow get away from us."

So began a crazy chase in and about the environs of Paris. Lanny's driver had been a dispatch rider on the upper Meuse front, so he called back to his passenger; he looked like an *apache*, and behaved like one. They turned corners on two wheels, and Lanny leaned out of the window to balance the cab. They dashed through cross-wise traffic—and they held onto the other car. More than once Lanny saw the passenger in front turning round to look— always holding his gray fedora below the level of his eyes. Lanny took off his hat and waved it, to give his friend every opportunity to recognize him. But it had no effect.

However, Lanny's *apache* was better than the other one. Kurt's taxi stopped suddenly in front of a department store, and Lanny's came up with screeching brakes behind it. Kurt got out, paid his driver, and turned to go into the store; Lanny came running, hav- ing also paid quickly. He realized the need of caution, and didn't call out; he came up behind the other and whispered: "Kurt, it's me—Lanny."

A strange thing happened. The other turned and gazed into Lanny's face, coldly, haughtily. "You are mistaken, sir." Lanny had spoken in English, and the answer was given in French.

Of course it was Kurt Meissner; a Kurt with features more care- worn, stern, and mature; his straw-colored hair, usually cut close, had grown longer; but it was Kurt's face, and the voice was Kurt's.

Lanny, having had time to think matters out, wasn't going to give up easily. He murmured: "I understand your position. You must know that I am your friend and you can trust me. I still feel as I have always done."

The other kept up his cold stare. "I beg your pardon, sir," he said, in very good French. "It is a case of mistaken identity. I have never met you."

He started away again; but Lanny walked with him. "All right," he said, his voice low. "I understand what is the matter. But if you get into trouble and need help, remember that I'm at the Crillon.

But don't think that I've turned into an official person. I'm doing what I can to help make a decent peace, and you and I are not very far apart."

One of the clerks of the store came forward with inquiry in his manner, and Kurt asked for some gloves. Lanny turned and started to leave. But then he thought: "Maybe Kurt will think it over and change his mind." So he waited, just inside the door of the store. When the other had completed his purchase and was going out, sure enough, he said: "You may come with me, sir, if you wish."

VII

The two of them went out to the street, and walked in silence for quite a while, Kurt looking behind them to make sure they were not being followed. Then they would take a glance at each other. More than four years had passed since their last meeting in London; they had been boys and now they were men. The German officer had lines in his long thin face; he walked as if he were bowed with care—but of course that might have been because he was trying not to look like a military man. It was plain that he was deeply moved.

"Lanny," he exclaimed, suddenly, "may I have your word of honor not to mention this meeting to any person under any circumstances?"

"I have an idea of your position, Kurt. You can trust me."

"It is not merely a matter of my own life. It might have extremely unpleasant consequences for you."

"I am willing to take the risk. I am sure that you are not doing anything dishonorable."

They walked on; and finally Kurt broke out: "Forgive me if I am not a friend at present. I am bound by circumstances about which I cannot say a word. My time is not my own—nor my life."

"I promise not to misunderstand," replied the other. "Let me tell you about my job, and perhaps you can judge about trusting me." He spoke in English, thinking it would be less likely to be caught

by any passer-by. He told how he had come to be at the Crillon,
and gave a picture of the Peace Conference as it appeared to a
translator-secretary.

Kurt couldn't bear to listen to it. He broke in. "Do you know
what is being done to my people by the blockade? The food
allowance is one-third of normal, and the child death-rate has
doubled. Of course our enemies would like them all to die, so there
wouldn't be any more of us in the world. But is that what President
Wilson promised?"

Lanny replied: "There isn't a man I know in the American
delegation who doesn't consider it a shame. They have protested
again and again. Mr. Hoover is in Paris now, wringing his hands
over the situation."

"Wringing Mr. Hoover's hands won't feed the starving babies.
Why doesn't President Wilson threaten to quit unless Clemenceau
gives way?"

"He can't be sure what that would do. The others might go on
and have their way just the same. It's hard to get a sane peace
after a mad war."

Said the captain of artillery: "Are you aware that our people
still have some of their gold reserve? They don't ask anybody to
give them food, they ask merely to be allowed to buy it with their
own money. And there's plenty of food in America, is there
not?"

"So much that we don't know what to do with it. The government has agreed to take it from the farmers at fixed prices, but
now there's no market. There are millions of pounds of pork that
is going to spoil if it isn't used."

"But still our people can't spend their own money for it!"

"The French say they want that gold to restore their ruined
cities with."

"Don't you know that we have offered to come and rebuild the
cities with our own hands?"

"That's not so simple as it sounds, Kurt. The people here say
that would throw their own workers out of jobs."

"Maybe so; and again maybe it would let them find out how decent our people are—how orderly and how hard-working."

The two strolled on, arguing. Lanny guessed that his friend was sounding him out; and presently Kurt said: "Suppose it became known to you that there were some Germans in Paris, working secretly to try to get this wicked blockade lifted—would that seem to you such a bad thing?"

"It would seem to me only natural."

"But you understand that in the eyes of military men they would be spies, and if they were discovered they would be shot?"

"I realized that as soon as I saw you. But I don't see what you can possibly accomplish here."

"Hasn't it occurred to you that you can accomplish something anywhere in the world if you have money?"

A light dawned on Lanny. So that was it! He had heard his father say many times that you could get anything you wanted in Paris if you had the price.

Kurt went on: "There are people here who won't let our babies have milk until they themselves have gold. And even then you can't trust them—for after they have got the gold they may betray you for more gold. You see, it's a complicated business; and if one happened to be in it, and to have a friend whom he loved, it would be an act of friendship to be silent. It might be extremely inconvenient to know about these matters."

Lanny didn't hesitate over that. He declared with warmth: "If that was all that was being done, Kurt, I should think that any true friend would be willing to know and to take a chance at helping. Certainly I would!"

VIII

The walk prolonged itself to several miles. Lanny decided that his duties at the conference could wait. His friend was questioning him as to persons who might be interested in helping to get the blockade of Germany lifted. There were two kinds whom a secret agent might wish to know: journalists and politicians who might be bought, and idealists and humanitarians who might be trusted to expend money for printing or other such activities. Lanny told about Alston and others of the staff—but they were doing all they could anyhow. He told about Herron, who was being called a Red because he wanted a truce with the Bolsheviks, and a pro-German because he didn't want the French to keep the Rhineland. He told about Mrs. Emily, who was kind and charitable, also influential; too bad that a German officer couldn't come to her home and be properly introduced and invited to set forth his case! Kurt hinted that perhaps she might be useful as a distributor of funds. It was hard to give much money without having the French police make note of the sudden increase of spending power of some group. But if a wealthy American lady were willing to furnish funds to help make known the plight of the starving babies of Germany . . . ?

Presently Lanny, racking his mind, mentioned another person who was an idealist and propagandist of a sort, however perverted. That was his uncle. "I never told you about him, because I've been taught to be ashamed of him. But it appears that he's a personage of a sort here in Paris." Kurt was interested and asked many questions. Just what were Jesse Blackless's ideas? What group did he belong to? Was he an honest man—and so on.

Lanny answered: "Really, I hardly know him at all. Most of my impressions have come from my father's calling him names. Robbie thinks his ideas come from the devil, and the fact that he really believes them only makes it worse."

"How much money has he?"

"He lives like a poor man, but he may give money away. I suppose he'd have to, believing as he does."

"Do you suppose I could trust him with my secret?"

"Oh, gosh!" Lanny was staggered. "I wouldn't dare to say, Kurt."

"Suppose I were to go to him and introduce myself as a musician from Switzerland, interested in his ideas: how do you suppose he'd receive me?"

"He'd probably guess that you were a police agent, and wouldn't trust you."

They walked on, while Kurt pondered. Finally he said: "I have to take a chance. Can you do this for me? Go to your uncle and tell him that you have a friend who is interested in pushing the demand for the lifting of the blockade throughout Europe. Tell him that I have money, but there are reasons why I do not wish to be known. Tell him that you know me to be a sincere man— you can say that, can't you?"

"Yes, surely."

"Tell him someone will come to his room at exactly midnight and tap on his door. When he opens it the person will say the word 'Jesse,' and he will answer the word 'Uncle,' and then a package will be put in his hands. He will be under pledge to spend the money in the quickest and best way, for leaflets, posters, meetings, all that sort of thing. I'll watch, and if I see signs of his activity, I'll bring more money from time to time. Would you be willing to do that?"

"Yes," said Lanny, "I don't see why I shouldn't."

"You understand, both you and your uncle have my word that never under any circumstances will I name you to anyone."

"How much money will it be?"

"Ten thousand francs should be enough to start with. It will be in hundred-franc notes, so it can be spent without attracting attention. You will be able to see your uncle before midnight?"

"I don't know. I'll try."

"You know the park of captured cannon in the Place in front of the Crillon?"

"I see them every day."

"There is a big howitzer, directly at the corner as you enter the center lane of guns. It happens to be one that I had charge of; I know it by the marks where it was hit. It's directly across from the main entrance of the hotel, so you can't miss it."

"I think I know it."

"Can you be standing in front of it at exactly eleven tonight?"

"I guess so."

"If you lean against the gun, it means that your uncle says all right. If you walk up and down, it means that he says no, and the deal is off. If you're not there, it means that you haven't been able to find him, or that he wants more time before he gives his answer. In that case I'll look for you at the same hour tomorrow evening. Is that all clear?"

"Quite so. Isn't there any way I can get hold of you again?"

"Your mail at the hotel comes without censorship?"

"Oh, surely."

"I'll write you some time, a note in English, just saying, meet me at the same place. I'll sign an English name—shall we say Sam?"

"All right, Sam," said Lanny, with a grin. It promised to be great fun. Lanny's mother would be dancing tonight in behalf of charity, and Lanny would be conspiring in the same cause!

IX

The conspirator paid another call on his Uncle Jesse. This time no one answered his knock, so he poked a note under the door, saying he would return at seven. He had pressing duties, and the only time he could get free was by skipping his dinner; he bought a couple of bananas and ate them in the taxi, donating the dinner to the German babies. On his second call the uncle was waiting; Lanny, explaining that he had to attend a night session of one of the commissions, got down to business at once. "Uncle Jesse, do you agree that the blockade of Central Europe should be lifted?"

"I am an internationalist," replied the other. "I am opposed to every such interference with human liberty."

"You know people who are working to have it lifted—I mean they are writing and publishing and speaking in support of that demand, aren't they?"

"Yes; but what—?"

"I have a friend, who for important reasons cannot be named. It's enough that I know him intimately, and trust him. He feels about this blockade as you do, and it happens that he has a great deal of money. He asked me to suggest some way that he could put money into the hands of someone who would spend it for that purpose. I took the liberty of naming you."

"The devil you did!" said Uncle Jesse. "What then?"

"You realize that I don't know you very well—I haven't been allowed to. But I have the impression that you have real convictions, and wouldn't misapply funds that you accepted for such a cause."

"You have guessed correctly in that."

"No doubt you have friends who are trying to raise money for promoting your party, or whatever it is?"

"We get it by persuading poor workingmen to cut down on their food. We don't have rich people coming and dropping it into our laps."

"Well, this is one time it may happen—if you say the word."

"How much will it be?"

"The first payment will be ten thousand francs, in bank notes of small denominations."

"Jesus Christ!" said Uncle Jesse. Lanny had heard that these Reds were nearly all hostile to the accepted religion, but they still had one use for its founder.

"You have to pledge your word to spend it in the quickest and most effective way to promote a popular demand for the lifting of the blockade throughout Europe. If there are signs that you are spending it effectively, more will come—as much as you can handle."

"How will I get it?"

"Someone will knock on your door at midnight tonight. When you open the door the person will say 'Jesse,' and you will answer 'Uncle,' and a package will be put into your hands."

The painter sat eying his young nephew. "Look here, Lanny," said he. "The police and military are busy setting traps for people like me. Are you sure this isn't a scheme of some of the Crillon crowd?"

"I can't tell you whose scheme it is, but I assure you that the Crillon knows nothing about it, and neither do the police. They'll probably take notice as soon as you begin spending the money. That's a risk you have to run."

"Naturally," said Uncle Jesse, and pondered again. "I suppose," he remarked, "this is some of the 'German gold' we read about in the reptile press."

"You mustn't ask any questions."

"I'm free to spend the money according to my own judgment?"

"For the purpose agreed upon, yes."

The painter thought some more. "Son, this is wartime. Have you thought what you're getting in for?"

"You take risks for what you believe, don't you?"

"Yes, but you're a youngster, and you happen to be my sister's son, and she's a good scout, even if her brains don't always work. This could get you into one hell of a mess."

"If you don't mention me, there's no way it can get out. Wild horses couldn't drag it out of my friend."

Again a pause; and the bald-headed painter smiled one of his crooked smiles. "Perhaps you read in the papers how Lenin was in Switzerland when the Russian Revolution broke out, and he wanted very much to get into Russia. The German government wanted him there and sent him through in a sealed train. They had their reasons for sending him and he had his reasons for going. His reasons won out."

Lanny got the point and smiled in his turn. The uncle thought for a while and then told him how, many years ago, there had been a big fuss in America over the fact that multimillionaires who had corrupted legislatures and courts were trying to win public favor by giving sums of money to colleges. It was called "tainted money," and there was a clamor that colleges should refuse such donations. One college professor, more robust than the rest of the tribe, had got up in a meeting and cried: "Bring on your tainted money!" The painter laughed and said: "That's me!"

30

Out of the Depths

I

ON the fourteenth of February the Supreme Council ratified the
Covenant of the League of Nations at a stately ceremony; and
immediately thereafter President Wilson took the night train for
Brest, to return to Washington for the closing sessions of Congress.
He and his purple-clad lady walked on red plush carpets spread
all the way to the train, between rows of potted palms set out by
a polite government. All official France attended to see him off;
and thereafter it was as in a barn when the cat has departed and
the mice come out to devour the stores of grain. The diplomats of
the great states began helping themselves to German and Russian
territory, and the reactionary newspapers of Paris declared with
one voice that the foolish and utopian League was already dead
and that the problems of Europe were going to be settled on a
"realistic" basis.

Professor Alston said that this was the voice of Clemenceau, who
controlled a dozen newspapers of the capital and could change
their policies by crooking his finger. Alston and his friends were
greatly depressed. What was the use of meeting all day and most
of the night, wrestling over questions of fair play and "self-
determination," when it was evident that those who held the reins
of power would not pay the least attention to anything you said?
The French delegates now wore a cynical smile as they argued before the commissions; they had their assurance that their armies were
going to hold the Rhineland and the Sarre, and that a series of buffer
states were to be set up between Germany and Russia, all owing

their existence to France, all financed with the savings of the French peasants, and munitioned by Zaharoff, alias Schneider-Creusot. France and Britain were going to divide Persia and Mesopotamia and Syria and make a deal for the oil and the laying of pipelines. Italy was to take the Adriatic, Japan was to take Shantung—all such matters were being settled among sensible men.

Lanny continued to attend sessions and listen to tedious discussions of imaginary boundary lines. His chief was called in to advise the American delegates on the commission which was trying to pacify the Italians and the Yugoslavs, who for a month or two had been taking pot-shots at one another. The revolting Yugoslav sailors had seized the Austrian war vessels, and the Italians wanted them, but the Yugoslav sailors wanted the Americans to take charge of them. The Italians were trying to seize Fiume, a city which hadn't been granted to them even in the secret treaty. They were like the man who said he wasn't greedy for land, he just wanted the land adjoining his own. They made a fuss, they interrupted proceedings, they blocked decisions on other questions—and how execrable was their accent when they tried to speak French!

A pathetic victim of this system of muddle was George D. Herron. He had been formally appointed a member of a delegation to travel to Prinkipo; but now President Wilson had set out for America without even taking the trouble to let him know that the project was dropped. The poor man, whose arthritis made moving about an ordeal, was left to spend his money and time holding preliminary consultations with various Russian groups in Paris; he would convince them one day and the French would unconvince them the next. The first hint he got that he had been laid on the shelf was when his friend Alston brought him a report that the President had appointed a mission which was already on its way to Moscow, to find out the situation and report.

Watching Herron and listening to him, Lanny learned how dangerous it was to have anything to do with unpopular ideas. The prophet was called a Red, when in truth he looked upon Bolshevism as his Hebrew predecessors looked upon Baal and Moloch. He had heard about Jesse Blackless and was worried for fear Lanny might be lured by the false faith of his uncle. He told the youth, in his biblical language, that dictatorship was a degradation of the soul of man, and that anyone who took that road would find himself in the valley of the shadow of death. Either Socialism must be the free, democratic choice of the people, or it would be something worse than the rule of Mammon which it sought to replace. Lanny promised very gravely that he would remember this lesson. Privately, he didn't think he was going to need it.

II

The conspirator for charity expected every day to have a note from Kurt, but none came. He spent some time trying to figure out what Kurt would be doing, and wondering if it would be possible for a German spy in Paris to be apprehended and shot without anything getting into the papers. There were great numbers of persons of German descent living in Switzerland, in Holland and the Scandinavian countries, so it was possible for Germans to pass as citizens of these countries. All through the war German spies had been doing this, and there was no reason to imagine that they had all gone home when the armistice was signed. Kurt must be a member of such a group; and being young, he would have a superior who told him what to do.

When the weather was decent and Lanny had time, he liked to walk, to get the air of the overheated conference rooms out of his lungs. One of his walks took him to Montmartre, and he climbed the musty stairs of the old tenement, and found his uncle covered up on his cot to keep warm, absorbed in the reading of a workers' newspaper. The first thing the uncle said was: "Well, by God, from now on I believe in Santa Claus!"

It really had happened: the knock on his door, the exchange of passwords, the package placed in his hands! He chuckled as if it was the funniest thing that had occurred to a Red agitator since the birth of Karl Marx. "Every sou has been honestly spent, so tell your friend to come again—the sooner the better!

"Did you notice the *affiches?*" continued the painter; and Lanny said he hadn't seen any referring to the lifting of the blockade against Germany, but on the kiosks he had noticed in big red letters a call for a *réunion* that evening, to demand government action against the rise in food prices. "That is ours," said the uncle. "We couldn't post anything on behalf of Germany—the *flics* would be down on us before we got started. But they can't prevent our defending the rights of French workers and returned soldiers."

"As a matter of fact, Uncle Jesse," asked the youth, "if they allow food to be exported into Germany, won't that make it scarcer in France?"

"The Germans don't want any food from France," replied the other. "They can buy it from America. What we want the French government to do is to get after the middlemen and speculators who are holding food in warehouses and letting it spoil because they can make more when prices are high."

Jesse Blackless launched upon an exposition of his political views. He had been a "syndicalist," which meant that he supported the left-wing labor unions, whose aim was to take over industry for the workers. But recent events in Russia had convinced him that the Bolshevik program represented the way to victory, even though it might mean the surrender of some liberties for a time. "You have to have discipline if you expect to win any sort of war," said the rebel painter. It was practically the opposite of what Herron had said.

Lanny really wanted to oblige his father; but how could he hold his present job without giving thought to the ideas of these Bolsheviks? In the Crillon people talked about them all the time. You couldn't discuss the problems of any state or province of Central Europe without their being brought up. "If you don't lend us money, if you don't give us food, our people will go over to the Bolsheviks. . . . If you don't give us guns, how can we put down the Bolsheviks? . . . If you take our territory away from us, we will throw ourselves into the arms of the Bolsheviks." Such were the utterances in every conference room. Often it was a form of black-mail, and the French would resent it with fury. The ruling classes of Germany, Austria, and Hungary were playing up this fear in order to get out of paying for the ruin they had wrought in Europe. "All right!" the French would answer. "Go to Moscow or go to hell, it makes no difference to us."

But this was a bluff. As soon as they had said it, the French would look at one another in fear. What if the Red wave were to spread in Poland, as it had spread in Hungary and Bavaria? If the Reds got the upper hand in Berlin, with whom would the Allies sign a treaty of peace? The Americans would ask this, and French and British diplomats didn't know what to answer, and took out their irritation on the persons who asked the questions. They must be Reds, too!

III

"Would you like to come to the *réunion* tonight?" asked Uncle Jesse; and Lanny said he would if his duties left him a chance. "I won't offer to take you," said the other. "It'll be better for the Crillon if you're not seen with me."

It happened that the staff at the Majestic was giving a dance that evening, and Lanny had a date with a fair-haired English secretary who reminded him of Rosemary. He thought she might find it romantic to take in a Red meeting, and do the dancing later. Lanny could call it a matter of duty, for he had told his chief about it and Alston had said: "Let me have a report on it."

The *salle* was in a teeming working-class quarter, and apparently not large enough for the thousand or two who wanted to get in. Lanny and his young lady were among the fortunate ones, because they were recognized as foreigners, and people made way for them. The place was hazy with tobacco smoke, and up on the platform, among a dozen other men and women, Lanny saw his uncle. He saw no one else whom he knew, for these were not the sort of persons one met at Mrs. Emily's teas. There was a sprinkling of intellectuals, art students, and others whom you could recognize by their garb, but for the most part those present were workers and returned soldiers, their faces haggard from long years of strain.

Lanny would be in a position to report to his chief that the workers of Paris were bitterly discontented with their lot. Hardly had the speakers got started before the shouting began, and he was a poor speaker indeed who could not cause some auditor to rise and shake his clenched right hand in the air and shout "*à bas*" somebody or something. There were no poor speakers, by that standard; they all knew their audience and how to work it into a fury, how to bring first murmurs and then hoots and jeers against bureaucrats and bemedaled militarists who feasted and danced while food was rotting in the warehouses and the poor in their dens were perishing of slow starvation.

Especial object of their hatred appeared to be Georges Clemenceau. Traitor, rat, Judas, were the mildest names they called him; for the "tiger of France" had been in his youth a *communard*, one of themselves, and had served a term in prison for his revolutionary activities. Now, like the other politicians, he had sold out to the capitalists, now he was a gang leader for the rich. Lanny was interested to discover that these workers knew most of the facts about Clemenceau which his father had been telling him. One of the speakers mentioned Zaharoff—and there was booing that might have brought a shudder to the Grand Officer. They knew about Clemenceau's control of the press; when the speaker said that journalists were bought and sold in Paris like rotten fish the crowd showed neither surprise nor displeasure.

Lanny was surprised to discover that his uncle was an effective orator. The sardonic, crooked smile became a furious sneer, his irony a corroding acid that destroyed whatever it touched. The painter was there to see to it that the real theme of the evening was adequately covered; he pointed out that the workers of France were not the only ones who were being starved, the same fate was being deliberately dealt to the workers of Germany, Austria, Hungary. All the workers of Europe were learning that their fate was the same and their cause the same; all were resolving that never again would they fight one another, but turn their guns against the capitalist class, the author of their sufferings, the agent of their suppression, the one real enemy of the people throughout the world. The English girl, of course, didn't know he was Lanny's uncle, and after she had listened to his tirade for a while, she exclaimed: "Oh, what a vicious person!"

IV

Lanny told himself that he was observing this *réunion* professionally; he was going to make a report. Every day for seven weeks and more he had been translating reports, revising reports, filing reports. And now he was going to report on the sentiments of the working classes of Paris. Should he say that they no longer had any feelings of enmity against the *sales boches*, but that all their fury was turned against Clemenceau and his government? Hardly that—for it was obvious that this was a special group, who had come to listen to the sort of speeches they enjoyed. And even they were not unanimous. Every now and then there were cries of dissent; a man would leap up and shout contradictions and others would howl him down. More than once there was uproar and confusion, men seizing the impromptu orator and pulling him into his seat; if he resisted, there would be fist-fighting, and perhaps chairs wielded as a convenient weapon. It appeared that much of the opposition was organized; there were groups of protestants looking for trouble. They were the *Camelots du Roi*, the royalists of France; their inspirer a raging journalist named Maurras, who in the paper which he edited did not hesitate to call for riots and murders.

Lanny, as he listened, kept thinking of the French revolution. Jean Marat, "friend of the people," living in the sewers of Paris to escape his enemies, had come forth to deliver just such speeches, denouncing the aristocrats and demanding their blood. Here too one saw the *tricoteuses*, grandmotherly-looking old women who sat knitting, and at the same time listening attentively; every once in a while one of them would open her mouth and scream: *"Mort aux traîtres!"*—and without missing a single stitch.

Lanny watched the faces. Sinister and dark they seemed, but full of pain, so that he was divided between fear and pity. He knew there were whole districts of Paris which were vast "cabbage patches," in which the poor were housed in dingy, rotting buildings centuries old. They had suffered privations so that Zaharoff and his friends might have their war to the finish; and now, with production almost stopped and trade disorganized while diplomats and statesmen wrangled—could it be expected that they would not complain?

Among those packed against the walls of the *salle* was a youth whose violent gestures caught Lanny's attention. You could know that he was a workingman by the fact that he wore a corduroy suit and a cotton shirt with no collar or tie. His face was emaciated, unshaven, and unkempt, but there was a light in his eyes as of one seeing visions. He was so wrought up by the oratory that his lips kept moving, as if he were repeating the phrases he heard; his hands were clenched, and when at the end of a climax he shouted approval, he shook not one but both fists in the air.

Lanny tried to imagine what life must seem to a youth like that. He was about Lanny's age, but how different in his fate! He wouldn't know much about the forces which moved the world; he would know only suffering, and the fact that it was caused by those in authority, the rulers and the rich. Maybe that wasn't the truth, but he would think it was, and Lanny would have a hard time contradicting him. The well-educated young Englishwoman, whose father was a stockbroker at home, had called Jesse Blackless a "vicious person"; and maybe he was that, but all the same, Lanny knew that what his uncle was saying was true. When he raged at the Clemenceau government because it had stopped in Berne a shipment of Red Cross medical supplies intended for the ailing children in Austria, Lanny knew it had happened, and that Mr. Herbert Hoover, most conservative of businessmen, was uttering in the Hotel Crillon censure fully as severe—and far more profane.

When the meeting was over, Lanny saw the young workingman

elbowing his way to the front. He went onto the stage and grabbed Jesse Blackless by the hands and shook them. The painter patted him on the back, and Lanny wondered, was this unkempt youth a friend of his uncle's, a member of his group, or just a convert, or a prospect? Lanny continued to reflect upon it, only half hearing the shocked comments of Penelope Selden, his lady friend.

They got into a taxi to drive to the Majestic, and on the way she forgot politics and put her hand in his. They danced together in the onyx-lined ballroom; a gay and festive scene, with half the men and many of the women wearing uniforms. They too had suffered, and been under strain; they too needed relaxation from heavy duties, and it wasn't fair to blame them for dancing. But Lanny was haunted by the faces of the angry workers; he was haunted by the millions of children who were growing up stunted and deformed, because of things which these dancing ladies and gentlemen had done and were still doing.

The young English girl, with soft brown hair and merry eyes and disposition, was pleasant to hold in your arms. Lanny held her for an hour, dancing with no one else; she made plain that she liked him, and he had got the impression that she would be his for the asking. So many of the women were in a reckless mood, in these days of deliverance from anxieties too greatly prolonged. Lanny couldn't very well say to her: "I've had an unhappy love affair, and I've sworn off the sex business for a while." What he said was: "Don't you think maybe your chief could do something with Lloyd George, if he told him about this meeting, and what a fury the people are in? Really, you know, it's a very bad state of affairs!"

V

Lieutenant Jerry Pendleton showed up in Paris, having got a week's leave. He had won promotion in the Argonne Forest by the method of being luckier than other sergeants of his outfit. In his new uniform he looked handsome and dignified, and Lanny at first thought he was the same gay and buoyant red-head from whom he had parted back at Camp Devens. But soon he noticed that Jerry had a tendency to fall silent, and there would come a brooding, somber look. Apparently going to war did something to a man. Lanny had been expecting to be entertained with accounts of hairbreadth 'scapes i' the imminent deadly breach; but his former tutor said: "Let's not talk about it, kid. All I want is to go home and try to forget."

"Aren't you going down to see Cerise?"

"I haven't enough time."

Lanny knew that wasn't true, for Jerry could have taken the night express and been in Cannes in the morning. The youth let the subject drop; but later, after he had told about his misadventure with Gracyn in Connecticut, the lieutenant warmed up and revealed what was troubling his mind. "The plain truth is, I just don't like the French. I'm sore at the whole damn country."

"What have they done to you?"

"It's just that we're so different, I guess. I'm always stumbling on things I dislike. I realize I don't know Cerise very well, and I'm never going to be allowed to know her until I've married her; and then what will I find out?"

"My mother married a Frenchman, and they were very happy."

"Your mother lived here a long time and probably knew how to choose. I've seen so many things in France that I want to get away from. Manure-piles!"

Lanny laughed. Having spent nearly all his life in France, he assumed that this national institution was necessary to the agricultural process. But Jerry said they ordered things differently in Kansas; everything there was clean and agreeable, even the hogs. Lanny was amused, because when Jerry Pendleton had first made his appearance on the Riviera he had described his home state as a dull, provincial place, and had earnestly desired not to go back and help run two drug stores.

But now what a change! "I fought to save these people," said the lieutenant of a machine-gun company, "and now I have to bite every franc to see if it's made of lead."

"That can happen anywhere in Europe," replied his friend.

"It doesn't happen in Koblenz," declared the other, emphatically. He was part of the army which had gone into the Rhineland to guard the bridgeheads pending the signing of a treaty. Jerry's brigade was covering a semicircle of German territory, some forty miles in diameter on the far side of the river, and his company had been quartered for three months in a tiny village where they had every opportunity to know the population. The lieutenant himself was billeted in a farmhouse where everything was so neat, and the old couple so kind, so patient and humble, grateful for the tiniest favor—it was exactly as Kurt had told Lanny it would be, the dough-boys had learned that the Germans were not the Huns they had been pictured. More and more the Americans were wondering why they had had to fight such people, and how much longer they were going to have to stay and blockade them from the rest of the world.

The Rhineland is a rich country and produces food and wine in abundance; but it had been just behind the fighting front for four years and the retreating German armies had carried off all they could. Now the people were living on the scantiest rations and the children were pale and hollow-eyed. The well-fed Yanks were expected to live in houses with undernourished children and preg-nant women and never give them food. There were strict orders against "fraternizing with the enemy"; but did that include stuffing half a load of bread into your overcoat pocket and passing it out to the kids?

And what about the Fräuleins, those sweet-faced, gentle creatures with golden or straw-colored braids down their backs, and white dresses with homemade embroidery on the edges? Their fellows had been marched back into the interior of Germany, and here were handsome upstanding conquerors from the far-off prairie states, with chocolates and canned peaches and other unthinkable delicacies at their disposal. Lieutenant Pendleton chuckled as he told about what must surely have been the oddest military regulation ever issued in the history of warfare; the doughboys had been officially informed that entering into intimate relations with German Fräuleins was not to be considered as "fraternizing" within the meaning of the army regulations!

"Is that why you've lost interest in Cannes?" asked Lanny, with a grin.

"No," said Jerry, "but I'll tell you this. If somebody doesn't hurry up and make up his mind about peace terms, a lot of our fellows are just going to take things into their own hands and go home—and their Fräuleins with them. What's the matter with these old men in Paris, Lanny?"

"I'll introduce you to some of them," answered the youth, "and you can find out for yourself."

VI

Jerry Pendleton having lunch at the Crillon; a piece of luck that rarely fell to the lot of a "shavetail," even one who had fought through a war! It would be something to tell at the officers' mess in the Rhineland; it would be something to tell to his grandchildren in Kansas, in days when all this was in the history books—the "First World War."

Lanny sat at table with his chief, because meals were times for confidential chats and informal reports, and perhaps for helping to translate the excited French of somebody who wanted more territory for his tiny state. A young officer on leave from the front might hear things that would give him a jolt—for these college professors had opinions of their own, and did not hesitate to bandy about the most exalted names.

The young lieutenant was asked to what unit he belonged and what service he had seen. When he said that he had been through the Meuse-Argonne—well, it was no great distinction, for more than a million others could say the same, not counting fifty thousand or so who would never speak of that, or anything else. The conversation turned to that six weeks' blood-bath, hailed as a glory in the press at home. What was the real truth about it? Had Foch wished to set the Americans a task at which no army could succeed?

Had he been punishing General Pershing for obstinacy and presumption?

The young lieutenant learned that from the hour when the first American division had been landed in France there had been a war going on between the American commander-in-chief and the British and French commands, backed by their governments. It had been their idea that American troops should be brigaded in with British and French troops and used to replace the wastage of their battles; but Pershing had been determined that there should be an American army, fighting under the American flag. He had declared this purpose and hung onto it like any British bulldog. But the others had never given up; they had used each new defeat as an excuse for putting pressure; they had pulled every sort of political wire and worried every American who had any authority or influence.

So, by the summer of 1918, they had managed to acquire a pretty complete dislike of the jimber-jawed Missouri general. When Baker, Secretary of War, had visited England, Lloyd George had tactfully suggested that President Wilson should be requested to remove Pershing; to which the secretary had replied coldly that the American government was not in need of having anyone decide who should command American troops. Clemenceau had written a long letter to Foch, insisting that he should appeal to President Wilson to remove Pershing, on the ground that he had proved himself incompetent to handle armies in battle. Alston said he had seen a copy of that letter, though he wasn't at liberty to tell who had shown it to him. What more likely than that the generalissimo of all the Allied forces had said to himself: "Well, if this stubborn fellow is determined to have his own way, we'll give him something to do that will keep him busy."

After listening to such conversation, Lanny and his friend strolled down the Champs-Élysées, between the mile-long rows of captured cannon, and for the first time and the last the lieutenant was moved to "open up" to his friend. "My God, Lanny!" he exclaimed. "Imagine fifty thousand lives being wiped out because two generals were jealous of each other!"

"History is full of things like that," remarked the youth. "Ten thousand men march out and die because the king's mistress has been snubbed by an ambassador."

The ex-tutor went on to pour out the dreadful story of the Meuse-Argonne, a mass of hills and rocks covered with forest and brush. "Of course that's all gone now," said Jerry, "because we blasted every green thing from a couple of hundred square miles; we even blew off the tops of some of the hills. The Germans had been working for four years making it a tangle of wire, with machine guns hidden every few yards, and dugouts and concrete shelters. We were told to go and take such and such places, no matter what the cost, and we took them—wave after wave of men, falling in rows. I saw a man's head blown off within three feet of me, and I wiped his brains out of my eyes. We had whole regiments that just ceased to exist."

"I heard about it," said Lanny.

"You might, because you met insiders; but the folks at home haven't the remotest idea, and won't ever be told. Military men say that troops can stand twenty percent losses; more than that, they go to pieces. But we had many an outfit with only twenty percent survivors and they went on fighting. There was nothing else you could do, because you were in there and the only way out was forward. The hell of it was that the roads ran crossways to our line of advance, so there was never any way to get in supplies except on men's backs. You took a position, and flopped down into a shell hole, and there you lay day and night, with shells crashing around you and bullets whining just over your head. The rain drenched you and near froze at night, and you had no food, and no water but the rain you caught in your tin hat; all around were men groaning and screaming, and nothing to do but lie there and die. That's modern war, by God, and if they give me any more of it, I'm going to turn Bolo."

"Be careful how you say it, Jerry," warned his friend. "There really are Bolos, you know, and they're working in our army."

"Well, tell those old fellows at the Crillon to hurry up and settle it and send us home, or my outfit will turn Bolo without anybody having to do any work at all."

VII

Next morning Lanny had his light French breakfast and went to Alston's office. He was standing by the latter's desk, going over their schedule for the day, when in came Professor Davisson; the big, stout man was hurrying, greatly excited. "Clemenceau's been shot!"

"What?" exclaimed Alston, starting up.

"Anarchist got him as he was on his way here to see House."

"Is he dead?"

"Badly hurt, they say."

Others of the staff came in; the building was like an ants' nest when something upsets it. Everybody's plans were bowled over; for what was the use of holding conferences and making reports, when the whole thing would have to be done over? If the Tiger died, Poincaré would take his place; and the professors who had been scolding Clemenceau now had a sickening realization that he was a man of genius and a statesman compared with his probable successor, a dull pasty-faced lawyer who came from Lorraine, and therefore had drunk in hatred of Germany with his mother's milk. If Poincaré got the reins of power in his hands there would be no more talk of compromises, but a straight-out campaign to cripple Germany forever.

Clemenceau had been driving from his home, and as his limousine turned into the Avenue du Trocadéro, a young worker wearing corduroy clothing had stepped from behind a kiosk and fired eight or ten shots at him. Two had struck the elderly premier, one in the shoulder and one in the chest; it was believed that a lung had been penetrated, and there seemed little chance of life for a man of seventy-eight, a diabetic, weakened by four years of terrific strain.

"Well, that's the end of peace-making," said Alston. The staff agreed that it would mean a wave of reaction in France and the suppression of left-wing opinion.

But the old man didn't die; he behaved in amazing fashion—with a bullet hole in his lung he didn't want even to be sick. Reports came in every few minutes; the doctors were having a hard time persuading him to lie down; he could hardly speak, and a bloody foam came out of his mouth, but he wanted to go on holding conferences. The Tiger indeed; a hard beast to kill! Of course he became the hero of France and people waited hour by hour for bulletins as to his fate.

A messenger brought in newspapers with accounts of the affair. The assassin had been seized by the crowd, which mauled him and tried to kill him; the papers gave pictures of him being held by a couple of gendarmes who had protected and saved him. His name was Cottin, and he was said to be a known anarchist; the photographs showed a frail, disheveled, frightened-looking young fellow. Lanny studied them, and a strange feeling began to stir in him. "Where have I seen that face?" As in a lightning flash it came to him: the youth whom he had watched in the *salle* while Jesse Blackless was making his speech! No doubt about it, for Lanny had watched the face off and on for an hour, taking it as a symbol of the inflamed and rebellious masses.

Lanny's last glimpse of the young worker had been on the platform, with Uncle Jesse patting him on the back. Lanny had wondered then, and wondered now with greater intensity, did that mean that he was a friend of the painter, or merely an admirer, a stranger moved by his speech? Was this attempted killing the kind of political warfare that Uncle Jesse favored, whether publicly or secretly? Lanny remembered what his father had said, that syndicalism was for practical purposes the same as anarchism. Now Uncle Jesse had said that he had adopted the theories of the Bolsheviks. Did this by any chance include taking pot-shots at one's opponents on the street?

Decidedly a serious question for a youth getting launched upon a diplomatic career! To be sure, his chief had told him to go to the meeting and report; but nobody had told him to go secretly to the home of a syndicalist-Bolshevik conspirator and arrange for him to receive ten thousand francs of German money to be used in stirring up the workers of Paris to commit assassinations. Of course nobody at the meeting had directly advised the killing off of unsatisfactory statesmen, but it was an inference readily drawn from the furious denunciations poured upon the statesmen's heads. The orators might disclaim responsibility, but certainly they must know the probable result of such speeches.

Lanny's thought moved on from his uncle to his intimate friend. How much had Kurt known, and how far was he responsible for what had happened? It had become clear to Lanny that Kurt's money was being used for a lot more than the lifting of the blockade of Germany. Uncle Jesse had explained by saying that the police wouldn't allow a meeting on behalf of Germans, so the subject had to be brought in under camouflage. Lanny hadn't thought about the matter long before realizing that he had been extremely naïve. The obvious way to relieve French pressure on Germany was to frighten France with the same kind of Bolshevist disturbances that were taking place throughout Central Europe. Kurt and his group were here for that, and they were using camouflage just as Uncle Jesse was.

VIII

A lot of complications to occupy the thoughts of a secretary supposed to be marking for his chief's attention a dozen conflicting reports on the proper boundary between the city of Fiume, inhabited by tumultuous Italians, and its suburb Susak, on the other side of a creek, inhabited by intransigent Yugoslavs! Lanny sat with a stack of documents before him: American, British, and French recommendations, and translations of Italian charges and Yugoslav countercharges. He sat with wrinkled brows, but it wasn't over these problems. He was saying to himself: "What does Kurt think about assassination of statesmen as a means of influencing national

decisions? And would he be willing to use me for such a purpose?"
Lanny's sense of fair play compelled him to add that Kurt had given
him warning. Kurt had said: "Forgive me if I am not a friend at
present. My time is not my own, nor my life."

Of course the attempt on Clemenceau would rouse the French
police and military to vigorous action. They would begin a round-up
of the associates of the anarchist youth; they would subject them
to inquisition, trying to find out if there had been a conspiracy, and
if there was danger to other statesmen. No doubt they had spies
in Uncle Jesse's movement and must know of his sudden appearance
with a large sum of money. Perhaps they had him already and were
questioning him about the source of those funds! Lanny was sure
that his uncle wouldn't "give him away"; but still, he got a sudden
realization how close to a powder magazine he had been walking.
Yes, modern society was something dangerous and insecure, and a
youth who strolled blandly along, feeling safe because he was well
dressed and his father was rich—such a youth might see the earth
open up in front of him and masses of searing flame shoot out into
his face. Lanny decided that for the present he would repress his
curiosity as to the relationship between his uncle and the anarchist
Cottin; also that if he should meet his friend Kurt Meissner again
he would be extremely reserved and cautious.

IX

Two days passed, and Clemenceau didn't die, but on the contrary
was announcing that he would be back on the job of peace-making
in half a week. Then one afternoon in Lanny's mail he found a note
reading: "Meet me at the same place, same time. Sam."

Professor Alston was to advise some American delegates on the
Fiume problem that evening. They probably wouldn't get through
by eleven o'clock; but Lanny had been working faithfully, and felt
justified in asking to be excused at five minutes before the hour.
Wrapped in his warm trench overcoat, which had a detachable
sheepskin lining, and wearing a waterproof hat against the driving

rain, the youth strolled out of the hotel, across the wide avenue, and past the great gun which Kurt had once used to blow entrenchments and poilus to Kingdom Come. The German officer came from the other direction and fell in beside him, and they walked between the rows of monstrous engines rusting in the rain. "Well, Kurt?" said Lanny, seeing that his friend didn't speak at once.

"I have no right to call on you," said the other, at last. "But I'm in danger, and I thought you might wish to know it."

"What is it?"

"The police have raided the group with whom I have been working. I went last night to the place where I stay. I always make it a practice to walk on the other side of the street, looking for a window signal indicating that everything is all right. I saw a police van drawn up in front and they were taking people out of the house. I walked on, and I've been walking the streets most of the time since. I don't know any place to go."

Lanny didn't need to be told how serious this danger was. "Have you any reason to think the police know about you?"

"How can I tell what they know? I'm sure my leader won't talk, and we never kept any papers in the place. But one can never be sure what has happened in this business."

"I've been watching the newspapers. There's been nothing in them."

"The police would surely not make anything public about spies."

"How long have you been at this work, Kurt?"

"Only since the armistice. I got into it because of you."

"Of *me*?"

"My father has a friend in Switzerland—the man who used to forward my letters to you. After the armistice he asked me to come and see him. He told me he had been doing government work, and offered me an important duty to help the Fatherland. I accepted."

"How many others of your people know about you?"

"I don't know for certain. The other side may have had a spy among us. It's the attempt on Clemenceau that has stirred them up, of course."

"You must tell me the truth about that, Kurt. It's been worrying me a lot."

"What do you mean?"

"Whether you had anything to do with that attack."

"Oh, my God, Lanny! What put that idea into your head?"

"Well, I have realized that you are trying to stir up revolt here. And it's fair to assume that some of your agents would be in touch with people like that anarchist."

"I don't know whether they are or not, Lanny, but, granting it, we have nothing to gain by such an attempt. It has set us back, it may have ruined everything. I assure you my associates are not fools. Would they want to put Poincaré in power?"

"I can have your word of honor, Kurt, that you and your people had nothing to do with that attack?"

"You have that absolutely."

"It's a mighty serious matter for me, you know."

"I understand that fully. That's why I walked the streets all day, trying to make up my mind to call upon you. I'm not sure that I have the right to, and if you decline to touch the matter, I'll not blame you."

"I want to help you, Kurt, and I will."

"You know what would happen if you were caught aiding an enemy agent."

"I'm willing to take a chance on that—provided I know that neither you nor your friends have been destroying life or property."

"The truth is, Lanny, I have no idea what they did before the armistice. I suppose they were doing everything they could to help the Fatherland. But now they are trying to soften the French government by promoting political opposition. We have such troubles to deal with at home, and why shouldn't the French have their share?"

"That's all right with me," said the French-American, with a grin.

X

They had come to the embankment of the Seine, and were walking along the *quais*, close together, talking low, with wind and pelting rain to absorb their voices. When a passer-by came, they fell silent until he was gone. Lanny was thinking busily: "What shall I do? Kurt can't stay out on a night like this." Already the rain was turning to sleet.

"Let's get down to the problem," he said. "I can't take you to my rooms, because I share them with two other fellows. I can't take you to my uncle, because the police may have him already."

"That is true."

"Wherever we go, we'll have to take somebody into our confidence. It wouldn't be decent to introduce you under a false name. One can't play a trick like that on one's friends."

"I suppose not."

"I believe Mrs. Chattersworth would be sympathetic, but she has so much company, and you'd have to meet people, otherwise the servants would think it strange."

"The servants will make trouble anywhere."

"I might get a car and drive you down to Juan; but the servants know you, and have heard my mother and me talking about you during the war."

"That's out."

"I thought of Isadora Duncan, who's in Paris. She's an internationalist and has queer people around her all the time. But the trouble is, she's irresponsible. They say she's drinking—the war just about drove her crazy."

There was a pause while he thought some more. "I believe our best guess is my mother. She's not very good at keeping secrets, but she'd surely keep this one because it means danger for me also."

"Where is she?"

"In an apartment in a small hotel. Most of the time she's invited out to meals, but she has breakfast sent to her rooms. She has no servant except a maid, and could find some excuse to get rid of her. That's the one way I can think of to get you hidden."

"But, Lanny, would your mother be willing to have a strange man in her apartment?"

"You aren't a stranger; you're my friend, and my mother knows how dear you are to me. It would be inconvenient, of course; but it's a matter of life or death."

"But don't you see, Lanny—the hotel people would be sure that she had a lover. There couldn't be any other assumption."

"They don't pay so much attention to that in Paris; and Beauty knows what it is to be gossiped about. You see, she lived with Marcel for years before they were married. All her friends know that story, and you might as well know it too."

"I only saw your mother for a few hours, Lanny, but I thought she was a wonderful person."

"She's been through a lot since then, and it's left her sort of distracted and at loose ends. She's only recently got reconciled to the idea that she's never going to see her husband again. Now she's figuring how the world may be persuaded to recognize his genius. He really had it, Kurt."

The gusts of icy rain were blowing into their faces from across the river, and Lanny turned into a side street. "The hotel is up here," he said.

"You mean to take me there without telling her?"

"I'll phone and make sure she's alone. She won't want you left out in this rain, that I know. Tomorrow the three of us will have to figure out some way to get you out of France."

31

In the Enemy's Country

I

PRESIDENT WILSON was back in the United States, taking up the heaviest of all his burdens, that of persuading the American people to accept his League of Nations. He had wrought them into a mood of military fervor, and the war had ended too suddenly. In the November elections, a few days before the armistice, they had chosen a majority of reactionary Republicans, determined to have no more nonsense about idealism but to think about America first, last, and all the time. President Wilson invited the opposition chieftains to a dinner party, and they came, but neither good food nor moral fervor moved them from their surly skepticism. Wilson had, so he told the world, a "one-track mind." Now he was traveling on that track, and the Senate leaders were digging a wide and deep ditch at the end of it.

Of course the election results were known in Paris, and were one of the factors undermining the President's position. Both Lloyd George and Clemenceau had consulted their people and had their full consent to the program of "making Germany pay." Their newspapers were taunting the American President with the fact that his people were not behind him; now they printed the news about his failures in Washington, and on that basis went ahead to remake the world nearer to their hearts' desire.

Already they had fourteen little wars going—one for each of the Fourteen Points, said Professor Alston, bitterly. They were getting ready for the really big war, the Allied invasion of Russia. The blockade was screwed down tighter than ever; the Allies refused to lift it even from Poland and the new state of Czechoslovakia, for fear that supplies might get into Germany, or that Red agents might get out through the *cordon sanitaire*.

Clemenceau got out of his sick bed and resumed his place in command of the conference. He sat slumped in his chair, a pitiful, shrunken figure—but try to take anything from under his claws, and hear the Tiger snarl! This statesman aged in bitterness had performed a strange mental feat, transferring all that he had of love to an abstraction called *la patrie*. Individual Frenchmen he despised, along with all other human creatures; he humiliated and browbeat his subordinates in public, and poured the acid of his wit upon the pretense of idealism in any person in public life. But France was glory, France was God, and for her safety he was willing to destroy everything else in Europe and indeed in the world.

Colonel House was representing the President. The "little white mouse" didn't have a one-track mind, and hadn't come to Europe unprepared; he knew the age-long hatreds which made life a torment on that continent. He was trying to placate and persuade, and was sending long cablegrams to his chief about his great failures and his small successes. The staff at the Crillon watched and whispered, and the hundred and fifty registered newspaper correspondents from America hung about on the outskirts, gathering rumors and sending long wireless messages about secret covenants being secretly arrived at.

II

Meanwhile Lanny was taking all the time his chief could spare to run over to his mother's hotel and try to solve the embarrassing problem of his German friend. First he had the bright idea that Jerry Pendleton was the trustworthy person who would take this charge of dynamite off his hands. Jerry was going back to his regiment; surely he could take with him a Swiss musician friend, and find some pretext, a concert or something, to get him into Koblenz. Let him entertain the regiment! After that it would be easy for him to disappear into Germany, for the American lines were loosely held and peasants and others came freely into Koblenz.

Lanny even worked up a likely story for the lieutenant to tell about how he had met this musician; he phoned to the Hotel du Pavillon—one of the "Y" shelters, where Jerry had been staying—and to his vexation learned that his friend had departed, leaving no address. Next morning came a post card marked Cannes. After all that scolding at the French, and all those doubts and fears, Jerry had gone running off to his girl!

Lanny's mother wasn't surprised. Lovers were like that, she declared: full of agonies and uncertainties, embarrassments and extravagances, impulses and remorses; quarreling bitterly, parting forever, and making it up next day. You just couldn't tell what unlikely sort of partner anyone would pick, or what crazy thing he or she would do. Lanny could understand that a man who had been drilled and disciplined for a year and a half, and had fought through one of the greatest battles in history, was apt to be restless and moody—and very much in need of feminine society.

Lanny sent his friend a telegram: "Don't fail to see me before you return to duties." A couple of days later he was bowled flat by a letter from the lieutenant, saying that he was never going to return to his duties, and that Uncle Sam could come and get him if and when he could find him. Jerry was going to marry his Cerise, and settle down to helping run a boarding house without boarders. "Tell those old buzzards to hurry up and sign the peace," said the ex-tutor from Kansas, "so that tourists can begin coming back to the Riviera!"

Lanny was much worried about this, for he knew that desertion in wartime was a serious matter. He took occasion to bring up the subject with one of the military men at the Crillon, and learned that the army had been severe with the A.W.O.L.'s at the outset, but was becoming less so every day as a matter of sheer necessity. Men who had submitted cheerfully to the draft now considered that their duty was done, and wanted to go home before some other

fellow got their girls and their jobs; there were so many deserters
in Paris that the M.P.'s couldn't bring them in nor the guardhouses
hold them. Lanny wrote his friend for heaven's sake to take off his
uniform and not show himself in public places until after the peace
was signed. Then, presumably, the army would go home and forget
him!

Lanny and his mother had also discussed Johannes Robin, prosperous speculator in cast-off armaments. He journeyed frequently
to Paris and other places; surely he must know persons at the border, and could arrange to import a competent Swiss musician to
play duets with his son! Lanny composed a nice sociable letter, telling the news about himself and his parents, and saying that he
hoped to see Mr. Robin when he came to the city, and did he have
any plans to come? So tactful was this letter that Mr. Robin
missed the point and replied even more sociably, telling how happy
his whole family was to hear from Lanny, and all about what they
were doing and thinking. Only at the end did he mention that he
had no plans to come to Paris just now, but that when he did,
Lanny would be sure to hear from him. What Lanny said was:
"Damn!"

III

On account of her secret "house guest," Madame Detaze was
compelled to receive her friends in the parlor of the hotel, a circumstance which sooner or later was bound to awaken their curiosity. Only two persons, her brother and her son, were accustomed
to come up unannounced; the next afternoon, when Lanny entered
his mother's drawing room, he found his Uncle Jesse seated there.
Kurt wasn't visible, so Lanny assumed that he must be hidden in
Beauty's boudoir. The youth couldn't get away from the feeling
that he was playing a part in a stage comedy. Suppose the German
captain of artillery should happen to be seized by a fit of coughing
or sneezing—there would be quite a job of explaining to Beauty's
brother!

But this calamity did not befall. With more than one of his twisted smiles the brother told about his adventures with the agents of the Sûreté Générale, who had descended upon him within a couple of hours after the attack upon Clemenceau. Jesse hadn't heard about the incident, and was caught with a letter half-written on his table—fortunately it dealt with American affairs! The police took him to the Préfecture and gave him a grilling, threatening among other things to expel him from the country. The painter had taken a high stand, declaring that this would make more propaganda than he could achieve by a hundred speeches.

"They wanted to know about my sister and my nephew," added Jesse. "I gather that few things would please them more than to be able to tie the Crillon up with the attempt on Clemenceau."

"They all think we're pro-German," replied the youth. "Or at any rate they say they do."

Beauty had been told about the *réunion*, so Lanny was free to ask his uncle: "Do you know that fellow Cottin?"

"Never heard of him," was the reply. "I don't go much with anarchists. It's my judgment they nearly always have a screw loose."

Lanny had been taught by his father that all varieties of Reds were in that condition. Said he: "Do you remember a young workingman who came onto the platform at the meeting and shook hands with you?"

"There were several who did that."

"This one talked to you and you patted him on the back."

"Probably he was praising my speech," said Uncle Jesse. "If so, I liked him."

"Don't you remember one who wore corduroys?"

The painter searched his memory. "I believe I do. A rather frail chap, looking as if he'd been sick?"

"That was Cottin."

Jesse exhibited astonishment—and his nephew watched him closely. Was it genuine, or was it good acting? No doubt many comrades of the young anarchist were forgetting him just now. Distrust of his uncle had been so deeply ground into Lanny's mind that he was never sure if any of the painter's emotions were genuine.

Beauty interrupted the drama with some remark about the wickedness of shooting that poor old man who was doing so much for France. This caused her brother to turn upon her with what certainly seemed a genuine emotion. He said that attempts at assassination were foolish, because they didn't accomplish the purpose desired; but so far as wickedness was concerned, how about statesmen and diplomats who had caused the murder of ten million innocent persons and the destruction of three hundred billions of dollars' worth of property? And what were you going to say about bureaucrats and politicians who left the poor to stand in line for hours waiting for a chance to buy a few scraps of half-spoiled food at twice the prices charged before the war?

Jesse Blackless was started on the same speech he had made at the meeting. He told about food rotting in warehouses at Le Havre and Marseille, about freight cars rusting idle—and all because speculators reaped fortunes out of every increase in prices. "What does it mean to you that the cost of living in Paris has doubled, and that some foods cost five or six times as much? All you have to do is to ask Robbie for another check."

"I assure you you're mistaken," said Beauty, spunkily—for she had had plenty of practice quarreling with her brother. "I've lost ten pounds since I came to Paris."

"Well, it's probably due to dancing all night, not to going hungry. I don't go into the smart restaurants, but I pass them and see they're crowded all night with bemedaled men and half-naked women."

"That's because Paris is so full of strangers. People sit packed at the tables so that they haven't room to move their elbows."

"Well, they manage to get the food. But the people I know haven't tasted a morsel of sugar in four years, and now they stand in the rain and snow for hours for a loaf of bread or a basket of fuel. Is it any more wicked to kill a cynical old politician than to starve a million women and children so that they die of anemia or pneumonia?"

IV

Jesse Blackless went on in this strain until he saw that he was hurting his sister without helping his cause. Then he remembered that he had come to advise her on the subject of the exhibition of her late husband's paintings. He calmed down, and said that he had been thinking the matter over, and it would be better to wait until peace had been signed, when the newspapers would have more space to devote to painting. June would be a good month; the elderly vultures could hardly take that long to pick the bones of the German carcass. When Beauty answered that she couldn't stay away from Baby Marceline, Jesse advised her to go home and come back. When she said she wanted to be with Lanny, her brother said that her problems were too complicated for any man to solve.

He arose to take his departure, signing to Lanny to follow him. In the passage he said: "My comrades have got the habit of coming to me for funds, and I don't know what to tell them. Is your friend coming again?" What a sensation Lanny could have made if he had said that the friend had been in the adjoining room!

Having seen his uncle out of the building, Lanny went back and found Kurt talking to his mother. Kurt had heard the conversation, and made up his mind that he was no longer going to impose upon Beauty's too great kindness. "You try to hide your fears," he said; "but I know what a scandal it would make if the police were to arrest me here. I'm ashamed of myself for having stayed so long."

"You may be going to your death," protested Beauty.

"The worst of the storm has blown over. And anyhow it's wartime, and I'm a soldier."

There was another reason, which Lanny could guess. Kurt had written a letter to Switzerland and Lanny had mailed it for him. Now it was time for a reply to be at *poste restante*, and there was no keeping Kurt from going for it. "The letter will tell me a new place to report," said he, "and no one else must take the risk of getting it."

He thanked his two friends, and it was the old Kurt speaking, the man of conscience and exalted feelings. "I told you, Lanny, that life is a dedication; but neither of us knew how soon we'd have to prove it."

There were tears in Beauty's eyes. The poor soul was sending another man away to death! She was living again the partings with Marcel; and the fact that Kurt was fighting on the other side made no difference whatever. "Oh, God!" she exclaimed. "Will there never come a time on this earth when men stop killing one another?"

She tried to keep Lanny in the apartment, and he knew what that meant. The police might be waiting in the lobby of the hotel, and would get both of them! Lanny said: "I won't go very far; just escort him outside and make it respectable!"

What Lanny wanted was to deliver his uncle's message to Kurt; also to follow him at a safe distance and make sure of what happened at the post office. He watched his friend receive a letter and put it into his pocket and walk away. Lanny went to a telephone and told his mother that all was well. Then he returned to his safe job of trying to stop the fourteen little wars and one big one.

V

The Supreme Council decided to go ahead and complete the treaty with Germany, and ordered all the various commissions to deliver their reports and recommendations within a few days. That meant rush times for geographers, and also for secretaries and translators. Professor Alston's French was now equal to all demands, and Lanny's geography had improved to such an extent that he could pretty nearly substitute for his chief. There was work enough for both, and they hurried from place to place with briefcases and portfolios. A fascinating game they were playing, or rather a whole series of games—like the chess exhibitions in which some expert keeps a dozen contests in his head at the same time. In this case the chessboards were provinces and the pawns were national minorities comprising millions of human beings. Some games you were winning and some you were losing, and each was a series of surprises. At lunchtime and at dinner you compared notes with your colleagues; a busy chatter was poured out with the coffee, and human hopes were burned up with the cigarettes.

On the whole it was exhilarating, and contributed to the sense of importance of gentlemen whose domains had hitherto been classrooms with a score or two of undergraduates. Now they were playing parts in the great world. Their names were known; visitors sought them out; newspaper reporters waylaid them in lobbies and begged them for news. What a delicious thrill it gave to the nineteen-year-old Lanny Budd to say: "Really, Mr. Thompson, I'm not supposed to say anything about that; but if you will be careful not to indicate the source of your authority, I don't mind telling you that the French are setting their war damages at two hundred billion dollars, and of course we consider that preposterous. Colonel House has said that they play with billions the way children play with wooden blocks. There's no sense in it, because the Germans can never pay such sums."

When Lanny talked like this he wasn't being presumptuous, as you might imagine; rather he was following a policy and a technique. Over a period of two months and a half the experts had observed that confidential information leaked quickly to the French press whenever it was something to French advantage; the same was the case with the British—and now the Americans also were learning to have "leaks." Trusted newspapermen had found out where to come for tips, and would carefully keep secret the sources of their treasures.

Lanny didn't even have to have explicit instructions. He would hear his chief say to some colleague: "It mightn't be a bad thing if the American people were to know that one of the great powers is proposing to get rid of a large stock of rancid pork by selling it to the Germans and replacing it with fresh pork from America." Going out for a walk Lanny would run into Mr. Thompson of the Associated Press, and they would stroll together, and next day a carefully guarded secret of state would be read at twenty million American breakfast tables. A howl of protest would echo back to Paris, and Lanny's chief would remark to his colleague: "Well, that story got out, it seems! I don't know how it happened, but I can't say I'm sorry."

VI

In such ways the youth was kept so busy day and night that he had little time to think about his German friend. Beauty called up to ask if he had any news, and Lanny understood that his tender-hearted mother had taken another human fate into her keeping and had a new set of fears to mar her enjoyment of fashionable life in La Ville Lumière. Lanny made note how little politics really meant to a woman. Beauty had been an ardent pacifist so long as she was hoping to keep Marcel away from the fighting; she had been a French patriot so long as that seemed the way to get the war over; now, tormented by the image of Lanny's friend being stood against a wall and shot, she was for letting bygones be bygones and giving the German babies food.

The youth didn't have time to call upon his uncle, but he got a little note saying: "Your friend called again. Thanks." That seemed to indicate that Kurt had got in touch with his organization and was carrying on as usual.

At one of the luncheons in the Crillon, Lanny met Captain Stratton, and brought up the subject of the spread of discontent in Paris. The intelligence officer said it was a truly alarming situation: a succession of angry strikes, and protest meetings every night in the working-class districts; incendiary speeches being made, and the city plastered with *affiches* containing all the standard Bolshevik demands—immediate peace, the lifting of the blockade, food for the workers, and the suppression of speculators.

"Aren't those all reasonable demands?" asked Alston; and so came another installment of the controversy among the staff. The young captain said the demands might be reasonable enough, taken by themselves, but they were mere camouflage for efforts to overthrow the French government and seize the factories and the banks.

"But why not grant the reasonable demands?" asked Lanny's chief. "Wouldn't that weaken the hands of the agitators and strip off their camouflage?"

"That's outside my province," replied the other. "My job is to find out who the agitators are and keep track of what they're plotting."

The stoutish and pugnacious Professor Davisson broke in. "My guess is you'll find they're operating with German gold."

"That's what we assume," replied the other. "But it's not easy to prove."

Said Alston: "My opinion is, you'll find that German gold in the eye of Maurras and his royalists. The French masses are suffering and they have every reason in the world to complain and to agitate."

Lanny smiled to himself. His chief called himself a "liberal," and Lanny had been trying to make up his mind just what that meant. He decided that a liberal was a high-minded gentleman who believed the world was made in his own image. But unfortunately only one small part of it was deserving of such trust. He had been looking for such a spot, and the only one he had found was the tiny country of Denmark, whose delegates had come to the conference determined not to take on any racial minorities. Others were trying hard to persuade them to accept a chunk of Germany down to the Kiel canal; but they would have no land of which the population was not preponderantly Danish—and they would insist upon a plebiscite before they took even that. If only the whole of Europe had been "liberal" according to that formula, how simple all the problems would have been!

VII

President Wilson returned to Paris in the middle of March, one month after his leaving. There were no tumultuous receptions this time; the various peoples of the world had learned that he wouldn't give them what they wanted, and couldn't if he would. He came a beaten man; for the expiring Congress had left unpassed three vital appropriation bills, in order to make certain that he would have to summon a special session of the new Congress. He arrived at a Peace Conference which had laid all his Fourteen Points on the shelf, and also its own resolution of seven weeks earlier, whereby the Covenant of the League of Nations was to become a part of the peace treaty.

Wilson set his long Presbyterian jaw and went into a three-hour conference with the two head malefactors, Clemenceau and Lloyd George. When he came out from it he gave out a statement to the effect that the Covenant was a vital part of the treaty and would remain in. Then what a steaming and stewing, a bubbling and boiling of diplomatic kettles! Pichon, French Foreign Minister, issued a declaration to the effect that the Covenant would not have any place in the treaty; and when the reporters asked him about President Wilson's statement, he said he hadn't heard of it. There was a great scandal, and Clemenceau was forced to "throw down" his foreign minister and stop the publication of his communiqué. Then Lord Robert Cecil gave out a statement supporting Wilson's side, and the clamor of the Tories forced Lloyd George to throw him down. So it went, back and forth; those elderly gentlemen met and argued until they were sick of the sound of one another's voices. The shrill clamor penetrated to the attachés outside, and caused them to look at one another with anxious faces, or perhaps with mischievous grins.

The "Big Four" were meeting by themselves now, resolved to push things through and get done. A more oddly assorted quartet of bedfellows had rarely been chosen by political fate. Woodrow Wilson was a stiff and grave person, of principles which he held as divinely ordained. He kept his sense of humor for his private life; in public it was his function to deliver eloquent discourses in favor of righteousness, and at this there was no one in the world to rival him. He brought his great talent to every session and exercised it upon Georges Clemenceau, who sat hunched in his chair with eyes closed, the picture of agonized boredom; every few minutes the Tiger would open his heavy-lidded eyes and reply with any one of half a dozen French words, the equivalent of four-letter English words which every guttersnipe knew, but which few had ever seen in print.

This form of political argument was something hitherto inconceivable to the Presbyterian professor. He had been brought up to the idea that scholar and gentleman formed an inseparable combination; but here was a scholar who was perfectly content to be a blackguard and a rascal. His political career had been that of a Tammany Hall boss—so Robbie Budd had told his son. As Lanny didn't know much about New York City's political history, the father explained that forceful men of the people went into politics, their hearts bleeding for the wrongs of the poor; so they collected votes and built up a political machine, which they used to blackmail their way to fortune.

The Tiger, now seventy-eight, had seen a great deal of the world, but here was a phenomenon the like of which he had never encountered: a politician who in the presence of other politicians pretended to mean what he said in his speeches! At first Clemenceau had found it absolutely infuriating; he had raged and stormed, and there was a dreadful story going the rounds that he had struck the President in the face and that Lloyd George had had to separate them. You met people who declared that they knew this story was true; but how did they know it? Others reported that as the battles of the Big Four went on, the Tiger began to take a humorous attitude; at the end he had actually grown fond of this odd phenomenon, as one might of some human freak, a man with two heads or four arms.

The mediator in the battle was Lloyd George, one of those superpoliticians who could be on both sides of every question. Lloyd George had begun as "a little squirt of a Welsh lawyer," friend of the people and a terrifying demagogue. When he got power he had kept it by the device of selling titles of nobility to beer barons, press lords, and South African diamond kings. In his recent "khaki election" he had become the slave of a Tory majority, and he swung back and forth between what they told him to do and what he thought would please the public. He was gay and personally charming, and possessed what was called a "mercurial temperament"—meaning that he didn't mind saying the opposite of what he had said yesterday, if in the meantime he had found that he was in danger of losing votes. In this he was the twin brother of Orlando, the Italian Premier, a good-looking and amiable old gentleman whose one thought in all issues was to gain some advantage, however tiny, for his native land.

VIII

A terrifying world in which this duel of wills went on. The war upon the Soviets was continuing on a dozen fronts, but without notable success. A Red Hungary had been added to a Red Bavaria and an almost Red Berlin. The Poles were fighting the Ukrainians for the possession of Lemberg. The Italians were threatening to withdraw from the conference unless they were permitted to fight the Yugoslavs for the possession of Fiume. The Armenians were in Paris demanding freedom from the Turks, and the Turks were trying to settle the problem by killing the last Armenian before a decision could be reached. Not one, not a dozen, but a hundred problems like that, all being dinned into the ears of four bewildered and exhausted old men.

They wrangled over the question of Danzig and the proposed Polish Corridor to the sea. They decided it, and then, when the clamor rose louder, they undecided it and referred it back to the commission. So geographers and ethnographers and their assistants were summoned once more, and Lanny Budd lugged his portfolios into the high-ceilinged, overheated conference rooms at the Quai d'Orsay, and stood behind his chief for hours—there being not enough chairs for secretaries and translators. Lanny couldn't help but feel grave, for there was a consensus among the American experts that here was where the next war would start.

The real purpose of that corridor had by now become clear to all; the French were determined to put a barrier between German manufacturing power and Russian raw materials, which, if combined, might dominate Europe. So give the Poles access to the sea by driving a wedge through Germany, with Danzig for a port. But the trouble was that Danzig was a German city, and the proposed corridor was inhabited by more than two millions of that race. When this was brought to President Wilson's attention, he produced a report from Professor Alston, pointing out that this district had been Polish, but had been deliberately "colonized" by the Germans, by the method so well known in Europe of making the former inhabitants so miserable that they emigrated. At a conference with his advisers President Wilson said that this appeared to be a case where one principle conflicted with another principle.

Alston reported this remark to Lanny, and the youth asked questions of his chief. Could two principles be principles when they contradicted each other? Apparently it was necessary for men to have such moral maxims; but there would seem to be something wrong when they betrayed you in an emergency. The highly conscientious gentlemen at the Crillon racked their brains for some way to prevent fighting in that corridor. Most of the scholars were inclined to sympathize with the Poles—perhaps on account of Kosciuszko, and because in their youth they had read a novel called *Thaddeus of Warsaw*. But, alas, their sympathies were weakened by the fact that the Poles were carrying on dreadful pogroms against the Jews; and if they were that sort of people, what were the chances for the two million Germans of the corridor? The time was out of joint: O cursèd spite, that ever college professors were born to set it right!

BOOK SIX

They Shall Reap the Whirlwind

32

I Have Seen the Future

I

PARIS was dancing. It was a mania that had seized all "society"; in hotels and cafés, in private drawing rooms, wherever men and women met, they spent their time locked in one another's arms, swaying and jiggling this way and that. These modern dances seemed to have been invented to spare the necessity of any skill, any art; if you knew how to walk, if you were sober enough so that you could stagger, then you could dance, and you did.

Lanny didn't have much time for diversion, but his mother went out now and then, and when he called on her, she would tell about her adventures. More than once she had left the room because of disgusting things she had witnessed. Beauty's world seemed to be coming to an end; that world of grace and charm for which she had spent so many years equipping herself. She had learned all the rules—and the result was she was out of date. Men no longer wanted coquetry or subtlety, elegance, even intelligence; they wanted young females to hug, and that was too cheap and easy, in the opinion of Beauty. She said that apparently the real horrors of war didn't begin until it was over.

Her old friends were scattered. Sophie, Baroness de la Tourette, had lost her lover in the last dreadful fighting on the Marne, and had gone back to visit her relatives in Ohio. Margy Eversham-Watson was at her country place in Sussex, his lordship having been struck with a bad attack of gout. Edna Hackabury, now Mrs. Fitz-Laing, was on the Riviera, waiting for her husband to return from a military expedition in the Near East. All these persons were unhappy in one way or another, and Beauty, who craved pleasure

as a sunflower craves the light, seemed as if trying to flee from her
world. A horrible world! She told Lanny how, sitting at dinner
next to Premier Orlando, that genial statesman had declared himself
displeased that so lovely a woman had waited eighteen years between children. In his family it was different, he gravely assured her;
his wife never got up from her accouchement bed without being
pregnant again.

More and more she was coming to rely upon Emily Chattersworth, a tower of strength in times such as these. Emily had money
enough and force of will enough to make a world of her own. Emily
had learned the rules, and persons who didn't know them and obey
them got no share of her hospitality. In her home you met intellectual people and heard serious talk of the problems of the day, as
well as of literature and art and music. Beauty would remark sadly
that she was coming to an age where it was necessary for her to
be intellectual; she would go to one of Emily's soirees, and listen
while more brilliant persons talked, and come home and tell Lanny
whom she had met and what compliments they had paid her.

Lanny accompanied her when he could find time. He realized
that Mrs. Emily was performing an important service in bringing
people together in gracious ways. When the American delegates
and advisers met the French, it was always for business, and too frequently the discussions ended with bitterness. But in the drawing
room of a woman of the world they could discuss the same problems with urbanity and humor; their shrewd hostess would be
watching, ready to help the conversation past a dangerous corner.
Here the women came; and the Americans found it easier to like
the French when they met their women.

Mrs. Emily was fond of Lanny Budd, who from childhood had
learned to behave in a drawing room. She considered him extraor-
dinarily fortunate in his present role, and permitted him to bring
members of the staff to her affairs without special invitation, an
honor she granted to few. She came to have lunch with his friends
at the Crillon, and this too was a distinction. Professor Alston remarked that many women had money, but few knew how to use it;

if there were more persons like Emily Chattersworth in the world there wouldn't be so many like Jesse Blackless.

II

The British and the French were taking unto themselves those portions of Asia Minor which had oil, phosphates, and other treasures, or through which oil pipelines had to travel to the sea. Since the Fourteen Points had guaranteed the inhabitants of these lands the mastery of their own destinies, the subtle statesmen had racked their vocabularies to find some way of taking what they wanted while seeming not to. They had evolved a new word, or rather a new meaning for an old word, which was "mandate." The scholars at the Crillon had an anecdote with which to divert their minds from sorrowful contemplations. Some diplomat newly arrived in Paris had inquired: "What's going to be done about New Guinea and the Pacific islands?" and the answer was: "They are to be administered by mandatories." "Who is Mandatories?" inquired the newcomer.

Mister Mandatories—or was it Lord Mandatories?—was going to take over Syria and Palestine and Iraq, the Hejaz and Yemen and the rest of those hot lands which had been promised to the people of the young Emir Feisal. The brown replica of Christ had taken off his multicolored silk robes, his turban and veil, and put on the ugliest of black morning coats, in the hope of impressing the Peace Conference with his civilized condition—but all in vain. Behind the scenes Grand Officer Zaharoff had spoken, and Clemenceau was obeying; Henri Deterding, master of Royal Dutch Shell, had spoken, and Lloyd George was obeying.

One portion of the former Turkish empire had no oil or other mineral treasures of consequence; it had only peasants, who were being slaughtered daily by Turkish soldiers, as they had been off and on, mostly on, for ages. To stop this slaughter there was needed another Mandatory—a kind, idealistic, high-minded Mandatory, who cared nothing about oil nor yet about pipelines, but who loved

poor peasants and the simple life. The British and French brought
forward a proposal in the name of humanity and democracy: an
elderly gentleman named Uncle Samuel Mandatory was to take
charge of Armenia, and doughboys singing "Onward, Christian Soldiers" would drive out the Turks and keep them out.

This proposal was sprung, and President Wilson promised to consider it and give his decision promptly. There was a rush call to the
staff for everything they had on Armenia, and a hundred reports
on history, geography, language, population, resources, production,
trade, government, had to be dug out and read, digested, summarized,
headlined, so that a busy statesman could get the whole thing in his
mind in ten minutes' reading. Professor Alston had to do his part,
and Lanny had to help—which was the reason he missed a musical
evening at Mrs. Emily's town house.

Beauty attended; and shortly before midnight she telephoned her
son at the hotel. "Lanny, the most amazing thing has happened."

He knew from the tone of her voice that she was upset. "What
is it?"

"I can't tell you over the phone. You must come here."

"But I'm not through with my job."

"Isn't it something that can wait till morning?"

"It's for the Big Boss himself."

"Well, I must see you. I'll wait up."

"Any danger?" His first thought, of course, was of Kurt.

"Don't try to talk now. Come when you can."

III

So Lanny rather stinted the Armenians, and maybe let more of
them die. So many poor peasants were dying, in so many parts of the
world—there came a time when one just gave up. He omitted from
his report some of the Armenian charges and some of the Turkish
admissions, and slipped into his big trench coat, ran downstairs, and
hopped into a taxi.

His fair blond mother was waiting in one of those bright-colored silk dressing gowns from China—this time large golden dragons crawling clockwise round her. She had taken to smoking under the strain of the past year, and evidently had done it a lot, for the air in the room was hazy and close. Beauty deserved her name almost as much as formerly, and never more so than when tenderness and concern were in her sweet features. After opening her door she looked into the passage to see if anyone had followed her son, then led him into her boudoir before she spoke.

"Lanny, I met Kurt at Emily's!"

"Oh, my God!" exclaimed the youth.

"The first person I saw, standing at her side."

"Does she know who he is?"

"She thinks he's a musician from Switzerland."

"Who brought him?"

"I didn't ask. I was afraid to seem the least bit curious."

"What was he doing?"

"Meeting influential Frenchmen—at least that's what he told me."

"You had a chance to talk to him?"

"Just a moment or two. When I went in and saw him, I was pretty nearly bowled over. Emily introduced him as M. Dalcroze. Imagine!"

"What did you say?"

"I was afraid my face had betrayed something, so I said: 'It seems to me I have met M. Dalcroze somewhere.' Kurt was perfectly calm—he might have been the sphinx. He said: 'Madame's face does seem familiar to me.' I saw that he meant to carry it off, so I said: 'One meets so many people,' and went on to explain to Emily why you hadn't come."

"And then?"

"Well, I strolled on, and old M. Solicamp came up to me and started talking, and I pretended to listen while I tried to think what to do. But it was too much for me. I just kept quiet and watched Kurt all I could. By and by Emily called on him to play the piano and he did so—very well, I thought."

"Whatever he does he does well."

Beauty went on to name the various persons with whom she had observed their friend in conversation. One was the publisher of one of the great Paris dailies; what could a German expect to accomplish with such a man? Lanny didn't try to answer, because he had never told his mother that Kurt was handling money. She continued: "Toward the end of the evening I was alone with him for just a minute. I said: 'What are you expecting to accomplish here?' He answered: 'Just meeting influential persons.' 'But what for?' 'To get in a word for our German babies. I pledge you my honor that I shall do nothing that can bring harm to our hostess.' That was all we had time for."

"What do you mean to do?"

"I don't see what I can do. If I tell Emily, I am betraying Kurt. If I don't tell her, won't she feel that I've betrayed her?"

"I'm afraid she may, Beauty."

"But she didn't meet Kurt through us."

"She met him because I told him about her, and he found some way to get introduced to her under a false name."

"But she won't ever know that you mentioned her."

"We can't tell what she'll know. We're tying ourselves up in a knot of intrigue and no one can guess what new tangles may develop."

A look of alarm appeared on the mother's usually placid features. "Lanny, you're not thinking that we ought to give Kurt up!"

"Telling Mrs. Emily wouldn't be quite the same as giving him up, would it?"

"But we promised him solemnly that we wouldn't tell a soul!"

"Yes, but we didn't give him permission to go and make use of our friends."

A complicated problem in ethics, and in etiquette too! They discussed it back and forth, without getting very far. Lanny said that Mrs. Emily had expressed herself strongly against the blockade of Germany; she would, no doubt, be deeply sympathetic to what Kurt was doing, even while she might disapprove his methods.

The mother replied: "Yes, but don't you see that if you tell her you make her responsible for the methods. As it is, she's just a rich American lady who's been deceived by a German agent. She's perfectly innocent, and she can say so. But if she knows, it's her duty to report him to the authorities, and she's responsible for what may happen from now on."

Lanny sat with knitted brows. "Don't forget," he remarked, "you're in that position yourself. It ought to worry you."

Said Beauty: "The difference is that I'd be willing to lie about it; but I don't believe Emily would."

IV

When in doubt, do nothing—that seemed to be the wise rule. They had no way to communicate with Kurt, and he didn't make any move to enlighten them. Was he arguing the same way as Beauty, that what they didn't know wouldn't hurt them? It was obvious that in trying to promote pro-German ideas among highly placed persons in Paris he was playing a desperately dangerous game, and the fewer dealings he had with friends the better for the friends.

Many ladies in fashionable society become amateur psychologists, and learn to manipulate one another's minds and to extract information without the other person's knowing what they are after—unless, perchance, the other person has also become an amateur psychologist. Beauty went to see her friend in the morning; and of course it was natural for her to refer to the handsome young pianist, to comment on his skill, and to ask where her friend had come upon him. Emily explained that M. Dalcroze had written that he was a cousin of an old friend in Switzerland who had died several years ago, and that he had come to Paris to study with one of the great masters at the conservatory.

"I asked him to come and play for me," said the kindly hostess. "He's really quite an exceptional person. He plans to be a composer and has studied every instrument in the orchestra—he says that you have to be able to play them if you are going to compose for them."

"How interesting!" said Beauty, and she wasn't fibbing. "Where is he staying?"

"He tells me he's with friends for a few days. He's getting his mail at *poste restante*."

Said the guileless friend: "I only had a chance for a few words with him, but I heard him talking with someone about the blockade of Germany."

"He feels deeply about it. He says it is sowing the seeds of the next war. Of course, being an alien, he can't say much."

"I suppose not."

"It's really a shocking thing, Beauty. The more I hear about it the more indignant I become. I was talking to Mr. Hoover the other day; he has been trying for four months to get permission for a small German fishing fleet to go out into the North Sea—but in vain."

"How perfectly ghastly!" exclaimed Lanny's mother.

"I am wondering if I shouldn't get some influential French people to come here some evening and hear Mr. Hoover tell about what it means to the women and children of Central Europe."

"I've thought of the same idea, Emily. You know Lanny talks about that blockade all the time. The people at the Crillon are so wrought up about it."

"Our French friends just can't bring themselves to realize that the war is over."

"Or perhaps, as Professor Alston says, they're fighting the next one. We women let the men have their way all through, but I really think we ought to have something to say about the peace."

"I know just how you feel," said the grave Mrs. Emily, who had had Beauty weeping on her shoulder more than once during the days of Marcel's long-drawn-out agony.

"Let's you and me take it up, Emily, and make them let those women and children have food!" It was farther than Beauty had meant to go when she set out on this visit; but something in the deeps of her consciousness rose up unexpectedly. A woman with a loving nature may try her best to dance and be merry while other women are bearing dead babies, and while living babies are growing up with twisted skeletons; but all of a sudden comes a rush of feeling from some unknown place and she finds herself exclaiming, to her own surprise: "Let's do something!"

V

The discussions among the four elder statesmen were continuing day and night and reaching a new pitch of intensity. They were dealing with questions which directly concerned France; and the French are an intense people—especially where land or money is involved. There was one strip of land which was precious to the French beyond any price: the left bank of the river Rhine, which would save them from the terror which haunted every man, woman, and child in the nation. They wanted the Rhineland; they were determined to have it, and nothing could move them; they could argue about it day and night, forever and forever, world without end; they never wearied—and they never gave up.

Also they demanded the Sarre, with its valuable coal mines, to make up for those which the Germans had deliberately destroyed. The French had suffered all this bitter winter; other winters were coming, and who were going to suffer—the French, or the Germans who had invaded France, blown towns and cities to dust and rubble, carried away machinery and flooded mines? The French army held both the Sarre and the Rhineland, and General Foch was omnipresent at the Peace Conference, imploring, scolding, threatening, even refusing to obey Clemenceau, his civilian chief, when he saw signs of weakening on this point upon which the future of *la patrie* depended.

The British Prime Minister very generously took the side of the American President in this controversy. Alston said it was astonishing how reasonable Lloyd George could be when it was a question of concessions to be made by France. England was getting Mesopotamia and Palestine, Egypt and the German colonies; Australia was getting German New Guinea, and South Africa was getting

German Southwest Africa. All this had been arranged by the help of the blessed word "mandatory," plus the word "protectorate" in the case of Egypt. But where was the blessed word that would enable the French to fortify the west bank of the Rhine? That was not to be found in any English dictionary.

Lanny got an amusing illustration of the British attitude through his friend Fessenden, a youth who was gracious and likable, and infected with "advanced" ideas. Lanny had been meeting Fessenden off and on for a couple of months, and they had become one of many channels through which the British and Americans exchanged confidences. Among a hundred other questions about which they chatted was the island of Cyprus, which Britain had "formally" taken over from Turkey early in the war. What were they going to do with it? "Self-determination of all peoples," ran the "advanced" formula; so of course the people of Cyprus would be asked to whom they wished to belong. Young Fessenden had been quite sure that this would be done; but gradually he became less so, and the time came when he avoided the subject. When it became apparent that the island was "annexed" for good, young Fessenden in a burst of friendship confessed to Lanny that he had mentioned the matter to his chief and had been told to stop talking nonsense. If the British let the question of "self-determination" be raised, what would become of Gibraltar, and of Hong Kong, and of India? A young man who wanted to have a diplomatic career had better get revolutionary catchwords out of his head.

VI

Such was the atmosphere in which Mrs. Emily Chattersworth and her friend Beauty Detaze set out to change French opinion on the subject of the blockade. They had resolved upon getting persons influential in French society to gather in Mrs. Emily's drawing room and hear an appeal from Mr. Herbert Hoover, who had been in charge of Belgian relief and now had been put in charge of all relief by the Supreme Council. The persons whom Mrs. Emily planned to invite were many of them intimate friends, frequenters of her salon for years; but when she broached this proposal to them, they were embarrassed, and certain that it couldn't be done.

They would start to explain to her, and it would turn into an argument. The blockade was cruel, no doubt, but all war was cruel, and this was part of the war. The Germans hadn't signed the peace, and the blockade was a weapon to make them sign; so the army chiefs said, and in wartime a nation took the advice of its general staff. Yes, it might be that German babies were dying; but how many French babies had died in the war, and how many French widows would have no more babies as a result of the German invasion? The famous critic who had been Mrs. Emily's lover for a decade or more told her that every German baby was either a future invader of France, or else a mother of future invaders of France; and when he saw the look of dismay on her face he told her to be careful, that she was falling victim to German propaganda. It didn't make any difference whether one got this propaganda direct from Germans, or from Americans who had been infected with it across the seas.

Such was the mood of the people of France. Those two or three friends who were sympathetic told Mrs. Emily that her action would be misunderstood, and that her future career as a *salonnière* would be jeopardized. As soon as the treaty was signed something would doubtless be done; but few French people, unless they were tainted with Bolshevist ideas, would attend an assemblage where pro-German arguments were to be voiced. The French were grateful for American help, but people who lived in safety three thousand miles away shouldn't presume to give advice about the problems which France faced every day and every hour.

The fact was that the French regarded the Peace Conference as an intrusion, and they watched all foreigners suspiciously. One of Mrs. Emily's friends asked her: What did she really know about the tall and severe young musician who looked so much like a German and spoke with a trace of German accent? He had been discussing the blockade in her drawing room, and more than one person had made note of it. "Enemy ears are listening!" Mrs. Emily mentioned this warning to her friend Beauty, as an example of the phobias which tormented people in Paris. Beauty said, yes, it was really pitiful.

VII

The four elder statesmen met in the morning in President Wilson's study and in the afternoon at the headquarters of the Supreme Council at Versailles. Members of their staffs accompanied them and waited in anterooms; sometimes they were summoned to the presences, but most of the time were forgotten for hours on end. The proceedings of the Big Four were supposed to be completely secret; only one secretary was present. The meeting place became a whispering gallery, with awe-stricken subordinates pricking their ears for every sound, watching the expressions and gestures of those who emerged from the holy place.

The slightest anecdotes spread like wildfire among the staff. Marshal Foch had come rushing out of the chamber, his face red, his eyes dark with storm. He would never go back there, never, never! —so he shouted. Frightened members of his staff whispered to him, begged him, implored him; finally he went back. Professor Elderberry, whose specialty was Semitic dialects, and who had been on a "field commission" to Palestine, had witnessed Lloyd George and Clemenceau in a near fracas. Wilson had interposed, his outstretched arms between them, exclaiming: "I have never seen two such unreasonable men." Lanny, waiting outside for his chief, saw Clemenceau coming out in a rush and being helped into the big gray fur-lined overcoat which protected his chilly old bones. "How are things going?" someone asked, and the Premier of France replied: "Splendidly. We disagreed about everything."

Professor Alston, summoned to one session, described to his colleagues the curious spectacle of four elderly gentlemen who had spread a big map on the floor and were crawling round on their hands and knees, looking for bits of territory which they were going to assign to one nation or another. They were ignorant on many points of geography, and invented names for foreign places when they couldn't remember the right names; when the right ones were given they forgot, and went on using their inventions. Alston was violating no confidence in telling this, for Lloyd George had asked in Parliament: "How many members ever heard of Teschen? I don't mind saying that I never heard of it." Now, having heard of it, he took it from Austria and divided it between the Czechs and the Poles.

For ten days they had wrangled over the French and German boundary and got nowhere. They were exhausted, their tempers badly frayed. The peoples too were becoming hysterical; for where news was lacking rumor took its place. All parties continued to whisper the things they wanted to have believed, and the dozen Paris papers which Clemenceau controlled were denouncing the American President, lampooning him, cartooning him with shocking bitterness. Wilson was ill equipped for a struggle such as this; he was gentle, courteous, anxious to oblige people, and could hardly be brought to realize the nature of the forces being mobilized against him.

Clemenceau had his formula, from which he never varied: "This —or France has lost the war." Of course the President didn't want France to lose the war; he didn't want the responsibility of causing it to happen. He just hadn't realized what an inferno he was coming into. Many of his staff now urged him to go home; others begged him to take the American people into his confidence, telling them the real situation. He might not get what he wanted, but at least he would save his ideals intact and give the peoples of the world a glimpse of the forces that were wrecking Europe.

VIII

George D. Herron, distressed over these developments, left his home in Geneva and returned to Paris. He saw the President and afterwards told Alston and Lanny about it. Wilson was a sick man, paying the penalty of his temperament. As Herron explained it, he was lacking as an executive. "He knows how to judge himself, but not others; he knows how to drive himself, but not others; he can't trust anyone to write his speeches and memoranda, or even to type-write them. The result is that he's overwhelmed. He and he alone is the American Commission to Negotiate Peace, and the number of matters he has to consider and decide are more than can be got into one human brain."

What troubled the President in this crisis was the fear of seeing Europe fall prey to Bolshevism. The French assured him that this would happen; and might it not be true? The American staff had prepared a map, with terrifying large red arrows pointing into Lithuania, Prussia, Poland, Hungary, the Ukraine, Georgia. If Wilson were to break off negotiations and take the American army home, the Germans might refuse to sign the peace treaty, the war might start again, and revolts might follow in Paris and even in Britain.

A young member of the Crillon staff had been picked by the President and sent to Moscow. "Bill" Bullitt was his name, and he had taken with him a journalist friend, once famous as a "muck-raker." In the days when Lanny had been a toddler on the beach at Juan, this man had been traveling over the United States probing into political corruption, interviewing "bosses" and their big-busi-ness paymasters. Latterly his work had been forgotten, and Lanny had never heard the name of Lincoln Steffens until he was told that the "Bullitt mission" had set out for the land of the Reds.

They had come back with surprising news. Lenin wanted peace, and was ready to pay almost any price for it. He would give up all Siberia and the Urals, the Caucasus, Archangel, and Murmansk, even most of the Ukraine and White Russia. He would recognize all the White governments. But, alas, President Wilson had a severe headache that evening, and Colonel House also was ill. Bullitt saw Lloyd George first and told him the terms; Wilson, on the verge of a nervous breakdown, was so angry at this slight that he wouldn't see Bullitt, he wouldn't hear of peace with wicked Bolsheviks. And Lloyd George stood up in the House of Commons and denied that he had ever known anything about the Bullitt mission!

All this suited the French, who didn't want peace under any cir-cumstances. They were being beaten, but dared not admit it. They were having to back out of the Ukraine; their armies were becoming unreliable—this dreaded new kind of war, fought not merely with guns but with ideas. War-weary soldiers listened, and began to whisper that maybe this was the way to end matters. There were mutinies in the French fleet in the Black Sea, and when Colonel House was asked by newspapermen about Odessa, he replied: "There's no more Odessa. The French are clearing out." British troops, ordered to embark at Folkestone for Archangel, refused to go on board. No use to look for such events in newspapers, whether British or American; but the staff at the Majestic knew, and Fessenden gossiped to Lanny with wide-open startled eyes. "For God's sake, what's going to happen next?"

IX

Lanny kept thinking he ought to hear from Kurt; but no word came. He wondered about his Uncle Jesse, whether he was getting more money and what he was doing with it. Having a couple of hours off one afternoon, Lanny yielded to the temptation and turned his steps in the direction of Montmartre.

It was the first day of April; bright sunlight, blue sky, fleecy white clouds; crocuses blooming in the gardens, daisies in the grass of the parks; the trees just far enough in the bud to show a pastel green. The poor frightened world was coming out of the winter of war; Lanny, climbing the hill, carried a thought which by now had become his familiar companion: Why, oh, why did men have to make their lives so ugly? What evil spell was upon them that they wrangled and scolded, hated and feared?

He climbed the stairs in the dark hallway which hadn't yet learned that winter was over. He knocked on his uncle's door, and a voice called: "Come in"; he did so, and saw there was a visitor, seated in the extra chair from which a load of books and papers had been dumped. He was a short, compactly built man with brown hair and small gray imperial and mustache trimmed neatly; a rather square face with glasses, and small blue-gray eyes with many wrinkles around them, giving him a quizzical appearance. The visitor was plainly but neatly dressed, and you would have taken him for a small business-man, or perhaps a college professor. Said Uncle Jesse: "This is Lincoln Steffens."

Lanny was surprised, also pleased, and showed it. "I've been hear-ing about you at the Crillon!"

"Indeed," said the other. "I've been trying to figure out a way to let them know I was in town."

When Lanny knew him better he would understand such teasing remarks. As it was, he decided to be frank, and said: "You know how it is—they're a bit afraid of you."

"That's why I came to see your uncle," replied the journalist. "One man who might be interested to hear about the future."

"Stef has spent a whole week in the future," explained the uncle, with one of his twisted smiles.

Lanny took his seat on the cot, which had become familiar to him. Because it sank down in the middle it cut his knees, so pres-ently he stretched out on it, leaning on one elbow. In this position he listened for an hour or more to an account of one of the great events of human history.

For a matter of seventeen months now Lanny had been hearing about the Bolshevik Revolution. Again and again he had been told how one-sixth of the earth's surface had been seized by blood-thirsty ruffians, more cruel and cunning than any that had ever before plagued the earth. He had seen all the policies of his own country and a number of others based upon that certainty. The fact that his Uncle Jesse believed in and supported these devilish creatures merely meant that his uncle was "cracked" in some seri-ous way, and must be dealt with as you would with an inmate of a home for mental patients.

But here sat this correct-looking middle-aged gentleman, who had been sojourning among these Reds, and not merely hadn't had his throat cut or his watch stolen, but apparently hadn't even got his clothes wrinkled. He had an unusually pleasing voice and poured out the details of what he so oddly called "the future." Apparently this wasn't one of his jokes; he really thought the world was going to be like that. Lanny, who was going to live in the future, naturally wanted to know about it.

He learned that in this new world everybody would have to work. That didn't trouble him so much as it would have done three months earlier, for now he was working. As it happened, he was being paid by the state, so it didn't worry him to hear that this was the way among the Soviets. When he heard that the state was preparing and serving meals to workers in factories, it sounded very much like what was happening to him and the rest of the staff at the Crillon. In Russia, to be sure, they had only one meal a day, and that scanty; but "Stef" said that was due to five years of war and revolution, and to civil wars now going on over a front of ten thousand miles. What there was, all shared alike; that being the first principle of "Communism."

What, then, was the difference between America and Moscow? The "muckraker" said it was a question of who owned the state. In America the people were supposed to own it, but most of the time the big businessmen bought it away from them. "It is privilege which corrupts politics," was his phrase. He explained that among the Soviets it was soldiers and sailors, workers and peasants, who had seized power; capitalists had been abolished. Now there was war between these two kinds of states, and it looked as if it was going to be a war to the finish.

X

Lanny Budd was interested in this news, and no less in the envoy who brought it. What an eccentric little man, he thought. Why should a scholarly person, of breeding and presumably of means, take the side of those underworld figures against his own class? He took it only partly, as Lanny soon began to understand; there appeared to be a war between his heart and his head, and you could almost watch this conflict going on. Stef would become eager and excited, and then would check himself. "If I go too fast," he would say, "people won't listen to me. And, besides, I may be wrong." He would proceed to put some "ifs" and "buts" into his discourse.

Steffens was like Herron, a pacifist and a moralist first of all. He wanted a revolution, but one of the mind and spirit; he was pained by the thought that it might have to be bloody and violent. Did we want such an overturn in western Europe? Could we pay the price?

Jesse Blackless, for his part, was sure that we were going to pay it, whether we wanted to or not. There developed an argument between the two men, to which Lanny listened with close attention. The painter foretold how the Allied armies would continue to decay, and the Red movement would spread to Poland and Germany, and from there to Italy and France. The painter knew it was coming; he knew the very men who were preparing to do the job. Stef looked at Jesse's nephew with a twinkle in his little blue-gray eyes and said: "It's nice to have a religion, Budd. Saves all the trouble of having to think."

A curious experience to Lanny to hear Bolshevism referred to as a "religion," even in jest. But he understood when the reporter described the wave of fervor which had seized upon the people of Russia, victims of many centuries' oppression, sunk in unspeakable degradation—and now suddenly finding themselves masters of a mighty empire, and setting to work to make it into a workers' and peasants' co-operative. People were hungry, they were ragged, half-frozen all winter, but in their eyes was a feverish light and in their hearts was hope, vision, a dream of the future. From the unformed, unregarded mass, from soldiers and sailors and factory workers and peasants, had come new leadership, new statesmanship. . . .

Steffens had talked for hours with Lenin: that studious, shrewd little man who had watched the storm gathering and seized the proper hour to strike. "From now on we proceed to build Socialism," he had said quietly, the day after the coup. As Steffens described him, he knew more about the Allied statesmen than they knew about themselves. He understood the forces confronting the

Soviets; and while the bourgeois world sent armies against him, he would send fanatics, men and women who hated capitalism so much that they were willing to give their lives to undermine and destroy it. "Men like your Uncle Jesse," said Stef, with his sly smile; and Lanny understood, even better than Stef could have imagined.

Lanny was sorry that he had to leave. He summoned his courage and asked if Mr. Steffens would have lunch with him at the Crillon. The other advised him to think it over for a day and then call him. "Colonel House is the only other member of the staff who would have the courage to invite me just now!"

XI

The young fellow who had attempted to kill Clemenceau had been tried and sentenced to death, but the Premier had been persuaded to commute his sentence. The one who had killed Jaurès had been held in prison for nearly five years, because the authorities were afraid to try him during wartime. Now the trial was held, and the lawyers who defended him did so by seeking to prove that Jaurès had been disloyal to his country. So it became in effect a trial of the Socialist leader, and he was found guilty, while the assassin, whose name, oddly enough, was Villain, was acquitted.

The result was a mighty demonstration of protest by the workers of Paris, culminating in a parade in which the red flag was carried for the first time since the armistice. Lanny stood on the street corner and watched it go by, in company with his new friend Steffens. Each of them had his thoughts and did not say them all. Lanny saw his Uncle Jesse marching in the front ranks, looking very determined—but doubtless quaking inside, because no one knew if the police would try to stop the parade, and it might be a killing matter if they did. The nephew thought: "Kurt had something to do with this"; and again: "I wonder if he's watching."

The same crowd that Lanny had observed at the *réunion;* the same sort of persons, and in many cases no doubt the same individuals: men and women, hungry, undernourished from childhood, with pale faces set in grimmest hatred. Lanny knew more about them now; he knew that they meant blood, and so did their opponents. The submerged masses were in revolt against their masters and sworn to overturn them. A few weeks ago Lanny would have thought it was a blind revolt, but now he knew that it had eyes and directing brains.

He noticed how few of the marchers looked about them, or paid any attention to the watching crowds. They stared before them with a fixed gaze. Lanny remarked this to his companion, who replied: "They are looking into the future."

"Do you really want it, Mr. Steffens?" Lanny asked him.

"Only half of me wants it," replied the muckraker. "The other half is scared." He meant to say more, but his words were drowned by the menacing thunder of the "Internationale":

> Arise, ye pris'ners of starvation,
> Arise, ye wretched of the earth;
> For justice thunders condemnation,
> A better world's in birth.

33

Woe to the Conquered

I

THERE was another question which the Big Four had to settle, and which they kept putting off because it contained so much dynamite. The problem of money, astronomical sums of money, the biggest that had ever been talked about in the history of mankind. Who was going to pay for the rebuilding of northeastern France? If this peasant people had to do it out of its own savings, it would be crippled for a generation. The Germans had wrought the ruin—a great deal of it quite wanton, such as the cutting of vines and fruit trees. The French had set the cost of reparations at two hundred billion dollars, and thought they were generous when they reduced it to forty. The Americans were insisting that twelve billions was the maximum that could be paid.

What did it mean to talk about forty billion dollars? In what form would you collect it? There wasn't gold enough in the world; and if France took goods from Germany, that would make Germany the workshop of the world and condemn French industry to extinction.

This seemed obvious to an American expert; but you couldn't say it to a Frenchman, because he was suffering from a war psychosis. You couldn't say it to a politician, whether French or British, because he had got elected on the basis of making Germany pay. "Squeeze them until the pips squeak," had been the formula of the hustings, and one of Lloyd George's "savages," Premier Hughes of Australia, had come to the conference claiming that every mortgage placed on an Australian farm during the war was a part of the reparations bill. Privately Lloyd George would admit that Germany couldn't pay with goods; but then he would fly back to England and make a speech in Parliament saying that Germany should and would pay. The Prime Minister of Great Britain had Northcliffe riding on his back, a press lord who was slowly going insane, and revealing it in his newspapers by clamoring that the British armies should be demobilized and at the same time should march to Moscow. Lloyd George pictured the Peace Conference as trying to settle the world's problems "with stones crackling on the roof and crashing through the windows, and sometimes wild men screaming through the keyholes."

The time came when Clemenceau lost his temper and called Woodrow Wilson "pro-German" to his face. It may have been a coincidence, but right after that the President was struck down by influenza and retired to his bed under doctor's orders. When next he saw the Premier and the Prime Minister it was in his bedroom, and they had to be considerate of an invalid. Once more the fate of the world waited upon the elimination of toxins from the bloodstream of an elderly gentleman whose powers of resistance had been dangerously reduced.

Everybody quarreling with everybody else! General Pershing in a row with Foch, because he wouldn't obey Foch's orders as to the repression of the Germans on the Rhine; Americans wouldn't treat a beaten foe as the French demanded. The Marshal was in a row with his Premier, and Poincaré, President of France, was at outs with both. Wilson was snubbing his Secretary of State, who agreed with none of his policies, yet didn't choose to resign. There was open conflict with the Senate opposition, which now had couriers bringing news from Paris, because it didn't trust what President Wilson was telling the country. There were even rumors among the staff to the effect that a coolness was developing between Wilson and his Texas colonel. Had the latter made too many concessions? Had he taken too much authority? Some said yes and some said no, and the whispering gallery hummed, the beehive quivered with a buzz of gossip and suspicion.

II

The question of the blockade had narrowed down to this: was America willing to sell the Germans food on dubious credit, or would she insist on having some of the gold which the French claimed for theirs? A deadlock over the issue, while mothers hungered and babies died of rickets. The American government had guaranteed the farmers a war price for their food, and now the government had to have that price. At least, so the Republicans clamored—and they controlled the new Congress that was going to have no more nonsense about "idealism."

Lanny listened to controversies among members of the staff. What would our government do with the gold if we took it? Already we had an enormous store which we couldn't use. Alston insisted that when it came to a showdown the French wouldn't dare to take Germany's gold, because that would wreck the mark, and if the mark went, the franc would follow; the two currencies were tied together by the fact that French credits were based upon the hope of German reparations.

Lanny was finding out what a complicated world he lived in; he wished his father could be here to explain matters. But the father wrote that he expected to be busy at home for quite a while. Budd's had been forced to borrow money and convert some of the plants to making various goods, from hardware and kitchen utensils to sewing machines and hay rakes. For some reason Robbie considered this a great comedown. Incidentally he was in a fresh fury with President Wilson, who had failed to repudiate the British demand that increases in the American navy, already voted by Congress, should be canceled and abandoned.

Mrs. Emily hadn't heard again from "M. Dalcroze," and an invitation addressed to him in care of *poste restante* had been returned. Lanny said: "He must have gone back to Germany," and Beauty said: "Thank God!" But Lanny was only half convinced, and was troubled by imaginings of his friend in a French prison or a French grave.

One hint Lanny picked up. At luncheon the professors discussed the amazing change in the attitude of one of the great French dailies toward the subject of reparations and blockade. Actually, it appeared that light was beginning to dawn in French financial circles. A Paris newspaper pointing out editorially that Germany couldn't pay unless she acquired foreign exchange, and that to do this she had to manufacture something, and to do this she had to have raw materials! A miracle, said the hardheaded Professor Davisson—who ordinarily didn't believe in them.

Lanny got a copy of the paper, and did not fail to note that the publisher was the man with whom Kurt had been getting acquainted in Mrs. Emily's drawing room. Lanny hadn't forgotten what his father had told him concerning the method by which "miracles" were brought about in the journalistic world. Before the war the Russians had sent gold to Paris and paid cash for the support of French newspapers; and now the Germans were trying to buy mercy! Could it be that Kurt had moved into those higher regions where a man was safe from both police and military authorities?

<h1 style="text-align:center">III</h1>

One couldn't talk about such matters over the telephone, so Lanny went that afternoon to call upon his mother. He rode up in the lift unannounced and tapped on her door. "Who is it?" she called; and when he answered she opened the door cautiously, and after she had let him in, whispered: "Kurt is here!"

The German officer gave no sign until Beauty went to the door of the inner room and called him. When he emerged, Lanny saw that he had adopted fashionable afternoon garb, in which he looked handsome. He wore a little mustache, trimmed close in English fashion, and his straw-colored hair, which had been perhaps a quarter of an inch long when Lanny first met him at Hellerau, was now of a length suited to a musician. Kurt was pale, but easy in manner; if the life of a secret agent was wearing on his nerves, his friends were not going to be troubled with the fact. "I thought I owed it to you both to let you know I'm all right," he said to Lanny.

"Isn't it dangerous to come here, Kurt?"

"Things are all right with me so far as I know. Don't ask more."

The other held up the newspaper, saying: "I was bringing my mother a copy of this." There was a flash of the eyes between the two friends, but no more was said.

They seated themselves, and Kurt drew his chair close, so that he could speak in a low tone. He asked first what Lanny knew about the intentions of the Peace Conference regarding the district of Stubendorf; Lanny had to tell him the worst, that it was surely going to the Poles. Then Kurt wanted to know about the blockade; Lanny outlined different projects which were being discussed, and the attitude of various personalities he knew or knew about. Kurt repaid his friend by talking about developments in Germany, information which might be valuable to the Crillon staff.

This talk went on for quite a while. When there came a lull, Beauty remarked: "Kurt has told me something that I think you ought to know about, Lanny—his marriage."

"Marriage!" exclaimed Lanny, dumfounded. The smile went off the other's face.

Another of those tragic tales of love in wartime—*amor inter arma.* The affair had begun when Kurt lay in hospital after his second wounding, some pieces of his ribs torn out by a shell fragment.

"It was a small town near the eastern border," said the officer. "The front had shifted back and forth, so there was a lot of wreckage and suffering. The nurse who took care of me was about a year younger than I, a fine, straight girl—her father was a schoolteacher, and poor, so she had been obliged to work for her education. I'd got a touch of gangrene, so I had a long period of convalescence and saw a great deal of her, and we fell in love. You know how it is in wartime——"

Kurt was looking at Beauty, who nodded. Yes, she knew! Lanny said: "The same thing happened to Rick. Only it wasn't a nurse."

"Indeed! I must hear about that. Well, I was going back to duty and the time was short, so I married her. I didn't tell my parents, because, as you know, we pay a good deal of attention to social status in Germany, and my parents wouldn't have considered it a suitable match. My father was ill with influenza and my mother was under heavy strain, so I just sent my father's lawyer a sealed letter, to be opened in the event of my death, and I let the matter rest there until the war was over. Elsa wouldn't give up her duties as nurse, even though she was pregnant; and in the last weeks of the war she collapsed from undernourishment. So you see this blockade meant something personal to me."

Kurt stopped. His face was drawn, which made him look old; but he gave no other sign of emotion. "There wasn't enough food for anybody, unless it was speculators who broke the law. Elsa kept the truth from me, and the result was the baby was born dead, and she died of hemorrhages a few days later. So that's all there was to my marriage."

Beauty sat with a mist of tears in her eyes; and Lanny was thinking a familiar thought: "Oh, what a wicked thing is war!" He had lived through the agony of France with Marcel and his mother, and the agony of Britain with Rick and Nina; now in Germany it was the same. The younger man, thinking always of patching matters up between his two friends, remarked: "Nobody has gained anything, Kurt. Rick is crippled for life and is seldom out of pain. He crashed in a plane."

"Poor fellow!" said the other; but his voice sounded dull. "At least that was in a fight. His wife hasn't died of starvation, has she?"

"The British had their food restrictions, don't forget. Your submarine campaign was effective. Both sides were using whatever weapons they had. Now we're trying to make peace."

"What they call peace is to be just another kind of war. They are taking our ships and railroad stock, our horses and cattle, and saddling us with debts enough to last a century."

"We are trying to make a League of Nations," pleaded the American; "one that will guarantee the peace."

"If it's a league that France and England make, it will be a league to hold Germany down."

Lanny saw that it wouldn't do any good to argue. For a German officer, as for a French one, it was still war. "We Americans are doing everything in our power," he declared. "It just takes time for passions to cool off."

"What you Americans should have done was to keep out of it. It wasn't your fight."

"Maybe so, Kurt. I wasn't for going in, and now most of our men at the Crillon are doing their best to reconcile and appease. Do what you can to help us."

"How can we do anything when we're not allowed near your so-called 'conference'?"

A hopeless situation! Lanny looked at his watch, recalling that there would be an Armenian gentleman waiting for him at the hotel. "My time isn't my own," he explained, and rose to go.

Kurt rose also. But Beauty interposed. "Kurt, you oughtn't to go out until after dark!"

"I came before dark," he replied.

"I don't want you to go out with Lanny," she pleaded. "Why risk both your lives? Please wait, and I'll go with you." She couldn't keep the trembling out of her voice, and her son understood that for her too the war was still being fought. "I want to talk to you about Emily Chattersworth," she added; "she and I are hoping to do something."

"All right, I'll wait," said Kurt.

I V

The deadlock among the Big Four continued; until one day came a rumor that shook the Hotel Crillon like an earthquake: President Wilson had ordered the transport *George Washington* to come to France at once. That meant a threat to break off the conference and go back to his own country, which so many thought he never should have left. Like other earthquakes, this one continued to rumble, and to send shivers through many buildings and their occupants. Denials came from Washington that any such order had been received. Then it was rumored that the British had held up the President's cablegram for forty-eight hours. Had they, or hadn't they? And did Wilson mean it, or was it a bluff?

Anyhow, it sufficed to send the French into a panic. Clemenceau came hurrying to the President's sickroom to inquire, and to apologize and try to patch matters up. Even though he had called the stiff Presbyterian "pro-German," he couldn't get along without him, and his departure would mean calamity. A whole train of specters haunted the French: the Germans refusing to sign, war beginning again, and revolution spreading to both countries!

They resumed meeting in the President's room, and patched up a series of compromises. They decided to let the French have the

Sarre for fifteen years, during which time they could get out the coal and keep their industries going until their own mines were repaired. Then there would be a plebiscite, and the inhabitants would choose which country they preferred. The Rhineland would go back to Germany after fifteen years, permanently demilitarized. Marshal Foch went on the warpath again, and it wasn't long before he and his friends were trying to start a revolt of the French population in the Rhineland, to form a government and demand annexation to *la patrie.*

It was easy to understand the position of a man who had spent his life learning to train armies and to fight them. Now he had the biggest and finest army ever known in the world; troops from twenty-six nations, and more races and tribes than could be counted. Two million Americans, fresh and new, magnificent tall fellows, utopian soldiers, you might call them—and now they were being taken away from their commander, he wasn't going to be allowed to use them! The generalissimo had worked out detailed plans for the conquest of Bolshevism in Russia, and in Central Europe, wherever it had shown its ugly head; but the accursed politicians were turning down these plans, demobilizing the troops and shipping them home! The voluble little Frenchman was behaving like one demented.

Three subcommissions had been studying the question of reparations, but all in vain; so finally they decided to dodge the issue of fixing the total amount. Germany was to pay five billion dollars in the first two years, and after that a commission would decide how much more. Another job for the League of Nations! Woodrow Wilson was having his heart's desire, the League and the treaty were being tied together so that no one could pry them apart. But Clemenceau had his way on one basic point—Germany was not to be admitted to the League.

This last decision filled the American advisers with despair. They had been working day and night to devise an international authority which might bring appeasement to Europe, and now it was turning into just what Kurt had called it, a League to hold Germany down! There were rumors that the President was going even farther and granting the French demand for an alliance, a promise by England and America to defend her if she was again attacked. President Wilson had given way on so many points that Alston and others of the "liberal" group were in despair about him. All agreed that any such alliance would be meaningless, because the American Senate would never ratify it.

V

All day long and most of the night Lanny listened to arguments over these questions. He was not just a secretary, carrying out orders; he was concerned about every step that was being taken, and his chief dealt with him on that basis, pouring out his hopes and fears. Lanny had the image of Kurt Meissner always before him, and he pleaded Kurt's cause whenever a chance arose. He couldn't say: "I have just talked with a friend who lives in Germany and has told me about the sickness and despair." He would say, more vaguely: "My mother has friends in Germany, and gets word about what is happening. So does Mrs. Chattersworth."

These, of course, were grave matters to occupy the mind of a young man of nineteen. With him in the hotel suite were two other secretaries, both college graduates and older than he. They also carried portfolios, and filed reports, and made abstracts, and kept lists of appointments, and interviewed less important callers, and whispered secrets of state; they worked overtime when asked to, and when they grumbled about low pay and the high cost of cigarettes, it was between themselves. But they didn't take to heart the task of saving Europe from another war, nor even of protecting Armenians from the fury of Turks. They enjoyed the abundant food which the army commissary provided, mostly out of cans—and found time to see the night life which was supposed to be characteristic of Paris, but in reality was provided for foreign visitors.

Lanny listened to the conversation of these roommates, which was frank and explicit. To them the sight of a hundred women dancing on the stage stark naked, and painted or enameled all the hues of the rainbow, was something to stare at greedily and to gossip about afterwards. To Lanny, who had been used to nakedness or near it on the Riviera, this mass production of sex excitement was puzzling. He asked questions, and gathered that these young men had been raised in communities where the human body was mysterious and shocking, so that the wholesale exposure of it was a sensational event, like seeing a whole block of houses burn down.

To these young men the need for a woman was as elementary as that for food and sleep. Arriving in a new part of the world, they had looked about for likely females, and exchanged confidences as to their discoveries. They wanted to know about Lanny's love life, and when he told them that he had been twice jilted and was nursing a broken heart, they told him to forget it, that he would be young only once. He would go off and ponder what he had heard —in between his efforts to keep the Italians from depriving the Yugoslavs of their one adequate port.

"Take the good the gods provide thee!"—so had sung an English poet in the anthology which Lanny had learned nearly by heart. That seemed to apply to the English girl secretary, Penelope Selden, who enjoyed his company and didn't mind saying so. Lanny found that he was coming to like her more and more, and he debated the problem: what was he waiting for? Was he still in love with Rosemary? But that hadn't kept him from being happy with Gracyn. It was all very well to dream about a great and permanent love, but time passed and there was none in sight. Was he hoping that Rosemary might some day come back to the Riviera? But she was expecting a baby, the future heir to a great English title. Lanny had written to her from Paris, and had a nice cool friendly reply, telling the news about herself and their common friends. All her letters had been like that, and Lanny assumed it was the epistolary style of the English aristocracy.

He reviewed all over again the question of his sexual code, and that of his friends of the *grand monde*. The great and permanent love theory had gone out of fashion, if indeed it ever had been in fashion with anybody but poets and romancers. Rich and important persons made what were called marriages of convenience. If you were the son or daughter of a beer baron or diamond king, you bought a title; if you were a member of the aristocracy, you sold one, and the lawyers sat down and agreed upon what was called a "settlement." You had a showy public wedding, as a result of which two or three new members of your exclusive social set were brought into the world; then you had done your duty and were at liberty to amuse yourself discreetly and inconspicuously.

Was Lanny going to play second fiddle in some fashionable chamber concert? The invitation had been extended and never withdrawn. Assuming that he meant to accept, what about the interim? Live as an anchorite, or beguile his leisure with a refined and discreet young woman secretary? He was sure that if Rosemary, future Countess of Sandhaven, ever asked questions about what his life had been, it would be with curiosity as friendly and cool as her letters. Such were the agreeable consequences of that "most revolutionary discovery of the nineteenth century," popularly know as "birth control."

VI

The Big Four were deciding the destiny of the Adriatic lands and finding it the toughest problem yet. President Wilson had traveled to that warm country and been hailed as the savior of mankind; he had thrown kisses to the audience in the great Milan opera house, and had listened to the roaring of millions of throats on avenues and highways. He had got the impression that the emotional Italian people really loved him; but now he learned that there were two kinds of Italian people, and it was the other kind which had come to Paris: those who had repudiated their alliance with Germany and sold the blood and treasure of their land to Britain and France, in exchange for a signed and sealed promise of territories to be taken in the war. Now they were here, not to form a League of

Nations, not to save mankind from future bloodshed, but to divvy the swag.

The British and French had signed the Treaty of London under the stress of dire necessity, and now that the danger was over they were not too deeply concerned to keep the bargain—on the general principle that no state ever wants to see any other state become more powerful. But they lacked an excuse for repudiating their promises, and regarded it as a providential event when a noble-minded crusader came from overseas, bearing aloft a banner inscribed with Fourteen Points, including the right of the small peoples escaping from Austrian domination not to be placed under some other domination. The British, who had repudiated the idea of self-determination for Cyprus, and the French, who had repudiated it for the Sarre, were enthusiastic about it for the Adriatic—only, of course, it must be President Wilson who would lay down the law.

The crusader from overseas did so; and Premier Orlando, that kindly and genial gentleman, wept, and Baron Sonnino scowled, and the whole Italian delegation stormed and raved. They said that Wilson, having lost his virtue on the Rhine and in the Polish Corridor, was now trying to restore it at the expense of the *sacro egoismo* of Italy. There were furious quarrels in the council halls, and the Italians packed up their belongings and threatened to leave, but delayed because they found that nobody cared.

In the early stages of this controversy the hotels and meeting places of the delegates had swarmed with charming and cultivated Italians whose pockets were stuffed with banknotes; anybody who had access to the Crillon might have expensive parties thrown for him and enjoy the most delicate foods and rarest wines. The Hotel Édouard VII, where the sons of sunny Italy had their headquarters, kept open house for the diplomatic world. Later, when the thunder clouds burst, they didn't sever friendships, but were heartbroken and made you understand that you and your countrymen had shattered their faith in human nature.

The dispute broke into the open in a peculiar way; the Big Three agreed that they would issue a joint statement opposing the Italian demands, and the American President carried out his part of the bargain, but Lloyd George and Clemenceau didn't, so the Americans were put in the position of standing alone against Italy. Wilson's picture was torn from walls throughout that country, and the face which had been all but worshiped was now caricatured *sub specie diaboli*. The Italian delegation went home, and the French were greatly alarmed; but the Americans all said: "Don't worry, they'll come back"; and they did, in a few days.

VII

Lively times for experts and their secretaries! Professor Alston would be summoned to President Wilson's study, where the elder statesmen were on their hands and knees, crawling over Susak or Shantung. There would come a call to Lanny, asking if he could hurry over to the Quai d'Orsay to bring an important document to some associate who was assisting in the final revision of the League of Nations Covenant. An extremely delicate situation there, because the American Congress had insisted upon a declaration that the League was never going to interfere with the Monroe Doctrine; this provision had to be slipped in as quietly as possible, for there were other nations having "regional understandings" which they would have liked to put into the Covenant, and there was danger of stirring them up.

A group of the professors would meet at lunch, and Lanny would hear gossip about arrangements being made for the reception of the German delegation, now summoned to Paris to receive the treaty. The Germans were to be regarded as enemies until the document had been signed; they were not allowed to wear uniforms, and all intercourse with them was forbidden under military law. They would have the Hotel des Réservoirs, and building and grounds were to be surrounded with a barbed-wire stockade. This, it was explained, was to keep the mob from invading the premises; but it would be difficult to keep the Germans from feeling that they were being treated like wild beasts.

The delegation arrived on the first of May, the traditional holiday of the Reds all over Europe. A general strike paralyzed all Paris that day: métro and trams and taxis, shops, theaters, cafés—everything. In the districts and suburbs the workers gathered with music and banners. They were forbidden to march, but they poured like a hundred rivers into the Place de la Concorde, and the staff of the Crillon crowded the front windows to watch the show. Never in his life had Lanny seen such a throng, or heard such deep and thunderous shouting; it was the challenge of the discontented, a voicing of all the sufferings which the masses had endured through four and a half years of war and as many months of peace-making.

Lanny couldn't see his uncle in that human ocean, but he knew that every agitator in the city would be there. It was the day when they proclaimed the revolution, and would create it if they could. Captain Stratton had told how Marshal Foch was distributing close to a hundred thousand troops at strategic points. The Gardens of the Tuileries were a vast armed camp, with machine guns and even field-guns, and commanders who meant business. But with the example of Russia only a year and a half away, could the rank and file of the troops be depended on? Fear haunted everyone in authority throughout the civilized world on that distracted May Day of 1919.

VIII

Lanny Budd had come to be regarded by the Crillon staff as what they called half-playfully a "pinko." It amused them to say this about the heir of a great munitions enterprise. The rumor had spread that he had a full-fledged Bolshevik for an uncle; and hadn't he brought that avowed Red sympathizer, Lincoln Steffens, into the hotel dining room? Hadn't he been observed deep in conversation with Herron, apostle of free love and Prinkipo? Hadn't he tried to explain to more than one member of the staff that these wild men and women, marching and yelling, might be "the future"?

What the Crillon thought of the marchers was that they wanted to get into the streets where the jewelry shops were. The windows of these shops were protected by steel curtains for the day, but such curtains could be "jimmied," and doubtless many of the crowd had the tools concealed under their coats. None knew this better than the commander of the squadron of *cuirassiers*, in sky-blue uniforms decorated with silver chains, who guarded the line in front of the hotel. The cavalrymen with drawn sabers were stretched two deep across the Rue Royale, blocking the crowd off; there was a milling and moiling, shrieks of men and women mingled with sounds of smashing window glass. Lanny watched this struggle going on for what seemed an hour, directly under the windows of the hotel. He saw men's scalps split with saber cuts, and the blood pouring in streams over their faces and clothing. It was the nearest he had come to war; the new variety called the class struggle, which, according to his Uncle Jesse, would be waged for years or generations, as long as it might take.

The Crillon staff took sides on the question as to the seriousness of the danger. Of course if the Reds succeeded in France, the work done by the Peace Conference would be wiped out. If it succeeded in Germany, the war might have to be fought again. The world might even see the strange spectacle of the Allies putting another Kaiser on the German throne! But apparently that wasn't going to happen, for Kurt Eisner, the Red leader of Bavaria, had been murdered by army officers, a fate that had also befallen Liebknecht and "Red Rosa" Luxemburg in Berlin. The Social-Democratic government of Germany hated the Communists and was shooting them down in the streets; and this was rather confusing to American college professors who had been telling their classes that all Reds were of the same bloody hue.

Strange indeed were the turns of history! A government with a Socialist saddlemaker at its head·was sending to Versailles a peace delegation headed by the Imperial Minister of Foreign Affairs, Count von Brockdorff-Rantzau, member of the haughty old nobility who despised the German workers almost as much as he did the French politicians. He and his two hundred and fifty staff members were shut up in a stockade, and crowds came to look at them as they might at creatures in the zoo. The count hated them so that it made him physically ill. When he and his delegation came to the Trianon Palace Hotel to present their credentials, he became deathly pale, and his knees shook so that he could hardly stand. He did not try to speak. The spectacle was painful to the Americans, but Clemenceau and his colleagues gloated openly. "You see!" they said. "These are the old Germans! The 'republic' is just camouflage. The beast wants to get out of his cage."

34

Young Lochinvar

I

THE tall and stately Mrs. Emily Chattersworth was going shopping, and called at her friend Beauty's hotel rather early in the morning. "Such a strange thing has happened, my dear," said she. "Do you remember that young Swiss musician, M. Dalcroze?"

"Yes, very well," said Beauty, catching her breath.

"I had a visit last night from two officials of the Sûreté. It seems that they are looking for him."

"What in the world for, Emily?"

"They wouldn't tell me directly, but I could guess from the questions they asked. They think he's a German agent."

"Oh, my God!" exclaimed Beauty. Almost impossible to conceal the surge of her emotion. "How horrible, Emily!"

"Can you imagine it? He seemed to me such a refined and gentle person."

"What did they ask you, Emily?"

"Everything, to the remotest detail. They wanted to know how I met him and I gave them the letter he had written me. They wanted a description of him, height and weight and so on, which it's so difficult to remember. They wanted a list of the persons he had been introduced to at my home; they were much disturbed because I couldn't remember them all. You know how many persons I entertain—and I don't keep records."

"Did you give them my name?" asked Beauty, quickly.

"I'm happy to say I realized in time how that might point the finger at the Crillon."

"Oh, thank you, Emily—thank you! Lanny's whole future might depend on it!" Beauty got herself together, and then rattled on: "Such an incredible idea, Emily! Do you really suppose it can be true?" A woman doesn't spend many years in fashionable society without learning how to conceal her emotions, or at any rate to give them a turn in a new direction.

"I don't know what to think, Beauty. What could a German be trying to do now? Blow up the Peace Conference with a bomb?"

"Didn't you tell me that M. Dalcroze talked a great deal about the evils of the blockade?"

"Yes; but it's no crime to do that, is it?"

"It would be for a German, I suppose. The French would probably shoot him for it."

"Oh, how sick I am of this business of killing people! I hear there were several hundred killed and wounded in those May Day riots. The papers don't give us the truth about anything any more!" The kind Mrs. Emily, whose hair had turned snow-white under the stress of war, went on to philosophize about the psychology of the French. They were suffering from shellshock. It was to be hoped that when this treaty was signed they would settle down and become their normal selves. "If they have the League of Nations to protect them—and surely it can't be possible that the American Congress will reject such a great and beneficent plan!"

Beauty controlled her trembling and added a few reflections, derived at second hand from Lanny's professors. After a decent interval she said: "You haven't any idea what's become of that young man?"

"Not a word from him since he left my house that night. I thought it very strange."

"I'll ask Lanny about him," suggested the mother. "He knows many musical people, and might find him. Do you suppose he's related to Jaques-Dalcroze?"

"I asked him that. He told me no."

"Well, I'll see if Lanny can find him."

"But why, Beauty? Isn't it better not to know, under the circumstances?"

"Then you wouldn't want to give him up?" inquired the devious one.

"Surely not—unless I knew he had committed some serious crime. The war is over, so far as I am concerned, and I've not the least interest in getting anybody shot. Let the Sûreté find him if they can."

"Are you satisfied that they believed your story, Emily?"

"It hadn't occurred to me that they wouldn't," was the great lady's reply. She was a most dignified person, and did not have to assume this role. "Apparently they knew all about me, and they talked as if they were gentlemen. They are high officials, I am sure."

"Of course they'd find out how to approach you, Emily. But they probably don't tell anybody all they know, and they might take it for granted that you wouldn't either."

"What on earth are you driving at, Beauty?"

"Well, Lanny keeps telling me how the French are always calling the Crillon staff 'pro-German'; and if there should be German agents in Paris trying to make propaganda on behalf of lifting the blockade, wouldn't it please the French to be able to tie them up with us?"

"What a witch you are!" exclaimed her friend. "You look so innocent and trusting and then you talk like a Sherlock Holmes!"

"Well, Lanny told me the other day that since I have no money I have to develop brains."

"I wonder what Lanny is thinking about me!" reflected the *salonnière;* and in their laughter Lanny's mother found a chance to hide the nervous tension under which she was laboring.

II

Beauty declined to have lunch with her friend, saying that she wasn't feeling well and wouldn't dress. As soon as the visitor had departed, she called the Crillon, and said: "Come at once, Lanny. Tell the professor your mother is ill."

The youth had no trouble in guessing what that meant. He made the necessary excuses and reached the hotel as quickly as a taxi could bring him. He found his mother weeping uncontrolledly, and he guessed the worst, and was both relieved and puzzled when he learned that the Sûreté hadn't yet got hold of Kurt, so far as Beauty knew. "Certainly they didn't have him last night," he argued. "And he may be out of the country after all."

"I just know he isn't, Lanny! Something tells me!" Beauty sobbed on; her son hadn't seen her in such a state of distress since the days when she was struggling with Marcel, first to keep him alive, and then to keep him from plunging back into the furnace of war.

Suddenly she looked up, and the youth saw a frightened look in her eyes. "Lanny, I must tell you the truth! You must manage to forgive me!"

"What do you mean, Beauty?"

"Kurt and I are lovers."

Those were the most startling words that Lanny Budd had heard spoken up to that moment of his life. His jaw fell, and all he could think of to say was: "For God's sake!"

"I know you'll be shocked," the mother rushed on. "But I've been so lonely, so *distraite* since Marcel died. I've tried to tell myself that my baby was enough, but it isn't so, Lanny. I'm just not made to live alone."

"I know, Beauty——"

"And Kurt is in the same state. He's lost his wife and baby, he's lost his war, and his home—the Poles are going to have it, and he says he'll never go back to be ruled by them. Don't you see how it is with us?"

"Yes, dear, of course——"

"And did you think that Kurt and I could be shut up here in three rooms, and not talk about our hearts, or think about consoling each other?"

"No, I must admit——"

"Oh, Lanny, you were such a darling about Marcel—now you must manage to be it again! Kurt is the best friend you have, or he will be if you'll let him. I know what you think—everybody will say it—that I'm old enough to be his mother; but you've always said that Kurt was older than his years, and you know that I'm much too young for mine. Kurt is twenty-two, and I'm only just thirty-seven—that's the honest truth, dear, I don't have to fib about it——"

Lanny couldn't keep from laughing, seeing this good soul! desperately defending herself against all the gossips she had ever known. And taking a year or so from her own age and adding it to Kurt's!

"It's all right, dear. I was a little taken aback at first——"

"You don't have to feel that you've lost either your mother or your friend, Lanny. We will both be to you just what we were before, if you will forgive us and let us."

"Yes, Beauty, of course——"

"You mustn't think that Kurt seduced me, Lanny!"

The youth discovered himself laughing even more heartily. "Bless your dear heart! I'd be a lot more apt to think that you seduced Kurt!"

"Don't make fun of me, Lanny—it's deadly serious to both of us. You must understand what a gap there's been in my life ever since your father left me—or since I made him leave me. You'll never know what it cost me."

"I've tried to guess it many times," said the youth, and put his arm about her. "Cheer up, old dear, it's perfectly all right. Come to think of it, it's a brilliant idea, and I'm ashamed of my stupidity that I didn't think of it. Are you two going to marry?"

"Oh, that would be ridiculous, Lanny! What would people say? I'd be robbing the cradle!"

"Does Kurt want to marry you?"

"He thinks it's a matter of honor. He thinks you'll expect it. But tell him that's out of the question. Some day soon I'll be an old woman, and then I'd be ashamed of myself, to be a drag on his life. But I can make him happy now, Lanny. He's been coming here · nearly every day, and we've both been embarrassed to tell you."

"Well, I don't think this was a very good time for you to turn into a prude," said the youth, severely. "But anyhow, that's done, and the question is how we're going to get you two sinners out of the country."

III

Beauty was like a person in a nightmare in which one is possessed by an agonizing sense of helplessness. She had no way to reach Kurt; he had given no address; he was under pledge, so he told her. He would come again—but when? And would he find police agents waiting for him in the hotel? Lanny must go downstairs and see if any suspicious-looking men were sitting in the lobby. Of course there are often men sitting in hotel lobbies, and how are you to say whether they look suspicious? Are police agents chosen because they look like police agents, or because they don't?

Beauty had to have help; and who was there but her son? She was terrified at the thought of involving him. Not on account of the Crillon—she didn't care a sou for them, she said, let them look out for themselves! But if the police were to take Lanny with Kurt? If he were to be punished for her guilty love—so she persisted in regarding it, being a woman who had been brought up respectably, a preacher's daughter, knowing the better even while she followed the worse!

Somebody must stay in the room, to be there when Kurt came, to warn him and hide him until night. Then they must get him out of Paris, and the safest way seemed to be by car. Beauty would go out and buy one, hers having been commandeered in the spring of the previous year. She supposed it would now be possible to get one if you had the price. Gasoline was still rationed, but that too could be arranged with money. She had only a little in the bank, she always did; but Lanny had a supply, and could draw on his father's account in an emergency. He offered to go out and attend to these matters; but the mother's terror took a leap—the police might trace all this, and Lanny would be guilty of helping a spy! No, let him wait here; she would run the errands.

Where would they go, he asked, and when she didn't know, he suggested Spain. If you went to Switzerland you were traveling toward Germany, and the authorities would be on the alert; but Spain was a neutral country, a Latin country, and a natural place for a rich American lady to be motoring with a lover. Or had it better be a chauffeur? They discussed the problem. A lover would appeal to Latin gallantry, but probably a chauffeur in uniform would be passed by the guard at the border with fewer questions.

Beauty had no passport, that evil device having been invented during the war, and she hadn't been out of France all that time. She would have to apply for one, and have a little picture made. She decided she would go back to the name of Budd, a powerful name, and foreign, more suitable to a tourist. Kurt doubtless had a passport, forged or genuine; if it was under the name of Dalcroze, it would have to be changed. No use to discuss that until he came.

In the meantime Beauty's heart would be in her mouth every moment. Oh, why, why did the life of men have to be an affair of danger, of obsessing and incessant terror?

Lanny promised to wait in the room, and positively not to leave it unless the hotel burned down. If a German officer were to arrive, what should be done with him? Hide him in the boudoir? Or send him out to walk in the parks? Lanny argued for the former. What chance was there of the Sûreté connecting Kurt with them? But Beauty was ready with an answer. Emily had named the other guests at that musicale. The agents would interview them, and ask the same questions they had asked Emily; surely some of them would remember Beauty! Perhaps already the police had her name and were on the way to question her! If her son were in the room, that would be all right; but Kurt must go out into the Parc Monceau, take a book, sit on a bench, and look like a poet; watch the rich children playing, and flirt with the *bonnes* like a Frenchman. "All right, all right," said Lanny.

IV

He wrote his mother a check, and while she dressed they discussed makes of cars, probable prices, and routes to Spain; also the possibilities of Kurt's evading the police or soldiers at the border, by paying a guide and climbing through the mountain passes. It would be the Basque country, which Beauty had traveled in happier days; but no day ever so happy as that one, if she lived to see it, when she and her new lover would be free in Spain. Again Lanny remembered his anthology. Young Lochinvar had come out of the east this time, and the steeds that would follow were swifter than any hero of Sir Walter Scott could ever have dreamed: sixty miles per hour on the roads and a hundred and fifty through the air— to say nothing of messages that traveled round the earth in the seventh part of a second.

Beauty telephoned; she was making progress; was there any news? Lanny said no, and she hung up. Another hour, and she tried again; more progress, but still no news. So it went through the longest of days. She came back late and reported she had a car safely stored in a garage. All the formalities had been attended to; she had paid, five francs here, ten francs there, and petty functionaries had hastened to oblige her. She had a passport in the name of Mabel Budd. That had been arranged through an influential friend to whom she had explained that she didn't want to be a widow any more; he had smiled, and offered to relieve her of the handicap forever. Many matters could be arranged in France if you were a beautiful woman and able to have clothes which did you justice.

She had had the passport visaed for Spain, and had bought a map. With her to the hotel came a man carrying a large package containing a uniform for a tall chauffeur. They stowed it under the bed, where perhaps the Sûreté Génerale would overlook it. That completed everything that Beauty and her son could think of; all that was needed now was a chauffeur to put inside the uniform.

Lanny, having done his part, must return to the Crillon and forget this dangerous business. If anyone questioned him, he was to say that he knew nothing about it whatever. The mother sat at the escritoire and wrote a note on hotel stationery: "Dear Lanny: I have gone away on a short trip; will wire you soon. Have a chance to sell some of Marcel's paintings. Adieu." That would be his alibi in case he should be questioned. When she got into Spain, she would wire him. If she or Kurt got into trouble, he must go to Emily Chattersworth and make a confession of the whole affair and beg for her help with the French authorities. Beauty kissed him many times, and told him he was a darling—no news to him.

He went back to the question of Shantung, which now was destroying the peace of mind of the Crillon staff. His mother went to packing her belongings, and then to pacing the floor and smoking one cigarette after another. She couldn't eat anything, she couldn't think anything but: "Kurt! Kurt!" She saw him in a score of different places with the hands of French police agents being laid upon his shoulders. She saw herself weeping in Emily's room, pleading for forgiveness, explaining how she had kept this dreadful secret from her friend for the friend's own good. She saw herself on her knees before French officials, weeping, begging for mercy which they wouldn't or couldn't grant. Always she saw herself hating war, going to live in some part of the world where it wasn't —but what part was that? Why had God made so many wretched creatures, born to trouble as the sparks fly upward? Because of a pious upbringing, Beauty had phrases like this in her mind.

V

All through the proceedings of the conference the little Japanese delegates had sat listening, polite but inscrutable. They had tried to get into the Covenant of the League a provision for "racial equality," intended to get them access to California and Australia. That proposal having been turned down, they waited, studying the delegates and learning all they could. Which meant what they said and which could be bluffed or cajoled? Japan had taken the rich Chinese province of Shantung and meant to keep it unless it meant war with somebody. Would it, or wouldn't it?

The American staff was agog over this problem. If the Japanese had their way, it meant that the Fourteen Points had gone up in smoke. The patient, ever-smiling Chinese delegates haunted the Crillon corridors, morally and intellectually when not physically. Would "Mister Wilson" stand by them, or wouldn't he? The staff couldn't guess. They knew that "Mister Wilson" had been harried by seven unbroken weeks of wrangling, and was a badly exhausted man. Did he have one more fight left in him? Everybody speculated; and Lanny heard them as if in a dream. An absentminded and far from satisfactory secretary, he was excused because he was so worried about his mother's illness. Every hour he would go to the phone. "How do you feel, Beauty?" She would say: "Not very well."

In the middle of the evening the mother called: "Come at once, please." He went, and found her in a state of tension. Kurt had come, and now had gone to interview someone who had authority over him, to get permission to leave. He had said no more, except that he was sure he could get a passport into Spain. "He says he has friends there," Beauty explained.

Lanny hadn't thought of that. Of course the Germans would be working through Spain as well as through Switzerland, and if they could buy or manufacture passports in one country, they could do it in another.

Beauty was to meet Kurt at an agreed place on the street. "In one hour," she said. "But let's get out of here at once."

Her bags were packed and ready. Lanny paid the hotel bill, explaining that his mother had been called back to her home on the Riviera. The car had been phoned for and was at the door; the bellboys stowed the luggage, and Lanny tipped them generously. The couple stepped in, the car rolled away—and Beauty put her face into her hands and burst into sobbing. So much she had feared in that well-appointed family hotel; and nothing of it had happened!

They drove slowly about the boulevards, still unlighted, as in war days. After a while Beauty told him to drive to the spot where Kurt was supposed to come. "Draw up to the curb," she requested, and when he did so, she said: "Please go quickly."

"I don't like to leave you here," he objected.

"I'll lock the car. And I have a gun."

"I wanted to wait and see you off."

"Don't you understand, Lanny? The police may be following Kurt! They would want to get his associates, too."

He had to admit that this was reasonable. Since she didn't know how to drive, he asked: "What'll you do if he doesn't show up?"

"I'll lock the car and find some place to telephone you."

Lanny had hoped to see Kurt and give them both his blessing; but the most important thing was to calm his tormented mother. He got out, and said: "Tell him that if he isn't good to you I'll turn him over to the Sûreté."

She gave a little broken laugh. "Good-by, darling. Go quickly, please. Don't hang around."

VI

It was late, but Lanny returned to his desk, because documents were piling up and he was a conscientious secretary; also, he doubted if he could sleep. His mind was traveling the Route Nationale that ran south by west from Paris to the Bay of Biscay. He had never traveled it, but knew it would be good, for the safety of *la patrie* depended upon her roads. The distance was some five hundred miles, and if all went well they would cover that during the night and part of the next day; probably the border would be closed at night. There was a little town called Hendaye, and a bridge, and not far on the Spanish side was a popular resort called San Sebastián. Early in May it might be chilly, but those two had means to warm their hearts. No use thinking about possible mishaps—better to see Alston and work out the next day's schedule.

It was the day of a strange ceremony, the formal presentation of the peace treaty to the German delegation, taking place in the great hall of the Trianon Palace Hotel. The Allied delegates were received with drums and trumpets, which made more awe-inspiring the deathlike silence when the Germans were ushered in. Upon the table in front of their seats had been placed copies of an elaborate printed volume of close to a hundred thousand words, the Treaty about which the whole world had been talking and writing for half a year. The official text, in both French and English, was supposed to be the inspired word; but the Crillon heard strange rumors to the effect that numerous changes agreed upon at the last moment hadn't been got in, and even that the French had fixed up some things to read the way they wanted them. Whose business had it been to study the document line by line and compare it— with what? How could there be any checking up when three elderly gentlemen had met in the bedroom or study of one of them and kept no record, except for notes made by a trusted friend of Mr. Lloyd George who himself was not always to be trusted?

Anyhow, there was the volume, and Clemenceau arose and made

a brief speech to the Germans, informing them that they would have fifteen days in which to make their written observations. Said he: "This second treaty of Versailles has cost us too much not to take on our side all the necessary precautions and guarantees that the peace shall be lasting."

When it came the turn of Count von Brockdorff-Rantzau to answer, he did not rise, but sat motionless in the big leather chair. Perhaps this was because he was ill; but in that case he might have said so, and it appeared that his action was a studied discourtesy. The Allies had put into the treaty a statement to be signed by the Germans, assuming sole responsibility for the war. This filled the count with such fury that his voice shook and he could hardly utter the words: "Such a confession on my part would be a lie."

At the same time the Crillon gave out the news that President Wilson had made an agreement, jointly with Britain, to guarantee France in the event of another attack by Germany. The great master of words had searched his vocabulary once more, and this was not to be an "alliance," but an "understanding"; and of course that made it different. Many of the advisers were in a state of excitement about it, and wherever two of them met there were arguments. "If the treaty were just," declared Alston, "the whole world should help to defend it. But this treaty is going to cause another war; and do we want to obligate ourselves to be in it?" He pointed to the news from Germany, where the government had declared a week of national mourning in protest against the war-guilt declaration.

Lanny Budd wasn't supposed to have opinions; so he ran errands among the excited advisers who had stopped speaking to one another. He noted black looks and listened to angry words, and was unconcerned—because all the time his thought was: "Why don't I get that message?" He knew that the telegraph service of the French government was shockingly disorganized. Why hadn't he thought to tell Beauty to telephone? But he hadn't; so maybe they were safe in Spain, or maybe they were in jail in Tours, or Bordeaux, or Hendaye. Lanny couldn't keep his mind on his work.

Until late the next day, when the telegram arrived. Short and sweet it was: "Lanny Budd, Hotel Crillon, Paris: Peace love beauty." Highly poetical—but the important point was that the message was marked from San Sebastián!

VII

How was that oddly assorted couple going to make out? Lanny tried in his spare moments to imagine it. He had learned that you never could tell about other people's guesses in love; you just had to let them guess. Kurt would find that he had taken into his life a woman who hadn't much real interest in his ideas—only in him. Whatever he believed would be the truth and whatever he did would be important. Beauty would be loyal to her man; would take up his cause and fight for—not it, but him.

She talked a great deal and would certainly bore him while motoring over Spain. But she had sense enough to let a man alone if he asked it. If Lanny said he wanted to read, all right, he could go off in a corner of the garden and stay half a day. If Marcel had wanted to paint, or Robbie to play poker, that too was all right. If Kurt could only realize that the war was over, and get his musical instruments together and go on with his work, Beauty would be content to hear him tootling and tinkling all day. She had learned her formula from Emily: Kurt was a composer, and in order to write for any instrument you had to know its range, what fingerings were easy, what were impossible, and so on.

The day that Kurt produced his Opus 1, he would become for Beauty the greatest composer in the world; she would take up that composition and fight for it as she had fought for Marcel's art, and for the selling of munitions. She would inquire around and find out who was the topmost conductor of the hour, and somehow she would manage to be in his neighborhood and have him invited to tea. Maybe he would know what was up or maybe he wouldn't, but, anyway, he would hear Kurt's Opus 1, and soon it would be performed by a great symphony orchestra, and Beauty would see to it that all the critics were there, and that they met the *crème de la crème* of Paris or London society. Kurt would be dressed for the occasion, and presented to everybody—or would he? Maybe he'd be eccentric, like Marcel, despising smart society, wanting to hide himself! If so, Beauty would fall on her knees and tell him that she was a crude and cheap person, that he might have it his way—any way in the world, so long as he didn't go to war again! (Lanny, living over those days of anguish with his stepfather at Juan-les-Pins!)

Now it was Kurt who was going to be stepfather. What an odd thing! Of course Kurt had always taken the attitude of an elder and Lanny had thought of him as a mentor. As they grew older, fifteen months' difference in their ages would matter less; but probably Kurt would always know what he wanted to do, whereas Lanny might never be sure. Lanny had imaginary whimsical conversations with his friend, in which they adjusted themselves to the trick which fate had played upon them. Anyhow, they wouldn't be jealous of each other; and they would have lots of music in the house! Lanny began to reflect that he ought to concentrate upon that great art and try to make something of himself with Kurt's help.

VIII

The German delegation was bombarding the conference with notes, protesting against the terms of the "monstrous document," as the treaty was called by the President of the German Republic. They said that it was impossible of fulfillment; that in failing to fix the amount of the indemnity the Allies made it impossible for Germany to obtain credit anywhere; that in taking all her colonies and her ships, and requiring her yards to make new ships for the Allies, they were making it impossible for her to have any trade and so condemning millions of people to starvation. The better to continue this bombardment, the Germans brought in a special train with linotype machines and printing presses, and set about preparing a volume of their own, a "counter-proposal." Clemenceau replied with cold rejection of most of the German notes, and the experts and secretaries and translators worked at preparing ammunition to repel this new kind of bombardment.

It became Lanny's duty to take the files referring to Upper Silesia, and help the staff to digest them all over again, and prepare answers to the strenuous arguments of the German delegation, that this province was overwhelmingly German, and that giving it to the Poles was merely a move of power politics, to deprive Germany of coal and manufacturing power. A lot of extra work fell upon Lanny's shoulders, because Alston was giving so much time to discussing whether it was his duty to resign his position as a public protest against what he felt was a breach of faith with Germany.

There were signs of wavering among those responsible for the drastic terms of the treaty, and Lanny had the exciting idea that by some stroke of superdiplomacy he might be able to save the castle and district of Stubendorf for Kurt and his family. At any rate, Lanny would make special mention of it in the data he got together; he would underscore the name if it occurred; he would make notes on the margin of reports. When he had a chance to talk with his chief he told how he had visited that beautiful country— and assuredly every man, woman, and child that he had seen was German.

Professor Alston shook his head sadly. Lanny wasn't telling him anything new; it was just such blunders which were tormenting the conscience of the Americans, and of some Britons, too. But what could they do? It might be possible to persuade the Big Four to grant a plebiscite for the bulk of Upper Silesia, but Stubendorf lay too far to the east, and was surely going to the Poles. Paderewski, President of the new Polish Republic, had come to Paris, to fight for every foot of territory he could get, and the French were backing him. As Robbie had so carefully explained, this new republic was a French creation, to be armed with weapons manufactured by Zaharoff.

Lanny had been too busy to return to the mansion on the Avenue

Hoche; but every now and then he would come upon another strand of the web of that busy old spider. Right in the midst of the bright dream of saving Kurt's home came news that gave everybody at the Crillon a poke in the solar plexus: a Greek expedition had landed at Smyrna and taken the city, with British and French warships supporting them, and—here was the part which the Americans could hardly believe—the battleship *Arizona* and five United States destroyers lending aid! The French took the harbor forts, the British and Italians held the suburbs, while the Greeks invaded the center of the city and slaughtered the Turkish inhabitants.

Turkey was going to be dismembered, of course. The British and French were going to quarrel over the oil. The Italians were going to hold some of the islands. The Greeks were going to get Smyrna, as a reward for sending troops to Odessa to help fight the Bolsheviks. But what was America getting out of it, and why were American warships assisting against Turks, upon whom we had never declared war?

These developments had been foreseen by Robbie Budd, and Lanny now passed his information on to Alston and others of the staff. Zaharoff was a Greek, and hatred of Turkey was, next to money-making, the great passion of his life. Zaharoff controlled Lloyd George through the colossal armaments machine which had saved Britain. Zaharoff controlled Clemenceau through Schneider-Creusot—to say nothing of Clemenceau's brother and son. The Grand Officer of the Legion of Honor had practically an official status at the Peace Conference, and was now getting himself a port for the future conquest of Turkey and the taking of its oil. America was to accept a mandate for Constantinople, which meant sending an army and a navy to keep the Bolsheviks shut up in the Black Sea; also a mandate for Armenia, which meant blocking them off from the Mosul oil fields. Lloyd George had a map showing all this—young Fessenden had revealed the fact to Lanny without quite realizing its importance.

One fact Lanny failed to grasp—what he was doing to himself

by talk such as this in the Crillon. His mother was fondly imagining that he might have a diplomatic career, something so distinguished and elegant. He himself was finding it thrilling to be behind the wings and at least on speaking terms with the great actors. But he forgot about the whispering gallery, the busy note-takers and filers of cards. Zaharoff had tried to hire him as a spy. Did he imagine that Zaharoff had failed to hire others? Did he imagine that one could sit in with the Alston malcontents and discuss the project of resigning, and not have all that noted down in one or many black-books?

35

I Can No Other

I

LANNY BUDD was in a state of mental confusion. He had absorbed, as it were through the skin, the point of view of his chief and the latter's friends, the little group who called themselves "liberals." According to these authorities, the President of the United States had muffed a chance to save the world and that world was "on the skids"; there was nothing anybody could do, except sit and watch the nations prepare for the next war. George D. Herron went back to his home in Geneva, sick in body and mind, and wrote his young friend a letter of blackest depression couched in the sublimest language. Uncle Jesse, on whom Lanny paid a call, had the same expectations—only he didn't worry, because he said it was the nature of capitalism on its way to collapse. "Capitalism is war," said the painter, "and what it calls peace is merely time to get ready. To try to change it is like reforming a Bengal tiger."

A very young secretary listened to these ideas, bandied back and forth among the staff. He tried to sort them out and decide which he believed; it was hard, because each man was so persuasive while he talked. And meanwhile Lanny was young, and it was May in Paris, a beautiful time and place. Rains swept clean the streets and the air, and the sun came out with dazzling splendor. The acacia trees in the Bois, loaded with masses of small yellow blossoms, were bowed in the rain and then raised up to the sun. Children in bright colored dresses played on the grass, and *bonnes* with long ribbons dangling from the backs of their caps chatted together and flirted impartially with doughboys, Tommies, Anzacs, and chocolate soldiers from Africa. The beautiful monuments and buildings of Paris proclaimed victory, the traffic hummed and honked, and life was exciting, even though it might be on the way to death.

Lanny, walking on the boulevards, thought about his mother and Kurt, safe in Spain, and having a magical time. A letter had come from his friend, full of needless apologies, signed by that oddly unsuitable name of "Sam" which he had chosen without a moment's thought. Beauty had written also; no more about the past and its perils, but personal and happy news. A rugged and inspiring coast—the Bay of Biscay, O! Fascinating old towns, picturesque inns, sunshine and white clouds floating; peace and safety, heavenly anonymity, and, above all, love.

Lanny understood each of these words in its secret inner meaning. Voices told him that he was missing something in his life. Other people were finding it, but he was alone; no mother, no father, no girl—only a group of middle-aged and elderly gentlemen looking at the world through dark glasses, no two of them able to agree as to what they wanted to do—and powerless to do it anyhow!

II

"Society" was reviving. The fashionable folk were coming out of their five years' hibernation, hungry for pleasure as the bears for food. The Grand Prix was to be run at Longchamps, and President Wilson would attend, the first holiday that harassed man had allowed himself in a couple of months. Lanny resolved to attend, and to do it in style—with the help of the complaisant little army officer who had charge of the nice big open Cadillacs with army chauffeurs who took people on "official business" to the races or anywhere else in or near Paris.

His thoughts turned to that agreeable lass at the Hotel Majestic. She could get time off, and so could young Fessenden and the female member of the staff who was his special friend. The English are a sporting people, and the severe chaperon who looked after the welfare of the young ladies of their delegation would regard watching horses race under the eyes of President Wilson as a form of social duty. It is amazing how young women on very small salaries can manage to look as gay and new as the richest ones; they don't tell you how they do it, and Lanny had no means of guessing, but he saw that the *toilettes* of the professional beauties which were featured in the newspapers could hardly be distinguished from those of girls who worked all day typing letters and keeping files. It was democracy.

To look at that racetrack and its throngs of people, you would have had a hard time realizing that Paris had been in deadly peril less than a year ago; that long-range cannon had been peppering her streets and houses with shells, and that hundreds of thousands of her sons had given their lives to save her. The women who wore mourning did not attend the races; only those fortunate ones whose men had made profits out of the war. Now they wore hats full of flowers, and the most striking ensembles that dressmakers had been able to invent at short notice; they flaunted striped parasols and waved handkerchiefs which represented a month's wages for one of the working girls who made them. The beautiful sleek horses strained and struggled for their entertainment and roars of cheering swept over the stands and around the track.

In short, life had begun again for the leisure classes. The mood was to spend it while you had it, and Lanny's father had it. So the youth drank in sunshine and warm spring air and felt his soul expanding. He strolled among the smiling, chattering throngs, bowed to distinguished persons whom he knew, and told his friends who they were. The *grand monde* at its very grandest was here: important persons not merely of Paris and London and Washington, but of Greece and Egypt, Persia and India, China and Japan, Australia and New Zealand—and back to Paris by way of San Francisco and New York.

Penelope Selden was slender and quick-moving, with hair that glinted without dye and cheeks that were bright without rouge. Certainly she was happy without any effort that afternoon; they all made jokes, and bubbled with laughter at the poorest of them, and no shadow of the world's trouble crossed their souls. They bet no more money than they could afford to lose, and oddly enough they won, and enjoyed the delight of getting something for nothing.

Fessenden had an engagement for the evening, so they were driven back to town. Then, because all the restaurants of Paris would be packed to the doors on the evening of the Grand Prix, Lanny and Penelope took a taxi to the suburbs and found a little inn, having outdoor tables in a garden, an obliging moon to provide the right amount of light, and a host who was not obtrusive. The cooking was good, the wine tolerable, and afterwards they strolled in the garden and sat on a bench. Someone in the inn was playing a concertina—not the highest type of music, but it sufficed.

Lanny reflected upon the dutiful life he had been living these past five months or so; and also that in places such as this were rooms which could be hired with no questions asked. He had already made up his mind that he would take the good the gods provided him. He permitted the conversation to become personal, and when he put his arm on the top of the bench behind the girl, and then about her shoulders, she did not withdraw. But when he began to whisper his feelings, she exclaimed, in a voice of pain: "Oh, Lanny, why did you wait so long?"

"Is it too late?" he asked.

'I've gone and got myself engaged!"

"Oh, damn!" thought Lanny—to himself. Aloud he replied: "Oh, dear! I'm sorry!" Then, after a pause: "Who is it?"

"Somebody in England."

She didn't tell him more. Did that mean that she wasn't altogether pleased with her choice? They sat for a while, watching the tree shadows in the moonlight, which had become suddenly melancholy; the concertina was playing *adagio lamentoso*.

"What was the matter, Lanny? Did you think I was a gold digger, or something horrid?"

"No, dear," said he, truthfully. "I was afraid I mightn't be fair to you."

"Couldn't you have left that to me?"

"Perhaps I should have. It's hard to be sure what's right."

"I wouldn't have made any claims on you—honestly not. I've learned to take care of myself, and I mean to." They were silent once more; then she put her hand on his and said: "I'm truly sad about it."

"Me too," he replied; and again they watched the wavering shadows of the trees.

III

They talked about the relationship of the sexes, so much in the thoughts of young people in these days. They had thrown overboard the fixed principles of their forefathers, and were groping to find a code which had to do with their own happiness, the thing they really believed in. If you were going to have babies, that was another matter; but so long as you couldn't afford to have babies, and didn't mean to—what then?

Lanny told about his two adventures; and Penelope said: "Oh, those were horrid girls! I would never have treated you like that, Lanny."

"There's something to be said for both of them. The English girl belongs to a class and she owes a duty to her family. Don't your parents feel that way?"

"A stockbroker isn't so much in England—unless he's a big one, and my father isn't. He has other people to take care of besides me; that's why I went out on my own. So long as I earn my way, I think I've a right to run my own life. At any rate, I'm doing it."

"Have you ever had an affair?" he made bold to inquire.

She answered that she had loved a youth in the business school she had attended. His parents were well-to-do, and wouldn't let him marry. "I guess we didn't really care enough for each other to make a fight for it," she said. "Anyhow, we didn't. It messes things all up when one has more money than the other. That's why I was afraid to let you know that I liked you so much, Lanny. A girl can generally start things up if she wants to."

"I haven't much money," said he, quickly.

"I know, you say that. But you have what looks like it to a girl on the salary our Foreign Office pays. I waited, hoping you would speak, but you didn't."

It was a dangerous conversation. Their hearts were bared to each other and their feelings were stirred; it wouldn't have taken much to "start things up." But something like an alarm bell was ringing in the young man's soul. This was a lovely girl, and she was entitled to a square deal. It might be that she would call off her engagement and take a chance with him; from vague hints he guessed that the man in London was in business, and was not glamorous to her. But to break with him would be a serious step. If Lanny caused her to do it, he would be under obligations—and was he prepared to keep them? The Peace Conference was drawing to its close and their ways would part. Did he want to invite Penelope to Juan? If so, what would become of her job and her boasted independence? On the other hand, would he follow her to London?

No, he hadn't intended anything so serious. He had been thinking about a little pleasure, in the mood of these days, when men and women had the feeling that life was cheating them. Penelope said something like that; she was leaning closer to him, practically in his arms, and all he had to do was to close them.

"Listen, dear," he said; and his tone forecast what he was going to say: "If we do this, we'll get fond of each other, and then we'll be unhappy."

"Do you think so, darling?"

"You may be thinking you can go back to that chap at home. But perhaps you'll find you don't care for him any more, and you'll make yourself miserable, and him too."

"I've thought about it a lot, Lanny. We do what we think is right—and then we go off and spend many a lonely hour wondering if we didn't make a mistake."

"I'm judging by the way I am with that English girl I told you about."

"You can't forget her?"

"I've tried to, and I ought to, but I just don't."

"I suppose that's what's the matter between us," reflected Penelope. "There's a German poem that tells about a youth who loved a maiden who had chosen another."

"I know—Heine. And whom it just touches, his heart breaks in two."

"I don't suppose there'll ever be a remedy for that," said the girl.

They sat listening to the concertina player, who was evidently a returned poilu; he played their songs, which Lanny knew from Marcel and the other *mutilés*. Many of them dealt with love, and as a rule were sad; the toughest old campaigner would sit with a mist of tears in his eyes, hearing about the girl he had left behind him and wouldn't see again. Lanny told Penelope what was in these songs, and with echoes of them in their ears they strolled to the car and drove back to the city. Afterward, it was just as she had said—they both wondered if they hadn't made a mistake.

IV

The Germans were continuing their bombardment of the treaty, and were getting the help of liberal and "radical" groups all over the world. The statesmen in Paris who had pledged themselves to "open covenants openly arrived at" were now doing their best to keep the terms of this treaty from reaching the public; the text was unobtainable in America, and even in France, but you could buy a copy for two francs in Belgium, and protests against it arose more loudly every day in the neutral lands. The British Labour Party denounced it, which meant many votes and had a disturbing effect upon the "mercurial" Prime Minister. He began wobbling again and caused an amusing situation.

Through all the battles, it had been the Presbyterian President against the cynical Tiger, with Lloyd George holding the balance of power, and generally giving the decision to the Tiger. But now, here was the little Welshman fighting the Tiger, and President Wilson having the decision—and he too giving it to the Tiger! This amazed the people at the Majestic. One of the staff, Mr. Keynes, said that Lloyd George had set out to bamboozle the American President and had succeeded too well; now, when he set out to "debamboozle" him, it couldn't be done. The agile-minded little Welshman was helpless before the stiff "Covenanter" temperament, which had to convince itself that what it did was divinely inspired, and then, having acquired that conviction, had to stand by it, no matter how many votes it might cost.

Lanny heard the President's side from Davisson and others who were defending him in hot arguments with Alston. At the time when Wilson had needed Lloyd George's help it had been refused. Now the treaty had been presented to the enemy, and it was a question of making him sign it. What time was this for the Allies to start weakening? Clemenceau couldn't give way, for he had Foch on his back, and Poincaré watching for the moment to trip him. All that could be brought about was another deadlock, such as they had had two months ago, and starting the whole weary wrangle all over again.

One aspect of the problem could be mentioned only in whispers. General Pershing wasn't sure how long he could control his troops. His armies were melting away. All over France, Belgium, Switzerland, were not merely doughboys but also officers who had quit in disgust. No need for Jerry Pendleton to hide, or for Lanny to worry about him any more! And if the Germans should refuse to sign the treaty, would the men still under arms consent to march and fight? Congress had been summoned in special session, and there was a resolution before the Senate declaring that a state of peace existed with Germany. Just as easy as that!

Clemenceau and Marshal Foch wouldn't yield an inch; no, not an inch; but having said that and sworn it, they began to yield, a fraction of an inch here and a fraction there. Germany was going to be admitted to the League of Nations after all. And there was going to be a plebiscite for a part of Upper Silesia—not the part containing Schloss Stubendorf, alas, but the part with the coal mines, which the Poles wanted so badly, and which the French wanted to use against Germany the next time. So it went, and each small concession was a bite out of the body and soul of France; the screams were loud and terrifying—and Lanny, most of whose life had been lived among the French, couldn't make up his mind whether to listen to his boyhood friends, or to these new ones who talked so impressively about justice, chivalry, democracy, and other abstractions.

It was a complex problem that taxed the mental powers of the ablest minds in the world, and would continue to be argued about by historians. Professor Davisson and others to whose arguments Lanny listened declared that these were not questions of right and wrong, of morality or immorality, but of statesmanship. Of course it wasn't just that Germany should be shut off from East Prussia; but wouldn't it be equally unjust if Poland should be shut off from the sea? The real question was, which course would provide for international security. Said Davisson: "The main lines of this settlement have been established by the processes of history. It is fighting against these processes not to recognize the successor states, especially Poland and Czechoslovakia, and give them the territory and resources to maintain and defend themselves."

There were those who went even farther, driven by the mood of war; they insisted that the Allied armies should have marched to Berlin, to let the Germans know what war is really like, and

cure them of their fondness for it. The peace terms should now
provide for the dividing of Germany into a number of small states,
as in the days before Bismarck. The Prussians were a tribe incapable
of understanding any ideal save that of conquest, and it should be
made impossible for them to use the peace-loving Germans of
Bavaria and the Rhineland in their adventures. Lanny didn't associate with persons who held such views, because Alston and his
group considered them outside the pale; but he met them among
his mother's friends, and among those who came to Mrs. Emily's.
They seemed to know a lot of history.

V

Bullitt and Steffens had journeyed to Russia on a mission, of a
sort contrived by statesmen who wish to keep themselves free either
to accept the results, in which case it was an official mission; or to
reject the results, in which case the statesmen had nothing to do
with the mission and didn't even know about it. In the case of the
expedition to Russia, Wilson and Lloyd George had chosen the
latter course; and now what were the expeditioners going to do?

Lincoln Steffens had already had his experience of martyrdom,
and was having it still. He had written too sympathetically about
various "radicals" in trouble, and as a result no magazine of any
circulation was willing to have his name appear in its pages. Here
he was, a highly trained journalist in Paris, enjoying contacts such as
no other had; every day he collected marvelous stories—and could
do nothing with them but hand them over to less competent men.

Lanny sat in Stef's room, listening to some of these tales, when in
came Bill Bullitt; bouncing, eager young newspaper fellow, now
being suddenly matured and sobered. His was an old and wealthy
family of Philadelphia, and young men of exalted social position
perhaps have their own way too easily, and are impatient of neglect
and frustration. Also, they can afford the luxury of moral scruples.
It made young Bullitt furious when Lloyd George would send for

him, and pump his mind of everything he had seen and heard in the land of the Soviets, express deep appreciation of the service which Bullitt had performed—and then get up in Parliament and officially lie about him. The young aristocrat was like a man who strolls in a lovely garden, picking the fruit and tasting it, and suddenly falls through the sod and discovers that the garden is made over a charnel pit. When Lanny first met him, Bill had just scrambled out, his eyes and mouth full of horrors. He was hating it in a blind fury, and determined to expose it to the world.

And here was Stef, middle-aged, sad, and accustomed to the odors of charnel pits; they were ancient institutions, all the national gardens of Europe were built over them. If any young fellow wanted to go on a crusade against lying and cheating in diplomacy, all right, but let him know what he was fighting. It was nothing less than the property system, which was the foundation of modern western culture; and were you prepared to scrap it? If not, why all this fuss about a few of its by-products?

Stef told about two French journalists who had come to him at the outset of the Peace Conference, obviously sent by Clemenceau or one of his agents, putting up to the Americans the question: Just how much of his Fourteen Points did President Wilson really mean, and how far were the Americans ready to go in support of these exalted principles? Did they mean to apply them to India, to Hong Kong, Shanghai, Gibraltar? Of course they didn't; of course they meant to let the British Empire keep on going—so why not a French empire? This put the Americans in a hole, as it was meant to do. The whole world saw, the first thing President Wilson did when he reached London was to begin hedging on his "freedom of the seas," making plain that it didn't mean what everybody but statesmen had supposed it meant.

"All right," said Stef, "go in and fight; but don't start until you know who your enemy is, and have some idea of his strength. The war on Russia which we denounce, and the peace treaty, are parts of the same imperialist program. The Polish Corridor, the new

Baltic states, and all the rest of it, are meant to keep Germany and Russia apart, so that the British Empire and the French Empire can deal with them separately. That's what empires do, and must do if they are to go on existing. What we Americans have to get clear is that the same forces are building the same kind of empire at home, and we'll be doing the same thing as the British and French, because we have to have foreign trade, and outposts like the Panama Canal and Hawaii. So why not start reforming ourselves, Bill?"

Young Bullitt didn't see that; and Lanny only half saw it. He listened to the muckraker talking in his quizzical fashion, teasing people with paradoxes, often saying the opposite of what he really meant; Lanny decided all over again that these radicals were damned irritating. But at the same time he was embarrassed to discover how much they knew, and how often their unpleasant predictions came true. He decided that maybe he'd agree with them after they were able to agree among themselves.

VI

In a private dining room of the Crillon a small group met to choose their future course. They were in a painful situation, and some were wishing they had never crossed the seas. They had to choose whether to let their names and reputations be used in support of what they believed to be falsehoods and blunders, or to get themselves called unpatriotic and eccentric, to be looked upon as unreliable, perhaps touched with the poison of "radicalism."

It was a not too luxurious dinner, for most of them were not well off. Even for those who had private fortunes it was a grave decision, for they didn't want to live idle lives—they had come with a fond dream of helping to make the world better, and the course they now contemplated might put them on the shelf for a long time, perhaps for life. Their wives came with them, and over a dinner table decorated with yellow jonquils and red roses they talked more solemnly and frankly than Lanny had ever heard from persons of their clever sort. Were they going to ride along on the bandwagon, or climb off as a gesture of protest?

It was a young people's party; the only middle-aged ones were Steffens and Alston. Bullitt was twenty-eight, and Adolf Berle, acting chief of the Russian Section, was only twenty-four; there were others of that age, and their wives were still younger. You could feel the spiritual wrestling going on; but they all tried, in the modern fashion, to take it lightly and not look or act like martyrs, or heroes, or anything that was bad form. Over the liqueurs and coffee everyone had his say, and heard what the others thought about his arguments, and even about his moral status.

Those who were not resigning built themselves a defense mechanism. They were members of a team and had to stand by their captain. He had done the best he could, and they had to exclude from their minds all arguments against his many surrenders. Or else they declared that they were subordinates, employed to furnish information, not to make decisions. Certainly they weren't signing any treaties. Some were in the army, and for them to resign would mean courtmartial!

Those who were resigning were none too patient with these excuses. Being young, their judgments were harsh; black was black and white was white, and no half-tones between. "Oh, yes!" they said. "Be a good boy and do what you're told! Feather your own nest and let the world go to hell!" One of the group had decided at the last minute not to attend; it was rumored that he had been promised a job on the Secretariat of the new League of Nations, which seemed the way to a glamorous European career. "He has his thirty pieces of silver!" exclaimed the resigners.

They had been sold out; that was the general sentiment of the rebels. Each had his own department, about which he knew, and on which he contributed information. Samuel Morison of the Russian Section was furious because the Allies were trying to use his favorite Baltic states as a springboard for White Russian interventions. Bullitt's anger was because the French General Staff had a mandate to run Europe. Berle was indignant because the Allied and associated powers remained untouched by the high moral principles which they were applying to their enemies. Said Alston: "It is not a new order in Europe but a piece of naked force." Because of his age his words carried weight.

The non-resigners fought back, and their wives helped them. They talked about "futile gallantry"; one woman compared them to a group of mosquitoes charging a battleship. It was an old, old question, which Lanny had confronted in talks with Kurt and his father. What part do moral forces play in history? Is there any real use in making yourself uncomfortable for a lot of people who will never hear about it, and wouldn't appreciate it if they did? "It's going to be a long, long time before the verdict of history is rendered on this treaty," said one; and when Alston appealed to the public at home, another said: "All they are thinking about is to punish the Germans; if you try to stop it, you're 'pro-German,' and that's the end of you."

When it came Lanny's turn, he said that Alston was his chief, and he meant to follow him. Alston answered that it might be better if Lanny stayed, because he knew the files and the contents of many reports, and could be of help to whoever took over the job. But Lanny said: "I joined on your account. If you go, I'm sick of the whole business." When the voting was over, one guest reached out and took some of the flowers which decorated the table and, pulling the blossoms off the stems, tossed one to each person—red roses to the resigners, and yellow jonquils to the "good boys" and their girls. It was highly poetical.

When they broke up, close to midnight, Lanny and young Berle walked twice around the Place de la Concorde, in the blue fog and between the rows of looming guns. The acting chief of the Russian Section reminded his still more youthful companion of the saying of Count Oxenstjerna, Swedish diplomat of nearly three hundred years back: "Go forth, my son, and learn with how little wisdom the world is governed!"

VII

The few protestants were in the mood of Martin Luther at the Diet of Worms: "God help me, I can no other!" Carefully and conscientiously each one composed a letter to the State Department, setting forth the reasons which impelled him to the grave step. These letters were duly handed in, and copies were given to the press representatives. Having fired the shot which was supposed to be heard round the world, each patriot held his breath and waited for the echoes.

Alas, they had things to learn about the world they lived in. One of the great New York papers gave an inch or two to the report of some resignations, naming no names; the rest of the press gave not a line to the matter. And then—a pathetic sort of anticlimax— the tactful secretary-general of the American Commission sent for each of the resigners separately and said that their objections had been duly recorded on the books of history; so their honor must now be considered to be satisfied. Wouldn't they kindly consent to stay on and perform their duties during the short time still remaining? No one else knew what they knew; they were really indispensable. Amateurs in diplomacy, they could hardly evade this trap. A couple of days later the department in Washington gave to the press a denial that anyone had resigned except Bullitt, and one professor who was returning on account of pressing duties at home.

Lanny parted from his friend Alston, who was going to teach summer school—a humble professor once more, with no presumptuous ideas of guiding the destiny of states. He had had a great influence upon his secretary, and would not be forgotten. That is the consolation of professors.

Lanny stayed resigned, and so was loose and alone in Paris. He no longer had the use of a room, paid for by the government; no more free meals, and no more honors. The doormen of the Crillon knew him, and would still let him in, but he became aware that persons who talked to him were a bit uneasy. It wasn't quite the safe thing to do.

More to his surprise, Lanny found the same sense of discomfort when he went to see his friend Fessenden. The American had understood, of course, that he was being used as a source of information, but he had assumed that the friendship was real, even so. Now the young Englishman wanted him to understand that it was really real, but Fessenden was dependent upon his career for a living— he wasn't a playboy like Lanny, and couldn't afford to get himself marked as a "pinko." He was very busy now; but when the conference was over there would be time for sociability.

Mrs. Emily invited the homeless youth to be her guest, and he was glad to accept. Here was a comfortable place to stay, and quiet friendship to smooth his ruffled plumage. His hostess was nearing sixty, and with her white hair was a dignified and impressive figure. In her home he met mostly French people; and oddly enough, cultivated Frenchmen paid very little attention to his revolt. The French are a well-insulated people, and seldom bother to know what is going on outside their own world unless it is forced upon them. Disputes and disagreements among the American staff? Yes, they are a rather violent people; their cinema reveals it; they still have wild Indians, don't they? The French would shrug their shoulders.

Lanny was a man of leisure, with time to stroll on the boulevards and watch the sights of a great city and reflect upon them. He himself didn't realize to what extent his point of view had changed; how different his reflections from what they would have been a year ago. For example, the painful spectacle of the women of Paris. In the early days of the Peace Conference you hardly saw a spot on the Champs-Élysées where a person could sit that didn't have a doughboy with a French girl in his lap; now, when the doughboys were disappearing, the competition among the women had become ravenous. Three or four would sight Lanny at once, and come to him swiftly, each looking ready to tear the eyes out of her rival; when he politely told them in good French that he was living a chaste life, their enmity to one another would vanish, and they would gaze mournfully after him, saying: "Oh, but life is hard for the women!"

Six months ago, Lanny would have attributed all this to natural depravity, of a sort peculiar to the Gallic race; he would have recalled some phrases which M. Rochambeau had quoted from Tacitus, censuring the moral code of that race in its then barbaric state. But now Lanny had the phrases of Stef and his Uncle Jesse in his mind. His attention had been called to the fact that municipal authority under the stress of war had set the wages of French workingwomen at six francs per day; whereas to go into a restaurant and have a poor dinner would cost one of them at least seven. Yes, it was the stark, simple fact that hunger was driving them to sell their bodies; hunger was driving the poor of Europe to madness, and making the ferocious class struggles.

What about the women of more prosperous classes, so many of whom were selling themselves for silk gowns, fur coats, and jeweled slippers? "Well," Lanny could hear his uncle saying, "aren't these the tools of their trade?" The gentle and refined scholars whom Woodrow Wilson had brought to Paris were appalled at the behavior of females who wore the clothes of ladies and had been expected to behave that way: females of all nations, American included, some of them in Red Cross costumes. In the Crillon order was maintained, but in other hotels they peddled themselves from door to door like book agents. The shocked professors repeated a story about the American Ambassador to Belgium, who was lodged in the ultra-magnificent Palace Hotel of Brussels, owned by the King of Spain. Said the ambassador to his friends: "It is the custom in European hotels to leave your boots outside the door, to be gathered up by the porter and polished in the early morning hours. So I have bought myself a pair of ladies' shoes, and every night I place them outside my door along with my own boots!"

VIII

There were other aspects of life in Paris less depressing. There were theaters with more to show than troupes of naked women. There were concerts, to remind one that the life of the spirit still continued. Most interesting to Lanny was the spring salon in the Petit Palais. To think that in the midst of the last desperate agony of war, with several "Big Berthas" dropping shells into the city every twenty minutes, with food scarce and fuel unobtainable, more than three thousand men and women had sat at easels and maintained their faith that art could not be destroyed, but was and would remain the supreme achievement and goal of life!

Lanny went to this show day after day. There were many kinds of paintings, many subjects, many techniques; he studied them, and tried to understand what the artist was telling him. Beauty had had three of Marcel's last works brought to Paris, and they had been hung; Lanny now compared them with the work of other men, and confirmed his opinion that there was nothing better being shown. You could see how the crowds felt, for there were always people looking at Marcel's work, and asking questions concerning the painter. Not many knew about him, but they were going to; that would be one of Lanny's tasks, and his mother's—when she came back from her new honeymoon.

Lanny knew many of the artists at this show. Some came to the Cap and worked; for others Beauty had posed in her very young womanhood. They came to see how their work was being received, and to compare it uneasily with work that might be better. Lanny talked with them, got their addresses, and went to visit their studios and talk shop. They were glad to welcome a rich young man who might be a customer, or could send others. As a stepson of Marcel Detaze and nephew of Jesse Blackless, he was an insider; they talked freely, and it was like old times. He had expected to find them all starving and was happy to hear that art activities had come back with an astonishing rush. The bourgeoisie had money and wanted portraits of their beautiful ladies and their eminent selves; they were planning palaces and villas and wanted them made elegant. Artists, eternal enemies of the bourgeois, spoke of them with condescension; another form of the class struggle.

Beautiful things, always touched with sadness. Lanny would stop before a certain painting, and the thought would come to him:

what would Marcel think of this? His stepfather's spirit hovered at his shoulder, and would do so at every exhibition for the rest of his life; pointing out brushwork, atmosphere, composition, meaning, all the things that painting conveys to the trained intelligence. If Lanny was puzzled, he would wait and Marcel would tell him; if Lanny had a conclusion to announce, it would take the form of a dialogue with Marcel. So it is with impressions which form our childhood, and which we pass on to others in their turn.

Kurt Meissner was here in Lanny's thoughts, because they had attended a salon the year before the war; Rick, too, because they had attended the one of 1917. With these two friends Lanny was hoping to resume the life of art, in London, on the Riviera, all over Europe—when finally the statesmen had settled their squabbles and men could begin to think about the things that mattered. Lanny was in a mood of intense repugnance toward politics and everything that had to do with it. He had been on the inside, and never again would he believe in a statesman, never would a stuffed shirt or a uniform decorated with medals produce the slightest stir in his mind. Lanny's dream was to build himself an ivory tower and invite his chosen friends; they would live gracious lives, such as you read about in the days of the Medicis, and the Esterhazys, and other patrons of the arts.

The future patron had in his pocket a letter from Rick, begging him to come to England for a visit. Lanny had replied that he would do so as soon as he could arrange it. He had written to both his mother and his father, telling them about his resignation and asking as to their plans. From Robbie the reply came in the form of a cablegram—the old familiar kind that had made life such an adventure: "Sailing for London steamer Ruritania meet me Hotel Cecil Monday."

36

The Choice of Hercules

I

WHEN Lanny left Paris, at the beginning of June, the Allies and the Germans were still exchanging notes about the treaty, and all the world was waiting to know, would they sign, or wouldn't they? The railwaymen of France were threatening to tie up the country with a strike against low wages, long hours, and the high cost of living; so Lanny took his departure by plane, a new and adventurous way of traveling, if you had the price. This was one good thing that had come out of the war; air travel had become quick and easy, and top members of the British delegation found it swanky to fly to London in the morning, have lunch and a conference, and return to Paris in the afternoon.

Private passengers paid eighty dollars for a one-way trip. You were bundled up in a heavy sheepskin coat and robe and wore a helmet with goggles. A marvelous sensation to feel yourself being lifted off the ground and see the earth falling away. What hath God wrought! The wind roared by at a hundred miles an hour, and the noise of the engine made it necessary to write a note to the pilot if you had anything to say. Down below were the farms of France, little checkerboards of green and brown and yellow. Then the Channel, made safe for traffic, the submarines having been surrendered to the English fleet. Fishing boats were tiny specks on the smooth blue and the heavy coal lighters trailed streamers of black smoke.

When Lanny got off the train at the station near The Reaches, Rick and Nina were waiting in a little car, Nina driving; Rick could never drive because of his leg. He had it in a steel brace, but even with this support it pained him to walk, and now and then he would go white and have to lean against something. But he didn't want anybody to help him; it was his own trouble and he would attend to it. Just oblige him by going on with the conversation, quietly and indifferently, English fashion.

Lanny had expected to find his friend emaciated, but he was stouter than he had been. That was on account of the lack of exercise; he couldn't go into the water, and the only form of work he could perform was to lie on his back and wave his arms, or raise himself to a sitting position—all of which was a bore. He couldn't play the piano very well, because of the pedals. Most of the time he read, and he was exacting of his authors, also of people who came to talk with him. Nina said he had fretted himself near to death, but gradually he was learning to get along with what fate would allow him.

A little more than two years had passed since Lanny had seen him, strong and confident, hopping into a railway car with a load of cigarettes and chocolate for the "corps wing." Now you'd have thought ten times as many years had passed; his face was lined and melancholy and there were touches of gray in his wavy dark hair. But inside him was the same old Rick, proud and impatient, critical and exacting for himself as well as for others, yet warm-hearted in his reserved way, generous and kind in actions even when he was fierce in words. He was pathetically glad to see Lanny, and right away on the drive began asking questions about the Peace Conference, what it had done, what it was going to do.

Lanny could talk a lot about that and he found himself an important person, having been on the inside, and knowing things which the papers didn't tell. Even Sir Alfred wanted to hear his story. In the twilight they sat on the terrace of that lovely old place, and friends came, young and old, whom Lanny had met five years ago. What strange things they had been through—and how little they had been able to guess!

A basic question which they discussed at length: Could you by any possibility trust the Germans? Would they be willing to settle down, let bygones be bygones, take their part in a League of Nations, and help to build a sane and decent world? Or were they incurable militarists? If they got on their feet again, would they start arming right away, and throw the world into another Armageddon? Manifestly, the way you were going to treat them depended upon the answer to these questions. Lanny, having heard the subject debated from every possible angle, was able to appear very wise to these cultivated English folk.

Some had had experience with Germans, before and during the war, and had come to conclusions. Sir Alfred Pomeroy-Nielson, pacifist and radical of five years back, had now become convinced that Germany would have to be split up, in order to keep her from dominating Europe. On the other hand Rick, who had done the fighting and might have been expected to hate the people who had crippled him, declared that the dumb politicians on both sides were to blame; the German and the English people would have to find a way to get rid of these vermin simultaneously. With his usual penetration, Rick said that the one thing you couldn't do was to follow both policies at the same time. You couldn't repress Germany *à la française* with your right hand, and conciliate her *à l'américaine* with your left. That, he added, was exactly what the dumb politicians were attempting.

II

Next day they went punting. Rick spread himself on cushions on the bottom of the boat, with Nina at his side, and Lanny took the long pole and walked them up the Thames. They recalled the boat races, which had been postponed for five years, but would be held again next month. They stopped under an overhanging tree and ate lunch, while Lanny told about his stay in Connecticut, and the great munitions industry and the trouble it was in; he told about Gracyn, whose play had run all winter in New York.

Lanny thought how much better it would have been if he'd had the luck to find a girl like Nina, who so obviously adored Rick, and watched over him and waited on him day and night. They had a lovely little boy toddling about on the green lawns and Nina was expecting another. That was all Rick was good for, he said; to increase the population and make up for the losses of war. It wasn't any fun making love without a kneejoint, but he could manage it as a patriotic duty. Nina didn't make any objection to this form of conversation; it was the fashion among these young people, who went out of their way to say exactly what they meant.

Rick told about his family's affairs. When Lanny went for a walk he would discover that those old cottages which had shocked him had been razed and the ground planted to potatoes. A part of the estate had been sold to pay war taxes, and they might have to part with the whole thing if government didn't let up on them. The poor fools who imagined they were going to make Germany pay for the war would pretty soon begin to realize that Germany had nothing to pay with, and wouldn't do it if she could. Lanny agreed with that; he reported that the Crillon expected the Germans to sign with their fingers crossed and begin every possible method of evasion.

They drifted back with the current. While Rick lay down to rest, the other two sat under a tree on the lawn, and Lanny made friends with the baby while Nina told about her life. She didn't have to say that marriage and motherhood had agreed with her; her frail figure had filled out and her eager, intense manner had changed to one of repose. Rick's exacting ways didn't trouble her too greatly; she had learned to understand him, and managed him as an expert would a problem child. She counted herself fortunate, because she had love, which so many others had lost or had never found.

"At least they can't take him to war," she said, and added: "Now that we women have got the vote, if we allow any more wars, we'll deserve the worst that comes to us. Do you think women will get the vote in America?"

Lanny answered that President Wilson had been strongly against it, as a federal measure; but it had been shown that he could be made to change his mind. "I have seen that happen," said the youth, with a touch of malice.

"What are you going to do with yourself?" Nina wanted to know. When he told her that he was trying to make up his mind, she said: "You can't just drift around; if you do, some woman will get hold of you and make you miserable. Why don't you come and live near here, and let Rick and me find you a wife?"

He laughed and said he'd have to find a way to earn his living first; he didn't want to live on his father indefinitely. "Why don't you and Rick come to the Riviera next winter, and let him stay outdoors in the sunshine?"

"I don't believe we'll be able to afford any travel, Lanny."

"You'll be surprised how cheaply you can live, if you don't put on side. There are lots of little villas, and food will be cheap again when Europe settles down." Lanny was figuring on bringing Kurt and Rick together again. Such a clever intriguer he was!

III

He had asked Rosemary if he might come to see her. She answered that she was expecting a baby in a couple of months, and was "a sight," but if he could stand her she'd be delighted. Sir Alfred lent him the small car, and he drove for a couple of hours through the lovely English countryside, now at its best, and so peaceful you would think there had never been a war in the world: soft green meadows and fields of ripening grain, villages with broad commons and sheep grazing, great estates with parks, villas with well-kept hedges full of blossoms and singing birds. In most of those houses there would be gracious and kindly people, good to know; yes, maybe he would come to England—and learn to drive on the wrong side of the road without so much effort of mind.

Rosemary was now the Honorable Mrs. Algernon Armistead Brougham, pronounced Broom, and she lived in what was called a "lodge," a fairly large house on the estate of her husband's grandfather. She enjoyed the scenery of a beautiful park without the trouble or expense of keeping it; an ideal environment for the incubating of a future member of the ruling class. The visitor was ushered into a sun parlor full of flowers and the song of a canary; presently Rosemary came in, wearing an ample robe of pink silky stuff, and looking so lovely that Lanny felt the blood start in warm currents all over him.

A strange thing to see the woman he loved carrying another man's child! But then, stranger things had happened to Lanny already; and in this part of the world, whatever you felt you didn't show it. Certainly the future mother of a future earl was going to show no signs of worry. "The sons of Mary seldom bother, for they have inherited that good part"—and the daughters the same. Rosemary was gracious, she was kind, and for the time being she was an elder sister to this youth who had had the good fortune to please her.

She wasn't much interested in politics, and he didn't even bother to mention his resignation from the Crillon. What she wanted to hear about was the members of the British delegation he had met; she knew some of them, and had heard talk about others. She wanted the latest news about Nina and Rick and their common friends. She asked politely about Lanny's mother, and when he said that she was traveling in Spain, that sufficed; for the leisure class went traveling when the mood took them, and no other reason was required. Nor had she much curiosity about his visit to America—a remote and provincial place that people came from but didn't go to.

Most of all she wanted to know about Lanny himself; what was the state of his heart, and what was he planning to do with himself? He didn't tell her about Gracyn, being ashamed of it. When she asked the direct question whether he had fallen victim to the lures for which La Ville Lumière was famous, he answered that he had lived a well-disciplined life, but had been sorely tempted by the charms of a stockbroker's daughter on the British staff.

"Poor darling Lanny!" said she. "He's going to be meat for some designing woman!" She was not to be persuaded that any man could ever see through the wiles of her sex.

The advice she gave him was the same as Nina's—to come and live in England. Rosemary, also, would like to find some "nice girl" to take care of him! "They can't fool us with their tricks, you know."

She had given him an opening, and he said: "Tell me—are you happy with your husband?"

"Oh, we get along," was the reply. "He's a very good boy—not vicious at all, only a bit soft." Her frank blue eyes met Lanny's. "He had a love affair, too."

"I see!" replied the youth. He had lived in France most of his life and wasn't naïve; but all the same, he was in revolt against the property marriage. Perhaps it was because he had read so many novels and dramas—impractical inventions which attempted to maintain the rights of the heart over those of great estates and family fortunes! Few indeed among the heroines of these works had been able to take the complications of their sex life with the serenity of the future Countess of Sandhaven.

"Lanny, darling," said she, "I feel for you just what I used to; and maybe some day things will be so that we can be happy again. But don't be silly and try to wait for me. It may be a long time. Take things as they are and don't wear yourself out trying to change them all at once."

IV

Lanny went up to town early on Monday morning, and was waiting in the hotel lobby for his father. It amused him to sit in the same chair which he had occupied under the same circumstances almost exactly five years earlier. In that far-off time people had been wont to complain that life had become commonplace, that civilization had taken all the romance and excitement out of it. But very certainly Lanny hadn't found it so during those five years!

Robbie came in, looking prosperous and well cared for as always. His son gave him a hug and some pats on the back, and they went upstairs, and after Robbie had unpacked his whisky bottle and got his ice and soda, he said: "Now what the dickens is this about Beauty going to Spain?" Lanny had written cryptically, for he couldn't give any hint about Kurt in France, and he thought it better not to allude to a love affair which would require a lot of explaining.

Now he told the story, and Robbie sat astonished, forgetting his drink. The younger man wasn't at liberty to tell the part about Uncle Jesse and the money, even to his father; but he told about the duel with the Sûreté, and the father said: "Look here, kid, did all this happen, or did you dream it?" When Lanny began to picture Kurt's life in Beauty's apartment, Robbie exclaimed: "You left those two people shut up together for a week?"

So the "love interest" in the story didn't require as much explaining as the younger man had anticipated. Robbie knew his former mistress from top to toe, as he said, and he had never imagined that she could live without a man. "Even if she tried, the men wouldn't let her," said he.

What he was interested in was trying to guess the chances of her finding happiness in this oddest and most unexpected of liaisons. He had met Kurt only a few times, in London five years back; what had he turned into, and what could Beauty have to offer him, apart from the arts of love? Lanny, of course, defended his friend ardently, and read his father the brief letters which had come from his mother in Spain, indicating her perfect happiness. Robbie said: "Of course, if they can hit it off together, it's all right with me. But don't count on it for too many years."

The father gave some of the news from home. Esther and the children were well and sent messages of affection; they lived uneventful lives over there. As happens in all large families, one or two old Budds had died and several new ones had made their entrance upon the scene. The family was having the devil's own time making over the plants. They had had to go into debt; but

Robbie was hopeful, for the world was half a decade behind in every form of production except guns and shells, and there was sure to be a terrific boom as soon as order was restored.

"Then we're not going to sell out to Zaharoff?" said Lanny; and his father authorized him to bet his boots that it would not happen.

V

Of course Robbie wanted to hear about the Peace Conference. Nearly three months had passed since he had left, and Lanny hadn't been able to put the confidential things into letters. The father plied him with questions about those aspects which were important to a businessman. Was Wilson really going to stand by that preposterous guarantee which Clemenceau had wangled out of him? Were we really going to get ourselves tied up with Constantinople and Armenia? Were France and Britain likely to get anywhere with the scheme they had been trying to work from the outset, to tie up German reparations with the money they had borrowed from America for the prosecution of the war? To make the paying of their own just and lawful debts dependent upon their collections from Germany—and thus, in effect, get America to do their collecting for them!

Lanny replied that a lot of people at the Crillon were questioning whether either form of debts could ever be paid. Even if the Allies took all the livestock and the movable wealth out of Germany, they couldn't get more than a billion or two; the gold reserve was much less than anyone believed, and to take it would mean to destroy Germany as an industrial power, and hence her ability to pay anything more. Lanny quoted what Steffens had said, that every dollar the Allies collected would cost them a dollar-five. He talked a lot about Steffens and Bullitt, in many ways the most interesting men he had met.

Gradually the younger man began to notice a shift in the conversation. The father stopped asking what the Peace Conference had done, and began asking about what Lanny thought. Lanny, who wasn't slow-witted, caught the meaning: his father was worried about the sort of company he had been keeping. Lanny was in the position of a man who has been out in the woods or some place where he hasn't had the use of a mirror; now suddenly one was held up before him and he saw the way he looked. To put it plainly, the way he looked was pink with red spots—a most unpleasing aspect for a young gentleman of leisure and good family.

The change had happened so gradually—a little bit one day and next day another little bit in another part of his mind—that Lanny hadn't had time to become aware of it, and now couldn't believe it, wouldn't admit it. He imagined that his father must be misunderstanding him, and tried to explain himself—thereby making matters worse than they were before. He would cite things that Robbie himself had told: what the big businessmen had done to cause the war and to prolong it and to get advantages out of the settlement. The Crillon was full of talk about *concessionnaires* from every nation who were in Paris, pulling wires more or less openly, telling statesmen what to do to protect these coal mines or that oil territory. Grabbing this and threatening to grab that—surely Robbie must know that as well as anybody! Surely he must realize that these were the things which had wrecked the conference!

Yes, Robbie knew all that. Robbie knew that right now Britain and France were squabbling behind the scenes over the oil in Mesopotamia. Robbie knew as well as the Crillon that nothing in the world but fear of Germany would keep Britain and France from turning against each other in that dispute. Robbie knew that the two nations were still trying to hold on to Baku with its oil, and had even succeeded in having a vessel flying the American flag in the Caspian Sea, in the effort to overawe the Bolsheviks and keep them out of their own country's oil fields. And knowing all that— why was Robbie so disturbed when his son named the big oil promoters among the enemies of a sane peace?

There was a very special reason, which had to do with Robbie's crossing the ocean. Perhaps he had made a mistake in not mentioning it earlier in the conversation. An oil geologist whom he had known for many years, and who had worked for the big companies in the Near East, had come to Newcastle on purpose to interest him in a project for getting a concession in Eastern Arabia. After hearing his story, Robbie had got together a group of his friends, men who had made money out of Budd dividends and were looking for a place to invest it; they had formed a syndicate, and Robbie was here to work on the project, to interview representatives of the Arabs and pull wires with the British and French officials, as he knew so well how to do. Some Americans were going to get more than paper promises out of all the blood they had poured into the soil of France, and the billions of dollars' worth of food and clothing, oil and machinery, guns and shells and what not which they had ferried across the ocean to France and England!

VI

Robbie behaved like the battalion chief of a fire department who arrives on the scene and discovers that he has a dangerous conflagration on his hands; he sent in a second and a third alarm, brought up all his apparatus, and started to flood his incandescent son with arguments. Surely Lanny couldn't have watched modern war without realizing that oil was vital to a nation! Not a wheel in a Budd plant could turn without it; and what was going to become of America, what would be the good of dreams about liberty, democracy, or other sorts of ideals, if we failed to get our share of a product for which there was no substitute? All over the world the British were grabbing the territories in which there was any chance of oil; they were holding these as reserves and buying our American supply for immediate use—it was their deliberate policy.

"Look at Mexico!" exclaimed the father. "Right at our own doors they are intriguing, undermining us, freezing us out. Every official in the Mexican government is for sale and the British are there with the cash. That is 'law and order,' 'freedom of trade,' 'peace'—all those fine phrases! Everywhere an American businessman goes his British competitor is there with his government behind him—and we might as well quit and let them have the world. Fine phrases make pleasant week-end parties, Lanny, but they don't lubricate machinery."

"The Crillon is hoping to adjust such matters through the League of Nations," argued the son.

"Did anybody at the Crillon ever persuade the British to give up anything in the final showdown? And if you had an insider to advise you, you'd see that one demand after another is to protect the oil they have or to get more."

"But what's to be done about it, Robbie? The British and French are begging to continue the Supreme Economic Council, but the Americans insist upon ending it and going back to unrestricted competition."

"That's because we know the British are bound to dominate the Council. Imagine the nerve of them—each of their dominions to have a vote in the League, while the United States has only one!"

"One vote will be enough for a veto," countered Lanny, who knew that League Covenant pretty nearly by heart.

"That's the silliest thing in the whole scheme," declared the father; "it means that the machine will be stalled from the outset. I read somewhere that they had such an arrangement in old-time Poland—any knight could rise in the assembly and veto any measure and kill it. A nation couldn't survive on such a basis, and neither can a League of Nations."

Lanny had heard all these arguments; he knew his father's mind inside out. Nor was he conscious of any disagreement. What Robbie said was true, and likewise what Lincoln Steffens said; it was just that they drew different conclusions from the facts. But Lanny had better not say that, because then the father would repeat his arguments all over again. Better agree with him as far as you could, and keep the rest of your ideas to yourself. That was the course which Robbie had recommended during the years that Lanny had lived in France at war; and now Lanny would apply the method to its teacher.

VII

Robbie told all about his business project: who was backing it in America and who was to be approached in London. It wasn't a big one, as oil projects went; only about eight million dollars, but there would be more where that came from if Robbie continued to be satisfied about the prospects. It was a fast game they were going to break in on; in telling about it the father used the language of sport, of gangsters, of war—it was all of those things. Zaharoff had gone into oil; no munitions people could stay out, for it was oil that had won the last war. Did Lanny realize why the German armies had so suddenly begun clamoring for an armistice? It wasn't because they couldn't fall back and defend a new line; it wasn't because of revolts at home; it was because the Rumanian oil field had been destroyed, and the surrender of Bulgaria had cut them off from the southeast, and there was no more oil to run the tanks and trucks without which armies were stalled.

Lanny perceived that the money his father had made was burning a hole in his pocket. The idea of settling back and resting hadn't occurred to him, and it would do no good to suggest it. The purpose of having money was to get more. Money was power, the ability to do things. Money was patriotism, also. Robbie told about a Dutch bank clerk of the name of Henri Deterding who had forced his way into the oil industry and now was the master of Royal Dutch Shell; it was he who had kept the British fleet supplied with fuel all through the war. The British had had to meet his terms, and, as a result, little Holland was one of the most prosperous countries in the world—and with hardly any army or fleet of its own!

American money had made it possible for the British to take Mesopotamia from the Turks and keep it. Said Robbie: "If we hadn't sent our men and supplies, the Germans would be getting that oil right now. So why shouldn't our country have a share? We'll take in some influential Britishers and give them a chance to co-operate; but if they won't we'll use the power of the government and make them give up."

"You mean you'll threaten them?" asked Lanny.

"Not even an argument," said the father, smiling. "Just a little understanding among gentlemen."

"You'll have to get a new administration in Washington," ventured the youth; and Robbie said he hadn't overlooked that. Wilson's peace treaty was going to be dumped into the ashcan, and his fool League with it. There would be a Republican President, and a State Department that would understand businessmen and back them up.

"Believe me," said Robbie, "the haughty gentlemen of this 'City' know how to give up when they have to. Some day you'll see them make Robbie Budd a Knight Commander of the Bath—as I'm told they're planning to do for a Greek ex-fireman who's got hold of their munitions industry!"

VIII

Hitherto in the life of this father and son the younger had been bubbling over with interest in the elder's affairs, eager to go with him and share what he was doing. And here was another chance. Lanny would only have to say: "Can I help you with this, Robbie?" and his father would let him attend the conferences, would give him a block of stock in the enterprise, and make him, in effect, a partner. Perhaps Robbie had been counting upon it—for now, having been trained in the duties of a secretary, the son could be of real help. But the father was too proud to ask; he waited for his son to speak—and Lanny didn't speak.

Only six months had been needed to make that difference; to fill Lanny's mind, not merely with doubts and questionings, but with a distaste which startled him when he came face to face with it. He just didn't want to be in the oil business! The very thing which made it so important to Robbie had made it in the eyes of the

Crillon liberals the arch-malefactor of the time. Five years ago it had been possible for Lanny to think of intrigues and battles over the selling of guns and cartridges as romantic and exciting; but now it was impossible to get up such feelings about an oil concession and pipeline.

So, while the father went to keep the first of his appointments, Lanny walked on the Embankment, watching the traffic on the river and saying to himself: "What is it that I really want to do?" He pictured his life if he should become Robbie's London representative. He would have a sumptuous office and meet the important men of the City, also of Whitehall; Rosemary, Margy Petries, and others of the ladies would put him into the social whirl; they would find him a rich wife, and his father would see that he made all the money he wanted. He would spend his time figuring how to outwit Zaharoff and Deterding and lesser men of that sort; he would be in a game, or racket, or battle, in which there was no rest, no let-up—it was dog eat dog, and if you didn't get your grip on the other dog's throat, he would get his grip on yours, and that would be your finish.

Lanny's fancy moved on to that peaceful Côte d'Azur, with sunshine and blue water, and air always warm, except at night, or when the mistral blew. There were a lot of fashionable goings-on, noise and distraction, gambling and vice, and doubtless it would be worse since the war; but you didn't have to bother with it, you could go your way and let the wasters go theirs. In the living room was a piano, good enough when it had been tuned, and a great stack of music which Lanny had played through and would like to tackle again. He had been to concerts, and heard new music which he would try out. In the storeroom of the studio were all but a few of Marcel's paintings; and now, fresh from an exhibition, Lanny would view his stepfather's work all over again and compare it with what he had seen. Also there were a score or so of wooden cases, containing the books which his Great-Great-Uncle Eli had willed to him; Lanny promised himself an adventure unpacking these and having shelves made for them. He hadn't liked New

England any too well, but he thought he might come to know it better through its poets and sages than through its country club gentry and munitions makers.

He had it planned out in detail. His mother and his new step-father would come back from Spain as soon as it was safe, and they would build another studio for Kurt on the other side of the grounds—if both of them were going to tootle and tinkle they would want as much distance between them as possible. Some day Rick and Nina would come to visit them; and—still farther in the future—Rosemary would come. Lanny remembered the spot where they had sat in the darkness and watched the lights over the water and listened to the distant music from the casino orchestra; the thought of it sent little shivers coursing up and down his nerves. *"Ein Jüngling liebt ein Mädchen, Die hat einen Andern erwählt!"*

IX

A delicate situation between a devoted father and an equally devoted son: one calling for a lot of tact—and fortunately Lanny had been in the polite world long enough to acquire it. Never would he say a word against the oil industry; never would he argue, but let Robbie have his say. Lanny would think his own thoughts—one of the great privileges of man. He would lunch or dine with his father and meet some of the "big" men—interesting personalities, provided you entered into their world and didn't expect them to enter into yours. An oil magnate discussing the market prospects or the international situation might be an authority; but discussing a book or a play he wasn't so hot. Lanny would say that he had a date, and would go look at an art show or hear a concert.

He had told about these plans before they crossed the seas, so there could be no complaint. Robbie was a fair man, and wouldn't try to compel his son; Robbie's own father had made that mistake, with results which Robbie would never forget or forgive, and he was not going to repeat the offense. He had promised Lanny an allowance, what he would have had if he had been going through college. So long as he was improving himself and not wasting his life, he was free to choose his own course. Lanny did really mean to make something of his opportunities—even though he wasn't sure just what it was going to be. The world was so big, and there were so many things he wanted to see and to understand; so many interesting people, to start new ideas going in his mind!

He accepted an invitation to a week-end with Beauty's old friends, the Eversham-Watsons, and practiced riding and jumping some more, and learned about the gout from his lordship, and had an amusing time fencing off the efforts of Margy Petries to find out what his blessed mother was doing in Spain. No use trying to fool that eager chatterbox and manipulator of men—she knew it was a "romance"—she knew that Beauty Budd wasn't going to remain a widow—and who was it, some grandee of that land of castanets and cruelty? Lanny would just smile and say: "Beauty will tell you some day. Meanwhile, be sure that anything you guess will be wrong!"

He walked, and saw London at the beginning of the peace era. He knew what he was looking at now; he could recognize the signs of that poverty in the midst of luxury which was the plague of the modern world, and perhaps, as Stef thought, the seed of its destruction. He walked in Piccadilly and saw hordes of women peddling themselves, as in Paris—only they lacked the *chic* and *esprit* of the French. In the fashionable shopping streets he saw returned soldiers, hundreds of them, wandering listless and depressed; England had needed them, but now they peddled pencils, boxes o' lights, any trifling objects that would keep them from being beggars within the meaning of the law. Prosperity was coming back, everybody insisted—but for these men it was a marshlight, flitting out of reach.

As in Paris, all the smart forms of play had been resumed with a rush. A horde of people had got money, and the newspapers assured them that the way to help the poor was to spend it fast. Benevolent souls, they labored hard to do their duty. They acquired new outfits of costly clothing, thus making work for seamstresses and tailors; they motored to the racetracks, thus making work for jockeys and trainers, for salesmen and chauffeurs of automobiles; they swarmed into the expensive restaurants, ordered lavishly, and tipped the waiters generously. To assist their efforts were shows and pageants, balls and festivals, events with historic names— "Wimbledon" and "Henley," a "Peace Ascot" and a "Victory Derby," a Cowes regatta coming for the first time in six years. There would be no "Courts," but there were six Royal Garden Parties at Buckingham Palace, gay and delightful affairs at which the ladies were forbidden to wear *décolleté* in the afternoons. In the days of Jane Austen it would have been proper, but the present Queen considered female arms and bosoms improper until after sundown.

Pearls were the gems of the day, and fashions were "anarchical"; dresses might be anything so long as skirts were short and waistlines nonexistent. Capes had come back; they were pleated, and large at the waist—built in imitation of barrels, so Margy Petries declared. The keynote of a day costume was plumes; not the curled ones, but lancer plumes, glycerined plumes, plume fringes, plume cascades, plume rosettes. Because of the great number of gas cases, which healed slowly if ever, many entertainments were given and costumes worn for the benefit of the crowded hospitals.

Lanny missed his mother, or some girl to enjoy the society game with him. He persuaded Nina and Rick to motor to town, and put them up at the hotel, and took them to see the Russian dancers— not Bolsheviks, but good, old-time Russians, doing *La Boutique Fantasque*, enacting can-can dancing dolls. Nina managed to persuade her husband to forget his pride and look at the spring exhibition of art from a wheel-chair. Lanny, having read what the critics had said in Paris, was able to talk instructively about the relative merits of the two displays. Altogether he managed to pass the time agreeably, until one day his father said: "I have to go to Paris for a while."

"That's on my way home!" answered Lanny.

37

Peace in Our Time

I

THE day that Lanny and his father arrived in France was the last day of the last extension of time allowed to the Germans, to say whether or not they were going to accept the terms imposed upon them. At least so the Allies declared, and at each of their outposts, fifty kilometers beyond the Rhine bridgeheads, their motorized columns were packed up and ready to start. They were going to advance thirty-five miles per day into Germany, so it was announced; and meanwhile in every drawing room and *bistro* in France the leading topic of discussion was: Will they sign or won't they?

An Austrian peace delegation had come, and a Bulgarian one, and were submitting with good grace to having their feathers pulled out while they were still alive. Not a squawk from them; but the Germans had been keeping up a God-awful clamor for six or seven weeks; all over their country mass meetings of protest, and Clemenceau remarking in one of his answers that apparently they had not yet realized that they had lost a war. Their delegation was kept inside their stockade and told that it was for their safety; some of them, traveling back and forth to Germany, were stoned, and for this Clemenceau made the one apology of his career.

The Social-Democrats were ruling the beaten country. It was supposed to have been a revolution, but a polite and discreet one which had left the nobility all their estates and the capitalists all their industries. It was, so Steffens and Herron had explained to Lanny, a political, not an economic revolution. A Socialist police chief was obligingly putting down the Reds in Berlin, and for this the Allies might have been grateful but didn't seem to be. Stef said they couldn't afford to let a Socialist government succeed at anything; it would have a bad effect upon the workers in the Allied lands. It was a time of confusion, when great numbers of people didn't know just what they wanted, or if they did they took measures which got them something else.

In the eastern sky the dark cloud continued to lower; and here, also, what the Allies did only made matters worse. The Big Four had recognized Admiral Kolchak as the future ruler of Siberia—a land whose need for a navy was somewhat restricted. This land-admiral had agreed to submit his policies to a vote of the Russian people, but meanwhile he was proceeding to kill as many of them as possible and seize their farms. The result was that the peasants went into hiding, and as soon as the admiral's armies moved on they came out and took back their farms. The same thing was happening all over the Ukraine, where General Denikin had been chosen as the Russian savior; and now another general, named Yudenich, was being equipped to capture Petrograd. They didn't dare to give these various saviors any British, French, or American troops, because of mutinies; but they would furnish officers, and armaments which were charged up as "loans," and which the peasants of Russia were expected to repay in return for being deprived of the land.

At any rate, that was the way Stef described matters to Lanny Budd; and Lanny found this credible, because Stef had been there and the others hadn't. The youth had gone to call on this strange little man, whose point of view was so stimulating to the mind. Lanny didn't tell his father about this visit, and quieted his conscience by saying, what use making Robbie unhappy to no purpose? Lanny wasn't ever going to become a Red—he just wanted to hear all sides and understand them. Robbie seemed to have the idea that the only way to avoid falling into the snares of the Reds was to refuse to have anything to do with them, or even to know about them. The moment you started to "understand" them—at that moment you were becoming tainted with their hateful infection!

II

There came a 'letter from Beauty, now viewing the art galleries
and cabarets of Madrid. She was so, so happy; but her conscience
was troubling her because of Baby Marceline, left motherless on
the Riviera for so many months. To be sure, the servants adored
her, and Beauty had asked friends to go and look her over; but
still the mother worried, and wanted Lanny to run down and take
her place. "You know my position," she pleaded. "I dare not leave
our friend alone." Always she used the tactful phrase, "our" friend.
If a woman wrote *mon ami*, that had a special meaning; but *notre
ami* was chaste, even Christian, and took Lanny into the *affaire*.

There was much to be done at their home, Beauty informed him.
The house needed very much to be redecorated, and it was fortunate that Lanny had such good taste; his mother would leave it
to him, and be interested to see what new ideas he had acquired in
two years of journeying about. Lanny decided that he would surprise her by building that extra studio. The many relatives of Leese
would be summoned *en masse;* they were slow, but Lanny knew
them and liked them, and they would work well for him.

This was something the youth could present to his father as a
plausible substitute for a job in the oil industry. Robbie believed in
buildings, as something you could see, and if need be could sell;
he said to do the studio right, and he would pay for it. He added
that Baby Marceline would probably be better off if Beauty would
stay in Spain, or go back to Germany with Kurt; all she could do
with a child was to spoil it. She would have done that with Lanny
if Robbie hadn't put his foot down many times. Lanny said maybe
she had anyhow.

The youth wanted to remain in Paris until his father was through.
He was seeing the Crillon and all its affairs through a new pair of
eyes. The men with whom Robbie was dealing were not the statesmen, but those who told the statesmen what to do. Yes, even the
stiff-souled Presbyterian, the reformer to whom big business had
been anathema—even he had become dependent upon the masters of

money. A whole procession of them had been called over to Paris: prominent among them Lamont of the House of Morgan, whom Wilson had refused even to receive at the White House before the war. A score of such men had now become the President's confidential advisers on questions of reparations and the restoring of trade and finance.

Of course these businessmen were telling him to do the things which would enable them to go on making money, as they had been doing so happily before the war. The railroads were to be handed back to private management, and government controls over industry were to be abandoned. The Supreme Economic Council was to be scrapped, so that the scramble for raw materials could be resumed and Wall Street speculators could buy up everything in sight. To Robbie Budd all this was proof that the world naturally belonged to vigorous, acquisitive persons like himself. He was here to consult with others of his sort, and make certain that American diplomatic and naval authorities would co-operate with American oil men endeavoring to obtain their share of a product for which there was no substitute.

III

Johannes Robin came to Paris to consult his business associate. He brought with him a suitcase full of letters, contracts, and financial statements, and Lanny had lunch with the two, and listened while the Jewish enterpriser explained the various affairs in which he had been using Robbie's money. Things hadn't gone so well as he had hoped, because the delays in the peace settlement had held up transportation and credit. Meanwhile storage charges were eating up a share of the profits; but still, there would be goodly sums left, and Robbie professed himself as satisfied with what had been done.

They went upstairs to their suite, and Robbie settled down to look over the documents, with his associate explaining them. Lanny went along, because Mr. Robin said he had brought more snapshots of his family, also a present, a copy of Hansi's "Opus 1," a violin étude; the copy made by the fifteen-year-old composer's own hands. Lanny sat down to study it and became absorbed; he had heard so much about that talented and hard-working lad who wanted to be his friend and adorer. He could see right away what had happened: Hansi had learned to perform a number of difficult technical feats on the violin, and in his composition he had been concerned to give himself an opportunity to do them all. But then, most performers' compositions are like that; you take it for granted, as you do the make-up and mannerisms of a "professional beauty."

Mr. Robin was so interested in Lanny's interest that he could hardly keep his mind on the business documents. When Lanny said: "That's a lovely theme just after the cadenza," the fond father turned pink with pleasure. "Can you really get it without hearing it?" he exclaimed; and of course Lanny was pleased to have his musical accomplishments admired. Perhaps the Jewish businessman knew that Lanny would be pleased—thus human relationships are complicated by the profit motive! Anyhow, Lanny promised to take the composition home with him and master the piano part, in preparation for the day when he and the young composer would play their first duet.

Robbie told his new associate about his plans to break into the oil game, and the latter said he would like to put his profits into that venture. Living in the land of Henri Deterding, he knew quite a lot about the oil business, and the two of them talked as equals in the fascinating game of profit-hunting. To Lanny they resembled two sleek and capable panthers which have met in the jungle and decided to work together for the quicker finding and bringing down of their prey. One had been born in a mud hut in Poland and the other in an aristocratic mansion in New England, but modern standardization had brought them to a point where they talked in shorthand, as it were—they understood each other without the need of completing a sentence. Lanny had a lot of fun teasing his father about it afterward, and trying to decide whether the new firm was to be known as Robbie and Robin, or Robin and Robbie. A delicate point in verbal aesthetics—or was it in social precedence? Of course, said the youth, when they had conquered the world and possessed its oil, they would be known as "R. & R."

The Dutch partner in this combination said that as soon as peace was certain he was planning to move his office and family to Berlin. Hansi had learned about all he could in Rotterdam; and for the father there would be extraordinary opportunities of profit in Germany in the next few years. He would keep his Rotterdam office, and turn all his money into guilders and dollars. With the reparations settlement as it was, the mark was bound to lose value; the only way, short of repudiation, for Germany to reduce her internal debts. Incidentally, by inflation, she could collect large sums from foreigners, who believed in the mark and were buying it now. Johannes Robin said there was much argument among Dutch traders on this point, and of course fortunes would be made or lost on the guess. Robbie was inclined to agree with his new partner, but advised him that it would be safer to buy properties and goods, which would be thrown on the market for almost nothing in a collapse of the German money system.

IV

The ministry of the Socialist Scheidemann resigned; he wouldn't sign the treaty. Brockdorff-Rantzau wouldn't sign. But somebody had to sign, for it was clear that Germany had no other course. The new ministry sent word that it would bow to the inevitable; but still they didn't send anybody. President Wilson was impatient to return to Washington, where a special session of the new Congress had been waiting for him for more than a month. But the ceremony of signing had to be put off day after day. It was most annoying, and offensive to the dignity of the victorious Great Powers.

Lanny went to call on Lincoln Steffens at his hotel. After listening to his father and his father's new business associate, the youth wanted someone to tell him that the world wasn't created entirely to have money made out of it. Sitting in his little hotel room, confined by a cold, Stef said that the money-makers were having their own way everywhere; but the trouble was they couldn't agree among themselves, and kept flinging the world into one mess after another. So there were revolts; and the question was, would these revolts be blind, or would they have a program?

Stef told what had just happened to an artist friend of his, a brilliant cartoonist of Greenwich Village, the artists' quarter of New York. Robert Minor had gone in a fine state of enthusiasm to look at the new revolutionary Russia, and had then come to Paris. He visited the headquarters of the railwaymen, then threatening their strike, and told them what the Russians were doing. As a result, a couple of French *flics* had picked him up at his lodgings and taken him to the Préfecture and grilled him for half a day; then they had turned him over to the American army authorities at Koblenz, who had held him prisoner in secret for several weeks. They had talked about shooting him; but he had managed to smuggle out word as to his whereabouts, and the labor press of Paris had taken up the case. It happened that "Bob's" father was a judge in Texas and an influential Democrat; so in the end the army authorities had turned their prisoner loose.

Lanny mentioned how his Uncle Jesse likewise had been questioned by the police, and had threatened them with publicity. Jesse had been sure they wouldn't jail an American just for making speeches.

"This was a special kind of speech," answered Stef. "Bob advised the railwaymen how to stop the invasion of the Black Sea by calling a strike on the railroads to Marseille."

"Yes, I suppose that's different," the youth agreed.

The muckraker asked whether Lanny hadn't been spied on himself. Lanny was surprised, and said he hadn't thought about it. Stef replied: "Better think!" He imparted a piece of news—that two of those members of the Crillon staff who had tried to resign had had dictographs put in their rooms—presumably by the Army Intelligence. This news worried Lanny more than he cared to let his friend know.

"How do you know a spy when you meet him?" he asked, and the other answered that often you didn't until it was too late. It was generally somebody who agreed with your pinkest ideas and went you one or two better. Lanny said he hadn't met anyone like that as yet—unless it was Stef himself!

This world observer, whose ideas were so hard to puzzle out, told some of his own experiences since his return from Russia. The Intelligence had thought it necessary to dog his footsteps continually. "There is a Captain Stratton——"

"Oh, yes!" broke in the youth. "I saw a lot of him at the Crillon."

"Well, he and another officer took the trouble to get the next table in a restaurant where I was dining with a friend. I saw that they were listening to our talk so I invited them over, and told them all about what I had learned in Russia, and had reported to Colonel House. I tried my best to convert them."

"Did you succeed?" asked Lanny, delighted.

"Well, they stopped following me. Maybe the reason was what President Wilson did a day or two later. I suppose he had heard that I was being shadowed, and he chose a tactful way to stop it. You understand, he has refused to see me and hear what I have to report on Russia; having made up his 'one-track mind' that he's not going to stop the war on the Soviets, he doesn't want to be upset by my facts. But he knows how I came to go to Russia, and he has no right to discredit me. I was one of a crowd of newspapermen waiting in the lobby of the hotel, when he passed through and saw me, and he came and bent over me and pretended to whisper something into my ear. He didn't say a word that I could make out; he just made murmurs. Of course his purpose was to tell everybody that I still had his confidence."

"So now you can be as pink as you please!" chuckled the other.

V

The German delegation arrived, and the much-postponed signing was set for the twenty-eighth of June. The signers were two subordinates, but the Allies were determined to make a ceremony of it. The setting was the great Hall of Mirrors of the Versailles palace, where the victorious Germans had established their empire forty-eight years earlier, and had forced the French to sign the humiliating peace surrendering Alsace-Lorraine. Now the tables were turned, and with all pomp and circumstance the two distressed German envoys would put their signatures to the statement that their country alone had been to blame for the World War.

Every tourist in France visits the Versailles palace, and wanders through the magnificent apartment where once the Sun King ate his meals and the population had the hereditary right to enter and stare at the greatest of all monarchs gulping his *potage* and at his queen and princesses nibbling their *entremets*. Lanny had been there with his mother and Kurt, motored by Harry Murchison, nearly six years back; that lovely October day stood out in his memory, and as he recalled it he had many strange thoughts. Suppose that on that day he had been able by some psychic feat to peer into the future and know that his German friend, adoring his mother, was to become her lover! Suppose that Beauty had been able to perform the feat and foresee what was going to happen to Marcel—would she have married Harry Murchison instead? Or suppose that the Germans, at the signing of the first Peace of Versailles, had been able to foresee the second!

Only about a thousand persons could be admitted to witness the ceremony, and Lanny Budd was not among the chosen ones. If he had cared very much he might have been able to wangle a ticket from his Crillon friends, whom he still met at Mrs. Emily's and other places. But he told himself that he had witnessed a sufficiency of ceremonies to last the rest of his days. No longer had he the least pleasure in gazing upon important elderly gentlemen, each brushed and polished by his valet from the tips of his shoes to the roof of his topper. The colonel from Texas wore this symbol of honorificabilitudinitas on occasions where etiquette required it, but he carried along his comfortable Texas sombrero in a paper bag, and exchanged head-coverings as soon as the ceremony was com-

pleted. Nothing so amusing had happened in Paris since Dr. Franklin
had gone about town without a wig.

The important thing now was that the much-debated document
would be signed and peace returned to the world. Or would it? On
the table in his hotel room lay newspapers in which he could read
that the treaty to be signed that day left France helpless before the
invading foe; and others which insisted that it was a document of
class repression, designed to prepare the exploitation of the workers
of both Germany and France. Lanny had read both, and wished
there was some authority that would really tell a young fellow
what to believe!

VI

The telephone rang: the office of the hotel announcing "Monsieur Zhessie Bloc-léss"—accent on the last syllable. Lanny didn't
want to have his uncle come up, because that would look like intimacy, so displeasing to Robbie if he should happen to return. "I'll
be down at once," he said.

In the lobby of the marble-walled Hotel Vendôme he sat and
exchanged family news with his relative who didn't fit the sur-
roundings, but looked like a down-at-heels artist lacking the excuse
of youth. Uncle Jesse wanted to know, first, what the devil was
Beauty doing in Spain? When Lanny answered vaguely, he said:
"You don't have to hide things from me. I can guess it's a man."

But Lanny said: "She will tell you when she gets ready," and
that was that.

More urgently the painter was interested to know what had
become of that mysterious personage who had paid him three silent
midnight visits. At the risk of seeming uncordial, Lanny could only
say again that his lips were sealed. "But I fear he won't visit you
any more," he said. "You know about the public event which is to
happen today."

"Yes, but that isn't going to make any difference," insisted the
other. "It doesn't mean a thing." They were speaking with caution,

and the painter kept glancing about to be sure no one was over-
hearing. "Your friends are still going to be in trouble. They are
going to have to struggle—for a long, long time."

"Maybe so," said Lanny; "and it may be they'll call on you again.
But as matters stand, I'm not in a position to inquire about it, and
that's all I can say."

The uncle was disappointed and a trifle vexed. He said that
when the owners of hunting forests put out fodder for the deer
in winter, the creatures got the habit of coming to the place and
thereafter didn't scuffle so hard for themselves. Lanny smiled and
said he had observed it in the forests of Silesia; but when it was a
question of scuffling or starving, doubtless they would resume
scuffling.

"Well," said the painter, "if you happen to meet your friend,
give him these." He took a little roll of papers from the breast
pocket of his coat. "These are samples of the leaflets we have
printed. I've marked on each one the number of copies distributed,
so he can see that none of his fodder has been wasted."

"All right," said Lanny. "I'll give them to him if I see him." He
put the papers into his own pocket, and sought for another topic
of conversation. He told of visiting Stef and how Stef had a cold.
He repeated some of the muckraker's stories about espionage on
the Reds.

"I, too, have tried the plan of chatting with the *flics,*" said the
painter. "But I've found no idealism in their souls."

Lanny repeated the question he had asked of Stef. "How do you
recognize a *flic?*"

"I wouldn't know how to describe them," replied the other. "But
when you've seen a few you know the type. They are always
stupid, and when they try to talk like one of us it's pathetic."

There was a pause. "Well, I'll get along," said Jesse. "Robbie
may be coming and I don't want to annoy him. No need to tell
him that I called."

"I won't unless he asks me," replied the nephew.

"And put those papers where he won't see them. Of course you can read them if you wish, but the point is, I'm not giving them to you for that purpose."

"I get you," said Lanny, with a smile.

VII

The youth saw his visitor part way to the door and then went to the apparatus you called a "lift" when you were talking to an Englishman, an "elevator" to an American. At the same moment a man who had been sitting just across the lobby, supposedly reading a newspaper but in reality watching over the top of it, arose from his seat and followed. Another man, who had been standing in the street looking through the window, came in at the door. Lanny entered the elevator and the first man followed him and said to the operator: "*Attendez.*" The second man arrived and entered and they went up.

When they reached Lanny's floor he stepped out, and so did the other two. As soon as the operator had closed the door, one man stepped to Lanny's right and the other to his left and said in French: "*Pardon, Monsieur.* We are agents of the Sûreté."

Lanny's heart gave a mighty thump; he stopped, and so almost did the heart. "Well?" he said.

"It will be necessary for you to accompany us to the Préfecture." The man drew back the lapel of his coat and showed his shield.

"What is the matter?" demanded the youth.

"I am sorry, Monsieur, it is not permitted to discuss the subject. You will be told by the *commissaire.*"

So, they were after him! And maybe they had him! Wild ideas of resistance or flight surged into his mind; it was the first time he had ever been arrested and he had no habit pattern. But they were determined-looking men, and doubtless were armed. He decided to preserve his position as a member of the privileged classes. "You are making a very silly mistake," he said, "and it will get you into trouble."

"If so, Monsieur will pardon us, I trust," said the elder of the two. "Monsieur resides in this hotel?"

"I do."

"Then Monsieur will kindly escort us to his room."

Lanny hesitated. His father's business papers were in that room and Robbie certainly wouldn't like to have them examined by strangers. "Suppose I refuse?" he inquired.

"Then it will be necessary for us to take you."

Lanny had the roomkey in his pocket, and of course the two men could take it from him. He knew that they could summon whatever help they needed. "All right," he said, and led them to the room and unlocked the door.

The spokesman preceded him and the other followed, closed the door, and fastened it; then the former said: "Monsieur will kindly give me the papers which he has in his pocket."

.Ah, so they had been watching him and Uncle Jesse! Lanny had read detective novels, and knew that it was up to him to find some way to chew up these papers and swallow them. But a dozen printed leaflets would make quite a meal, and he lacked both appetite and opportunity. He took them out and handed them to the *flic*, who put them into his own pocket without looking at them. "You will pardon me, Monsieur"—they were always polite to well-dressed persons, Lanny had been told. Very deftly, and as inoffensively as possible, the second man made certain that Lanny didn't have any weapon on him. In so doing he discovered some letters in the youth's coat pocket, and these also were transferred to the pockets of the elder detective. Lanny ran over quickly in his mind what was in the letters: one from his mother—fortunately she had been warned, and wrote with extreme reserve. One from Rosemary, an old one, long-cherished—how fortunate the English habit of reticence! One from his eleven-year-old half-sister—that was the only real love letter.

Lanny was invited to sit down, and the younger *flic* stood by, never moving his eyes from him. Evidently they must be thinking they had made an important capture. The elder man set to work

to search the suite; the escritoire, the bureau drawers, the suitcases—
he laid the latter on the bed and went through them, putting everything of significance into one of them. This included a thirty-eight
automatic and a box of cartridges—which of course would seem
more significant to a French detective than to an American.

If Lanny had been in possession of a clear conscience, he might
have derived enjoyment from this opportunity to watch the French
police *chez eux,* as it were. But having a very uneasy conscience
indeed, he thought he would stop this bad joke if he could. "You
are likely to find a number of guns in my father's luggage," he
remarked. "That is not because he shoots people, but because he
sells guns."

"*Ah! Votre père est un marchand d'armes!*" One had to hear it
in French to get a full sense of the *flic's* surprise.

"*Mon père est un fabricant d'armes,*" replied Lanny, still more
impressively. "He has made for the French government a hundred
million francs' worth of arms in the past five years. If he had not
done so, the boches would be in Paris now, and you would be
under the sod, perhaps."

"*Vraiment, Monsieur!*" exclaimed the other, and stood irresolute,
as if he hadn't the nerve to touch another object belonging to a
person who might possibly be of such importance. "What is it
that is the name of your father?" he inquired, at last.

"His name is Robert Budd."

The other wrote it down, with Lanny spelling the letters in
French. "And Monsieur's name?"

The youth spelled the name of Lanning, which a Frenchman
does not pronounce without considerable practice. Then he remarked: "If you examine that gun, you will see that it has my
father's name as the *fabricant.*"

"*Ah, vraiment?*" exclaimed the detective, and took the gun to the
window to verify this extraordinary statement. Evidently he didn't
know what to do next, and Lanny thought that his little dodge had
worked. But when the detective took the bundle of leaflets from his
pockets and began to examine them; and so of course Lanny knew

that the jig was up. He hadn't looked at the papers, but he knew what would be in them. "Workingmen of all countries, unite! You have nothing to lose but your chains; you have a world to gain!"

The *flic* put the papers back into his pocket, and went on piling Robbie's papers into a suitcase. "It is a matter which the *commissaire* will have to determine, Monsieur."

38

Battle of the Stags

I

RIDING in a taxi to the Préfecture de Police, Lanny thought as hard as he had ever done in his life. Had these agents been following him because they had learned about his connections with a German spy? Or had they been following the notorious Jesse Blackless and seen him hand papers to Lanny? Everything seemed to indicate the latter; but doubtless at the Préfecture they would have Lanny listed in connection with Lincoln Steffens, and with Herron, and Alston—who could guess where these trails might lead? Lanny decided that he had talked enough and would take refuge in the fact that he was not yet of age. Even in wartime they could hardly shoot you for refusing to answer questions; and, besides, the war was coming to an end this very afternoon! Many, many times in five years he had heard Frenchmen exclaim: "*C'est la guerre!*" Now, for once, he would be able to answer: "*C'est la paix!*"

The Préfecture is on the Île de la Cité, the oldest part of Paris, having as much history to the square meter as any other place in the world. Like most old buildings it had a vague musty odor. They booked him, and took away his billfold, his watch, his keys; then they put him in a small room with a barred window high up, and an odor of ammonia, the source of which was obvious. The younger of the two detectives sat and watched him, but did not speak. In half an hour or so he was escorted to an office, where he found no less than three officials waiting to question him. All three were polite, grave, and determined. The eldest, the *commissaire*, was dressed as if he were going to have tea at Mrs. Emily's. At a second desk sat a clerk, ready to begin writing vigorously—the so-called *procès verbal*.

"Messieurs," said Lanny, "please believe that I intend no discourtesy; but I consider this arrest an indignity and I intend to stand upon my rights. I am a minor and it is my father who is legally responsible for me. I demand that he be summoned, and I refuse to answer any questions whatsoever until that has been done."

You would have thought that the three officials had never before in their lives heard of anyone refusing to answer questions. They were shocked, they were hurt, they were everything they could think of that might make an impression upon a sensitive youth. They demanded to know: was it the natural course for an innocent man not to tell frankly what was necessary to secure his liberty? They wished him no harm; they were greatly embarrassed to have to detain him for a moment; the simple and obvious thing would be for him to tell them for what innocent reason he had come into possession of documents inciting to the overthrow of *la république française*, the murder of its citizens, the confiscation of their property, and the burning of their homes. The three officials had the incendiary documents spread out before them, and passed them from hand to hand with exclamations of dismay.

Was all that really in the documents? Lanny didn't know; but he knew that if he asked the question, he would be answering a very important one for the officials—he would be telling them that he didn't know, or at least claimed not to know, their contents. So he said again and again: "Messieurs, be so kind as to send word to my father."

Never had courteous French officials had their patience put to a severer test. They took turns arguing and pleading. The oldest, the *commissaire*, was paternal; he pleaded with the young gentleman not to subject himself to being held behind bars like a common felon. It was really unkind of him to inflict upon them the necessity of inflicting this embarrassment upon a visitor from the land to which France owed such a debt of gratitude. In this the *commissaire*, for all his lifetime training, was letting slip something of importance. They took him for a tourist; they had not connected him with Juan-les-Pins, and probably not with Madame Detaze, *veuve*, and her German lover now traveling in Spain!

The second official was a man accustomed to dealing with evildoers, and his faith in human nature had been greatly weakened. He told Lanny that *la patrie* was at war, and that all men of right feeling were willing to aid the authorities in thwarting the murderous intrigues of the abominable Reds. It was difficult for anyone to understand how a man would have such documents in his pocket and not be eager to explain the reason. And what was the significance of the mysterious figures penciled upon each sheet? If a man refused to perform the obvious duty of clearing up such a mystery, could he blame the authorities for looking upon him as a suspicious character?

The third official was younger, wore glasses, and looked like a student. Apparently he was the one whose duty it was to read incendiary literature, classify it, and take its temperature. He said that he had never read anything worse in his life than this stuff which Lanny had had in his pocket. It was hard for him to believe that a youth of good manners and morals could have read such incitements without aversion. Was Lanny a student, investigating the doctrines of these Reds? Did he know any of them personally? Had he been associated with them in America? Lanny didn't answer, but listened attentively and asked questions in his own mind. Were they just avoiding giving him any clues? Or had the two *flics* really not known who it was that gave him the papers?

Certainly Lanny wasn't going to involve his uncle unnecessarily. To all attempts to trap him he replied, as courteously as ever: "Messieurs, I know it is tedious to hear me say this; but think how much trouble you could save yourselves if you would just call my father."

"If you refuse to answer," said the *commissaire*, at last, "we have no recourse but to hold you until you do."

"You may try it," said Lanny; "but I think my father will manage to find out where I am. Certainly if an American disappears from the Hotel Vendôme, the story will be in the American newspapers in a few hours."

The official pressed a button and an attendant came and escorted Lanny down a corridor and into a room that was full of apparatus. In the old days it might have been a torture chamber, but in this advanced age it was the laboratory of a new science. Lanny, to complete his education, was going to learn about the Bertillon system for the identification of criminals. The operations were carried out by a young man who looked like a doctor, wearing a white duck jacket; they were supervised by a large elderly gentleman wearing a black morning coat and striped trousers, and with a black spade beard almost to his waist. They photographed their prisoner from several angles; they took his fingerprints; they measured with calipers his skull, his ears, his nose, his eyes, his fingers, his feet. They told him to strip, and searched him minutely for scars and spots, birthmarks, moles—and noted them all down on an elaborate chart. When they got through, Lanny Budd could be absolutely certain that the next time he committed a crime in France, they would know him for the same felon they had had in the Préfecture on the twenty-eighth of June 1919.

II

Lanny Budd sat on a wooden stool in a stone cell with a narrow slit for a window, and a cot which had obviously been occupied by many predecessors in misfortune. Perhaps the police were trying to frighten him, and again, perhaps they were just treating him impartially. For company he had his thoughts: a trooping procession, taking their tone-color from the dismal clang of an iron door. Impossible to imagine anything more final, or more crushing! So far, emotions such as this had been communicated to Lanny through the medium of art works. But the reality was far different. You could turn away from a picture, stop playing music, close a book; but in a jail cell you stayed.

Lanny had no idea how old this barracks was. Had it stood here in the days when Richelieu was breaking the proud French nobility, and had some of them paced the floor of this cell? Had it stood when the Sun King was issuing his *lettres de cachet?* Had the Cardinal de Rohan been brought here when he was accused of stealing the diamond necklace? It seemed a reasonable guess that some of the aristocrats had sojourned here on their way *à la lanterne;* and doubtless a long string of those poisoners and wife stranglers who provided the French populace with their daily doses of thrill. All through the Peace Conference Paris had been entertained by the exploits of a certain Landru, who had married, murdered, and buried some eight or nine women. Every now and then the authorities would dig up a new one, and the press would forget the problems of the peace. This happened whenever the situation became tense, and it was freely said at the Crillon that it was done to divert attention from what the delegates were doing.

The jailers brought Lanny food and water; but he didn't like the looks of the former, and was afraid the latter might be drugged. He spent most of his time walking up and down—five steps one way and five the other—thinking about his possible mistakes and regretting them. Almost surely the bureau would be digging in its files, and coming upon the name of Lanning Budd as a nephew of Jesse Blackless, revolutionary. Would they find him as son of Beauty Detaze, mistress of Kurt Meissner, alias Dalcroze, much wanted German agent? Phrased in the language of police files, it was certainly most sinister. Lanny recalled the melodramas he had seen on

the screen, with the hero lined up before the firing squad and res-
cuers galloping on horses, or rushing madly through automobile
traffic. Invariably they arrived just before the triggers were pulled;
but Lanny had been told that the movies were not always reliable.
Ride, Robbie, ride!

The father was supposed to be in conference with some "big"
men. Sooner or later he would return to the hotel and find that his
belongings had been rifled. He would learn from the elevator boy
that Lanny had gone away with two strange men. Would he think
that his son had been kidnaped, and apply to the police? That,
indeed, would be funny. But Robbie had a shrewd mind, and he
knew about his revolutionary brother-in-law, also about Kurt
Meissner, alias Dalcroze. He wouldn't fail to take these into his cal-
culations. He had friends in high position in the city, and Mrs. Emily
had still others. The *commissaire* of the Sûreté Générale would
surely get a jolt before many hours had passed!

The trouble was, the hours passed so slowly. Lanny's watch was
gone, so he couldn't follow them. He could only observe the slit
of light; and at the end of June the days linger long in Paris. Lanny
recalled that at three o'clock the treaty was to be signed, and he
occupied his mind with picturing that historic scene. He knew the
Galerie des Glaces, and how they would fix it up with a long horse-
shoe table, and gilded chairs for the delegates from all the nations
of the earth. Most of them would be black-clad; but the military
ones would be wearing bright-colored uniforms with rows of
medals, and there would be silk-robed pashas and emirs and mahara-
jas and mandarins from where the gorgeous East showers on her
kings' barbaric pearl and gold. He could picture the equipages rolling up the great avenue, lined with cavalry in steel-blue helmets,
with red and white pennants fluttering on their lances. He visioned
the palace, with the important personages ascending the great flight
of steps, between rows of the Gardes Républicaines, clad in brass
cuirasses, white pants, and high black patent-leather boots; on their
heads the shiniest of brass helmets with long horsetails stuck in the
tops. There would be two of them to each step, their shining sabers

at present arms. Inside, the hall would be crowded, and there would be a babel of whispering, the polite chit-chat of the *grand monde* which Lanny knew so well. How everlastingly delightful to be in places where you were assured that only the really important could come!

The treaty would be bulky, printed on vellum sheets decorated with numerous red seals. Presumably somebody would have checked it this time and made certain it was right. The enemy signers would be escorted by those *huissiers* with silver chains who had been the bane of Lanny's life, because they were forever trying to stop a secretary-translator from entering rooms where his chief had told him to go. Lanny had seen pictures of the two unhappy Germans: one big and beefy, like the proprietor of a *Bierstube*, the other lean and timid-looking, like a private tutor. They were the scapegoats, carrying the sins of their people, and signing a confession on two dotted lines.

The *huissiers* would command silence, and a hush would fall while the pens scratched. A tedious ceremony, for the plenipotentiaries from all over the world had to fall in line and sign four documents: the treaty proper, the protocol with modifications extracted by the German clamor, an agreement regarding the administration of the Rhine districts, and an agreement with Poland regarding the treatment of minorities—she would keep the minorities but not the agreement, Professor Alston had remarked while helping to draft this document.

Lanny's imaginings were interrupted by the thunder of cannon. So! It was signed! Those would be the guns on the Place d'Armes; and then a booming farther away—that would be the old fort at Mont Valérien. Shouts from the crowds in the near-by streets— Lanny knew how people would behave, he had done it himself on Armistice day at St. Thomas's Academy in Connecticut. The biggest banker in that state had warned him that he might get into jail if he didn't mend his ideas; and sure enough, here he was! He got up and began to pace the floor again.

Better to go on thinking about the treaty. He had been told by some of the insiders that General Smuts, head of the South African delegation, was going to sign under protest, stating that "We have not yet achieved the real peace for which the peoples are looking." So, after all, the little group of liberals had not protested in vain! Alston had said that this treaty would keep the world in turmoil for ten years, twenty years, whatever time it took to bring it into line with the Fourteen Points. Was he right? Or was that French general right who had announced to the company at Mrs. Emily's: "This treaty is turning loose a wounded tiger on the world. He will crawl into a hole and nurse his wounds, and come out hungrier and fiercer than ever"?

Lanny couldn't make up his mind about it; nothing to do but wait and see. Some day he would know—provided, of course, the French army didn't shoot him at sunrise tomorrow morning.

III

The sun's rays do not linger very long in any place, and the light faded quickly from Lanny's cell. He sat in twilight, and thought: "Surely Robbie must have returned by now!" His stomach was complaining, and in many ways he was tiring of this bad joke. When at last he heard a jailer approaching his cell he was glad, even though it might mean a court martial. "*Venez*," said the man; and escorted him to the office of the *commissaire* again.

There were the same three officials, and with them, not Robbie, as the prisoner had hoped, but Uncle Jesse! So once more Lanny had to think fast. What did it mean? Doubtless his uncle had been brought in, like himself, as a suspect. Had he talked? And if so, what had he said?

"M. Budd," said the *commissaire*, "your uncle has come here of his own free will to tell us the circumstances by which you came into possession of those documents." He paused as if expecting Lanny to speak; but Lanny waited. "Will you be so kind as to answer a few questions in his presence?"

"*Monsieur le Commissaire*," said Lanny, "I have already told you that I will answer no questions until my father has come."

"You mean that you don't trust your uncle?" A silence. "Or is it that the gentleman is not your uncle?"

"It would be such a very simple matter to telephone to my father's hotel, Monsieur!"

"We have already done that; but your father is not there."

"He is quite certain to arrive before long."

"You mean you intend to force us to keep you in this uncomfortable position until we can find your father?"

"No, Monsieur, I haven't the least desire to do that. I am willing for you to release me at any time."

There was a long silence. Lanny kept his eyes on the *commissaire*, whose face wore a stern frown. The prisoner wouldn't have been entirely surprised if the man had said: "Take him out and shoot him now!" He was really surprised when he perceived a slow smile spreading over the features of the elderly official. "*Eh bien, mon garçon*," he said, finally. "If I let you have your way, will you promise to harbor no ill feelings?"

"Yes, sir," said Lanny, as quickly as he was able to take in the meaning.

"Don't think that we are naïve, M. Bloc-léss," said the *commissaire* to the painter. "We have investigated your story. We knew most of it before you came."

"I was quite sure that would be the case," replied Uncle Jesse, with one of his twisted smiles. "Otherwise I might not have come."

"You are playing a dangerous game," continued the other. "I don't suppose you wish any advice from me; but if we are forced to ask you to leave the country, it will not be without fair warning—now repeated for the second time."

"If that misfortune befalls me, Monsieur, I shall be extremely sorry, for France has been my home for the greater part of my life. I shall be sorrier still for the sake of the republic, whose reputation as a shelter for the politically persecuted is the fairest jewel in her crown."

"You are a shrewd man, M. Bloc-léss. You know the language of liberty and idealism, and you use it in the service of tyranny and hate."

"That is a subject about which we might argue for a long while, *Monsieur le Commissaire*. I don't think it would be proper for me to dispute with you in your professional capacity; but if at any time you care to meet me socially, I'll be most happy to explain my ideas."

There was a twinkle in the elderly Frenchman's eye. *Esprit* is their specialty, and he knew a good answer when he heard it. He turned to Lanny. "As for you, *mon garçon*"—taking Lanny into the family—"it appears that you have been the victim of persons older and less scrupulous than yourself. Next time I would advise you to look at papers before you put them into your pocket."

"I assure you, Monsieur," said the youth, respectfully, "I intended to do it as soon as I got to my room." This too had the light play of humor in which the French delight; so the *commissaire* said he hoped his guest hadn't minded his misadventure. Lanny replied that he had found the experience educational, and that stories of crime and detection would be far more vivid to him in future. The suitcase containing Robbie's papers was restored to Robbie's son, and the three officials shook hands with him—but not with Uncle Jesse, he noticed. "M. Bloc-léss" was one of the "older and less scrupulous persons."

IV

Nephew and uncle stepped out into the twilight; and it seemed to Lanny the most delightful moment he had spent in Paris. Very certainly the Île de la Cité with its bridges and its great cathedral had never appeared more beautiful than in the summer twilight. Flags were out, and the holiday atmosphere prevailed. To everybody else it was because of the signing of the treaty, but there was nothing to prevent Lanny Budd's applying it to his emergence from the Préfecture.

The moment was made perfect when a taxi came whirling up the Boulevard du Palais, and there was Robbie Budd peering forth. "Well, what the devil is this?" he cried.

"You got my note?" inquired Jesse, as Robbie jumped out.

"That—and your telegram."

"I wanted to be sure of reaching you. I was afraid they might hold me, too."

"But what is it all about?"

"Get back into the cab," said Uncle Jesse. "We can't talk about it here."

The two got in, and Lanny handed in the suitcase, and followed it. When the Préfecture was behind them, the painter said: "Now, Robbie, I'll tell you the story I just told the *commissaire*. You remember how, several months back, Professor Alston sent Lanny to me to arrange for a conference between Colonel House and some of the Russian agents in Paris?"

"I was told about it," said Robbie, with no cordiality in his tone.

"Don't forget that it was United States government business. Lanny did it because it was his job, and I did it because his chief urged me to. I have made it a matter of honor never to force myself upon your son. I have done that out of regard for my sister. Lanny will tell you that it is so."

"It really is, Robbie," put in the youth.

"Go on," said Robbie, between his clenched teeth.

"Well, this morning a French labor leader came to me. You know the blockade of Germany is still going on, the war on the Soviet government is still going on—and both are products of French government policy."

"You may assume that I have read the newspapers," replied the father. "Kindly tell me what the police wanted with Lanny."

"This labor man of course would like to have American support for a policy more liberal and humane. He brought me a bundle of leaflets presenting the arguments of the French workers, and asked if it wouldn't be possible for my nephew at the Crillon to get these into the hands of Colonel House, so that he might know how the

workers felt. I said: 'My nephew has broken with the Crillon, because he doesn't approve its policies.' The answer was: 'Well, he
may be in touch with some of the staff there and might be able to
get the documents to Colonel House.' So I said: 'All right, I'll take
them to him and ask him to try.' I took them, and advised Lanny
not to read them himself, but to get them to the right person if he
had a chance.''

Lanny sat rigid in his seat, his mind torn between dismay and admiration. Oh, what a beautiful story! It brought him to realize how
ill equipped he was for the career of an intriguer, a secret agent;
all those hours he had spent in the silence of his cell—and never once
had he thought of that absolutely perfect story!

"My friend told me how many of these leaflets had been printed
and distributed in Paris, and I jotted down the figures on each one,
thinking it might help to impress Colonel House. It appears the
Préfecture found those figures highly suspicious."

"Tell me how it happened," persisted Robbie.

"When I left the hotel I got a glimpse of a man strolling past
the window and looking into the lobby. He happened to be one of
the *flics* who had picked me up several months back. I saw him
enter the hotel, and I looked through the window and saw him and
another man go into the elevator with Lanny. I waited until they
came down and put him into a taxi. Then I set out to find you. I
was afraid to go into the hotel, so I used the telephone. When
I failed to find you, I sent you a note by messenger, and also a telegram, and then I decided to go to the Préfecture and try my luck.
It was a risk, of course, because Lanny might have talked, and I
couldn't know what he had said."

"You might have guessed that he would have told the truth,"
said the father.

"I wasn't that clever. What I did was to fish around, until they
told me Lanny had confessed that he was a Red——"

"What?" cried Lanny, shocked.

"The *commissaire* said that himself; so I knew they were bluffing
and that Lanny hadn't talked. I told them my story and they held

me a couple of hours while they 'investigated.' What they did, I assume, was to phone to Colonel House. Of course they consider that most everybody in the Crillon is a Red, but they can't afford any publicity about it. That's why they turned us loose with a warning."

Robbie turned to his son. "Lanny, is this story true?"

The next few moments were uncomfortable for the younger man. He had never lied to his father in his life. Was he going to do it now? Or was he going to "throw down" his Uncle Jesse, who had come to his rescue at real danger to himself—and who had invented such a beautiful story? There is an old saying that what you don't know won't hurt you; but Lanny had been taught a different moral code—that you mustn't ever lie except when you are selling munitions.

Great was the youth's relief when his uncle saved him from this predicament. "One moment, Robbie," he put in. "I didn't say that story was true."

"Oh, you didn't?"

"I said I would tell you what I told the *commissaire.*"

The father frowned angrily. "I am in no mood for jokes!" he exclaimed. "Am I to know about this business, or am I not? Lanny, will you kindly tell me?"

"Yes, Robbie," replied the youth. "The truth is——"

"The fault is entirely mine," broke in Uncle Jesse. "I brought Lanny those papers for a purpose of my own."

"He is going to try to take the blame on himself," objected Lanny. "I assure you——"

"He can't tell you the real story, because he doesn't know it!" argued the painter.

"Nobody really knows it but me," retorted Lanny. "Uncle Jesse only thinks he knows it."

Robbie's sense of humor wasn't operating just then. "Will you two please agree which is going to talk?"

Said Lanny, quickly: "I think we'd all three better wait until we get back to the hotel." He made a motion of the finger toward the taxi driver in front of them. To be sure, they were speaking English—but then the driver might have been a waiter at Mouquin's on Sixth Avenue before the war. The two men fell silent; and Lanny remarked: "Well, I heard the guns. Has the treaty really been signed?"

V

When they were safely locked in their suite, Robbie got out his whisky bottle, which the *flics* hadn't taken. He had been under a severe strain, and took a nip without waiting for the soda and ice; so did the painter. Lanny had been under a longer strain than either of them, but he waited for the ginger beer, for he wasn't yet of age, and moreover he thought that his father was drinking too much, and was anxious not to encourage him. Meanwhile the youth strolled casually about the suite, looking into the bathroom and the closets and under the beds; he didn't know just how a dictograph worked, but he looked everywhere for any wires. After the bellboy had departed, the ex-prisoner opened the door and looked out. He was in a melodramatic mood.

At last they were settled, and the father said: "Now, please, may I have the honor of knowing about this affair?"

"First," said Lanny, with a grin, "let me shut Uncle Jesse up. Uncle Jesse, you remember the Christmas before the war, I paid a visit to Germany?"

"I heard something about it."

"I was staying with a friend of mine. Better not to use names. That friend was in Paris until recently, and he was the man who came to call on you at midnight."

"Oh, so that's it!" exclaimed the painter.

"I gave him my word never to tell anybody. But I'm sure he won't mind your knowing, because you're likely to become his brother-in-law before long—you may be it now. Beauty and he are lovers, and that's why she's gone to Spain."

"Oh, my God!" exclaimed Jesse. And then again: "Oh, my

God!" He was speaking English, in which these words carry far more weight than in French.

"I told Robbie about it," Lanny continued, "because he has a right to know about Beauty. But I didn't tell him about you, because that was your secret. May I tell him now?"

"Evidently he's not going to be happy till he hears it."

Lanny turned to his father. "I put my friend in touch with Uncle Jesse, and my friend brought money to help him stir up the workers against the blockade. I thought that was a worthy cause and I still think so."

"You knew you were risking your life?" demanded the shocked father.

"I've seen people risking their lives for so long, it has sort of lost meaning. But you can imagine that I felt pretty uncomfortable this afternoon. Also, you can see what a risk Uncle Jesse took when he walked into that place."

Robbie made no response. He had poured out the drinks for the red sheep of his former mistress's family, but not an inch farther did he mean to go.

"You see how it was," continued Lanny. "When my friend stopped coming, Uncle Jesse wanted to know why; he brought me some literature so that this friend might see what he had been doing. He asked me to pass it on if I got a chance, and I said I would. He suggested that I didn't need to read it. I didn't say I wouldn't—I just said that I understood. Uncle Jesse has really been playing fair with you, Robbie. It was my friend and I who planned this whole scheme and brought it to him."

"I hope you don't feel too proud of it," said the father, grimly.

"I'm not defending myself, I'm trying to set you straight about Uncle Jesse. If I've picked up ideas that you don't like, it hasn't been from him, for he's avoided talking to me, and even told me I couldn't understand his ideas if I tried. I'm a parasite, a member of the wasting classes, all that sort of thing. What I've had explained has been by Alston, and Herron, and Steffens——"

"Whom you met in Jesse's room, I believe!"

"Well, he could hardly refuse to introduce me to his friend when I walked in. As a matter of fact I'd have met Steffens anyway, because Alston's friends talked a lot about his visit to Russia, and he was at the dinner where they decided to resign. So whatever I've done that was wrong, you must blame me and not Uncle Jesse. I don't know whether he hasn't any use for me, or whether he just pretends that he hasn't, but anyhow that's the way things have been between us."

Said Robbie, coldly: "Nothing alters the fact that he came to this hotel and brought a swarm of hornets down on both of us. Look at my room!" Robbie pointed to his effects strewn here and there. "And my business papers taken by the police, and copies made, no doubt—and sold by some crook to my business rivals!" Robbie knew how such things were done, having done them.

"You are perfectly right," said the painter. "It is my fault, and I am sorry as can be."

"All that I want to know is that I don't have to look forward to such things for the rest of my life. You are Beauty's brother, and if you decide to behave yourself as a decent human being, I'm ready to treat you that way. But if you choose to identify yourself with the scum of the earth, with the most dangerous criminals alive—all right, that's your privilege, but then I have to say: 'Keep away from me and mine.'"

"You are within your rights." Uncle Jesse spoke in the same cold tones as his not quite brother-in-law. "If you will arrange it with your son to keep away from me, you may be sure that I will never again invade his life, or yours."

VI

That was a fair demand and a fair assent; if only those two could have let it rest there! But they were like two stags in the forest, which might turn away and walk off in opposite directions—but they don't! Instead they stand and stare, paw the ground, and cannot get each other out of their minds.

The painter was moved to remark: "You may hang on to your dream of keeping modern thought from your son; but I assure you, Robbie, the forces against you are stronger than you realize."

To which the man of business was moved to answer, with scorn: "Leave that to my son and me, if you please! When Lanny learns that 'modern thought' means class hate, greed, and murder, he may decide to remain an old-fashioned thinker like his father."

"The fond father's dream throughout the ages!" exclaimed the other, in a tone of pity, even more exasperating than one of ridicule. "Let my son be exactly like me in all things! Let him think exactly what I think—and so he will be perfect! But the world is changing, and not all the fathers leagued together can stop it, or keep the sons from knowing about it."

"My son has his own mind," said the father. "He will judge for himself."

"You say that," answered the revolutionist, "but you don't feel nearly as secure as you pretend. Why else should you be so worried when someone presents a new idea to Lanny's mind? Don't you suppose he notices that? Don't you suppose he asks himself what it means?"

That was touching Robbie Budd on the rawest spot in his soul. The idea that anybody could claim to know Lanny better than his father knew him! The idea that the youth might be hiding things, that doubts and differences might be lurking in his mind, that the replica of Robbie's self might be turning traitor to him! In the father's subconscious mind Lanny remained a child, a budding youth, something that had to be guarded and cherished; so the feelings that stirred the father's soul were not so different from the jealous rage of the forest monarch over some sleek and slender doe.

"You are clever, Jesse," said he; "but I think Lanny understands the malice in your heart."

"I'm sorry I can't call you clever," retorted the other. "Your world is coming to an end. The thousands of your wage slaves have some other purpose than to build a throne for you to sit on."

"Listen, Uncle Jesse," interposed Lanny. "What's the use of all this ranting? You know you can't convince Robbie——"

But the stags brushed him aside; they weren't interested in him any more, they were interested in their battle. "We'll be ready for them any time they choose to come," declared Robbie. "We make machine guns!"

"You'll shoot them yourself?"

"You bet your life!"

"No!" said the painter with a smile. "You'll hire other men, as you always do. And if they turn the guns against you, what then?"

"I'll be on the watch for them! One of them was fool enough to forewarn me!"

"History has forewarned you, Robbie Budd, but you won't learn. The French Revolution told you that the days of divine right were over; but you've built a new system exactly like the old one in its practical results—blind squandering at the top, starvation and despair at the bottom, an insanity of greed ending in mass slaughter. Now you see the Russian revolt, but you scorn to learn from it!"

"We've learned to shut the sons-of-bitches up in their rat-holes, and let them freeze and starve, or die of typhus and eat their own corpses."

"Please, Robbie!" interposed the son. "You're getting yourself all worked up——"

Said the painter: "Typhus has a way of spreading beyond national boundaries; and so have ideas."

"We can quarantine disease; and I promise you, we're going to put the right man in the White House, and step on your Red ideas and smash the guts out of them."

"Listen, Robbie, do be sensible! You're wasting an awful lot of energy."

"Stay in France, Jesse Blackless, and spit your poison all over the landscape; but don't try it in America—not in Newcastle, I warn you!"

"I'm not needed there, Robbie. You're making your own crop of revolutionists. Class arrogance carries its own seeds of destruction."

"Listen, Uncle Jesse, what do you expect to accomplish by this? You know you can't convert my father. Do you just want to hurt each other?"

Yes, that was it. The two stags had their horns locked, and each wanted to butt the other, drive him back, beat him to the earth, mash him into it; each would rather die than give an inch. It was an old, old grudge; they had fought like this when they had first met, more than twenty years ago. Lanny hadn't been there, Lanny hadn't been anywhere then, but his mother had told him about it. Now it had got started again; the two stags couldn't get their horns apart, and it might mean the death of one or both!

"You and your gutter-rats imagining you can run industry!" snarled Robbie.

"If you're so sure we can't, why are you afraid to see us try? Why don't you call off your mercenaries that are fighting us on twenty-six fronts?"

"Why don't you call off your hellions that are spreading treason and hate in every nation?"

"Listen, Uncle Jesse! You promised Robbie you'd let me alone, but you're not doing it."

"They don't let anybody alone," sneered the father. "They don't keep any promises. We're the bourgeoisie, and we have no rights! We're parasites, and all we're fit for is to be 'liquidated'!"

"If you put yourself in front of a railroad train, it's suicide, not murder," said the painter, with his twisted smile. He was keeping his temper, which only made Robbie madder.

Said he, addressing his son: "Our business is to clear the track and let a bunch of gangsters drive the train into a ditch. History won't be able to count the number they have slaughtered."

"Oh, my God!" cried Uncle Jesse—he too addressing the youth. "He talks about slaughter—and he's just finished killing ten million men, with weapons he made for the purpose! God Almighty couldn't count the number he has wounded, and those who've died of disease and starvation. Yet he worries about a few counter-revolutionists shot by the Bolsheviks!"

VII

Lanny saw that he hadn't accomplished anything, so he sat for a while, listening to all the things his father didn't want him to hear. This raging argument became to him a symbol of the world in which he would have to live the rest of his life. His uncle was the uplifted fist of the workers, clenched in deadly menace. As for Robbie, he had proclaimed himself the man behind the machine gun; the man who made it, and was ready to use it, personally, if need be, to mow down the clenched uplifted fists! As for Lanny, he didn't have to be any symbol, he was what he was: the man who loved art and beauty, reason and fair play, and pleaded for these things and got brushed aside. It wasn't his world! It had no use for him! When the fighting started, he'd be caught between the lines and mowed down.

"If you kill somebody," Uncle Jesse announced to the father, "that's law and order. But if a revolutionist kills one of your gangsters, that's murder, that's a crime wave. You own the world, you make the laws and enforce them. But we tell you we're tired of working for your profit, and that never again can you lead us out to die for your greed."

"You're raving!" said Robbie Budd. "In a few months your Russia will be smashed flat, and you'll never get another chance. You've shown us your hand, and we've got you on a list."

"A hanging list?" inquired the painter, with a wink at the son.

"Hanging's not quick enough. You'll see how our Budd machine guns work!"

Lanny had never seen his father in such a rage. He was on his feet, and kept turning away and then back again. He had had several drinks, and that made it worse; his face was purple and his hands clenched. A little more and it might turn into a physical fight. Seeing him getting started on another tirade, Lanny grabbed his uncle by the arm and pulled him from his seat. "Please go, Uncle Jesse!" he exclaimed. "You said you would let me alone. Now do it!" He kept on, first pulling, then pushing. The uncle's hat had been hung on a chair, and Lanny took it and pressed it into his hand. "Please don't argue any more—just go!"

"All right," said the painter, half angry, half amused. "Look after him—he's going to have his hands full putting down the Russian revolution!"

"Thanks," said Lanny. "I'll do my best."

"You heard what I had to say to him!"

"Yes, I heard it."

"And you see that he has no answer!"

"Yes, yes, please go!" Lanny kept shoving his exuberant relative out into the hall.

A parting shot: "Mark my words, Robbie Budd—it's the end of your world!"

"Good-by, Uncle Jesse!" and Lanny shut the door.

VIII

He came back into the room. His father was staring in front of him, frowning darkly. Lanny wondered: was the storm going to be turned upon him? And how much of it was left!

"Now, see here!" exclaimed the elder. "Have you learned your lesson from this?"

"Yes, indeed, Robbie; more than one lesson." Lanny's tone was full of conviction.

"You put yourself in the hands of a fanatic like that, and he's in a position to blackmail you, to do anything his crazy fancy may suggest."

"Please believe me, Robbie, I wasn't doing anything for Uncle Jesse. I was trying to help a friend."

"How far will a man go to help a friend? You were bucking the French government!"

"I know. It was a mistake."

"A man has to learn to have discretion; to take care of himself. You want friends, Lanny—but also you want to know where to draw a line. If people find out they can sponge on you, there's no limit to it. One wants you to sign a note and bankrupt yourself. One gets drunk and wants you to sober him up. One is in a mess with a woman, and you have to get her off his neck. You're a soft-shell crab, that every creature in the sea can bite a chunk out of. Nobody respects you, nobody thinks of anything but to use you."

"I'll try to learn from this, Robbie." Lanny really meant it; but his main thought was: Soothe him down; cool him off!

"You have a friend who's a German," continued the father. "All right, make up your mind what it means. As long as you live, Germany's going to be making war on France, and France on her. It doesn't matter what they call it, business or diplomacy, reparations, any name—Germany's foes will be trying to undermine her and she will be fighting back. If Kurt Meissner is going to be a musician, that's one thing, but if he's going to be a German agent, that's another. Sooner or later you've got to make up your mind what it means to have such a friend—and your mother's got to make up her mind what it means to have such a lover."

"Yes, Robbie; you're right. I see it clearly."

"And those Reds you've been meeting—I don't doubt they're clever talkers, more so than decent people, perhaps. But think what must be in the minds of revolutionists when they waste their time upon a young fellow like you! You have money, and you're credulous—you're their meat, laid out on the butcher's block! Maybe those Russians are going to survive awhile; maybe the Allies are too exhausted to put them down. They can live as long as they can plunder other people's wealth. And you have to make up your mind, are you going to let them use you, and laugh at you while they play you for a sucker? What else can you be to them—a parasite, the son of Robbie Budd the bloated capitalist, the merchant of death! Don't you see that you're everything in the world they hate and want to destroy?"

"Yes, Robbie, of course. I've no idea of having anything more to do with them."

"Well, for Christ's sake, mean that and stick to it! Go on down to Juan and fix up the house and play the piano!"

The youth couldn't keep from laughing. "That's the program!"
He put his arm about his father—knowing him well, and realizing
how ashamed of himself he would be for having lost his temper and
roared at a man who wasn't worth it.

Lanny was beginning to feel gay. A great relief to be out of jail—
and also not to have to take any worse scolding than this. "The
treaty's signed, Robbie!" he exclaimed. "And we've a League of
Nations to keep things in order!"

"Like heck we have!" replied the father.

"Pax nobiscum! E pluribus unum! God save the king! And now
let's get this room in order!" Lanny took the suitcase which he had
brought from the Préfecture, and put it on the bed and began sorting out the precious papers, like the good secretary he had learned
to be. "Tomorrow night I leave for the Côte d'Azur, and lie on the
sand and get sunburned and watch the world come to an end!"

BOOKS BY UPTON SINCLAIR

THE JOURNAL OF ARTHUR STIRLING
MANASSAS, A NOVEL OF THE CIVIL WAR
THE JUNGLE
THE OVERMAN
THE MILLENNIUM
THE METROPOLIS
THE MONEY-CHANGERS
SAMUEL, THE SEEKER
THE FASTING CURE
LOVE'S PILGRIMAGE
SYLVIA
SYLVIA'S MARRIAGE
DAMAGED GOODS
THE CRY FOR JUSTICE
THE PROFITS OF RELIGION
KING COAL, A NOVEL OF THE COLORADO
   STRIKE
JIMMIE HIGGINS
THE BRASS CHECK
100%—THE STORY OF A PATRIOT
THEY CALL ME CARPENTER
THE BOOK OF LIFE
THE GOOSE-STEP—A STUDY OF AMERICAN
   EDUCATION
THE GOSLINGS—A STUDY OF THE AMERI-
   CAN SCHOOLS
MAMMONART
LETTERS TO JUDD

SPOKESMAN'S SECRETARY
OIL!
MONEY WRITES!
BOSTON
MOUNTAIN CITY
MENTAL RADIO
ROMAN HOLIDAY
THE WET PARADE
AMERICAN OUTPOST
UPTON SINCLAIR PRESENTS WILLIAM FOX
THE WAY OUT: WHAT LIES AHEAD FOR
   AMERICA
I, GOVERNOR OF CALIFORNIA
THE EPIC PLAN FOR CALIFORNIA
I, CANDIDATE FOR GOVERNOR AND HOW I
   GOT LICKED
WHAT GOD MEANS TO ME: AN ATTEMPT
   AT A WORKING RELIGION
PLAYS OF PROTEST
CO-OP: A NOVEL OF LIVING TOGETHER
THE GNOMOBILE
NO PASARAN
THE FLIVVER KING
OUR LADY
LITTLE STEEL
YOUR MILLION DOLLARS
EXPECT NO PEACE

Plays

PRINCE HAGEN
THE NATUREWOMAN
THE SECOND STORY MAN
THE MACHINE
THE POT-BOILER

HELL
SINGING JAILBIRDS
BILL PORTER
OIL (DRAMATIZATION)
MARIE ANTOINETTE

Printed in the United States
4508

9 781931 313131